CW00496521

A QUIET VENGEANCE

Samarak Tales Book 1

Tim Hardie

TJH Publications UK

ALSO BY TIM HARDIE

The Brotherhood of the Eagle

Hall of Bones
Sundered Souls
Lost Gods
Broken Brotherhood (due for release in 2024)

Samarak Tales

A Quiet Vengeance

This novel is dedicated to my wife, Liz
Thanks for all your love and support over the years

MAP OF SAMARAKAND

Map of Samarakand

Naroque

Kingdoms of Kalat

Emerald Isles

Urumesh

Mirak

Shaqran

Obani

Assur

Hamda

Culah

Wadinni

Karnac

Karnac Strait

Regesh

Abitek

Edeen

Amonduras

Kandarah

Shalanar

Halak

Sea of Fassin

Janir

Al-Narah

Lake Missah

Amjahran

Fujareen

Bengarath

Strait of Bezeen

Kaal

Tandos

Gost

Shannanu

The Shallows

Zirhidan

Dosaan

The Emirates of Murtak

Tim Hardie 09/01/2023

AUTHOR'S NOTE

A Quiet Vengeance is the first in a series of interconnected standalone novels, set in the fantasy world of Amuran. Each will focus on different characters and their own particular story, although figures from other books will make an appearance from time to time. This novel tells the tale of Nimsah and Dojan, and the secret they share.

At the back of this book is a character list and a glossary, both of which you may find useful.

PROLOGUE

Dojan held the hand of his nurse as he approached Her Royal Highness Tanah Bel-Doshok, wife of the emir of Fujareen. His mother was sitting in a high-backed chair in the shade of a walled garden within Bengarath Palace, her protectors, led by Khanir Shinva of the Blessed Swords, standing watch with five other women warriors at a discreet distance. In her arms, Tanah carried a wriggling cloth-wrapped bundle, which began to emit unpleasant, high-pitched wailing noises as Dojan drew closer.

"Hush, little one," she cooed, the gentle breeze rippling through long jet-black hair, which flowed down to reach her waist. "It's your eldest brother, Dojan."

The infant was mollified by the sound of his mother's voice, contenting himself with wriggling into her breast. Dojan peered closer, looking at the boy's stubby nose and tightly shut eyes. His youngest brother resembled a wrinkled prune.

"Say hello to Beneth, Dojan."

"Hello," said Dojan, pursing his lips in disapproval.

Tanah reached out, stroking his short dark hair. "Not like that. Smile. He's part of our family now, after all. Aren't you pleased to have another brother to play with?"

Dojan shrugged, unimpressed. "He can't even do anything yet. Except cry."

1

His nurse laughed. "The things young boys say! You were just the same, my prince, when you were Beneth's age."

"I'm older now," Dojan told her. "At least Adina and Saraj can play chase and hide and seek with me."

"And Beneth will join in the games with your siblings when he's older," his mother replied. "Here. Do you want to hold him?"

Dojan didn't, but one look from his mother told him this wasn't an argument he was going to win. He held out his hands and the nurse helped him to support the infant's head in one arm, his other holding the child's weight. Beneth whimpered, soft and warm, smelling of fresh linen and milk.

"Adorable," said Tanah, smiling at the nurse as a flock of tiny birds chose that moment to flit through the garden, making one of the Blessed Swords start as they flew inches from her nose.

Beneth started wriggling in Dojan's arms, a hesitant half-cry signalling his displeasure at being separated from his mother.

"I don't think he likes me," muttered Dojan, adjusting his grip on his tiny brother as the wailing noise grew louder.

"Nonsense," his mother told him. "We're family. You'll have and love each other, long after I'm gone."

Dojan stared down at baby Beneth, who was now bawling his lungs out, unconvinced.

CHAPTER 1

Spring 198 – Bengarath Market

Nimsah darted through the crowded docks, weaving her way past barrows and baskets, stalls and crates, bare feet skipping lightly over the stones. Bengarath teemed with activity, moored dhows and baghlahs taking up every available inch of space on the quayside, with even more ships bobbing on the waters of the harbour. She could hear the chattering sing-song Abitek tongue, dark-skinned sailors of Naroque gleaming with sweat as they hauled ashore their cargo. She could smell the spices of Amjahran merchants, who were showing their wares to a prospective buyer, his nose wrinkled with concentration as he took in the rich scents of cumin and sumac.

Spices put Nimsah in mind of food, her belly growling at the thought. There'd be nothing to eat until she earned some coppers, so she hurried to Fenara's stall, holding fast to the hope she would have work for her this morning. Her stand was found on the edge of the market in a shady spot, piled high with baskets of all shapes and sizes. Nimsah spied a heap of reeds on the floor next to her table and offered Fenara a sweet smile, which the older lady returned with a twinkle in her dark eyes.

"Good day to you, Nimsah."

Nimsah grinned, bouncing on her heels. "Good morning, Fenara. Do you need any help with your weaving today?"

Fenara smiled wider, crows' feet creasing the corners of

her eyes and mouth. She adjusted her green shawl, tucking away a few stray strands of black hair, shot through with grey. She gestured to the pile of dried reeds at her sandaled feet. "Well, those baskets aren't going to make themselves, are they, young lady?"

Nimsah didn't need a second invitation. She crouched down on the floor whilst Fenara took a seat opposite, minding her stall and occasionally giving Nimsah instruction on the more complex parts of her task. Nimsah was a quick study, and she was pleased Fenara needed to intervene less often than when the two of them had first met three years ago. Her deft fingers bent the reeds into the intricate patterns she had been taught, moving independently of her mind with well-practised ease. It was satisfying being able to create something in this way – turning a jumble of flat reeds into an object people would pay for. Nimsah had learned that folk came from all over Bengarath for Fenara's baskets, knowing she only used the best quality reeds. Her friend had boasted that the emir himself purchased her wares for his palace, a tale Nimsah wanted to be true with all her heart.

"He didn't come in person," Fenara told her with a laugh, when Nimsah asked about it that morning. "He's far too busy to worry about baskets for his storehouses. He sends his servants to the market. There's a young katib who often comes this way … Oh, Nimsah, if I were fifteen years younger…"

"If you were fifteen years younger, you'd still be an old woman," Nimsah joked, shrieking with fear and laughter in equal measure as Fenara reached out and playfully tried to slap her behind. Nimsah was too quick, darting around to the other side of the stall, squealing.

"How *dare* you, you cheeky little thing," Fenara cried in mock outrage. "When I was a young woman, which *wasn't* all that long ago, I turned the head of many a man in Bengarath."

Nimsah cocked her head on one side, looking more closely at Fenara. She'd been widowed several years ago, taking over her husband's business when he died. She had high cheekbones and delicate features, face tanned dark from working outside every day. Lamornna hadn't blessed Fenara with children, which was why the pair had been drawn together in the first place. Nimsah didn't need to worry about jealous rivals for Fenara's affections.

"It won't be long before you'll be thinking about young men," Fenara told her.

Nimsah grimaced. "I don't think so."

"What are you? Just shy of your teens? We'll have this conversation in three or four years' time and see who's right," the older lady replied with a knowing look, as Nimsah took her seat and resumed work.

The day passed quickly, most customers not even seeing Nimsah as she worked on the dusty market floor. The market closed as midday approached and people headed back to their homes to escape the baking heat. Fenara lived in a small house in the centre of Bengarath, and invited Nimsah inside to share a meal of figs, dates, smooth salty white cheese and fresh flatbreads, washed down with black tea. Nimsah put a little of everything into a small leather bag she carried with her everywhere.

"You know I'll pay your wages," Fenara said as she caught sight of what Nimsah was doing.

"I'm not hungry," Nimsah lied. "I'll save this for later."

"There's nothing of you. Here, take these as well, in case you find your appetite," Fenara replied, giving Nimsah another handful of dried dates. "For later."

The pair of them finished their meal and returned to reopen Fenara's stall for the afternoon trade. Fenara didn't need any more baskets making that day, so Nimsah occupied herself by watching how she dealt with each customer. Fenara knew each one by name, always asking after their families, talking about how business was going, which ships had docked at the port and who was planning to leave with the morning tide. When Nimsah asked her why that was important, Fenara explained that a merchant making ready to leave would want to sell the last of their wares before taking their new cargo on to their next destination.

"That's the best time to strike a bargain," Fenara told her with a knowing wink and a smile.

It was that ready, friendly smile, which drew prospective buyers in and made them relax in her company. The Bengarath market was like one huge family and it gave Nimsah a warm, safe feeling to be part of that – however fleetingly.

By late afternoon the market was closing for the day, merchants packing away their stalls, the more expensive stone-built shops closing their shutters. Fenara loaded her baskets onto a handcart with Nimsah's help, making ready to head home. She pressed some coppers into Nimsah's hand.

"Thank you for your help today, young lady. Will I see you again tomorrow?"

Nimsah dropped the coins into her bag, adjusting the strap across her shoulder. "I hope so. I'll have to ask Farooq, though."

Fenara scowled, and Nimsah instantly wished she hadn't mentioned him. "I don't like this Farooq. He has a reputation, young lady. From what I hear, you'd be best staying away from him."

Nimsah placed the last basket on her cart, wiping her sweaty fingers on her brown smock. She knew Fenara meant well – she just didn't understand.

"You don't have to leave," Fenara wheedled. "You could come home, with me. There's room enough ..."

"I'll see you in the morning, if I can," Nimsah replied, moving in quickly and kissing her cheek. She left Fenara standing there, fingers lightly brushing the spot where Nimsah's lips had been moments before.

***

Nimsah made her way through Bengarath's winding streets towards the Bridge of Sorrows, bare feet slapping on the hot stones. Fenara's words had made her angry, a feeling that grew with each step she took, even though Nimsah knew they'd been spoken out of love. She'd no right to speak about Farooq that way. Fenara could weave her own baskets tomorrow.

The Bridge of Sorrows spanned the River Namja that flowed through Bengarath, constructed using enormous magical steels fashioned during the Enlightened Age, a feat that confounded the magi and scholars of today. Previously known as the Bridge of Steel, it had acquired its new name a dozen years ago when Haraq Al-Souk became the emir of Fujareen, hanging his rivals and any foolish objectors over the river below for all to see. Farooq had told Nimsah and her friends that story late one night as they listened, wide-eyed. Farooq said that when the wind blew in the right direction you could hear the creaking ropes of the nooses, a ghostly echo of Al-Souk's murderous rise to power.

Underneath a great archway on the eastern bank of the Namja lay the City of Tents, Nimsah's home, which she shared with hundreds of others too poor to live in the stone houses of Bengarath. A stiff breeze coming in off the river carried away the worst of the smell, setting the rainbow coloured tent fabrics flapping. Nimsah called out a greeting to those she knew as she navigated towards the centre of the tent city. Farooq was waiting for her in the courtyard outside his grand blue tent made of patterned silks, surrounded by a crowd of children and young adults. Farooq was in his early twenties (although like most who lived in the City of Tents, including Nimsah, he couldn't say exactly which year he'd been born), a tall muscular man from Naroque who favoured the light blue traditional robes of the Halak sea-serpent tribe. He sported a variety of gold bangles and bracelets, an outward expression of the wealth he had amassed in his short life. Elsewhere in Fujareen he would have been a shekh, yet here he was simply Farooq, master of the tent city.

"Here comes my little flower," Farooq called out when he saw Nimsah, waving her over. The crowd parted to let her through. Farooq was sitting crossed-legged in front of a fire built of hot coals, over which spiced lamb and chicken were being cooked. A low table was set with bowls of fragrant rice, couscous, red and green peppers and fresh mango. Nimsah had to tear her eyes away from the food.

"What have you brought me?" Farooq asked with a white-toothed smile.

Nimsah reached into her bag and scooped out the coppers she'd earned in the market. Farooq held out his hand, bracelets jangling, and she dropped them into his palm. He raised an eyebrow and licked his lips.

"Not much reward for honest work, is there?"

Nimsah shrugged. "I heard word in the market today that Denek Bel-Haroom's baghlah is expected to arrive from Zirhidan tomorrow morning."

Farooq's smile widened. "Ah. Now, that is worth more than a meagre handful of copper shekels. You look hungry, Little Flower. I think you have earned a place at my table this evening."

Nimsah took a bowl proffered by one of Farooq's men. She piled it with food, including a skewer of lamb and a chicken leg, before taking her place at the far end of the circle gathered around Farooq. She watched him holding court as she ate; some rewarded with food and kind words, others sent away empty handed if they had nothing of value. When no one was looking Nimsah slipped the chicken into her bag as she finished off the succulent lamb.

"Farooq has a job for you." Kandilla's breath was hot on her neck as she whispered in her ear, making Nimsah jump. She set her empty bowl aside, reaching for her coffee cup when she was confident her hands would not betray her.

"It's rude to sneak up on people like that."

Kandilla threw back her head and laughed. "That's rich, coming from you." Of an age with Farooq, Kandilla was his latest lover, olive skin and tattooed cheeks marking her out as a native of the neighbouring Emirate of Zirhidan. People from all parts of Amuran could be found in the City of Tents.

"What does Farooq want?" Nimsah asked, blowing on her hot coffee before taking a sip.

"Nothing much," Kandilla explained. "A small errand to earn your keep, that's all. Farooq wants you to watch the docks tomorrow for Denek Bel-Haroom's arrival. He's keen to speak to him so they can conclude their business affairs. Since your sharp ears brought him this news, he thought you deserved to be rewarded. I'll come to fetch you at dawn."

Nimsah watched as Kandilla walked away, narrow hips swaying from side to side as she joined Farooq. Watching the docks was easy work and would guarantee a full belly. She finished her drink and left the courtyard, making her way towards the tent she shared with a number of other children. As she expected, Rogesh was already sitting there on his own, knees drawn up to his chest, looking bored. His face brightened when she came inside.

"You're back."

Nimsah smiled. "I am. Did you have a good day?"

Rogesh's face fell. He picked at a hole in his trousers over one knee.

"That good?" Nimsah said brightly, sitting down next to him and opening her bag. "Perhaps this will cheer you up?"

Rogesh snatched the chicken leg out of her hand, devouring it in moments. He was still sucking the last flesh from the bone as Nimsah brought out the dates, figs and cheese she'd saved at Fenara's house, wrapped in a flatbread. The pair shared the food, eating every morsel.

Rogesh fell onto his blanket with a self-satisfied air, putting his hands behind his head. "Thanks, Nimsah. You always look out for me."

"You'd do the same," Nimsah replied, although if she was being completely truthful Rogesh tended to be the main beneficiary of their friendship. The boy lacked the sharp instincts you needed to thrive in the City of Tents. Sometimes Nimsah worried about him.

"Listen," Nimsah said, dropping down next to Rogesh.

"I have a job to do for Farooq down at the docks tomorrow morning. You could help me."

Rogesh rolled onto his side, casually resting his head on his hand. "What sort of job?"

"Watching out for a merchant. Farooq wants a word with him."

Rogesh gulped. "Rather him than me."

CHAPTER 2

Summer 213 – Bengarath Palace

Crown Prince Dojan Al-Haraq turned to the side and looked at his reflection in the polished mirror, pursing his lips. The flowing purple silk robes *were* very fine – the question was whether it was his colour. He turned to the other side, his reflection giving him a regal frown as he pondered the dilemma, stroking his neatly groomed black beard.

"Very becoming," fawned Quizar Bel-Khandir, a young katib at his father's court and Dojan's personal assistant. "You cut quite the figure."

Dojan raised an eyebrow, admiring his friend's red tunic and trousers. Red and purple would never work together. He wanted to make a good impression on their guest, not commit a fashion faux pas.

"Let's try the yellow again," said Dojan. Quizar sighed quietly and went to fetch the first outfit they had tried on, much earlier that morning.

***

Dojan and Quizar walked through the corridors of Bengarath Palace dressed in yellow and red respectively. Any visitor who failed to be impressed by their exquisite tailoring would know Dojan was a man of importance by his honour guard – six armoured warriors of the Regiment of the Mighty Spears, led by their mubarizun, Hadir Al-Nadim. Dojan found him a dour fellow, although he wasn't there to provide sparkling conversation. Only the regiment's khan, Hengesh, was more skilful with the Samarak fighting spear.

Hadir led them towards the eastern reception room, which always looked at its best in the morning light. Quizar was prattling in Dojan's ear, and he realised he had probably missed some important facts concerning his audience with this banker. He considered asking Quizar to repeat what he was saying before dismissing the idea. His father was going to conduct the negotiations, which involved protecting the bank's interests in the city state of Kandarah. Dojan was perfectly capable of handling the pleasantries before the emir deigned to make his appearance.

One of the warriors opened the door at the end of the corridor, Hadir entering the room first, eyes sweeping left and right as he made sure there were no intruders waiting for the Crown Prince.

"I'm in my own palace, Hadir. If anyone was going to assassinate me they wouldn't do it while I have half a dozen members of the Spear guarding my back, would they?"

"It's your father's palace, Crown Prince," Hadir corrected, peering around a column inlaid with gold leaf. Only when he was satisfied did he nod to his companions, who stepped away from the door and allowed Dojan and Quizar to enter.

Dojan was pleased at how the sunlight scattered across the room through the diamond-shaped gaps cut into the cedar shutters. It was furnished with a variety of couches and cushions, those different fashions reflecting the fact they entertained visitors from the emirates, Naroque and distant Kalat. Dojan made to sit on one of the cushions, changing his mind immediately as he realised this would mean the banker would be looking down on him when he entered the room. The reclining couch would result in the same effect, so Dojan settled instead for clasping his hands behind his back and pacing around the chamber, pretending to be interested in the artwork on the walls. He stared at some dull frieze depicting events from two centuries ago, when Morvanos duelled with

Vellandir for control of Amuran. In the background people were fleeing from the burning cities left in the wake of the battle between the two avatars, misery etched on their faces. In the skies above, Vellandir's dragons had taken to the air, battling the new chimera race Morvanos had secretly bred to finally defeat them. The War of the Avatars, the god-like servants of the Creator who helped him form the world of Amuran at the dawn of time, brought an end to the Enlightened Age and the dragons' dominance. It must have been a truly ghastly affair and Dojan was glad he hadn't had the misfortune to live in those times, when the Emirates had stood with Morvanos as he challenged the old Tyranny. As the gods turned on one another they had reduced the Creator's world to ash and rubble.

He started at the sharp rap on the door. One of the palace guards pushed it open, announcing that the representative of the Bank of Illesh had arrived and craved the honour of an audience with the emir of Fujareen.

"Yes, yes. Show them in," Dojan said, waving the man away. The guard nodded stiffly and stepped aside, opening the door more widely to allow their guest to pass through.

Dojan took a moment to register that his visitor was a woman, dressed head to toe in dark blue robes, a light blue shawl covering her hair and a veil hiding her face. He peered over her shoulder, expecting her to be part of some retinue intended to make this banker feel more self-important. The woman paused a few feet away and bowed, clasping her hands together in a show of respect, while Dojan collected himself as he realised she was alone.

"My lady, may I introduce you to the Crown Prince, Dojan Al-Haraq," said Quizar. "First born son of our beloved emir, heir to his father's emirate of Fujareen. Crown Prince, this is Nimsah of the Bank of Illesh."

"I am honoured to be greeted by the emir's eldest son," replied Nimsah in flawless Fujareen. She was either a native or someone well-schooled in the languages of Samarakand.

"It is our honour to entertain Illesh's representative," Quizar responded with a smile. "I am Quizar Bel-Khandir, the prince's personal katib. I hope you had a safe and pleasant journey from Naroque?"

"Perfectly," said Nimsah, and the way her cultured voice sculpted that single word drew Dojan's attention. He couldn't help wonder what lay behind that veil. She sounded young, which was promising.

Quizar turned to Dojan, and he realised he had been asked something by his katib. Dojan swallowed and took an educated guess.

"We would be delighted to offer you refreshment after travelling all this way." He cast a swift glance at Quizar, who clapped his hands, summoning servants carrying trays of dried fruit and a large silver pot of steaming tea, which they set on a low table.

"Please, make yourself comfortable," said Quizar, gesturing towards the cushions next to the table. Nimsah lowered herself onto the nearest one, crossing her legs underneath her robes. Quizar joined her and a servant began serving them drinks, whilst Dojan took a seat opposite their visitor.

When Nimsah drew back her veil and set her shawl aside, Dojan felt a smile creep across his face. She was as attractive as he'd hoped; dark olive skin, an oval face with a small nose and jet-black hair that flowed halfway down her back. While the ladies at court were beautiful they presented little in the way of a challenge, and his latest dalliance was becoming a chore. This member of the banking clans offered an altogether more enticing prospect. Nimsah blew on the hot black tea, dark eyes framed in long eyelashes catching Dojan in the act of staring at her. He tore himself away and took the cup of tea Quizar was offering him. Nimsah was young to be speaking on behalf of the Illesh money lenders. He caught the scent of her perfume – a rich, complex musk that was undoubtedly eye-wateringly expensive.

With a start, Dojan realised he had fallen behind in the conversation yet again. Quizar was asking about Nimsah's sea crossing from Kandarah, where the Bank of Illesh had their headquarters. Dojan decided he needed to become more engaged with his guest and say something intelligent.

"Of course, the seas … Um. That is to say, at this time of year …" he felt his throat tighten as he tripped over his own words, ending in an unintelligible stammer. What was the matter with him?

Nimsah blinked and smiled, looking as if she was entranced by the stumbling wit of his interjection. Dojan frowned, sensing something else for the first time. Something half-remembered. That name.

He attempted to start a conversation once more. "Nimsah. You seem … I wonder, have we ever met before? Were you originally from Fujareen?"

Nimsah sipped her tea. "I was born here, yes."

"Of course. You must be from one of the older Fujareen families? Perhaps we have been introduced at one of my father's gatherings?"

"I think that would be most unlikely, Crown Prince. The Illesh set aside their family names, although I can assure you I come from far more humble origins than you appear to imagine."

Of course, the Bank of Illesh operated like a family of sorts. No one ever left the service of the bank – they worked there their entire lives. They had some odd customs, although that hadn't got in the way of them making an *awful* lot of money. Was Nimsah married? Perhaps that was one of the things Quizar had explained that Dojan had half-listened to and already completely forgotten. Dojan cursed himself for not paying more attention. If she was married, he didn't want to offend her husband and risk damaging his father's business affairs. However, he really was tiring of his latest lover at court and Nimsah was an enticing prospect – a gift from Meras. What were her employers *thinking*, sending a young woman all this way across the Strait of Bezeen on her own?

It was time to turn on the legendary Dojan charm. "I find it hard to believe a woman so beautiful could be anything other than a descendent of Meras, avatar of love. Your husband is a fortunate man."

"I see your reputation for flattery is deserved, Crown Prince. However, I've yet to meet a man who was able to capture my heart." Nimsah's admission sent a thrill through his body. Dojan felt his mouth go dry and pondered on this fact whilst drinking some more tea.

Quizar cleared his throat, a clear signal that the prince wasn't following some plan that had presumably been discussed, agreed and subsequently forgotten. Dojan glared at the katib, attempting a stare that would put him back in his place.

Quizar picked up a dried fig from the silver platter on the table and popped it into his mouth. Nimsah did the same, commenting on how flavoursome the fruit was.

"A gift from midsummer in Fujareen," Quizar replied. "The markets are swelled by the produce of our industrious farmers at this time of year. Fujareen is famous for its figs, dates, lemons and oranges – they are the envy of the other emirates of Murtak. Ah, but I forget myself. You're a native of these parts, and here I am boring you, telling you something you already know."

Nimsah smiled and Dojan became so distracted the date he was chewing almost fell out of his mouth. "You're not boring me in the slightest, Quizar. I have lived in Naroque for most of my adult life and it pleases me to hear someone speak of my homeland in this way. However, I doubt that Emir Haraq Al-Souk went to war with his predecessor because of Fujareen's succulent oranges."

Dojan choked down his date, trying and failing to find a witty comeback to such an outrageous remark. Quizar retained his composure, leaning back on his cushion and refilling his cup from the silver tea pot with a small chuckle.

"My lady, what you say is true. It was the former emir's delicious figs that stirred Haraq Al-Souk to war."

Nimsah laughed, eyes twinkling as Quizar met her gaze, his face a mask of seriousness. After a moment, he cracked into a smile. "Ah, you have me. I cannot maintain the pretence."

Nimsah reclined on her cushion, a mischievous smile of her own playing on her lips. "I make a serious point. I am here to do business and I would welcome your thoughts on this matter. Fujareen is wealthy, yes, with fertile lands, busy ports and growing trade links with its neighbours both in Murtak and increasingly with Naroque. The Bank of Illesh can do business with any of the Emirates of Murtak, or the southern Kingdoms of Kalat. Why does Haraq Al-Souk deserve the exclusive treatment he has requested? Crown Prince, what kind of man would you say your father is?"

"Unhappy," Dojan replied, feeling himself flush with horror that the word had escaped his lips. Quizar interjected before Dojan could say anything to make the situation worse.

"What the Crown Prince means to say, I'm sure, is that our emir still has so many unfulfilled plans. There is much more he wishes to do to build Fujareen and make it the envy of the Emirates of Murtak. These are matters where the assistance of the Bank of Illesh would be most welcome."

"I'm sure," Nimsah replied, never taking her long-lashed eyes off Dojan, who squirmed under her scrutiny. He reached for another date, fumbled it between his fingers and watched it bounce off the table and disappear amongst the cushions scattered on the floor.

"Here, Crown Prince, please take another," Nimsah said, holding out the silver tray. Dojan mumbled his thanks as he took a piece of fruit.

"Crown Prince, are you alright?" asked Quizar, a look of concern on his handsome features.

"I'm fine," snapped Dojan, more forcefully than he intended. It was hot in the chamber, even though the hour was early. Nimsah's perfume was cloying in his throat, making it hard for him to think clearly. He stood up, swaying a little as he tried to clear his head.

"My apologies," he told Nimsah and Quizar. "This room is a little warm for my tastes. Perhaps we could take a tour of the hanging gardens and fountains of the palace before my father receives you. I would certainly welcome some fresh air."

Quizar helped Nimsah rise, taking her delicate hand in his. "Of course, Crown Prince," she said. "That sounds delightful."

CHAPTER 3

Spring 198 – Bengarath Docks

"This way," Nimsah called out, weaving her way through the heaving market, Farooq and a dozen of his men puffing and sweating in her wake as they tried to keep up.

"Slow down," hissed Kandilla, catching up with Nimsah and putting a hand on her shoulder. Nimsah glanced up at the woman, noting the narrow stare. It was a warning sign Kandilla's bad temper, which always lurked below the surface, was about to bubble over.

Nimsah shook off Kandilla's tight grip with a twist of her body. "I don't want us to lose him," she explained. "I left Rogesh on watch down there, but it would be better if he was still on the boat, wouldn't it?"

Kandilla's face hardened, pink tongue licking her lips. "It's not your place to tell us what is or isn't *better*."

"Enough, Kandilla. Our little flower speaks the truth," said Farooq, his bracelet-covered arm snaking around her waist. "I don't want Denek slipping through our fingers. Best get this over with, and his baghlah is as good a place as any. Let's go."

Kandilla bent down, ruffling Nimsah's hair, leaning in close to whisper in her ear. "You may be his *little flower* – I know you for what you really are. A dirty little street rat." She stood and in a louder voice said, "Show us the way, Nimsah."

***

Rogesh was delighted to see Nimsah when they reached the docks, and she had to clap a hand over his mouth to stifle the noisy torrent of words spilling out of his mouth.

"Once more, slowly," Nimsah told the boy with a smile.

Rogesh took a breath and pointed to the baghlah moored at the quayside next to where he was standing, explaining Denek Bel-Haroom was still there. She was a large red-painted ship with three tall masts. A man Nimsah presumed was the captain or first mate was busy supervising the crew as they unloaded their cargo with the help of several dockhands. Denek was watching over proceedings, dressed in black robes set with a pattern of silver stars, a long grey beard reaching down as far as his belt. Nimsah remembered him from the last time he paid a furtive visit to Farooq in the City of Tents. She hoped for Denek's sake that he hadn't spent all the money he owed on fine clothes.

Farooq looked at the boy. "Well, young Rogesh, you've done your part. I trust our visit is going to come as a surprise for our friend?"

"He didn't see me," Rogesh replied, proud that Farooq knew his name.

"I was the one who told you when his ship was coming into port," Nimsah added, frowning at Rogesh and making Farooq laugh.

"That you did, young lady. And I won't forget that in a hurry. Now, wait here while we speak to Denek Bel-Haroom. Tell them we need a private audience with their master," Farooq said to Bizek, a huge bare-chested man assembled from slabs of hairy muscle with pale scars criss-crossing half of his face. Nimsah had heard that Bizek once took a beating for Farooq that gave him those scars, cost him one of his ears and left his eyes pointing in slightly different directions. Farooq said no man was more loyal than Bizek, paying him well for his service and always ensuring there was a place of honour for him in the evening when they ate together.

Bizek lumbered forward with five other men, while

Farooq spoke to Raqqath, telling him to take the rest of his gang and make sure no one disturbed them. Denek's face fell when he saw Bizek, and the dockers clearly recognised him instantly. The baghlah's captain looked confused as the dockhands melted away without so much as a murmur. His face froze when Bizek towered over him, laying a heavy hand between his shoulder blades and ushering him down the quayside towards Raqqath's men.

Farooq stepped forwards. "Denek Bel-Haroom. Welcome back to Bengarath. If you would be so kind, I would like a quiet word with you."

The captain, who was being manhandled away from his ship by Bizek, looked at his master uncertainly. Denek's crew numbered some thirty sailors, more than their visitors. However, no one looked keen to take on Bizek and the rest of Farooq's men.

"Go," Denek told his crew with only a faint tremor in his voice. "I'll handle this – it's a simple misunderstanding." Nimsah had to admire him for his composure, feeling a sense of grudging respect for the merchant.

The captain didn't look convinced as he was pushed beyond the line established by Raqqath. The rest of his crew skulked past, some hurrying away and others standing in small knots, waiting for further instructions.

Raqqath put a hand on the captain's shoulder, nudged aside his robes with his other hand and patted the hilt of the knife tucked into his belt. Raqqath was a handsome man, dark-haired like all those native to Fujareen. It was his pale blue eyes that set him apart; they had an unsettling effect on anyone subjected to that gaze for long. Nimsah could see the captain losing heart as he stared into them now.

"Run along, and take the rest of your crew with you," Raqqath told him with a smile.

The colour drained from Denek's cheeks as his crew walked away, leaving the docks deserted. The sound of trading from the nearby market drifted across, a different world separated from this scene by a few winding streets and houses.

"Let's speak inside," said Farooq, inviting Denek to make his way up the gangplank. The merchant gathered up his black robes and returned to his ship, followed by Farooq, Bizek, Kandilla and three more of his gang. Raqqath gave his orders and the rest of the men took up their positions on the docks to ensure no one stumbled on the scene.

"Come on," said Nimsah once Raqqath's back was turned, nodding towards the baghlah.

"He told us to stay," Rogesh protested, looking worried.

"Don't you want to see what's happening?"

Rogesh sighed and with a furtive glance over his shoulder, he followed Nimsah as she padded lightly over the gangplank and together they took up a spot overlooking the cargo hold. Peering down they could see Denek standing among piles of baskets, boxes and crates. Bizek was holding his arms tightly behind his back, while Farooq was sitting on a large trunk in the middle of the hold, decorated with ornate metal bands at the corners and locked with a heavy chain.

"You don't have to manhandle me," Denek protested. "We can discuss this like civilised men, I'm sure."

Farooq looked up. "Civilised? Civilised men keep their word. Civilised men honour their promises, rather than slipping away on their ship in the dead of night."

Kandilla laughed at that, prowling around the hold, looking at Denek like he was a cornered animal in the slaughterhouse. Nimsah had a sick feeling in her stomach, although she couldn't tear her eyes away from what she was seeing. Kandilla liked this part.

"I'm far from civilised," Farooq continued, lounging on the trunk. "I'm not called Bel-this or Bel-that. I don't come from one of Fujareen's old families, grown fat on wealth passed down from father to son, mother to daughter. I've had to earn every coin I've held – hard graft and hard choices – that's all there is in the City of Tents, a place the old families would like to forget ever existed. Your name counts for nothing, Bel-

Haroom – only your actions."

"This … This is ridiculous," Denek stammered, trying unsuccessfully to shake off Bizek's grip. "Let go of me and we can talk. Please. I didn't slip away – I'm a merchant. How do you think I raised the money I needed to pay you back, Farooq? I needed to trade my wares up and down the ports of the Bezeen strait. The Haroom family traces its line back to the great Emir of Murtak, it's true. However, that doesn't mean it comes with vast wealth – we lost everything during the uprising. What little I had paid for this ship."

Farooq made a show of looking around the hold. "It looks to me like business has been good to you. How much of this was bought with my own money, I wonder?"

"You can take it back. Take anything you want. Consider it a down payment and let me sell the rest. I'll be able to pile your coffers high with shekels of silver and gold by the end of the day, I promise you."

"What's in here?" Farooq asked, pulling a knife from his belt and pointing it at the trunk.

Denek hesitated and Bizek squeezed his wrists between his enormous hands, making the merchant squeal in pain. Nimsah glanced at Rogesh, who was watching events with wide eyes, knuckles stuffed into his mouth as he chewed them absent-mindedly.

"I'm not going to ask again," said Farooq.

"I have the key," Denek admitted. Farooq nodded and Bizek released Denek's arms. Rubbing his wrists, Denek reached into his robes and produced a key from one of the pockets. Kandilla held out her hand and took it.

Nimsah shuffled round as quietly as she could, trying to get the best vantage point from which to see what lay inside the trunk. The padlock turned and with a rattle the chains fell away. Farooq stood up and lifted the lid, hinges creaking. Nimsah gasped as she saw the pile of silver coins inside, glittering despite the gloom of the hold.

"Well, there's a sight," Farooq remarked, glancing at

Kandilla. Both of them laughed, making the hairs on the back of Nimsah's neck stand up. Denek tried to shrink away, although there was nowhere in the crowded hold for him to go.

"I struck some good bargains in Regesh, cashed in on some longstanding deals," Denek began, as Bizek seized him once more and dragged him over to the trunk, pushing him down onto his knees in front of Farooq.

"Oh, don't tell me. You were going to come and see me as soon as you'd finished unloading your cargo," spat Farooq, striking Denek across the face with a backhand blow. "You've been gone for almost a year. You think I would *forget* what you owed? There's enough money in here to pay me back four times over. How many others have you stolen from to build up this stash?"

Denek looked around wildly, a trickle of blood running down from his nose, which he wiped away with the back of his hand. "I owe other people money too. I told you, I needed to buy the ship. A few of my deals went the wrong way and before I knew it, I owed more money to more people than I could ever repay. I've wronged you, I know. I took your money to pay off someone else – someone worse."

"Worse?" muttered Kandilla. "This man's an idiot."

"Idiot," echoed Bizek.

"I owed money to the Bank of Illesh," Denek told them, half sobbing.

While the name meant nothing to Nimsah, the effect on Farooq was noticeable. He recoiled from Denek as if the man had transformed into a serpent. It took him a moment to recover his composure as Kandilla hissed, also backing away.

"You paid them off?" asked Farooq, his voice quiet. "Tell me you paid them every shekel you owed."

Denek nodded and Farooq appeared to relax. He stepped in closer, rubbing his fingers on Denek's dark robes. "This is fine cloth. Kandilla, help him take it off."

Denek started to protest, until he lost the ability to speak as Kandilla landed a hard punch to his guts that left his face pressed onto the deck. Kandilla took hold of him and removed the robes, passing them to Farooq who ran them through his hands, admiring the quality of the design.

"Lovely fabric. It would be a pity to spoil it."

Denek whimpered, looking pathetic in his grey undergarments, ribs and spine poking through the thin flesh of his bare back as he cowered at Farooq's feet. "Please. I can pay you back. I have more than enough. Take it all."

Farooq looked down on him with disdain. "This isn't about the money any longer, don't you understand? I thought a *civilised* man would know better. You made me look like a fool. You relied on your name and you stole from me, with no intention of ever repaying it. That's not something I can let pass, although it's been a lesson to me as well. Why else would you have come to me, in the City of Tents? Clearly I was far too trusting."

"Trusting," muttered Bizek, looking at Farooq much like a hound watching its master.

Farooq turned to Kandilla. "You know what you have to do."

Denek struggled to rise, only for Bizek to plant a hand on his neck, slamming his face into the deck. Denek gasped in shock as Bizek hauled him back onto his knees. Kandilla stepped forwards, dagger drawn, and plunged the blade up to the hilt into Denek's neck. His face contorted in pain, Denek swayed on his knees, looking up at the sky. With shock, Nimsah found he was looking straight at her, eyes wide. Kandilla opened his throat with a twist of the dagger, turning his grey beard red as a torrent of blood poured into the hold. Denek gave a choking sound, eyes never leaving Nimsah. She wanted to back away and at the same time knew she couldn't – she didn't want him to die alone.

The light faded in Denek Bel-Haroom's eyes as Nimsah watched life leave him. The merchant limply fell to his side, Bizek stepping away from the pool of blood that looked more like black oil in the dim light of the hold.

"Take everything," Farooq said to his men as Nimsah and Rogesh backed away, looking at each other with frightened eyes. The pair scampered down the gangplank, skidding to a halt when they found Raqqath waiting for them at the bottom.

"If you know what's good for you, you'll forget everything you just saw," Raqqath said, blue eyes boring into them.

CHAPTER 4

Summer 213 – Bengarath Palace

"What's the matter with you?" hissed Quizar, making sure he was out of earshot of Nimsah as she admired the palace gardens. Hadir and his men were prowling around the perimeter, hunting for any sign of danger in the foliage.

"I don't know what you mean," lied Dojan, hoping a more convincing answer would shortly materialise, enabling him to spare his blushes.

"You haven't uttered a single sentence that didn't have the effect of making you sound like an imbecile," Quizar retorted. "Don't make matters worse by pretending things are fine. Your father has entrusted us with something important – why are you determined to ruin it? This is the delegation at the summer palace of Jalar all over again."

"I'm not trying to ruin anything," Dojan protested, straight denial against Quizar's relentless use of logic and facts his only defence.

"You described the emir as 'unhappy'. Do you remember that? *Unhappy*." Quizar jabbed his finger at Nimsah's back as she walked around an ornate fountain, the sun shimmering where it reflected off the water, decorating her blue robes with dancing beams of light. "She'll report back everything she learns here to her masters in Kandarah. Everything. I told you this morning that she's not to be underestimated."

"She's only a young woman," Dojan muttered, staring after her. Nimsah looked up and smiled, light from the fountain sparkling on her skin. Dojan was glad she'd not put her veil back on.

Quizar made an odd, strangled sound. "Do you like her? Is that it? You want to bed this woman and that gives you the excuse to act … To act like a love struck boy? Tell me that isn't true, with everything we have at stake."

Dojan opened his mouth and let out a sigh of relief as Ulan Bel-Naraar appeared at one of the doorways, dressed in flowing black robes and wearing a red handari on his head in the Kalat style, calling out to Quizar. Normally Dojan tried to avoid the ambitious pasha; the personal assistant of his father's vizier with responsibility for foreign affairs, and the suitor of his younger sister, Adina. However, this Dinuvillan-sent opportunity gave him a chance to make his excuses, since Quizar, as a more junior katib, had little choice other than to attend to the palace's pasha.

The hanging gardens of Bengarath Palace were constructed on a series of mezzanine levels, trailing flowers and plants cascading from one layer to the next, interwoven with artificial waterfalls, marble statues and sweeping staircases that allowed a visitor to traverse each level. It had been a project for his mother from the moment she moved into the palace, and there were times when Dojan wondered if she loved the sanctuary she had created more than him. Its elegant setting was "A paradise for assassins," according to Hadir, although Dojan had always found it to be a relaxing place. Birds flitted between the trees and bushes, the swift movement catching Hadir's eye and threatening to give him a nervous twitch.

"Your mubarizun never ceases watching out for you, does he?" Nimsah said, making Dojan jump as she appeared noiselessly behind him.

"No," he replied, trusting that if he only used a single word at a time the chances of damaging relations between Fujareen and the Bank of Illesh would be kept to a minimum.

"Quizar worries about you too," Nimsah observed,

nodding in his direction as Ulan continued to talk, arms gesticulating wildly. Quizar glanced over, his face pleading for Dojan to join him. He waved instead before turning back to Nimsah.

"He does." Two words, spoken in the right order. No mishaps so far.

Nimsah began walking through the gardens, side by side with Dojan. Hadir followed a few paces behind, his Samarak fighting spear strapped across his back. Dojan managed to utter a few pleasantries, describing his mother's handiwork, pointing out her favourite flowers. He was sweating into his yellow silks despite the fresh breeze that circulated through the gardens.

"I don't mean to make you uncomfortable," Nimsah said quietly. "That question concerning your father – I had no desire to cause you any embarrassment." Again, there was that perfume, wrapped around her like an invisible robe, the scent powerful even in the fresh air of the gardens.

"I don't regret what I said – it's true. My father's unhappy. He's a warrior at heart, not an emir. I think it would have been better if he'd been appointed as the andral in charge of the Fujareen army. My mother has always enjoyed politics far more – she would have been a worthy emira, although she seems happier to act as the power behind the throne."

"The quest for power is more enticing than the reality of holding it," observed Nimsah.

Dojan frowned. "My father never desired power – it sought him out. It's no secret he opposed Emir Godan Bel-Deem after he ordered my uncle's death. I don't think he ever imagined it would lead to him becoming emir in his place when the war was over and Godan was dead. I'm sure you already know much of this."

"Your father avenged his brother and did what he thought was right. That shows commendable qualities. You should be proud of him."

Dojan paused and turned to look at Nimsah. "I *am* proud

of him. The affairs of state weigh heavily on his shoulders, that's all."

Nimsah lightly brushed Dojan's arm with her hand for a moment. "I appreciate what you've told me. You've been honest, which can be a rare thing to find in Samarakand. It's important I understand things here in Fujareen, and you've helped me. This meeting with your father is important for both of us – being able to read all the hidden patterns and undercurrents in your court could mean the difference between success and failure."

"I'm glad to have been of service," Dojan replied, aware of a lingering sensation on his forearm where Nimsah's fingers had been moments before. "You're ... easy to talk to. I think Quizar would have a fit if he could hear me being so candid."

"Knowledge is prized more highly than gold by the Bank of Illesh. It is important we understand *who* we are doing business with and what their impulses and motivations might be. We need to know their *heart*. It isn't enough to make a return measured in shekels – we are building a new world from the shattered remains of the lost Age of Enlightenment. We believe the Fallen Age is merely the prelude to a period of restoration and hope for all, if the foundations upon which we build are strong."

"My father is a good and honourable man," said Dojan. "I can think of no better man with whom you could do business."

"I see that you truly believe that," Nimsah told him, her smile making her appear even more beautiful in the tranquil surroundings of the garden.

"There's something ..." Dojan halted, wondering if Quizar was right and he was love struck. Nimsah was stunning – there was no denying that. It wasn't that, though, that was unsettling him. Words she had spoken earlier that morning came back to him.

"When I asked you if we'd met, you never actually answered the question."

"Didn't I?" she replied coyly.

Dojan cleared his throat. "No. Have I committed another embarrassing mistake? Am I imagining all of this? It feels … It feels as if we have some sort of connection. I'm sure of it."

Nimsah paused, and an odd expression passed across her face. "It was years ago, when we were both children. I would be surprised if you remembered me at all."

Dojan frowned, memories stirring in his mind as he struggled to place her. His mouth went dry, the truth striking him like a blow to the face. "*Nimsah*. You're *that* Nimsah, from the Bridge of Sorrows? The girl from the tent city."

"You remember me now," Nimsah said with a sweet smile, her voice dripping with refinement so at odds with her origins.

Dojan coughed, feeling his face flush. He glanced behind him, hoping to see Quizar and Ulan heading in their direction. Instead, there was only Hadir, standing at a discreet distance so as not to overhear their conversation. From wanting to spend time with this woman, now all he wanted to do was get away. Of course it was her. She had changed in so many ways, yet the shape of her face, the way her mouth moved when she smiled – it was all the same. Looking at those dark eyes he recognised the face of the girl he had met all those years ago. A shudder passed up his spine as memories he was trying to suppress filled his mind.

"There's no need to look so mortified," Nimsah chided.

"There's every reason. Nimsah, I'm so sorry," Dojan stared at her, trying to gauge her reaction. An awful thought struck him, one that half-paralysed his ability to speak. "I do hope … That is, I mean to say … Er. Your visit and our … shared history. I hope …"

Nimsah interrupted his fumbling words to spare him further embarrassment, if that were possible. "Crown Prince Dojan, please don't distress yourself. I was a street child – why would you have remembered me? Whereas I met the crown prince, hardly an event a child from the City of Tents was ever likely to forget. I knew you would be here when my masters sent me to Bengarath. I'll confess, I was intrigued at meeting you again and seeing what kind of man you had become."

"You're much changed," said Dojan. "Still just as beautiful, though. I should have remembered you straight away. What do you think of the man you found?"

Nimsah blinked, heavy lashes fluttering over those dark eyes. "I'm still making up my mind, Crown Prince."

Dojan's heart fell. He had destroyed his father's negotiations with the Bank of Illesh before they had even started. Quizar was right – he was about to ruin everything. Nimsah saw his growing discomfort, shaking her head in exasperation and amusement.

"I *jest* with you, Crown Prince Dojan. Remember I spoke earlier about how I prize honesty, so trust me when I say this. I hold no grudge against you. None at all. We were both children, from different worlds. You couldn't have prevented what happened any more than I could have stopped it. It was long ago, and my life has changed since then. Now my only concern is to represent my employer to the best of my ability. Nothing is going to alter that."

"I'm pleased to hear it," Dojan replied, unconvinced. Did he doubt her sincerity, or whether he deserved her forgiveness?

Nimsah leaned in close as Quizar hurried towards them, having finally concluded his discussion with the palace pasha. "Don't worry, Crown Prince. What's done is done, and belongs in the past."

Quizar must have sensed something had passed between them while he was talking to Dojan's prospective brother-in-law. Dojan struggled to meet his gaze, staring instead at his sandaled feet and allowing Quizar to lead the way from the gardens to the throne room. Nimsah walked at the katib's side, making admiring noises as Quizar pointed out various artworks, tapestries and statues, asking questions that showed a keen knowledge of the arts. The Bank of Illesh clearly schooled its employees well.

Dojan knew he should be pleased for Nimsah – she had escaped a life of poverty on the streets of Bengarath. Guilt gnawed at his stomach as he thought on how she had achieved this despite rather than because of him. With a heavy heart he followed the pair of them into the throne room, his undeserved honour guard at his side.

CHAPTER 5

Winter, late 198 – Bengarath Market

"Well then, young lady, where have you been hiding yourself?" Fenara probed as the pair sat together weaving by her basket stall.

"I've been busy," Nimsah told her, frowning as she concentrated on the reeds, forming the intricate patterns she had learned over the years.

"Busy?"

"Busy."

Fenara sighed, setting her basket aside as a customer approached. Nimsah continued working as the pair of women haggled in the cold. Fenara was wearing thick black woollen robes and a heavy blue shawl, which covered her hair and wrapped neatly around her neck. Nimsah had caught her looking sideways at her bare feet and thin, dirty smock – the same clothes she had been wearing throughout the summer. The older lady looked worried, leaving Nimsah feeling a little guilty. She was lying to this kindly woman, taking advantage of her good nature by pretending to be something she wasn't.

The two women gossiped for a time, Nimsah's sharp ears missing nothing as they spoke of inconsequential things. There was nothing of value in the potter's increased prices or who widow Nereel was sleeping with these days. At least, nothing of value *now*. Nimsah stored all those little secrets away, just in case Farooq took an interest in the young widow or the potter's wares. That was why she ate at his table every day – she was a good listener. The ones who prospered understood what knowledge was worth.

Nimsah looked up at the darkening sky, feeling a change in the air that heralded rain. She could shelter under the canopy of Fenara's stall for now and worry about getting wet on the way home later.

"My house is nearer," Fenara pointed out, as if she had read her thoughts.

"Let's see what the day brings," Nimsah replied, trying to ignore the disappointment on Fenara's face.

***

The storm had set in, rain bouncing off the cobbled streets as Nimsah helped Fenara pack up her handcart and close her stall.

"Are you sure you won't join me for something to eat?" coaxed Fenara, looking hopeful.

The downpour had already soaked through Nimsah's smock. She shrugged and made up her mind at the last moment. "Alright, if you're sure."

Fenara's face brightened instantly. "Of course I'm sure, Nimsah. Come on – jump in."

Nimsah hopped into the handcart, wriggling her skinny bottom down between the piles of baskets. She started to giggle as Fenara set off at a swift jog, the wheel of the cart clattering over the stones as they weaved through the narrow streets, dodging the deeper puddles.

"Faster," Nimsah shouted. Fenara obliged and by the time they reached her house the pair of them were laughing together. They dived through the door into the warmth and dry inside.

"I'll light a fire. You should get out of those wet clothes," Fenara told her, passing her a blanket. Nimsah wrapped it round her shoulders and wriggled out of her smock. Fenara took it and placed it over the back of a chair near the cook fire, which she lit so it could begin to dry.

"Sit, sit." Nimsah obeyed, plopping down onto a three-legged stool and stretching out her toes towards the coals, flames already licking around their edges.

Nimsah watched the flickering fire, feeling the warmth begin to spread through the small room as Fenara changed into dry clothes behind a screen. "Not much call for this, most days," the woman observed. "Still, this is where I dress myself every day. Funny how some habits never change."

Fenara emerged dressed in fresh clothes with her familiar green shawl covering her head. "That feels better. Are you hungry? What a question – of course you are. I'll prepare something for both of us."

Nimsah watched as Fenara cooked, enjoying the smell of onions, ginger and garlic as they filled the room, sizzling in a pan over the fire. They hadn't done this in a while. She liked Fenara's company and she felt safe in her home, far away from the City of Tents. The pair chattered as Fenara cooked, throwing a variety of vegetables into the pan, fragrant rice cooking in a pot nestled at the edge of the fire. Nimsah breathed in, enjoying the scents. There would have been meat and fish waiting for her at Farooq's table – finer fare, yet she knew she'd enjoy this meal more.

As they ate together Fenara spoke of her late husband, who had passed away nine years ago. It was a familiar subject for Nimsah – she must have heard all the stories concerning Biwan by now. She smiled as she listened again to how he had courted Fenara, becoming more persistent when she rejected his initial advances, and increasingly charming in the face of the opposition from her parents.

"I suppose they were worried for me. Biwan was only a weaver, and my parents always had such high hopes for me. Pah, you'd have thought their family name began with 'Bel' something or other, the way they carried on." Fenara laughed. "They meant well, but I was in *love*. That's a precious gift and not one to be cast away lightly. We had twelve wonderful years together and despite the pain of losing him I wouldn't have changed that for all the gold in Amuran. Life is strange, Nimsah. One day I couldn't have been happier – the next, I was thirty, alone and childless," Fenara mused, her gaze growing distant.

"Yet here you are. You made a life for yourself," Nimsah told her between mouthfuls of rice and spiced vegetables as she filled her belly. "You have your own home and run your business. Trade is good, I've seen how busy you are."

"The days are busy, yes. It's the evenings when I miss him most."

"If you're lonely you should think about marrying again," Nimsah told her, scraping the last of her food from her bowl.

Fenara looked scandalised. "Nimsah – the very *idea*."

"You're still good looking. You have lovely cheekbones. Did you know that? Men *love* a woman with high cheekbones like that, trust me."

Fenara managed to look both cross and amused. "And what, young lady, would you know of such things? Anyway, I have a treat for you," Fenara announced, setting aside her bowl and walking over to her bag.

"Don't think I don't know you're changing the subject."

Fenara had the decency to look embarrassed. "But what a subject to change it to," she replied, taking out a small parcel and returning to her stool.

Nimsah sniffed as Fenara began unwrapping the paper, catching the sweet smell of nuts and honey.

"Baklawa," Fenara revealed the pastries with a flourish, the pair of them sharing a delighted giggle. "I bought them at the market earlier today, while you were minding the stall."

"Fenara," Nimsah exclaimed. "It's a good job I came here tonight. You could never eat all this on your own."

As they shared the sweet pastries Nimsah felt a pang of guilt. She'd only come tonight on a whim. She couldn't help thinking of Fenara, staring at the unwrapped parcel of treats, alone in her house. She finished the baklawa, popping the last parcel of filo pastry flavoured with honey and almonds into her mouth with a smile. As Fenara cleared away the pans and bowls Nimsah rose and felt her smock, which was warm and dry.

As she dressed herself Fenara opened one of the shutters and peered outside. "The rain's stopped," she said, sounding disappointed. "You don't have to go, Nimsah. If you wanted to stay the night I could make up a bed for you –"

"My friends will be wondering where I am," Nimsah told her, straightening her smock and making for the door. "Thank you for the meal, Fenara. It was delicious."

"Child, wait." Nimsah turned in the doorway as Fenara rummaged in her purse, dropping a few coppers into her hand. "You worked hard today. You earned that."

Nimsah pocketed the shekels and gave Fenara a smile. "I enjoyed it. It was a good day."

"It was. Perhaps I'll see you tomorrow?"

"Perhaps," Nimsah told her, knowing she wouldn't. She span on her heel and ran down the darkened streets, feet slapping on the wet stones.

***

"Where were you today?" Rogesh muttered sleepily as Nimsah slipped into their tent. "Farooq was asking after you."

"Busy," Nimsah told him, stepping over the bodies of several other sleeping children and taking up her familiar spot next to him.

"Busy?"

"Busy."

Rogesh groaned and rolled over, turning his back on her. After a few moments his breathing slowed as he drifted off to sleep. Nimsah gathered up a thick woollen blanket and rummaged in the chest she kept by her bed. Inside was an assortment of fine clothes. Gifts Farooq had rewarded her with in return for the secrets she had heard, whispered on the streets. She didn't want those now, setting aside her smock and with a grin she wriggled into some warmer garments that would stave off the night time chill. When she travelled around Bengarath in her smock no one took any notice of the thin girl shivering on the street corner. It was the perfect disguise when she was working. When she returned home she would always change before going to meet Farooq. He liked to see her wearing the outfits he had chosen for her.

The other children had been jealous at first, especially the newer ones who were keen to make their mark. Farooq had his favourites, and Nimsah had no intention of losing her position. Chandra, a young girl from Naroque who had appeared in the City of Tents a month ago, now knew better than to try and take her stuff. Nimsah had caught her rummaging through her bag one day and had beaten her for it. After that, Chandra had learnt her place and attached herself to Nimsah and Rogesh. The younger child could be very funny, and Nimsah liked the idea of developing a following amongst the street children of Bengarath. A network of allies was bound to be useful, so she encouraged the younger children like Chandra, showing them how to survive, where to find food and shelter, explaining what Farooq needed from them.

The only thing she kept to herself was Fenara. While Farooq knew she sometimes worked as a weaver he had no idea how often Nimsah had been invited into her house and shared her food. Wrapped up under the blankets, with Chandra snoring softly nearby, Nimsah found herself thinking of Fenara. The woman was looking for someone to take the place of the daughter Biwan had never been able to give her – that much was obvious. There was another life waiting for her, if she wanted it.

Nimsah rolled over, trying to get comfortable. The image of Denek Bel-Haroom, throat cut as he bled to death in the cargo hold of his baghlah, swam before her eyes. She'd seen people die in Bengarath more times than she could count, knowing she'd played a hand in some of their deaths. Farooq treated her with clothes and the choicest food from his table and she'd seen how some of the children looked at her, envy and worse in their eyes. A hungry child will do terrible things to survive in the City of Tents. Why not slip away and find a simpler life, away from all of this?

Nimsah allowed herself to dream of such possibilities for a few moments, snuggled up next to her bedfellows. With a sigh she set them aside, knowing Farooq would never let his little flower go. There was an unspoken understanding between them – she knew what was important to him, sifting through the news from the streets for what he wanted to hear. She'd cultivated something he valued, and Farooq wasn't a man who surrendered an advantage. If she wanted another life it would have to be far away from Bengarath – not working as a basket weaver in the marketplace.

CHAPTER 6

Summer 213 – Bengarath Palace

Dojan watched his father, Haraq Al-Souk, slouch on the dais with a bored expression, overlooking the crowd of courtiers that filled every corner of the room. He perched uncomfortably on the ornate wooden throne, inlaid with gilt leaf and encrusted with gemstones that glittered as sunlight poured through the open windows. Next to him, sitting upright on a slightly smaller and moderately less elaborate throne, was his wife, Tanah, politely laughing at a joke made by one of her visitors. Her eyes met Dojan's as she surveyed the room, and Tanah gave her son the briefest of nods in recognition before turning to speak to Vizier Haman, who was standing in attendance at the side of the emir. A delegation of Fujareen merchants waited patiently for their turn, whilst Haman invited a group of white-robed Veiled Magi to approach the dais.

"Looks like *everyone* is here," Quizar observed.

"A show of the emir's importance," Dojan replied. "Nimsah will have to wait her turn."

The delegate from the Bank of Illesh was circulating the room, speaking to Nema Bel-Yangash, Haman's wife and a close friend and confidante of Dojan's mother. Nimsah kept her veil removed, face animated and eyes sparkling, as she engaged the older woman in conversation.

"Should we help her?" asked Quizar. "Nema can be sharp-tongued."

"Something tells me Nimsah can look after herself. Come on, I need a drink."

Dojan led the way towards a table laden down with fresh fruit, a mouth-watering multi-coloured display, piled high on silver platters and bowls. Dojan picked up a slice of orange, popping the juicy fruit into his mouth as a servant approached him, effortlessly carrying a jug and several gold goblets on a large tray.

"May I offer you some wine, Crown Prince?"

"You've read my mind. Go on, pour away."

Dojan took a moment to appreciate the fine red, feeling the tension ease across his shoulders. Nimsah was still talking to Nema, the pair speaking like they were old friends. Dojan had a momentary panic that Nimsah was telling the vizier's wife the story of how they had met, his fingers tightening around his goblet. Muttering to himself that he was being ridiculous, Dojan pushed the thought aside, downing the rest of his drink and barking at a servant to bring him another.

Quizar raised an eyebrow. "You seem to have quite a thirst. Why don't you eat something as well?"

Dojan frowned at the katib. "It's been a long day."

"It's only noon."

Dojan scowled as he picked up a fresh goblet, taking a more measured sip. On the far side of the throne room were his younger brothers, Saraj and Beneth. Saraj had recently joined the Regiment of the Mighty Spears, serving under Khan Hengesh. Hadir had taken some pleasure in telling Dojan his brother had the makings of a future mubarizun, his burgeoning skill with the Samarak fighting spear far superior to anything Dojan had managed to display half-heartedly in the training grounds. Saraj had a muscular arm around Beneth's shoulders, his slender build something he shared with Dojan. His youngest brother's eyes crinkled in a smile as he listened to whatever story Saraj was telling. At seventeen Beneth was already an adept scholar, studying under the vizier himself. Next year he would be old enough to join the ranks of students attending the University of Bengarath, where he would be studying history and politics – a future vizier in the making, as his mother was so fond of saying.

"Brother, why do you look so miserable?" Dojan turned to greet his sister Adina as she walked towards him, arm in arm with her future husband, Ulan.

"This is my thoughtful face."

Adina laughed, kissing Dojan on the cheeks as Ulan looked on, unamused. "Well change your expression. Father will think the wine is off."

Adina had her mother's good looks, long black hair wound into a single braid tied with gold thread that hung down as far as her waist. She was dressed in fine white silks, allowing just enough light to pass through the fabric to hint at her shapely body without causing a scandal. Pasha Ulan's black robes stood out in stark contrast to his fun-loving sister's attire. Haraq had recognised his talents soon after his arrival at court and he was the youngest pasha to hold the office with responsibility for foreign affairs. Descended from one of the old families, Ulan made a worthy match for Adina, whilst more importantly strengthening the ties with the Bel-Naraar dynasty.

"I still can't believe Illesh's representative came alone," Ulan remarked. "It almost seems … disrespectful, sending a single delegate to treat with our emir. The Veiled Magi have sent a dozen from their order, and I'm not sure they've even bothered to ask for anything."

"Perhaps they're here for the food," Quizar joked, a wry smile playing on his face.

"What do you make of her, Dojan?" Adina asked, nodding in Nimsah's direction.

Dojan hesitated, taking a sip of wine as he took a moment to compose a reply. "She's an intelligent woman. I suspect the Bank of Illesh sent her here alone because they knew she was perfectly capable of dealing with their affairs here in Fujareen."

"Ooh, I think Dojan likes our guest," Adina said with a knowing smile.

"Don't be ridiculous," Dojan snapped, more sharply than he had intended. Adina's eyes went wide.

"She's certainly made an impression on him," Quizar added with a chuckle.

"I hope that's as far as things go," Ulan muttered. "Nimsah's first loyalties lie with her employer. She's married to the Bank of Illesh as far as you're concerned, my prince."

"I don't recall asking for your advice, Ulan. Since when has a mere pasha had the right to speak to the crown prince in that way?" Dojan let the statement hang there, cutting the conversation dead.

A small frown creased Adina's smooth forehead. "I see we've hit a nerve. Clearly Quizar has the measure of things and you'd do well to listen to your future brother-in-law, Dojan. You know how important these discussions are for our father."

Dojan patted Ulan on the shoulder – the two men were of an age and similar in height. He could feel the tension in the pasha's muscles under his robes. "Family always comes first, of course. I meant no offence and I'm sure Ulan didn't intend to overstep the bounds of his position."

"My apologies, Crown Prince," Ulan replied, bowing his head. "I meant no offence."

Ulan and Adina excused themselves and moved off, arm in arm, to mingle with the crowd. Quizar sighed as he watched them leave. "Are you going to banish me from your side too?"

"Only if you forget your place."

"Ulan has a lot riding on these discussions with Illesh," Quizar pointed out, ignoring Dojan's barbed comment. "It's unfair to goad him when he's been involved in all the details for months. It's an important moment with the bank seeking our aid to resolve the Kandaran dispute. Once the papers bear the emir's seal the rumour is that Fujareen will be the richest of the four emirates.

"Anyway, all Ulan and Adina did was observe the same

thing I have. It's obvious from the way you've been behaving there's something between you and this woman. I've never seen you so distracted – tell me I'm wrong." Quizar folded his arms across his chest, daring Dojan to disagree.

Dojan was spared from answering Quizar's question when the doors to the throne room swung open and the attendant announced the arrival of Illana Bel-Jedesh, the emir's andral. Illana had fought with Dojan's father in the war that had usurped Godan, Haraq rewarding her loyalty by giving her command of the entire Fujareen army. A tall woman with long grey hair and a square jaw she wore her ceremonial armour with ease, silver helmet clasped under one arm, her other hand on the hilt of her scimitar, a knot of The Pure closely guarding her. Close on their heels strode Illana's most senior khans – Khan Hengesh of the Mighty Spears and Khanir Shinva of the Blessed Swords. The Spears were the personal regiment of the emir, Hadir as their mubarizun having the honour of guarding the crown prince. Shinva's Blessed Swords were a regiment of female warriors, sworn to protect Tanah and her daughter Adina.

Dojan glanced at Shinva, blinking as an image of blood spreading on hot stones in the afternoon sun intruded on his mind for a split second. He shook his head and looked away, drinking from his goblet and wondering if Nimsah recognised the khanir of the Blessed Swords. Nimsah had been joined by Adina and Ulan, talking to them as she watched proceedings. If she recognised Shinva she hid it well, as Ulan made the introductions between Nimsah, Illana and her khans.

"Hengesh will enjoy this. A chance to show off," Quizar muttered into Dojan's ear.

Dojan nodded, walking to the far side of the throne room so he didn't have to watch the spectacle of Hengesh and Shinva trying to outshine each other. Illana was only in her early fifties, still trim and fit. However, one day the emir would want to appoint a new andral and both khans were determined it would be them. Dojan suspected Shinva only wanted the position to please his mother, although thwarting someone as ambitious as Hengesh would also be its own reward.

On the throne, Haraq Al-Souk stroked his grey beard as he half-listened to the Fujareen merchants. Nearby, one of the Magi of the Farseeing stood watch over the emir, guarding his thoughts with the mysterious skill of the Sight. Haman would be the real arbiter of their dispute, which centred around the tedious subject of docking rights. His mother rose from her seat and excused herself, smoothing out the swathes of expensive silks that she wore before walking towards Dojan. Whereas his father's former stocky, muscular frame had run to fat as he overindulged in the finer things of life, Tanah was slender, carrying herself with a grace that was often copied and never bettered by the other women at court. She laid a gentle hand on Dojan's arm, the warm smile on her full mouth not reaching as far as her eyes.

"Don't you think you've had enough?"

Dojan grimaced. "Mother, one of the few things I *am* good at is enjoying Fujareen's vineyards."

"You share too many of your father's traits. I swear, you're one of the reasons for this," Tanah gestured to her long dark hair, now shot through with grey, a look she carried well. She laughed as she spoke, several of the katibs nearby politely joining in. Quizar smiled in sympathy, managing to appreciate the joke whilst simultaneously looking supportively towards Dojan.

"You were short with your sister earlier."

"You heard?"

"I saw all I needed to see," Tanah replied, arching one long, perfect eyebrow.

Dojan took a sip of wine, ignoring his mother's glare. "Brothers and sisters are born to fight, Mother. Yet the bonds of love are strong, and just as quickly their quarrel is forgotten."

"Is that from a poem, Crown Prince?" ventured Quizar, voice quiet and calm.

"If it is, I don't recall where I read it."

Tanah tutted. "Perhaps you should have been more attentive during your studies, like Adina or Beneth over there. Vizier Haman always said you had the ability. However, ability without application is rarely a breeding ground for success."

Dojan drank deeply this time, aware those surrounding them were listening to every word. As the crown prince he could bring Pasha Ulan down with a few well-chosen remarks. However, no title provided a sure defence against angering Her Royal Highness Princess Tanah Bel-Doshok, and his mother always took full advantage of that fact.

"We all have our own particular qualities," Dojan said at last, hoping the vagueness of his observation would deflect further criticism.

"True enough," remarked his mother with a sardonic smile.

The noise in the throne room suddenly began to subside, and Dojan turned to see that his father had risen from his seat, the merchants bowing and scraping as they backed away from the dais. Vizier Haman looked pleased at being given the opportunity to display his wisdom, although Dojan had no idea in whose favour he had ruled.

"If there are no other petitions to hear, then I will take my leave of you," Haraq announced. "Nimsah, representative of the Bank of Illesh, I believe we have some private business to attend to."

Nimsah left Adina's side and approached the dais, bowing low before the emir. "If it pleases you, padishah."

Haraq's gaze lingered on her for a moment as Nimsah rose. "It does. Haman, if you would be so good as to lead the way."

Nema slipped her arm inside Vizier Haman's as the pair walked towards the emir's private chambers. Illana's honour guard of the Regiment of The Pure took their place around Haraq, as the tall andral gestured towards Nimsah to accompany her. The throne room remained in silence, everyone standing to attention, until the doors of the emir's chambers closed behind them. At once there was a low murmur, which grew as everyone began discussing Nimsah's visit.

Tanah turned to her son. "It doesn't even bother you, does it?" she hissed in an undertone.

Dojan frowned. "What do you mean?"

"You're the crown prince, my son," she whispered, leaning in close. "Greeting and taking tea with our guest from Kandarah is the kind of task one might give a lowly katib. Now the real diplomacy begins and here you are, drinking your wine outside as they close the door in your face." Tanah tutted and gave her son a brief kiss on the cheek as she took her leave, Shinva and her warriors in close attendance.

"Crown Prince, is everything alright?" Quizar asked.

"It will be," Dojan growled. "Find me a servant and bring me another drink."

CHAPTER 7

Winter, early 199 – Bengarath, the City of Tents

Nimsah watched as Farooq beckoned Rogesh forwards with an impatient wave of his hand, Kandilla lounging back on the rug spread in front of the cook fire to his left, watching him through half-closed eyes as she rested on an assortment of silk pillows. In front of Farooq, platters were piled high with food – warm flatbreads, dishes of spiced rice, some served with goat, others with lamb. It was still winter, so Farooq gathered his followers within his large blue tent, the fire warding off the chill. At these times of year there was extra value in being amongst his closest advisors and Nimsah was afforded a place in the circle of men and woman sharing his food, about halfway from Farooq. She was wearing a warm red dress, thick woven shawl and fur-lined boots, all of them expensive. Rogesh stood there awkwardly, grey trousers torn at one knee, tunic frayed at the sleeves, a yellowing sheepskin armless jacket his most prized item of winter clothing.

Bizek propelled Rogesh forwards, hairy hand set between the boy's shoulder blades. "Your master hasn't got all day."

Farooq stared hard at Rogesh, whose eyes were drawn inexorably towards the food. Nimsah spooned some of the rice into her mouth, hoping he would be joining her.

"Are you hungry?" Farooq asked, gesturing towards the platters in front of his crossed legs.

"Yes," mumbled Rogesh.

"What do you have for me?"

Rogesh fished around in his pockets, drawing out a single copper shekel. Raqqath laughed, shaking his head as he took a drink of tea.

"You've been gone all day, working the markets, and this is all you have to show for your efforts?" said Farooq, his voice calm and quiet.

"I'm sorry, master," Rogesh dropped the small coin into Raqqath's outstretched hand. He placed it into a bronze pot, almost overflowing with copper and silver shekels.

"You're sorry. If you've been in the markets you will have heard people talk. What have they been saying today? What did you learn?"

Rogesh mumbled something inaudible and Nimsah had to concentrate on tearing off a piece of flatbread to avoid squirming in embarrassment. Several members of Farooq's gang started laughing, enjoying the spectacle of the boy's growing discomfort.

"This boy wastes our time," Kandilla said, a sour expression on her face.

"Where do you think this comes from?" asked Farooq, pointing at the food.

"You provide it?" Rogesh's self-doubt turned the statement into a question, diminishing him further in the eyes of his master.

"No. Our shared efforts provide this food. We live together in the tent city, doing what we can for one another. Looking out for each other, sharing our coin and listening to the word on the streets of Bengarath. Those who are unable to contribute don't deserve to share what has been earned by the hard work of others. You haven't brought me anything of worth these past three visits to my tent. Don't come back here again until you have something of value."

Rogesh hung his head in shame as Bizek steered him out into the cold. Nimsah tore her eyes away only to find Kandilla staring hard at her, the tattoos on her cheeks twisted by an evil smile. Nimsah drank a little tea, finishing her meal with some dried fruits and a handful of nuts. When no one was looking she surreptitiously wrapped some of the bread and fruit inside a small cloth, dropping it into her bag.

***

"Is that all I get?" whined Rogesh, disappointment written across his face as he unwrapped the cloth later that evening inside Nimsah's tent.

Nimsah breathed in through her nose, taking her time before answering. "Would you rather ask Bizek to fetch you something else to go with it?"

Chandra snorted with laughter, sitting in a corner of the tent. "You're lucky she got you anything at all. Farooq would have her whipped if he knew she was sneaking food from his table."

Nimsah shot the Naroque girl a venomous look. "You'll keep your mouth shut."

Chandra adopted an innocent expression, eyes wide. "I won't breathe a word."

"No, you won't."

"Thank you," mumbled Rogesh through a mouthful of bread. "I'm sorry, I was hungry."

Nimsah sat next to the boy as he crammed the rest of her food parcel into his mouth. He looked thin, nose and cheeks pinched. She put an arm around his shoulders, feeling a chill deep in his bones.

Chandra trotted over and sat on the other side of Rogesh, hugging him tight. "You're cold. You can share your blanket with me tonight."

Normally such a remark would have provoked a wave of giggles and teasing. Tonight Rogesh drew his knees up to his chest, muttering his thanks as he hung his head.

"Tomorrow, you're coming with me to the docks," Nimsah told him in a tone that brooked no argument. Rogesh had a beaten look as he nodded silently in agreement.

***

Nimsah's set aside her fine clothes, looking unremarkable in a brown smock, a patched woollen blanket her only concession to the weather. Rogesh was grumbling in her wake, breath smoking in the cold morning air. A mist hung over the docks, already busy at first light as the sun began to creep over the horizon, its light milky and weak.

"Why are we here?" Rogesh asked, blowing into his cupped hands.

"There's always *something* going on down at the docks," Nimsah replied with a grin, trying hard to hide her irritation at his lack of effort. It was like he'd given up and she had enough to worry about looking after herself.

The pair wended their way past moored dhows unloading fish and the larger baghlahs with their more exotic cargos, hailing from Al-Narah, Zirhidan and Kalat. The activity stirred Rogesh, his eyes coming alive as he looked for an opportunity to relieve the merchants of some of their wares. Both children knew how to move quietly, unseen as they darted around the busy dockers, ducking under ropes and using barrels, crates and sacks as cover, sticking to the shadows and slipping through the morning mist.

By the time the sun's watery light had begun to warm the morning air Rogesh had a smile on his face and a small sack laden down with a number of prizes. The most expensive of these, a stoppered earthenware bottle of olive oil, would be enough to fill his belly that night. They moved away from the docks, Nimsah slipping a stolen purse into her own bag, its weight a pleasing sensation. Together they sat down on a coiled rope in the corner of an alley, watching as barrows and carts were filled at the entrance, transporting goods from the ships into the wending streets of Bengarath.

"That was an easy morning's work," Nimsah said with a sigh, leaning back against the wall. "You're good at this when you put your mind to it. How come you only scraped a single copper shekel at the market yesterday?"

Rogesh shrugged. "I don't know. It's different when I'm

with you."

"How?"

Rogesh squirmed on the pile of rope. "You make it look so easy. When I'm with you ... it feels like I can do anything. I don't need to worry when you're around."

Nimsah thought about that for a moment. "I can't be with you every day. Farooq doesn't want me to spend my time stealing purses. Lots of people can do that."

Rogesh looked crestfallen. "You said we'd done well today."

"We have," Nimsah told him. "What I'm saying is there's something more valuable to Farooq than what we can lift from the docks. He wants to know what's happening."

Rogesh looked worried. "We should go – we've lingered here longer than we should. I don't want to get caught with all this stuff."

Nimsah grinned, springing to her feet. "I thought you said you felt like you could do anything? I'm your lucky talisman."

With a grumble, Rogesh stood and followed her as she hurried towards the alleyway entrance.

***

"You saw this for yourself?" Farooq asked, deep frown lines creasing his forehead.

Rogesh nodded, a sheen of nervous sweat on his face. "Kamjah has returned. I saw him in Surat's coffeehouse this morning with several members of his gang. They were talking about having taken passage on a ship from Amjahran."

Kandilla leaned forwards, sweeping her long hair out of her eyes. "And how do you know what Kamjah looks like?"

Rogesh rolled up his thin sleeve, pointing at his forearm. "I've never seen him before, it's true, but I've heard of him. He has a tattoo of a kraken on his right arm, just here. I saw it with my own eyes, I swear."

Farooq nodded as Kandilla folded her arms, looking displeased. "You see Kandilla, teach these young ones a harsh lesson and they will learn. You have done well, Rogesh. Come and join us, take tea or fresh coffee and share in our meal."

Nimsah wriggled over, making space for Rogesh to sit beside her. Raqqath leaned close to Farooq, though Nimsah's ears caught his quietly spoken words.

"The Kraken will seek you out. If he's returned from Amjahran he'll have a reason, and confidence he has enough men at his back to stand his ground."

"We'll not discuss this here," Farooq replied, placing a hand gently on his friend's shoulder. Raqqath nodded, returning to his meal, eating with little enthusiasm.

Rogesh grew in confidence as he ate with Farooq's inner circle, joking with some of the other children who had been honoured to stay in his tent that evening. Although Kamjah's return meant trouble, Nimsah couldn't help smiling. Farooq's mild disappointment when she presented her pilfered goods from the docks had been worth it to see the weight lifted from Rogesh's shoulders. Whilst olive oil was valuable, knowing an old enemy had returned to Bengarath was priceless. Perhaps she really *was* his lucky talisman.

It was dark when Farooq dismissed them, clearly wishing to talk privately with Raqqath. Nimsah was surprised that Kandilla also rose with the rest of them, kissing Farooq on the lips, fingers caressing his jaw and neck as she took her leave. Outside, Rogesh and Chandra were chasing each other around various tents to the annoyance of their occupants, enjoying a rare moment of childhood. Nimsah stiffened as she felt Kandilla's hand close around her upper arm.

"Not joining in, Little Flower?"

Nimsah tried unsuccessfully to shake off Kandilla's grip. "I don't want to spoil my dress."

"Oh, you think you're so special."

Kandilla was pretty, her charms having captured Farooq's attention far longer than his previous lovers. However, as Nimsah looked up into her face there was a hard glint to those dark eyes. Nimsah's heart began to beat harder as she remembered how Kandilla had cut Denek Bel-Haroom's throat.

"You're hurting me."

Kandilla cocked her head to one side, squeezing harder as Nimsah tried to twist away. "I don't care. You think I don't know what happened in there? You're mocking Farooq, do you understand that?"

"No," Nimsah replied through gritted teeth.

"I think you do. Who do you think you are, deciding who your master favours? Do you think I'm so stupid as to believe bone-headed Rogesh would recognise Kamjah and his crew?"

"Nimsah. Are you coming?" called Chandra, breathing hard, white teeth framed in an enormous smile.

Kandilla let go and Nimsah couldn't help rubbing her arm, glaring at the older woman.

"Go and play with your friends, Little Flower," Kandilla hissed. "Next time you try and play your games with us I'll leave a mark on you that won't fade so quickly. There's no room in the City of Tents for those who can't take care of themselves."

CHAPTER 8

Summer 213 – Bengarath Palace

Dojan climbed the winding staircase in Bengarath Palace, Hadir at his side, the warrior moving easily in his ceremonial chainmail with his fighting spear strapped to his back. Dojan's thighs were screaming in protest by the time they reached the top, and he had to dab his forehead with the corner of one sleeve to make himself presentable as Hadir knocked on the door.

"Enter." His father's voice. Hadir opened the door and stood aside to let Dojan pass before taking his position outside, guarding the entrance to ensure Dojan's audience with his father was undisturbed.

Emir Haraq Al-Souk had a number of private chambers throughout the palace, some of which were given over to honoured guests when they were entertaining delegations from the other emirates, or important visitors from Naroque or Kalat. However, this room, right at the top of the tallest tower in the palace, was the emir's personal sanctuary. Dojan could count on the fingers of one hand how many times he'd been in here. His father was crouched over a mahogany writing desk, papers scattered in front of him, unattended by his vizier or even the lowliest katib. Light flooded in from the open window, which led out onto a balcony that gave an excellent view of the Bay of Bengarath, the Namja River glittering in the sun. Dojan walked over to admire the landscape, waiting for his father to explain why he had been summoned here this morning.

"Please, take a seat, Dojan," his father said, still poring over his papers as he waved at the chair in front of his desk. Dojan sat down, stretching his legs out in front of him, rubbing his thighs. Despite the cool breeze flowing in from the window he could feel the prickle of sweat on his brow once more.

His father gave a sigh, leaning back in his chair and looking at Dojan properly for the first time. Above his head, mounted on the wall, was the Samarak fighting spear Haraq had used in the duel with his predecessor. Underneath hung a scimitar, polished steel catching the sun and making Dojan squint. He adjusted his position to move away from the beam, wondering how often Father had Illana's blade cleaned. The sword looked brand new, its glossy sheen giving no clue this weapon was last used twenty-seven years ago when Illana took Emir Godan's head in battle. The dynasty of Bel-Deem had ended that day, ushering in the era of Al-Souk. It was a minor point, whether someone used the honorific of Bel, Al or El, yet it made all the difference.

"Something troubling you, my son?" Haraq raised a bushy white eyebrow, hands folded over his belly. It was hard to believe he'd gone to war to avenge his brother, wresting the title of emir by force of arms. Dojan reflected it had been a very long time ago.

"I'm merely curious," Dojan replied before his father grew impatient. "I'm trying to remember the last time I was here. I don't think I'd turned twenty. You showed me Illana's blade and told me the story of how Godan fell – the *real* story."

Haraq smiled, shedding years of worries for an instant as his face brightened. "They were simpler times, when solving problems merely meant defeating my enemy. Little did I realise all I was doing was exchanging one set of easy problems for a host of others, far more fiendish. I've never told anyone else the story of how Godan died, you know – not even your mother. That's a secret only shared by the three of us."

"And that's the way it will stay," promised Dojan.

Haraq gave a satisfied nod as he began to tidy his papers. One neat stack on the corner of his desk bore his signature – various orders and agreements left for his attention by Vizier Haman. Haraq placed the scattered documents he had been working on onto the pile and took out a red leather-bound book from a drawer next to him.

"Do you know what this is?" he asked.

Dojan shrugged. "No. Should I?"

The corner of his father's mouth twitched. "Look closer my son, this is important."

Dojan sat forwards, squinting at the book as Haraq passed it towards him across the desk. It was heavy, perhaps some two hundred pages of parchment inside. There was no writing on the cover, although the leather was fine quality, soft to the touch. Dojan opened the book and read the title on the first page: *A binding agreement between the Bank of Illesh and His Royal Highness, Emir Haraq Al-Souk, detailing the terms upon which an extensive lending facility will be made available to the noble Emirate of Fujareen.*

"Only Haman and Ulan have read the entire thing," his father admitted.

"This is what you've been working on with Nimsah for the past week?"

Haraq nodded. "I've already sealed it, and Pasha Ulan bound the agreement himself. I can trust only my closest and most loyal advisors in this matter. What you're holding there is the future of the emirate. Your future, in fact."

Dojan flicked over the next few pages, skirting past the flowing script that described in glowing terms the personal qualities of his father. He frowned as he worked his way through the more important clauses. Quizar was right – the sum the Illesh bankers were prepared to lend was astonishing – worth more than all the taxes due to the emir over several years. As he read on, unease gnawed at Dojan's stomach, the words weighing heavy on the page.

"This is far more than an advance of credit," he

muttered, placing the book back on his father's desk.

"You don't approve?" asked his father.

"Do you?"

Haraq pursed his lips. "I have signed this in my personal capacity as the emir, after much consideration and, speaking frankly, heated debate with Vizier Haman. I consider this to be the best course of action – one that I intend to see carried through."

Dojan squirmed in his chair, forcing himself to voice his thoughts against his better judgement. "Father, you're committing us to war in Kandarah. This agreement places our army and navy at the disposal of the Bank of Illesh. Why would they require a military force, and why would you agree to such terms?"

"To unite Fujareen and establish a dynasty that you'll inherit one day," Haraq explained, sliding the book back into its drawer and locking it away with a solid click. "These funds will be used to consolidate our power, making us the most powerful of the Emirates of Murtak."

"You'll be beholden to Nimsah – you've effectively made her emira of Fujareen by putting your name to that. You're *robbing* me of my inheritance rather than preserving it."

Haraq glowered, eyes narrowing. "It's good there's some fire in your belly but have a care. I'm still the emir, though I won't always be and that's the point. With this wealth the ancient families will have no choice other than to admit us to their circle. They'll finally agree to us becoming part of the Bel-Doshok dynasty."

Dojan folded his arms and sank back in his chair. "I've never understood ..." His voice trailed off and he looked at his feet, trying to think of something else to say.

Haraq wagged an admonishing finger. "You've something on your mind, Son. Say it."

"I'm proud to bear the name Al-Haraq, you know that," Dojan began. "Yet, in twenty-six years of marriage, Mother has never made any effort to bestow her own children with her dynastic title. Why have you allowed her to slight us so? You're the emir."

His father looked at him for a long time before replying. "You think it is up to Tanah to decide such things? She's already risked much allying her ancient house to my rule. Don't forget we married in turbulent times, only a few months after Godan's death when the threat of rebellion hung heavy in the air. Do you really believe being emir means I have the power to overturn two thousand years of tradition? The ancient families of the emirate trace their origins back to the Enlightened Age – some of them personally served the avatars. The Bel-Deems refused to countenance the dishonour of acknowledging my rule, leaving me with no choice other than to give the order that extinguished their line forever. When you've watched men, women and children weeping as they walked towards the gallows every day for two weeks you begin to understand what's at stake."

"I've heard the stories," Dojan breathed. "I know what you had to do to avenge my uncle and protect our family. I've seen the Bridge of Sorrows for myself."

His father nodded, eyes distant. "I've never made any secret of where I came from. My father was a warrior and mubarizun, as was I. We didn't come from noble stock – our line was rooted in the skill we showed with the Samarak fighting spear. I was Godan's loyal subject until he turned against my brother, making me a traitor in the eyes of the old dynasties. If Tanah and her brethren had allowed me to become Haraq Bel-Doshok, only for me to lose power, they would have been bound to share the same fate as the house of Godan Bel-Deem."

"The ancient dynasties are bound by ties stronger than love and marriage," Dojan said, repeating a familiar Fujareen saying and understanding it properly for the first time.

"I never wanted to be emir," Haraq continued. "But with Godan dead Fujareen was teetering on the brink of another civil war, with the emirates of Zirhidan, Amjahran and Al-

Narah circling to pick over our bones. Illana was Bel-Jedesh, yet her reputation was forever tainted by spilling royal blood. You know that they even advised me against making her my andral, despite hers being the only one of the ancient houses that fought alongside me? They would never have accepted her as emira, so my case became stronger by default, supported by your mother allying the house of Bel-Doshok to our cause. Enough to bring most of the other ancient houses in line without permanently tying the Bel-Doshok dynasty to the throne; room for manoeuvre that they needed at the time."

Dojan rested his chin on his hands, pondering his father's words. "This political balance has worked up until now. What's changed?"

"I'm getting older," his father replied with a shrug.

"Father, you're fifty-five. You have many more years to look forward to."

"Not as many as those I've already seen. At my age, you start to think about what happens after you're gone. What are you now, Dojan, twenty-three? Twenty-four?"

"I'm twenty-five," Dojan clarified, needled that his father was struggling to remember the birthday of Fujareen's crown prince.

Haraq shook his head, eyes distant. "The years pass more quickly than I can believe. When I was your age I thought I was going to live forever, and there was always time to do everything I hadn't yet done. Well, I've squandered enough of those years and the time has come to formally unite our house with your mother's old family."

"And the other ruling families of Fujareen? If you do this, you're cutting off any claim they might wish to make to the throne, unless they plan on overthrowing the Bel-Doshok dynasty."

Haraq leaned forwards, a hawkish smile spreading over his face. "Which is where the Bank of Illesh comes in. With our coffers full of their shekels we can build an army that will be the envy of our neighbouring emirates. Might and the right to rule are inexorably linked – with Illesh as our backers they would be fools to challenge us."

"Which brings me back to my first point," Dojan countered. "Who is the real andral of our mighty new army? Is it Illana or Nimsah?"

"The Kingdom of Lagash has always paid handsomely for Samarak warriors to fight across the sea under the banner of Morvanos. How is this any different?"

"Those warriors volunteer. We have no choice if the Bank of Illesh summons us. I still don't understand – what does Illesh need with an army? What are you getting us into?"

"It was actually your mother who first saw the opportunity," Dojan's father explained. "Shekh Birizal of the City State of Kandarah has become embroiled in a complex dispute, involving the Naroque Abitek and Edeen tribes."

"There's been talk of this at court. And this concerns the Bank of Illesh, as their ruling council is based there," Dojan surmised.

"They're more deeply involved than that. Illesh financed Birizal to undertake an expedition deep into the jungle of Naroque, which has discovered a safe route to the lost city of Amonduras."

Dojan arranged his face to disguise the fact that this name meant little or nothing to him. There was only a distant tug from a long-forgotten memory stirring at the back of his mind. Was this something Vizier Haman had covered in his teachings of the Samarakand histories? Perhaps.

"So the Fujareen army will be used to help Shekh Birizal secure his claim over Amonduras," said Dojan, trying to move the conversation on without displaying his ignorance.

"Exactly, which is why I want you to go to Kandarah."

Dojan sat bolt upright in his chair, any attempt at mastering his expression forgotten. "Me?"

Haraq sucked in air through his teeth, giving his son a penetrating look. "I think the phrase you're groping for is something along the lines of it would be my honour, Father, to represent our house in this matter."

"*Me*?" Dojan repeated, aware his mouth was hanging open. He tried and failed to close it. "I've never even been to Naroque."

"Here's your opportunity."

"Father, I'm proud you've chosen me for such a mission. However, think about this. I know nothing of Naroque or Kandarah. Am I really best placed to represent you? What about Vizier Haman or Pasha Ulan? They'd do a far better job."

"Actually, it was your mother's idea to send you. A delegation from Fujareen led by its crown prince has a nice ring to it."

"I'm surprised she didn't send Adina instead."

His father's expression softened. "I know those two are close – that's how it can be with mothers and their daughters sometimes. That doesn't mean Tanah doesn't love you ..."

"She just needs me to do something that will make her proud of me," Dojan finished, shaking his head.

"It's not like that," Haraq argued. "I've explained to you why this is so important. Dojan, you're my eldest son and the crown prince. This is an opportunity for you to secure the future of my line and our kingdom – a chance to make a name for yourself."

"I'm not wrong, then."

Dojan knew at once he'd gone too far. Haraq stood up, hands quivering as he set them on the desk and looked down on his son. When he spoke, his voice was quiet and full of menace.

"And is your mother? What have you done with your life so far, my boy? Tell me – I'm waiting."

Dojan sat there, his face flushing hot with embarrassment. Under his father's fierce scrutiny he saw an echo of the warrior that had declared war on his own emir all those years ago. He swallowed, and to his shame no words came.

"I think I've made my point," Haraq said with a look of

disdain. "I'm not a fool, I realise this will be difficult for you, but it's time you lived up to your title, Dojan. I'll be sending Pasha Ulan as your advisor to help you with the negotiations with Birizal. If there is anyone you want to accompany you, it can be arranged. My blood runs through your veins, my son. You have it in you to succeed in this and when you return to Bengarath you'll be a better man in the eyes of your people. A crown prince they can look up to, knowing that one day, when you become their emir, they will be in good hands."

Dojan stood awkwardly, still trying to take in what had happened. "I'll make you and Mother proud, I promise."

His father's face broke into a smile, the storm of his anger abating. "I'm already proud of you, Dojan. It's time for you to put your studies to good use and assume your responsibilities, ready for the day when you'll lead our people."

CHAPTER 9

Spring 199 – Bengarath, the City of Tents

Chandra, sitting cross-legged on the floor of their tent with Nimsah and the rest of her friends, threw the stone high into the air. She swept up the six silver jacks in one easy motion, raising her hand in triumph, a wide grin splitting her face. Nimsah thought the Naroque girl looked cocky. She'd show her.

"Give me the stone," Nimsah muttered, holding out her hand. "And seven jacks."

There was an *oohing* from the crowd of onlookers as Rogesh passed Nimsah the pile of jacks, adding another from a pouch. Nimsah dropped them onto the ground, watching carefully where they rolled as she felt the weight of the stone in her palm. She tossed the stone, taking care not to throw it too hard and send it straight into the fabric roof.

"Farooq! Where are you?" Nimsah jumped, her hand hovering over the jacks as the stone fell with a thud onto a cushion.

Rogesh was the first to his feet, sticking his head through the tent flap and gasping in surprise. Several other children joined him, squirming at the entrance as they jostled for position.

"Out of the way," hissed Nimsah, squeezing past Chandra, the only one of the group bold enough to step outside. It was a fine spring morning, the sun poking out from behind fluffy white clouds. Several other denizens from the tent city were emerging to see the cause of the commotion in the square in front of Farooq's blue tent.

A crowd of armed men, perhaps a score in total, were facing off a smaller number of Farooq's gang members, led by Bizek and Raqqath. The leader of the visitors was a tall, rangy man with a broad scimitar at his hip and thinning black hair. Nimsah didn't need to see the kraken tattoo on the man's arm to know that this was Kamjah.

Farooq swept aside the flap leading to his own tent, Kandilla a step behind, hand on the hilt of her dagger. Farooq crossed his arms, gold and silver bangles glinting in the sunlight, muscles bulging under his black skin. Nimsah thought Farooq cut an altogether more impressive figure than Kamjah, whose face told a tale of hardship and privation.

"You're not deaf, then," Kamjah observed, a sour smile on his face.

Kandilla hissed, hand hovering above her knife. Farooq said nothing, turning to his lover and shaking his head. She scowled, straightening her back as she took a few steps backwards, breathing in hard.

"Did you think I'd forget?" asked Kamjah in a quiet voice. "Did you think this was over, when I had to flee to Amjahran?"

"It should have been," Farooq replied.

Kamjah swept his arm in front of him, taking in the City of Tents. "You took this from me, Farooq. That's not something I could ever forget or forgive. I helped raise you and you betrayed me."

"The Kraken was weak. I took it from you as easily as wrestling a sweetmeat from the fingers of a child. You should have stayed in Amjahran, where it was safe."

Kamjah bridled at the insult. "This was all mine. It will be mine again."

Farooq laughed, the sound echoed by Bizek in a tone that set Nimsah's teeth on edge. Violence was brewing, threatening to boil over at any moment. Nimsah knew she was in danger, hovering on the edge of the square crammed with Kamjah's fighters. She heard Rogesh whisper at her, calling her back inside. She took another step forward, trying to gain a vantage point where she could see Kamjah's face more clearly.

Kamjah's voice was deadly quiet. "You laugh? You *mock* me?"

Farooq shrugged, shaking his arms loose so his hands dangled near the scimitar and knife hanging from his belt. "What are you doing, Kamjah? Are you so foolish you think you can walk into the middle of *my* city and believe I will do nothing?"

"I have allies," Kamjah told Farooq, throwing back his shoulders. "I've not been idle in Amjahran. The name of the man behind Denek Bel-Haroom's death has travelled far across the emirates these past twelve months. You've overreached yourself, Farooq."

The smile on Farooq's face faltered for a moment, quickly masked as he turned away and began to pace in front of Kamjah and his men. Nimsah glanced at Kamjah, who looked satisfied as he saw his words had struck home.

"No quick comeback? Now you see. Now you understand." Kamjah laughed, revealing a mouth of rotting teeth. "Your time ruling the City of Tents is at an end, Farooq."

Farooq's head snapped up at the mention of his name. "No, Kamjah. You're mistaken."

Kandilla's hand moved faster than Nimsah could follow, the dagger a flashing blur as it sped through the air. Kamjah barely reacted in time, swaying to one side with a cry. The dagger thudded wetly into the throat of one of his men, who dropped, gurgling, to the ground. Bizek was already moving as Kamjah's men started to draw their weapons. He shouldered two of them out of the way, drawing his scimitar with a roar, lopping off the hand of the first member of Kamjah's gang to try and fight him. Nimsah stepped back with a cry, staring at the severed hand still clutching a bloodied sword, lying inches from her feet.

More of Farooq's followers emerged from their hiding places, stepping forwards and stabbing the Kraken gang members, blades plunging into backs and necks without mercy. Nimsah realised that Farooq had allowed Kamjah into the heart of his city deliberately, and now his trap was sprung.

Raqqath and Kandilla fought together, killing two Kraken fighters who tried to get near Farooq, spilling their blood onto the ground. Kandilla leaned in, plunging a dagger into the eye of her already dying opponent. She glanced up and saw Nimsah watching her from the far side of the courtyard. Her smile was chilling as she pulled the blade from the twitching body of her victim.

Farooq watched with a calm detachment as Kamjah's men were butchered. Despite the bloody violence he had not even drawn his sword, casually stepping to one side as Bizek hurled the broken body of one Kraken member down at his feet with a crash. The giant lumbered forwards as the injured man struggled to his knees, broken right arm flapping at his side. Bizek clamped his huge hands around his head, hauling him into the air. The man's screams were cut short as Bizek gave him a savage shake, breaking his neck with an audible pop that turned Nimsah's stomach.

Kamjah had drawn his scimitar, looking wildly about as the Kraken gang were slaughtered around him. Raqqath slid his scimitar out of the chest of his last opponent, watching him drop to the ground. Kamjah stood alone in the courtyard, surrounded by Farooq's gang.

Farooq finally drew his sword, cutting through the air with a couple of practice sweeps. "You shouldn't have returned."

Kamjah took a step backwards, halting as he remembered his retreat was cut off. Nearby one of his men managed to raise himself onto all fours, blood soaking his jerkin from several wounds to his stomach. Bizek approached him and brought a sandaled foot down hard on his head. Nimsah had to look away as he continued to stamp on his foe's head, skull crunching as the bones broke apart under the brutal assault. After a moment, all was silent save for Bizek's laboured breathing.

With a defiant shout Kamjah launched himself towards Farooq, sword raised high above his head. Kandilla and Raqqath could have blocked his attack, and Nimsah gasped as they stepped aside, allowing him to charge directly at Farooq. Steel rang as their scimitars met, Farooq blocking the blow and turning it aside, dagger snaking out and biting deep into Kamjah's hip.

Kamjah gasped in pain, turning with difficulty to face Farooq once more, clutching at the wound. "You've made a terrible mistake …"

Farooq snarled, launching into a flurry of complex sweeping strokes that drove Kamjah backwards as he desperately warded off a series of killing blows.

"No," hissed Farooq, voice cold. "You made the mistake stepping off your ship, boasting of your return and having the nerve to walk into my city and demand I step aside."

Farooq's scimitar cut Kamjah on the shoulder, blood spraying the blue fabric of his tent. His dagger missed Kamjah's neck by an inch as the man rolled away, gasping as the move forced him to stretch his injured side. Nimsah could see blood welling up between Kamjah's fingers as he tried to keep pressure on the wound, circling around to keep away from Farooq and find a way through the wall of men blocking his escape.

"Denek served Illesh," gasped Kamjah, pain and fear etched on his face. "I speak for them in this matter."

Farooq shook his head. "No, you don't. They sent you here to kill me, thinking they could replace me with someone as weak as you. They're testing us, and you've been found wanting."

Kamjah dragged in a ragged breath, his sword heavy as he tried to raise it with his injured shoulder. "Let me go. If you have a message for the Bank of Illesh, let me carry it for you."

Farooq smiled widely. "As you wish."

Kamjah let his sword drop with a sigh. "What would you have me say?"

Farooq stepped forwards and swung his scimitar through the air, taking Kamjah's head from his shoulders in a crimson arc, which drew several shouts of surprise from the watching audience. Kamjah's headless corpse fell forwards, blood mingling with the rest of his slaughtered gang.

"Bizek," Farooq shouted. "Take his head and leave it in the market square. I'm sure the Bank of Illesh will understand my meaning well enough."

***

"I've never seen so much blood," declared Rogesh, acting out Farooq's duel with Kamjah for the hundredth time inside their tent as the other children looked on.

"You didn't see *any* blood. You never left the tent," Nimsah observed, drawing a hurt look from her friend.

"I *did* see. I was …"

"Well?"

"I was peering through the tent flap," Rogesh admitted as the other children laughed. "I saw well enough."

Nimsah shook her head, drawing herself up tall as the crowd of children turned to listen. "I saw everything. I was right there, in the square. The hand of a Kraken fighter rolled in front of my feet and, when the battle was done, I saw Bizek lift up Kamjah's severed head."

The younger children lapped up her tale, enjoying the gory details. Nimsah found she had a knack for vivid description, drawing out Kandilla's evil stare as she fought for her life and that of her lover; Bizek crushing his foes with his bare hands; Farooq defiant in the face of Kamjah's challenge. Nimsah felt a swell of pride in her chest as she recounted how Farooq had stood his ground, even once he learned Kamjah was serving the banking clans. The significance was lost on the younger children, although Rogesh understood the importance of what had happened.

"This doesn't end today," he observed later that evening sitting at her side, watching as Chandra entertained their companions with another game of jacks.

"That's true," Nimsah replied.

"The Bank of Illesh sent Kamjah to avenge Denek's death. What do you think they'll do when they find Kamjah's head in the marketplace?"

Nimsah hugged her knees to her chest, thinking before answering. "I think they'll change their opinion of Farooq. They thought they could walk in here and take charge of the City of Tents. Farooq was never going to accept being turned out, after everything he's done to build his life here. That's what he was saying to Kamjah, at the end. The bank was testing both of them – Farooq proved the stronger."

Rogesh frowned, considering her words. "Won't they just come back and try to kill Farooq again?"

Nimsah shook her head. "That's not how this works. They're looking for someone to run things here. If they want control of the City of Tents, who do you think they need to do business with now?"

CHAPTER 10

Summer 213 – Bengarath Docks

Dojan watched Quizar run a hand through his thick hair, straightening it before retying his checked white and red handari in place with a black cord to keep the sun off his head and neck. The wind was strong as they stood on the deck of the warship *Jezar*, the largest baghlah in the fleet making ready for the journey to Kandarah.

"Go on, give me the details. Show me you've been paying attention."

Dojan scowled at the katib, resenting the suggestion that this was a matter of doubt. "Quizar, my father has placed his trust in me. It would be good if you displayed the same level of faith."

Quizar raised an eyebrow. "Crown Prince, I have every confidence in your abilities. In the specific matter of your *concentration*, however ..."

Dojan leaned out over the side of the vessel, watching the activity in the docks where provisions were being loaded onto several of the dozen ships that comprised his fleet. Sailors and dockers shouted and gesticulated at each other, whilst ropes and cranes swung sacks, crates and barrels into the holds. Khanir Shinva had won the argument about who would represent the emir's army, much to Khan Hengesh's displeasure. Half the Blessed Swords were making the journey, and had been pledged to protect Nimsah. It meant the Bel-Doshok house was represented, albeit tacitly via Tanah's personal regiment, on this delegation. Khan Hengesh had swallowed his pride, accepting Andral Illana's decision to send Shinva to speak on behalf of the Fujareen army. Hengesh's Mighty Spears had to be satisfied with the task of guarding the crown prince. Hadir's face remained inscrutable as he stood on deck nearby, the mubarizun silently watching over Dojan's efforts to master the political intricacies of Kandarah.

Dojan pursed his lips, watching Nimsah talking to Shinva down on the quayside. She was dressed in yellow this morning, a golden shawl of silk with a patterned veil covering her face and hair. The Bank of Illesh spoke as one – and the veil was a common custom amongst its representatives, reminding outsiders that they were dealing with the organisation, not the individual. Although he couldn't see her face, Nimsah stood out in the busy crowd – her clothes were the finest quality, telling a story of money, power and success.

"Why would the Bank of Illesh finance Birizal's expedition to find Amonduras?" Dojan mused. "The ruined capital of the fallen dragon race, destroyed by Morvanos and surrounded by poisoned lands. No doubt it's been consumed by the jungles of Naroque in the past two hundred years, its crumbling stones now surely only of interest to antiquarians and scholars. So, what's in it for Birizal and the Illesh bankers?"

"It's a good question," Quizar remarked. "The legends concerning the risks of trying to reach Amonduras are well-known. Any such venture would be highly dangerous and speculative, yet Nimsah doesn't strike me as the gambling type." With his father's blessing, Dojan had shared sufficient details of the purpose of their mission to Kandarah with Quizar so that his katib could properly advise him. Ulan hadn't liked it; recalling the look on his face when he'd found out gave Dojan cause to smile as he replied.

"Birizal must have known the consequences would be destabilising for the region. The Abitek and Edeen tribes' whole history is bound up with the dragon race. They consider Amonduras to be their birthright. The City of Kandarah doesn't have the military might to defend its walls and secure Amonduras in the face of opposition from both tribes. Eighteen months of increasingly fractious negotiations and skirmishes haven't resolved who has the better claim – now we're drawn into this mess."

Quizar nodded. "The Abitek are the most powerful of the Naroque tribes, able to call thousands of warriors to their banner. If their cousins, the smaller Edeen tribe, support them then, from a military standpoint, things look bleak. Kandarah may be the wealthiest of the independent city states of Naroque but their population and standing army is tiny. Before getting into all of this the financiers of Illesh must have known their coin would need to secure another power, ensuring they could settle such matters in their favour should it come to war."

"And Fujareen answered the call. One thing's for sure, the Abitek and Edeen will be no match for Andral Illana's army."

Hadir apologetically interrupted their discussion to introduce two new arrivals on the *Jezar*. "Arak Bel-Yangash of the Order of Veiled Magi and Tormindah El-Shan, representing the Magi of the Farseeing."

Dojan turned and inclined his head in greeting as they exchanged pleasantries. He knew Arak, despite the fact he was hidden behind his pure white robes and veil. A member of the Bel-Yangash dynasty, Arak was a distant cousin of Vizier Haman Bel-Yangash and the pair were close allies. The woman with him, Tormindah, was dressed in grey robes and wore a black headscarf. Olive-skinned like most Fujareen denizens, she looked to be about thirty and had an open, honest face, rather than being classically beautiful. Although she seemed friendly enough, Dojan instinctively found himself adopting the mental exercises Vizier Haman had drilled into him to ward off the unwanted intrusion of those with the Sight.

"Ah, I see you have already become acquainted with my advisors for this voyage." Pasha Ulan approached them with a cursory bow, black robes flapping in the wind, a small retinue of guards from the Tireless Shields at his back.

"Indeed, Ulan," Dojan replied, taking a few steps away from Tormindah. "Quizar and I were just discussing how important it is to take every precaution on this mission to Kandarah."

"The Abitek tribe has much skill in the Sight, a gift they share with the Edeen," Tormindah told him in a soft voice. "I know the gifts of the Farseeing can be … disconcerting for some," her black eyes bored into Dojan before she continued. "However, it will be my honour to guard your thoughts and those of your companions, Crown Prince."

"Knowledge is prized more highly than gold," Dojan replied, recalling something Nimsah had said.

"Just so," Arak agreed with a nod. "You'll be in safe hands with Tormindah, Crown Prince. I chose her personally." Dojan smiled, making a mental note of where her loyalties lay.

"Nimsah has advised that the Edeen recently tried to broker a peace between the Abitek and Shekh Birizal, which complicates matters," Ulan added. "One of the things I want Tormindah and Arak to try and uncover are the motivations of this tribe."

"The Edeen are descended from the Abitek, having split with them many centuries ago during the Age of Enlightenment," Quizar added. "Both tribes were dragon worshipers – the Abitek their warriors, the Edeen guardians of their knowledge. Amonduras is significant for both of them for different reasons."

Pasha Ulan stroked his beard. "Exactly. The question is what *does* lie in the ruins of Amonduras? Forgotten secrets of the dragon race? Gold and silver? An empty pile of broken stones buried in wind-blown ash?" Dojan nodded, relieved that Ulan appeared to have no clearer idea than he did on such an important point.

"One of our objectives is to prise such secrets from Shekh Birizal," said Arak. "If Fujareen is to go to war in support of Kandarah's cause it would be preferable to know what we are fighting for is worth it."

"Many questions where we still have to learn the truth," Dojan replied. "I'm sure that Pasha Ulan has chosen my advisors carefully, so that on our return to Bengarath we will have all the answers in our possession."

Arak and Tormindah bowed at Dojan's compliment, as Pasha Ulan smiled. "Thank you, Crown Prince. We will repay your faith in us, I promise."

Dojan watched as Ulan led away his crowd of followers. If Beneth was to become vizier one day, the only one who stood in his way was Pasha Ulan. Normally, being the emir's son would have been enough to secure Beneth's position. Ulan's masterstroke of proposing to Adina had put him back into contention. Second in line to the throne, Adina would want her future husband as the emir's closest advisor in order to maintain her influence. Dojan sighed, regretting his earlier sharp words to his sister. He knew he would pay for them, one way or another – perhaps sooner, now the opportunity to travel to Kandarah with Ulan had presented itself.

"Who do we ally ourselves with and who should we oppose?" mused Dojan. "This journey across the sea to Naroque is going to be testing, placing us in the middle of an argument we don't fully understand between the Kandarans, Abitek and the Edeen. I hope this alliance with Illesh is going to be worth all the trouble it's already caused."

Quizar laughed. "Crown Prince, I do believe I misjudged you. You're taking a keener interest in the outcome of our negotiations than I expected."

Dojan glared. "I've already told you how important this is to my father. I'll not have Pasha Ulan running things on this voyage, Quizar. Do you understand? This is my delegation, not his. I should have had a say in the advisors who accompanied me. Instead, they're presented to me whilst I'm standing on deck and about to depart."

"My apologies, Crown Prince," said Quizar, bowing with

more deference than usual.

Dojan sighed. "No. I'm sorry, my friend. I spoke harshly. I can see my sister's handiwork in this and I've let her take the initiative. The outcome of this mission is every bit as important to Adina and Ulan as it is to me. If Ulan does well it will cement his position at court and pave the way for him to become vizier when Haman stands aside. Ulan's always thoroughly prepared and he'll want to control every aspect of our visit to ensure its success. I'm glad you're with me, Quizar. You're the only one around here I can trust."

Quizar smiled and patted Dojan on the shoulder, a breach of royal protocol that Dojan appreciated. He clasped Quizar's hand for a moment before looking out across the dockside once more. Dojan's eyes wandered back to where Nimsah was standing with Shinva. They would be travelling separately on another vessel – another missed opportunity. All his father wanted was for Dojan to be the figurehead for a successful mission. No one really expected him to *do* anything – Pasha Ulan was already behaving as if this was *his* delegation.

Dojan reflected on whether he had been right to withhold the story of how he had first met Nimsah from his father. He wondered if Shinva had said something. Had the Khanir of the Blessed Swords even made the connection concerning their shared history? It had been a long time ago, and although the memory was fresh in Dojan's mind he'd never discussed those events with Shinva, acting in accordance with an unspoken agreement.

"If I may venture a question?" began Quizar.

"Ask it."

"I can't help notice your attention never strays far from young Nimsah. Is there something I should know?"

Dojan cleared his throat, reflecting that Quizar's question was uncomfortably close to the mark. "I've no intention of laying a hand on her, I promise you."

Quizar frowned. "I've seen the way you look at her. You do know that the bank's representatives never have relations with anyone outside their house? Nothing is allowed to compromise their loyalty."

"What did I just say? I understand how much is at stake and I'm not going to do anything that undermines what my father is trying to achieve. She's a woman of quality, Quizar – bright and ambitious. She sees … into my heart, in a very different way to a Sight user. When we speak she's always one or two steps ahead of me, that's all. I let her fluster me when we first met. It won't happen again, I promise you."

Quizar looked at Dojan, unconvinced, before deciding to change the subject. "The involvement of Sight users isn't a welcome sign. I only know Tormindah by reputation as one of the most gifted of the Farseeing. The fact that Ulan thinks someone of her skill is needed on this voyage should put us on our guard."

"It's an awful thought – the idea that someone can worm their way into another's mind to uncover their secrets," replied Dojan with distaste.

Quizar pursed his lips. "Without Sightwielders every nations' spymasters would be placed at a great disadvantage."

"A necessary evil, I suppose," agreed Dojan.

"Sight users and shamans of the avatars are both held in high regard by the Naroque tribes," Quizar added. "It may not be Birizal's advisors we need to be most wary of. The Bank of Illesh and Kandarah need our support because the Abitek and the Edeen are powerful, and have considerable influence with the other tribes in Naroque. We need to play all sides in this potential war carefully to secure our own advantage."

Dojan nodded in agreement and returned his attention to the quayside, deep in thought. When he looked in Nimsah's direction, he found her looking straight back at him. He offered her a wave that he hoped appeared sufficiently regal and imposing. He'd meant what he'd said to Quizar – he was determined to show a different side of himself to Nimsah. One she would approve of.

CHAPTER 11

Summer 199 – Bengarath Market

Nimsah sat crossed-legged at Fenara's feet as the pair chatted at the basket weaver's stall. Nimsah held up her finished basket and Fenara's face broke into a smile.

"That's perfect, Nimsah. Let me put it here, at the front of my display. Pride of place."

Nimsah grinned, enjoying the compliment. It felt good to be back in the marketplace, away from the City of Tents, although those two worlds had become much closer after Farooq's defeat of Kamjah. Nimsah had wandered into the central square of the market early that morning. She knew Bizek would have carried out Farooq's orders without question. However, the authorities had clearly been alerted early, and of Kamjah's head there was no sign. Of course, that didn't mean people hadn't seen what had happened. When Nimsah sought out Fenara it was all she talked about.

"What is Bengarath coming to, Nimsah, when a thing like that can happen here, a hundred yards from where I work?" Fenara had said, wringing her hands. "I heard someone say it was Kamjah's head – the leader of the old Kraken gang. They had a terrible reputation, until they vanished a couple of summers ago. People were so relieved and now they're back – it's the last thing Bengarath needs."

"Maybe they won't be back for long, if it was this Kamjah's head in the marketplace," Nimsah observed. Fenara looked horrified at her words. "I'm sorry, Fenara, I didn't mean to cause offence."

Fenara sighed. "I know you didn't, child. Just be careful, please."

Nimsah had to hide a smirk as she bent down over her half-made basket. Having learned all that she needed to, she steered Fenara back to her usual subjects. Soon she was fussing over Nimsah as usual, asking if she was eating well and looking askance at her thin smock. After a time, Fenara fell silent and Nimsah could tell there was something on her mind.

"Nimsah …"

"What is it, Fenara?"

"This business, in the marketplace this morning. Some people are talking about how the Kraken used to run things … in the City of Tents."

"Did they?" Nimsah asked, looking up at Fenara with an innocent expression.

"I know Farooq of Naroque is in charge these days and that's where you live. Nimsah, I'm worried about you."

Nimsah frowned. "I've told you, Farooq looks after me."

"Men like that don't do anything without good reason. He's only offering you his protection now because he has plans for you in the future. People aren't selfless and kind in this world – they always want something in return."

"And what is it *you* want from me?"

Nimsah immediately regretted her hasty words, wishing she could call them back as Fenara's face darkened. It was the first time she'd seen her angry. "How could you? I always pay you for your time. I've opened my house and shared my meals with you, never asking for anything back. And you have the nerve to compare me to that … evil man. Farooq has a reputation, Nimsah. Don't pretend I'm so stupid that I don't know you're well aware of the kind of man he is. Why do you think I'm worried about you?"

"I can look after myself." The words escaped Nimsah's lips much to her surprise. She'd been about to say something completely different.

Fenara's eyes narrowed. "Are you sure? You're a bright young woman, or at least I thought you were. Is the life Farooq offers one you really want?"

Nimsah was on her feet, without any idea of how that had happened. "I've worked a whole morning for you. I'll take my pay now, thank you."

Fenara looked at Nimsah's outstretched hand, wounded by her words, though she tried to hide it. She reached into her bag and dropped a few copper shekels into Nimsah's palm; more than she was due. Nimsah closed her hand around the coins and pocketed them anyway as she walked away from Fenara's stall.

Left at an unexpected loose end for the remainder of the day, Nimsah wandered through the market with little real purpose. She was cross at herself for how she'd spoken to Fenara; the woman was only trying to help, after all. As she walked, Nimsah noticed that a crowd of people were making their way towards the docks, some of them pushing and shoving to get to the front. Her interest piqued, Nimsah headed off in the same direction, taking advantage of her quick feet and skinny frame to squeeze through the throng and work her way towards the front.

With some pushing and shoving Nimsah found herself pressed up against a wall of warriors in ceremonial chainmail, their breastplates highly polished, some with swords and shields, others with ornate fighting spears strapped to their backs. They were standing on a quayside, where a space had been cleared of the ordinary rabble. Several men and women, all wearing fine silks and colourful robes, were waiting at the bottom of a wide gangplank leading to the largest baghlah Nimsah had ever seen. Calling it a gangplank was underselling the quality of the object linking the ship to the docks. It was fashioned out of polished mahogany, with a handrail to prevent the vessel's passengers from making a less dignified return to the shore. Each rail was a single piece of flowing wood, the intricate whorls and grain shown off through a lacquer that gleamed in the sun, finely tooled spindles decorated with gold leaf connected the whole structure together. Nimsah could see this object was worth more than many a merchant vessel on the docks. The crews of several neighbouring baghlahs and dhows were watching proceedings from their vantage point, the task of unloading their cargo momentarily forgotten.

"His Royal Highness the Emir of Fujareen, Haraq Al-Souk, and his beautiful wife, Her Royal Highness Princess Tanah Bel-Doshok," announced the ship's captain.

The dignitaries on the dockside bowed low as a khan led the emir and his wife down the mahogany bridge. Haraq was smaller than Nimsah had expected, an ordinary looking man with a greying beard and a paunch. In contrast Tanah, his wife, was a beautiful young woman, dark hair trailing down her back rather than protected from the sun by a shawl as was the custom in Fujareen. Tanah was animated and lively, waving to the crowd and flashing them a smile as she walked with poise, head held high. She lapped up their cheers as Haraq gently took her manicured hand to steady her as she placed a sandaled foot on the stone quayside.

In the wake of the emir and his princess were two children, a boy of perhaps ten or eleven and a girl a year or two younger than him. Nimsah, who was proud of the clothes she had back in the City of Tents, felt a pang of jealousy as she looked at the fine green silk gown of the girl, the boy in a black and silver tunic with loose black trousers. Surrounded by guards, the emir's children were clearly the most precious cargo on the royal baghlah after Fujareen's ruler. Nearby there was some pushing and shoving as some people tried to get closer and catch a glimpse of the emir and his wife. It sent a ripple through the cheering crowd, jostling Nimsah into the back of one of the guards, who glanced down and pushed her back.

"Keep your thieving hands out of my purse, street rat," he hissed, his beard framing a snarl under his silver helmet.

Nimsah glowered, biting back a retort that might earn her a cuff on the ear – or worse. The crowd surged forwards, the ceremonial warriors breaking etiquette and turning their backs on the emir as they interlocked their spears and formed a barrier to restrain the onlookers. Nimsah eyed the sharp steel, worried that by being at the front she might get pushed too close for comfort. As the mass of people on the dockside continued to shift and sway like choppy waters, Nimsah could see two sailors walking past the distracted guards towards the royal family. Both wore scarves over their faces and they rolled a barrel into place, stacking it carefully next to five others. One of them reached into his pocket, pulling out a small oil flask with a short length of cloth pushed into the neck at the top.

His dark eyes met with Nimsah's as her mouth dropped open. She shouted a warning, unheard in the din of the crowd, as she struggled back, fighting to get away from the line of guards who were occupied with holding back the throng.

"For the house of Bel-Deem," shouted the man holding the oil flask, which was now lit. He tossed it towards an open barrel right in the middle of the stack before turning and running away with his companion.

Nimsah watched with horror as the flaming oil flask arced through the air, unseen by the distracted guards, and dropped with a soft thud into the open barrel. Nimsah crouched down low, covering her head with her hands as the barrel hissed. There was a thunderous crash and a roaring noise that slammed into Nimsah's chest, hurling her backwards as a flash of heat seared her hands and arms. The cheering crowd began to scream, the sound reaching Nimsah as if from a distance, distorted and strange. She opened her eyes and fought to take a breath as she saw fire raging on the dockside, bodies strewn everywhere, several warriors of the royal household screaming as they clutched at the stumps of severed limbs, many of them burning.

Nimsah glanced at where the emir had been standing with his family. The gangplank was gone and several of those waiting to receive the emir were lying on the ground. Tanah was shrieking, clutching her daughter to her chest.

"Adina! Adina, talk to me," Tanah shouted, smoothing the girl's hair from her soot-stained cheeks as she tried to see if she was hurt.

"She's breathing. She'll be fine," gasped one of the guards, trying to help the princess to her feet. "Princess, we need to move, it isn't safe –"

The man's words were cut off as a group of black-clad attackers, again masked by scarves, emerged from a nearby building, knives drawn. The nearest one stabbed the warrior trying to help Tanah straight through the throat. The surviving royal guards had already formed a knot around the emir, who was shakily getting back to his feet. His eyes widened as his bodyguards fanned out, trying to hold back the onslaught of his assassins.

Nimsah spotted that the emir's son was wandering through the crowd, eyes glazed, clothes torn and bloody. Two of the attackers in black peeled away from the main fight, angling their way through the dispersing crowd directly towards him. Nimsah got to her feet and propelled herself forwards towards the boy, calling out at him to watch his back. He didn't seem to hear her, weaving his way through the dead and dying with a blank expression. A wounded guard also saw the danger, limping forwards to intercept the men advancing on the young prince. His scimitar cut through the first man, opening up a hideous red wound across his chest. The second man snarled, stabbing at him, plunging his dagger into the warrior's thigh.

The prince continued to walk through the thinning crowd, unaware of the fight raging behind him. A man and a woman, a screaming girl clasped tight in the man's arms, ran past, accidently clipping the boy as they ran. He sprawled on his face next to the body of a dead sailor, the assassin in black fixing his eyes on him as he killed the royal guard with a savage upwards cut into his stomach, right under the breastplate.

Afterwards, Nimsah couldn't have said why she did it. She ran forwards, springing over bodies, feet splashing through puddles of congealing blood. Half the dockside was on fire and thick smoke swirled through the air, moving with a will of its own as the wind changed its course, eddying around the quayside. Nimsah reached the boy and hauled him to his feet, looking up, heart hammering when she saw the man in black had retrieved his knife and was staring straight at them.

"Get up," Nimsah shouted, dragging the boy to his feet. He stood there, swaying, limp like a rag doll.

Nimsah growled and took his hand, hauling him forwards. She half-expected him to fall flat on his face again. However, something must have fallen into place and the prince began to run, hand clasped tightly in hers as Nimsah led them down an alley. She could hear the footsteps of the man following them and she didn't look back, putting her head down as she followed the route by memory, darting left and right, half-dragging the prince behind her, his breath increasingly ragged and loud.

After a few minutes Nimsah found a pile of crates stacked at the rear of an old warehouse. She glanced behind her and with no sign of pursuit she took a deep breath and pointed. "Up there."

"Up. Where?" gasped the boy, looking around, eyes wide.

"Follow me," hissed Nimsah, planting her foot on top of one of the crates as she began to climb. The boy hesitated, only starting to move as the echoing sound of running feet started to draw closer.

Nimsah scaled the crates with ease, crouching down below a window on the first floor of the warehouse. The rotting shutters drooped on their hinges, open half an inch. Nimsah knew they wouldn't be locked and prised them open, wincing as they creaked. She shoved the prince through the narrow gap before jumping in afterwards, pulling them shut and breathing hard.

The pair of them crouched in the shadows for a time, Nimsah waiting for the pounding of her heart and the ringing in her ears to subside. She looked down at her hands, unable to make out much in the gloom and the narrow shaft of light that came through the broken shutters. The backs of her hands and her arms were stinging and sore to the touch. Nimsah remembered the bodies strewn across the bloodied stones of the quayside, knowing it could have been worse.

"Thank you." The boy's voice sounded small and lost in the darkness of the warehouse.

"It was no trouble," Nimsah replied, thinking that it had been the exact opposite.

"Have we lost him?"

Nimsah let out a sigh. "Yes, I think he ran straight past us. This is a good hiding place."

"I'm Dojan," the boy whispered. He coughed and cleared his throat. "I'm Crown Prince Dojan Al-Haraq, son of the noble emir of Fujareen. They'll be wondering what's happened to me."

Nimsah grinned, although she didn't think Dojan could see her smile. "I'm Nimsah, from the City of Tents. Pleased to make your acquaintance, Crown Prince."

CHAPTER 12

Summer 213 – Bengarath Docks

Looking out over the quayside, Dojan tried to remember if this was the same place where the Bel-Deem loyalists had attacked his family all those years ago. His memories of those events were hazy. The only thing that stood out bright and clear was meeting Nimsah and that dizzying, headlong rush in the maze of alleyways threading their way through the docklands district. It reminded him of the legends Vizier Haman entertained him with, as a reward for doing well at his studies. As a child, Dojan thought his life would one day turn into another of those great adventures. His hands clasped the gunwale, knuckles white. There was nothing he could do to change the past.

Nimsah was walking towards the *Jezar*, Khanir Shinva in close attendance. Dojan wondered what the pair were discussing and how Nimsah was really feeling. Surely coming back here stirred the same painful memories? As he watched her approach he asked himself the question that should have been obvious from the moment they were reunited. How could a child of the streets, brought up in the foul City of Tents – a sore on the face of Bengarath – now be working for one of the most powerful banks in Samarakand? There was no delicate way to raise the question in front of Pasha Ulan and Katib Quizar, as Nimsah climbed aboard the *Jezar* and politely enquired how their preparations were going. Her refined voice was so different from the child he'd first met fourteen years ago.

"Yes, all goes well," announced Dojan, waving in the general direction of the ship and gesturing at its folded sails. He felt a prickle of heat rise up his neck as he realised he had absolutely no idea what the *Jezar's* crew were doing. Were they minutes away from departure or did they have to wait hours for the turning of the tide?

"The captain of *Farah's Wings* reports that the rest of the fleet is set to leave shortly."

"That's good," Dojan replied, aware he was grinning like an idiot. "Very good indeed."

"I wanted to wish you well for the voyage and look forward to meeting you again in Kandarah. I'll offer up a prayer to Nanquido and Culdaff for still waters and favourable winds."

"I thought the Bank of Illesh worshipped the new gods of shekel and commerce, rather than the disgraced avatars of the past," commented Pasha Ulan, looking pleased with himself. "They took no part in the War of the Avatars, refusing to side with Morvanos in his efforts to end the Tyranny, so please forgive me if I baulk at praying to those who didn't side with our noble cause."

Nimsah bowed her head slightly. "The Kandarans say that it does well to embrace the future whilst remembering the past. Nanquido poured out the waters upon Amuran whilst Culdaff stirred the winds and fashioned the weather, if the old stories told by the shamans are to be believed. Since they weren't banished to the Void at the end of the War by the Creator, I'd rather show my respect and curry favour with those avatars who still walk upon the face of Amuran."

Ulan inclined his head. "My observation was not meant as an insult, good lady. I wear the red handari of Morvanos, so I respect the avatars' teachings from the Enlightened Age. However, I'll put my trust in Morvanos and the eternal cycle of change, rather than in those avatars who stood by and did nothing as the fate of Amuran was decided."

Dojan tried to imagine Nimsah's expression behind her veil as she replied. "I've always wondered if prayers are heard across the vastness of the Void. Unless you are gifted as a shaman, of course?" Quizar drew in a sharp breath, for Nimsah's words were close to heresy. Such thoughts, though they might be tolerated in the emirates, would have provoked a stoning in the Kingdoms of Kalat.

"I'm no shaman," Ulan said with a regretful smile. "However, I was taught that prayers shape the thoughts and ways of those who offer them up, and so they are never wasted. Morvanos may be banished, yet his teachings and knowledge survive. His shamans have the honour of direct contact with those across the Void. I must be satisfied with listening to their guidance and following the decrees of the avatars from afar."

"Such a devout man, and yet you serve as pasha to one of the secular emirates, rather than one of the religious Kingdoms of Kalat. An interesting choice, both on your part and that of your emir."

"I had the privilege of studying for three years at the court of the Sultan of Urumesh in Kalat," Ulan explained. "Whilst I was offered a position in Urumesh, I felt I could do more good by returning here, to the land of my birth. The world needs to hear and understand Morvanos' wisdom. His teachings need to be shared with the neighbouring lands."

"Or imposed, if necessary?" asked Nimsah.

Ulan smiled, bowing low to signify that he was about to take his leave. "If necessary. I had no idea you had such an interest in religious matters, Nimsah. I look forward to continuing these discussions when we arrive at Kandarah. It will be a welcome distraction from trade and politics."

"Those evenings spent with Pasha Ulan will simply fly by," quipped Dojan in an undertone as he watched Ulan's retreating back, Arak and Tormindah in tow.

Nimsah laughed quietly. "Don't be cruel. I genuinely find the subject fascinating."

"Oh," said Dojan, surprised. "If you were to ask me

whether it was right for Morvanos to rise up against the suffocating and ossified ways of the self-styled Avatars of Light then yes, I agree wholeheartedly. The question is, does this mantra have any relevance today? After all, Morvanos overthrew Vellandir, Garradon and the others and ended the Tyranny. The fact the Creator banished *all* the avatars who fought in that terrible war to the Void was certainly unfortunate for Morvanos and his followers. However, they achieved their overall objective, bringing the old ways that consolidated power in the hands of an elite few to an end, whilst also freeing the human race from a life of servitude under the dragons. What is there left to fight about today, other than expanding the power and influence of the countries that arose in the aftermath of the War?"

"Such thoughts would be considered sacrilege in Kalat," said Quizar in a low tone.

"We're in the Emirates of Murtak, Quizar. As the crown prince I'm permitted to voice my thoughts in my own country."

"Of course you may, Crown Prince. My only concern was that you have a care about who is listening to such words. Not everyone is as wise or as tolerant as your good self."

"Quizar advises you well," added Nimsah. "Whilst I welcome your candour I suspect that Pasha Ulan would view things very differently."

Dojan shrugged. "The emirate should be tolerant enough to be the home of people with different views. It's something I intend to enshrine in law when I become emir."

"Do you think your future brother-in-law will support you?" asked Nimsah, looking in the direction of Ulan, who was making ready to board his own ship.

"If he wants to be vizier, then yes. Although that's a difficult subject in itself – who do I wish to favour? My sister's husband or my youngest brother? Part of me hopes that Vizier Haman decides to step down from his duties whilst my father is still the emir. At least that way it won't be my decision."

"I think your brother Beneth would accept being passed over," Quizar offered. "He has the brains to be vizier, no question. However, he could turn his hand to other things and be equally satisfied. I could see Beneth prospering as a scholar in the university, for example. Pasha Ulan lives and breathes the politics of Fujareen. Taking away the prospect of him becoming vizier would destroy him."

"He's young to be pasha," Nimsah observed. "Isn't it rather soon to be talking of him taking up an even more responsible position?"

Dojan nodded. "You're right, he's of an age with me. I suspect that Haman will want to continue for several more years before this issue arises. Ulan was promoted from katib when father announced his engagement to my sister. It wasn't such a surprise – he was schooled for many years by Vizier Haman before he was sent to Urumesh, and the two have worked together closely since his return. Ulan is extremely able, which is why Haman has entrusted him with the diplomacy of our foreign affairs. As a partner for my sister, however …" Dojan paused, finding that once again Nimsah had drawn out more than he had intended to reveal.

"You don't approve?"

"That's not what I meant. It's not for me to approve. They're very different, that's all. The first thing someone meeting my sister will notice is her energy and good humour. She has an easy way with people and she sparkles in any gathering. Ulan is more serious minded and incredibly dedicated and focussed. I can't recall a time when I ever saw the man relax. Don't be fooled, though – they're both very ambitious and complement each other well. As long as Adina is happy with the match, and I know she is, that's all that matters."

Nimsah turned, and when Dojan followed her gaze he could see a procession, flanked on all sides by armed guards. He recognised his father's royal carriage in the centre, inlaid with gold and pulled by eight horses. The carriage was reinforced with steel on all sides, an innovation after the attempted assassination on the docks.

"Your father has brought the whole Regiment of Royal Arquebusiers with him," Quizar observed, pointing at the force leading the procession, each man carrying an arquebus on his shoulder.

Dojan smiled. "You see, Nimsah. Illesh and Kandarah have chosen the right military partner. No other Samarak army can boast such innovative gunpowder weaponry. I'm told the arquebus musket can fire a deadly shot at a range of up to six hundred yards."

"Assuming they hit something," interjected Hadir, a scowl on his face. "Our archers in the Regiment of the Stooping Falcon have greater skill and are thus more deadly."

"Thank you, Hadir," replied Dojan with a note of finality which caused the mubarizun to stiffen and step back. "The point is you will have both military innovation *and* traditional skill at your disposal, should it be required."

"One of many reasons why Fujareen was our partner of choice in this particular endeavour," said Nimsah, bowing to the crown prince. "If you will excuse me, I must return to my ship."

"I'll offer up my prayers to Culdaff and Nanquido for a pleasant crossing," Dojan told her and, whilst he couldn't be sure, he thought that under her veil Nimsah smiled as she took her leave and left for *Farah's Wings*.

"You'll keep your opinions to yourself in future, Hadir," Dojan told the warrior once Nimsah was out of earshot. "Especially when I'm trying to make a good impression on an honoured guest."

"My apologies, Crown Prince," Hadir replied, his expression inscrutable.

Dojan nodded, satisfied, and watched as the royal procession stopped. His family emerged from the carriage once the guards had thoroughly swept the docks for any sign of danger. Royal Arquebusiers, Mighty Spears and Blessed

Swords formed an honour guard that protected the emir as he stood with Dojan's mother, sister and two brothers. He waved in their direction, smiling when Saraj and Beneth pointed at the *Jezar* and waved back. Adina and Tanah were deep in conversation as usual, his sister more interested in Ulan's ship moored further down the dockside.

"I suppose Adina has as much riding on this venture as I," Dojan mused.

"We all have," said Quizar. "If this goes well, I'd like to discuss my own position."

Quizar's remark stunned Dojan and he turned to his katib, open-mouthed. "I'm sorry? You'd like to discuss what?"

Quizar looked embarrassed. "Crown Prince, I meant no disrespect, I assure you. However, you must understand that I don't intend to serve in the emir's government as a katib forever."

Dojan shook his head, realising how short-sighted he was being. "No, Quizar, of course not. Naturally, I want you to prosper. It's just that I value your advice – whoever steps into your position will be a poor replacement after your dedicated service."

"A friend serving as a pasha will be more valuable to you in the long term than having me remain as your aide," Quizar explained, with a smile. "Ulan has a firm grip on the position of pasha for foreign affairs. However, I have wondered, if I may be so bold, whether there would be an opportunity for me to become pasha with responsibility for the Treasury? As our ties with the Bank of Illesh grow this will be an even more important position, where having a close ally in charge of such matters could prove valuable."

Dojan looked into Quizar's face, thinking over his words. "I see the sense in what you're saying. When we return from Kandarah, I'll speak personally to Haman and argue your case."

Quizar bowed. "Thank you, Crown Prince. I am your ever-humble servant."

CHAPTER 13

Summer 199 – Bengarath Docks

What do you do with a lost prince? Nimsah chewed on the question as she led Dojan out of the warehouse, both of them squinting in the bright sunlight. They'd run some distance from the docks and she had no idea whether the emir and his guards would still be there. The palace, then? A further, unwelcome, thought wormed its way inside her skull.

"We have to get back," said Dojan, staring up and down the alleyway, wary of a further attack. His face was smeared with soot, splashes of dark blood on his forearms and across his chest, covering his fine clothes, which were torn in places. Nimsah glanced down and saw that her smock was similarly ruined.

"Are you hurt?"

Dojan touched his chest, his fingers coming away bloody, his dark eyes widening. "Er … No. No, I don't think so. I don't think this is mine. Myshall be cursed – my family. What happened to them? I don't remember, there was so much noise … and …"

Nimsah put a hand on the prince's shoulder. "They're alright. I saw the guards protecting them after the attack. You'd wandered away from them, which is why I came to help."

"Adina," Dojan breathed. "She was lying on the floor."

"The guard said she was breathing," Nimsah told him. She had no idea if that was still the case, not that it mattered. She had to get Dojan moving, and away from this alley.

Dojan nodded. "That's good. We have to go and find her. We need to get back to the docks."

"No, you can't go back there. We don't know if they'll be safe," Nimsah reasoned.

Dojan thought on that for a moment. "I live at Bengarath Palace. That's where my mother and father will be going. We should head there instead."

Nimsah looked at the ragged boy in front of her, weighing up her options. He was a year or two younger than her and looked on the verge of tears, his hands shaking.

"Right. Right, then." Dojan paused. "Er ... I don't know where we are."

"That's alright. I do. I come here all the time."

"Do you know where the palace is?"

Nimsah nodded. "Of course. Follow me, Dojan."

Dojan hesitated, a small frown on his face. "Nimsah, I ..."

"What is it?"

Dojan cleared his throat. "I'm the emir's son. You can't just call me Dojan."

"That's your name, isn't it?"

"Well, yes, it is."

Nimsah flashed a smile at the boy. "We're friends now. Do your friends call you lord and majesty all the time?" She finished with a clumsy curtsy that made Dojan grin.

"Actually, they just call me Crown Prince."

Nimsah frowned as she stood straight. "I can't call you *Crown Prince* as we walk these streets. Dojan will have to do."

Dojan stared at her, bemused, and Nimsah wondered if anyone had ever said no to the boy before. "Well ... since we're friends ..."

Nimsah turned to the sound of voices at the entrance to the alley – a group of dock workers, walking slowly towards them. She didn't think they'd been seen, and in that moment Nimsah made her decision.

"Come on, Dojan, it's time to go."

Nimsah led the prince via the back alleys and narrow side streets of Bengarath. Their appearance drew sidelong glances whenever they passed people, although no one stopped either to challenge them or ask if they were alright. Dojan kept pausing, staring at each new sight – a shop, a coffeehouse, a beggar – they each provoked the same reaction. He was completely unaware that Nimsah's route was taking him away from the palace and towards the City of Tents.

"Look at all this," Dojan gasped, jogging up to Nimsah's side when she told him to hurry up. "I've been to the emirates of Amjahran and Zirhidan, and yet I could probably count on the fingers of one hand the times I've left the palace when I'm in Bengarath. This city is vast. How do you find your way around?"

"I've never lived anywhere else," Nimsah admitted.

"And you know my own city better than me. Me, the son of the emir."

Nimsah shrugged. "Is it so surprising, if you've never left the palace?"

"No, I don't suppose it is," Dojan replied, looking thoughtful. "Why do you live there? In the City of Tents, I mean. Does your family live there too?"

"I live on my own," Nimsah answered, not liking how Dojan's question had caught her off-guard.

"What happened to your parents?"

"They … I'm not sure. They left me there ten years ago, when I was a small child. It happens a lot, when people are poor or get sick. Sometimes they can't look after their children, and they have no choice except to leave them behind. I don't even remember their names."

"I'm sorry about that," Dojan replied, and they walked for a time in silence until he spoke again. "So who looks after you now? Who feeds you? Where do you sleep?"

Nimsah shot Dojan a look. "You ask a lot of questions."

He looked embarrassed. "I'm sorry. I didn't mean to pry. It's just … I've never met anyone …"

96

"Who lives on the streets?" Nimsah finished Dojan's fumbling sentence.

"Yes. No. Well ..." Dojan stopped in his tracks and folded his arms. "Listen, I'm sorry. I had no right to ask you those things. Why don't you ask me something?"

Nimsah pouted, looking the prince up and down. "Alright. How rich are you?"

Dojan laughed. "I've no idea."

"You've no idea?"

"Well, I've never really thought about it before. I don't really have my own money – Mother takes care of that sort of thing with the vizier and his pashas."

Nimsah snorted with laughter. "If you live in a palace and never have to even *think* about money, that means you're very rich."

Dojan bobbed his head, acknowledging Nimsah's point. "I don't have any money on me, but when we get to the palace I'll have a word with Vizier Haman. He'll be able to give you a reward for saving me and then you won't have to live in the City of Tents anymore."

Nimsah stared at Dojan, deciding after looking hard at his earnest face that he really was serious. "What makes you think I *don't* want to live in the City of Tents? It's my home."

"But it's where ..."

"Poor people like me live," Nimsah finished, feeling satisfied as Dojan shrank from her. Farooq would enjoy talking to this one. "I *am* people like me."

"I meant no offence," he said, mortified. "It's just with what you said about how your parents left you. It sounds like a hard life. You helped me, and I want to do something to make your life better in return."

"I have lots of friends my age, and there's someone who takes care of me," Nimsah explained. "There's a lady in the marketplace I work for sometimes, weaving baskets for her stall."

"Well, that's good then." Dojan chewed on his bottom

lip. "Having friends is … good, I suppose. I wouldn't know."

"You don't have any friends?"

Dojan shrugged. "I'm schooled with my sister and my two younger brothers by Vizier Haman. We play together sometimes, which is alright. The officials at the palace don't like us getting dirty – I can't imagine what the vizier's going to say when he sees me like this."

"Do you like this vizerah?"

"*Vizier*," Dojan corrected. "Haman's very strict. It's important I learn everything I need to understand so that one day I can take my father's place."

Nimsah stared at the dirty, blood-stained boy in front of her and tried to imagine him one day being the emir. She thought of the value his father would place on finding his son and wondered how Farooq would handle the situation once she'd handed Dojan over to him. A knot of worry settled in her stomach as she debated whether she was doing the right thing. She thought of the royal guards fighting the assassins. How they showed no mercy, sacrificing their own lives to protect the emir's family. A vision swam before her eyes of men armed with Samarak fighting spears bearing down on her home. Tents burning. Women and children screaming. Would Farooq reward her for bringing him a prize captive, or punish her for putting them all in danger?

"Are you alright?" Dojan asked. "Shouldn't we keep moving? How near is the palace?"

"There's still some way to go," Nimsah told him.

"I'm going to tell them all about you," Dojan said as they started walking again. "You were really brave earlier. Father will be pleased, knowing we still have loyal subjects in Bengarath, willing to risk their lives for us. He'll reward you handsomely."

Whilst that sounded like a fine idea, Nimsah felt a growing sense of disquiet. She wasn't sure she wanted to explain to the emir or this vizerah who she was or where she lived. Awkward questions could lead anywhere, shining a light on Farooq's activities that he might prefer went on undisturbed. Although Nimsah was an accomplished liar, one wrong step might have unintended consequences. She'd already been careless and told Dojan the truth. If she tried to spin a different tale Dojan, in his innocent, hapless way, might well contradict her. As for a reward, Farooq would still expect this to be shared with the rest of his gang in the usual way, which meant giving any coin to him. How would the emir feel about a heavy purse of gold or silver being placed in Farooq's palm?

Nimsah cursed herself for not thinking things through. She knew what to do when it came to being Farooq's eyes and ears in the city. Now she found herself involved in something much more serious, where the risks of making the wrong choice could cost her everything. Which was best? Returning the boy to the palace or giving him over to Farooq? It would have been better never to have become involved. With a quiet sigh, Nimsah made her choice.

After a while their new course brought them to the edge of the main highway that led to the gates of Bengarath Palace. Nimsah pressed on, taking Dojan by the hand and steering him through the crowds, intent on reaching the gates. As they drew closer one of the warriors on guard spotted them, although he didn't appear to immediately recognise the prince.

Nimsah squeezed Dojan's hand. "I have to go. They'll look after you now. Don't tell them I was involved. I don't want those assassins paying my friends a visit on account of you."

A strange expression passed over Dojan's face – relief mixed with disappointment. "Are you sure? That doesn't seem right, not after everything you've done."

Four armed guards began walking towards them, making straight for Dojan. Nimsah knew she didn't have much time.

"I'm sure. Goodbye Dojan. It was interesting to meet you."

"Wait," Dojan said. "Will I see you again?"

Nimsah shrugged, offering him a wry smile. "Maybe. Take care of yourself."

Before Dojan could reply, Nimsah turned and ran off down the main street, making sure she put as much distance as possible between herself and the Crown Prince before there was a chance to change her mind.

CHAPTER 14

Summer 213 – The Strait of Bezeen, separating the Emirates of Murtak from the land of Naroque

Dojan watched Bengarath recede into the distance from the deck of the *Jezar*, the air sharp and clear. The grey bulk of the Bridge of Sorrows, impossibly suspended from its network of interconnecting cables, was visible even as the *Jezar* took to open water across the Strait of Bezeen. Dojan wondered if Nimsah was looking at the same view from her cabin on *Farah's Wings*. Ulan was probably already talking to her about how they should approach their diplomacy when they reached Kandarah.

Nimsah had come a long way from the street rat, scratching out a living amongst the homeless and dispossessed. Dojan immediately regretted describing her that way, even in the privacy of his thoughts. The girl had acted bravely and selflessly, putting herself in harm's way to save him. If she hadn't intervened, he'd have been cut down by those assassins on the dockside. The Bel-Deem loyalists had fought to the death that day, making it impossible to trace who was ultimately behind the plot. That the emir and his family survived the attack, which claimed the lives of twenty people including a dozen royal guards, was a miracle. Tanah had lit a candle in thanks to Dinuvillan that evening following Dojan's safe return. Adina slowly recovered from her injuries, their mother nursing her back to health as she kept an ever-present vigil at her bedside.

After a while the sea breeze began to cut through the impractical silks Dojan had selected for the voyage. Retreating to his cabin, he stretched out on the hard bunk that would serve the passable function of a bed for the next two days and debated Nimsah's return into his life. He'd kept his promise to her that day of the attack, never mentioning her involvement. Was it an accident she was the one the Illesh bankers had sent on their behalf to Fujareen? Did her employers know her history? These were questions he needed to ask Nimsah, assuming he got the opportunity to do so privately.

***

Dojan's sea voyage passed without incident, the summer seas calm and clear, ensuring the Fujareen fleet arrived at Kandarah in good time. It was Dojan's first visit to Naroque, the vast landmass that formed the central part of Samarakand. As they drew closer to the shoreline Dojan was a little disappointed at the similarities with the emirates. The same yellow hues and dusty ground, whitewashed settlements looking no different to the villages outside Bengarath.

"Wait until we round the headland and Kandarah comes into sight," Quizar told Dojan. "They say the City of a Thousand Spires is best viewed from the harbour."

"Hmm. I was expecting something ... wilder."

"The dense jungles of Naroque are further inland, where it can rain for a whole season and the trees are the tallest in all of Amuran," Quizar explained. "Kandarah is on the northerly part of Naroque, so its weather and climate aren't so dissimilar to our own."

"I know where Kandarah is," Dojan said with annoyance. "I just had a different picture of what to expect in my mind, that's all."

Dojan's irritable mood lifted when Kandarah came into sight. Quizar was right – even from afar this city state reeked of wealth, making Bengarath look second-best. Sun glinted off a host of spires rising up towards the sky, each competing with their neighbours to be the most elaborate, decorative or downright decadent. Dojan gasped when he realised that some of the tallest towers were clad in silver and gold.

"Kandarah is a small city, where land is at a premium," Quizar explained. "If you own a plot, you build high."

"It's quite a view," Dojan admitted. "How do they construct such tall towers? I've never seen anything like it."

"They use the knowledge of metals, learned during the Age of Enlightenment. The same lost art that gives Bengarath its famous Bridge of Steel."

Dojan shook his head. "That's a paltry, rusting wonder compared with these structures. Are you telling me these spires are fashioned out of metal, not stone?"

Quizar nodded. "So I'm given to understand. The knowledge of how they can smelt steels light and strong enough to be used in this way is a closely guarded secret."

Dojan gawped, beginning to comprehend the true scale of the city as they drew closer. "Imagine if Bengarath had spires like these. We could keep an eye on our neighbouring emirates without ever needing to leave the city."

"Perhaps the price of our involvement in Kandaran politics should be a lasting monument, celebrating our new-found friendship?" mused Quizar.

Shekh Birizal didn't meet the Fujareen delegation in person as they docked their ships. Instead, they were greeted by a high-ranking official of the Kandaran army called Lemarr. As crown prince, Dojan was pleased to see that this man at least knew his etiquette, welcoming him first, as befitted his status as the most senior of their visitors from Fujareen. Pasha Ulan introduced the rest of their party and Dojan waited for the carriage that would take him to the palace of the shekh. Standing around at the docks brought back unpleasant memories and he tapped his foot, impatient to be on the move. He glanced at Nimsah, who was wearing the same blue outfit she'd worn on the day he greeted her at Bengarath Palace. With her veil in place it was impossible to tell if she was thinking of the same events that had first drawn their lives together.

Shinva's Blessed Swords formed an honour guard that led their procession out of the docks and towards the centre of the city. Hadir remained in close attendance at Dojan's side, a dozen Mighty Spears acting as his personal bodyguards for the duration of this visit. Most of them walked outside his carriage, with Hadir and Quizar enjoying a more comfortable ride inside, although the summer heat was stifling.

"What do you make of Kandarah so far, Hadir?" Dojan asked.

The mubarizun grunted, sweating inside his armour. "I'll be happier when we're indoors."

"They'd be fools to try anything when we have this many guards," replied Quizar. "And what would be the point? If they meant us harm, they would have been better attacking us whilst we were at sea. What Kandarah lacks in infantry it makes up for with one of the best navies in Naroque."

Hadir shrugged. "I'm not paid to understand why someone is attacking us. All that concerns me is that there's a myriad of street corners, high vantage points and darkened alleys where anyone or anything could be waiting."

"You said the same thing about my mother's flower garden," Dojan quipped. Hadir ignored the remark, and the three of them rode on in silence.

The shekh's residence wasn't a palace in the conventional sense of the word. Dojan's carriage deposited him outside the entrance to one of the tallest spires in the very centre of the city. Down at ground level, Dojan felt small and insignificant – undoubtedly an effect intended by the magi who had fashioned this structure. It was like being in a vast forest of stone, steel and polished metals, staring up at fantastical trees from the base of their roots. The white clouds scudding through the sky gave Dojan an unpleasant sensation of vertigo, enough that he had to look down at his feet, firmly planted on the baking white granite flagstones outside the palace.

"Crown Prince?" said Hadir, placing a steadying hand on his shoulder.

"I'm fine," Dojan muttered, taking a breath and standing up straight.

"Welcome to the palace of Shekh Birizal, ruler of the City State of Kandarah," announced Khan Lemarr with a broad smile. Dojan frowned, wondering if the man was mocking him as he continued. "We would be delighted to quarter your warriors on the lower floors, whilst we have prepared luxurious chambers for you, Crown Prince, and your closest advisors on the upper levels. If you will allow me to accompany you, I can take you there now and ensure everything is to your liking."

"Yes, of course," Dojan replied with a wave of his hand. "Please, lead on."

The Kandaran khan led them into a spacious waiting area on the ground floor of the spire, all white marble with comfortable couches and polished tables scattered about. The air was pleasantly cool inside, the receiving chamber filled with a low murmur as Dojan spotted numerous delegations sitting around some of the tables, drinking coffee and tea, some smoking tobacco. Khanir Shinva's warriors were directed to their chambers – whilst Shinva herself, as the Fujareen army's representative, joined Dojan's delegation. She was accompanied by her mubarizun of the Blessed Swords, Yanzin El-Tebir.

"The journey to the top of the shekh's spire requires us to take an elevator," explained Lemarr. "I'm unsure if you are acquainted with such a device?"

Pasha Ulan stepped forwards. "We have no need of such contraptions in Bengarath, although I am familiar with the concept." His eyes met with Dojan's for a fleeting moment. "I understand these are cages, raised and lowered by means of a complex set of winches and pulleys, which allow easy access to the highest parts of a spire."

"I will not allow the Crown Prince to walk into a cage,

Khan Lemarr," growled Hadir, squaring up to the Kandaran, the dozen warriors of the Mighty Spears forming a neat circle around Dojan.

"Ahh," Lemarr licked his lips, glancing between Ulan and Hadir.

"This is my fault," Pasha Ulan said, stepping forwards, touching his chest just above his heart. "I should have spoken to our loyal mubarizun about such matters so he knew what to expect. Hadir, you have done the right thing but here in Kandarah they have different ways. Elevators are the only way to ascend and descend a Kandaran spire in comfort."

"Are you telling me there are no stairs in this building?" Hadir asked, glaring at Lemarr.

The khan thought for a moment. "Yes, all spires are fashioned with stairs. However, there are fifty floors in this palace, each stacked one upon the other. I fear to ascend to the forty-fifth floor, where your chambers are located, will require a level of exertion that our honoured guests would find ... uncomfortable."

"Did he just say there are *fifty* floors in this building?" Dojan hissed at Quizar.

"Yes, that's exactly what he said," his katib whispered back.

"We'll ride in the elevator, thank you Khan Lemarr," Dojan said in a louder voice.

Hadir turned to Dojan. "Crown Prince, if I am to fulfil my duties I must understand how to escort you safely about this place."

Khanir Shinva cleared her throat. "I would be most intrigued to see this elevator in operation. However, Mubarizun Hadir has a point concerning the protection of the crown prince. Yanzin, take my company of Blessed Swords and ascend this spire via the stairways so that we can understand how to enter and leave this building in the conventional fashion. I will accompany the crown prince with the Mighty Spears, using the traditional methods of traversing a Kandaran spire, in order to ensure his protection."

Yanzin glanced at her fellow warriors, none of whom looked pleased at the prospect of such a climb. However, at a nod from their mubarizun the company of Blessed Swords followed Lemarr, who led them to the stairwell before returning and directing the rest of the Fujareen party towards a set of highly polished metal doors, guarded by two Naroque warriors.

"The entrance to this elevator?" enquired Dojan.

"Just so, Crown Prince," replied Lemarr as he pressed a glowing button inscribed with the number 45 in silver script in the centre. There was a whirr and the doors slid open via some unseen mechanism, revealing a softly-lit chamber within.

"We should be able to accommodate all of you," said Lemarr, stepping inside.

Pasha Ulan led the way with Arak and Tormindah. Hadir hesitated for a moment as Shinva followed, before ushering Dojan and Quizar into the chamber with the rest of the Mighty Spears. It was a squeeze to fit nearly twenty inside, and Hadir's face darkened at the prospect of so many people pressed up close against the crown prince. However, his only other option was to leave half Dojan's bodyguards outside, which meant even less protection now the Blessed Swords were climbing the stairs. Dojan gave Hadir a friendly nod, and his mubarizun relaxed a fraction as the doors slid closed. There was the faintest of movements within the elevator and Dojan had a momentary sensation of becoming heavier. A short while later there was a gentle bump and the doors opened again.

"Please, come through and I will show you to your chambers, Crown Prince," said Lemarr with a smile.

Hadir's warriors left first, Lemarr nodding to show he understood the mubarizun's duties took precedence over the hospitality of Kandarah. Dojan waited in the elevator with Ulan and the others. Now it was less crowded, the elevator took on a more intriguing aspect, illuminated by yellow lighting emanating through gaps from behind panels that formed the floors and walls. There were no lanterns or torches that he could discern, and Dojan decided he would try and find out how this effect was achieved. Such a thing would look very fine indeed in Bengarath Palace.

"Crown Prince," Hadir called, bowing low and inviting him to enter the chamber.

Dojan smiled as he took in the finely appointed chambers, which were artistically lit and decorated by mirrors that had the effect of making the room seem far bigger. A few servants were dotted about the place, one of them fussing over silver pots of tea and coffee at a counter in the corner.

"We have private sleeping quarters through these doors, here, here and here," Lemarr explained, pointing at a number of doorways that led off from the main chamber. "My servants will bring you some light refreshments shortly. They can also help you change and bathe before your audience with the shekh this evening. We would be honoured to have you as our guests at his table."

"We would be honoured to dine with him and look forward to the evening," said Ulan.

Lemarr turned to Nimsah. "My lady, if you will accompany me to the top of the spire, Shekh Birizal craves a private audience with you."

"Of course." Nimsah bowed to each of them as she took her leave. "Crown Prince. Pasha Ulan. Forgive me, but duty elsewhere calls me away. I look forward to seeing you later this evening."

Dojan watched her leave with a pang of regret. So many questions would have to wait until the end of the day. His gaze was drawn to a wide window at the far end of the chamber. He thought it was the entrance to a balcony at first, realising as he drew nearer that it was actually three separate pieces of glass. He reached out and let his fingers brush lightly over the surface, confirming the glass really was there – it was so clear and smooth.

"Quizar, have you ever seen the like?" he whispered.

A servant stepped forwards. "Crown Prince, would you like to step outside?"

Dojan stared at the three pieces of solid glass, seeing no way to progress to the small courtyard that lay beyond. The servant smiled and pressed lightly on the glass. There was a click and each panel slid away, folding up one upon the other until they disappeared into a small gap in the wall. Dojan and Quizar stepped out into the courtyard beyond, carefully fashioned to shield them from the wind despite their height. Various potted plants had been set in the courtyard, which was perhaps a quarter the size of Dojan's receiving rooms. Together the pair walked to the high railings set at the edge, Hadir and three other warriors following closely behind.

The height was dizzying and Dojan had to force himself to rest his weight against the metal rail, fighting his natural instinct to shy away. He began to relax as the warm metal stood firm, peering out across the forest of spires, each gleaming in the morning sunshine. Most were smaller than the shekh's palace, although he was able to count at least three from his vantage point that rose higher still.

"That's ..." Quizar's words died on his lips as they took in the view, truly understanding the scale of the city and its accomplishments.

"A sight we'll never forget," Dojan breathed. "The question we need to ask ourselves, Quizar, is why a city as rich as Kandarah needs our help?"

CHAPTER 15

Summer 199 – Bengarath, the City of Tents

Nimsah's belly was full with saffron rice and spiced potatoes, leaving her sleepy as she sat at Farooq's table in the courtyard outside his tent. The late afternoon sun beat down, only serving to increase her torpor. The canopy above was welcomed by those in Farooq's inner circle. It had been a good day, and both Rogesh and Chandra were with her, chatting and joking to each other as they ate. Nimsah noticed the pair were becoming closer each day – something to keep an eye on.

A small child in ragged clothes ran up to them and whispered something in Raqqath's ear. Raqqath's blue eyes widened and he rose and followed the child, disappearing amongst the tents. Kandilla's attention had also been drawn to Raqqath's sudden departure and she leaned in close, lips brushing Farooq's ear as she spoke in an undertone. A frown creased Farooq's forehead and he set aside the wine they were sharing, sitting up a little straighter on his cushion at the head of the low table.

A few minutes later, Raqqath returned with several members of Farooq's gang, escorting a tall person in dark brown robes, the upper and lower parts of his face hidden behind a black veil. Although his robes were plain, they were expensive, the bright sun revealing a complex geometric pattern of interlocking squares in the weave. His fingers, clasped together in front of him, sported a number of gold rings. The arrival of such wealth, though modestly displayed, was enough to turn the heads of most of those who sat at Farooq's table.

Raqqath cleared his throat. "Farooq, forgive me for interrupting your meal but we have a visitor."

Farooq remained seated, bare arms folded, showing off the muscles beneath his golden bracelets and bangles. He glanced at the man accompanying Raqqath. "So I see. Does our guest have a name?"

"Jandral," said the stranger, his dark eyes sweeping over Farooq's companions. They lingered on Nimsah for a moment before he turned his attention back to Farooq. "I speak on behalf of the Bank of Illesh, and have travelled from the City State of Kandarah to speak with you, personally."

Farooq's eyes widened in surprise. "You must be tired after such a journey. It's opportune that you arrived whilst I'm eating with my friends. Please, sit and join us. Have something to eat and drink. Some fresh coffee or tea, perhaps, or would you prefer wine?"

Nimsah watched the banker carefully as he considered his response. Jandral would have preferred to conduct whatever business he had with Farooq in the privacy of his tent. However, if he refused an offer of hospitality this would be an insult to Farooq as his host. Eating and drinking with him, though, meant removing his veil, allowing Farooq to get a better measure of his guest.

"You're too kind. Some tea and a little food would be most welcome," Jandral replied, bowing his head as Kandilla rose and offered him her seat next to Farooq. He took his place and unwound his face coverings, revealing a man of around forty with black hair and a long, oiled beard. Nimsah thought he was good looking for an older man, although his direct stare was disconcerting. Small crow's feet gathered around the corners of his dark eyes as he looked shrewdly at those seated around Farooq.

Farooq served Jandral himself, pouring him water from a stone jug and piling his plate with an assortment of delicacies, whilst Kandilla moved to sit on Farooq's other side. Jandral thanked him, listening politely as Farooq introduced those around his table.

"What's this banker doing here?" whispered Rogesh next to Nimsah.

"Shush. If you bother to listen, you might find out," she hissed, straining to hear Farooq and Jandral's conversation.

Jandral dabbed the corners of his mouth with a napkin after he had finished eating. "Thank you. That was most welcome – and superior to the fare I was offered during my crossing from Kandarah. I feel much restored."

"The City of Tents has an unfair reputation amongst the richer members of Bengarath society," said Farooq with a wide smile. "You'll not find us lacking in manners or hospitality."

"That's not the reception Kamjah received," Jandral replied, neatly folding his napkin and placing it on the table in front of him.

"Kamjah brought the Kraken with him, his only purpose being to spill blood," Kandilla answered, leaning in close to Farooq. "He received the reception he deserved."

"Deserved it," echoed Bizek with a grimace.

"And when you visited Denek Bel-Haroom last year?" Jandral asked, fixing his eyes on Farooq. "What did he deserve?"

The low conversation around Farooq's table fell silent, and Nimsah could feel Rogesh tense next to her. Did Jandral know the part they'd played in the merchant's death?

Farooq sighed, running a hand over the back of his head. "Denek cheated on me. Such things have consequences, whether one lives in your world or mine."

"Worlds that have become connected as a result," Jandral said in a low voice. "Denek served my masters, and their interests suffered following his demise."

"Denek was so afraid of your masters he cheated me and a dozen others up and down the Murtak and Naroque coast so he could repay them," Farooq explained. "I wasn't aware of the involvement of Illesh until we confronted him, here in Bengarath. He swore that he had paid off his debt to you, at the expense of making more enemies than was … prudent."

Jandral frowned. "You misunderstand me. Denek paid us what he owed, this is true. However, this is not just a matter of shekels to my masters. Denek was of the old family of Bel-Haroom, a name which opened up doors to us throughout the emirates. Doors that closed, due to your actions."

Nimsah glanced around, wondering if Jandral had brought anyone else with him. The banker spoke with a quiet, calm voice, yet the challenge was obvious. If Jandral knew about Denek's fate, why did he think that he could speak to Farooq in this way?

"I'm sorry to hear that," Farooq replied. "However, you're omitting the part of the story that brought the Kraken gang back to Fujareen. Kamjah didn't come here looking to discuss matters with me over a meal – he came to take back control of the City of Tents. Kamjah told me who he was working for, before he died."

"Yet you killed him anyway?" Jandral asked.

Farooq shrugged. "The Kraken were the past. You paid them to usurp me and they were found wanting. I've made something of this place, giving the people here a life with purpose and hope, when before there was none."

"You've certainly done well for yourself – you've come a long way from the Naroque waif who stowed away aboard a merchant dhow all those years ago."

"Done well," muttered Bizek, face strained with concentration as he listened to every word.

"All have prospered," argued Farooq. "Your masters played a clumsy hand and I beat it. Now what? You didn't come here alone to try and kill me, so why are you here? Could it be that whilst some doors are opened by the old names of the ruling dynasties, others can only be accessed by those living under the shadow of the Bridge of Sorrows?"

Jandral smiled, the effect softening his features.

"Perhaps you're right."

Farooq rose from his seat, patting Kandilla gently on the shoulder and shaking his head when she made to join him. "I think Jandral and I have more to discuss in private. Please, come with me to my tent and we can speak further."

Jandral rose, offering a small bow to Kandilla. "It would be my pleasure."

Bizek stood guard outside as the two men left the table. No sooner had Jandral disappeared inside Farooq's blue tent then everyone began talking to their neighbour in hushed tones.

"Why doesn't Farooq just kill him?" Rogesh asked.

Nimsah shook her head. "Don't be stupid. You don't cross the Bank of Illesh. Jandral's safer under their protection than if he walked in here with an army. Remember Farooq's face when Denek mentioned he owed money to the bankers?"

Rogesh frowned. "Farooq killed Kamjah and Denek."

"Kamjah was paid to do a job by the bank, whereas Farooq only thought that Denek was a debtor. The difference here is Jandral *is* the bank."

Rogesh and Chandra both looked thoughtful as they went back to their food. Nimsah felt too full to eat anything else, listening instead to the chatter around the table. She was pleased to hear the rest of Farooq's gang coming to the same conclusion as her.

"Nimsah," Bizek called out from the entrance to the tent, making her start. "Farooq wants you."

Everyone turned to look at Nimsah as she stood up, Rogesh and Chandra wide-eyed with surprise. Feeling self-conscious, Nimsah walked towards Bizek, ducking down low as his thick arm held aside the heavy blue fabric, allowing her to enter. Inside the tent was dark, her eyes taking a few moments to adjust from the bright afternoon sun.

"This is the girl?" said Jandral, sitting cross-legged on a rich Oomrhani rug opposite Farooq.

"She's the one."

"She's younger than I thought she'd be."

Farooq gave Nimsah a smile and waved her forwards. "Age isn't important. My little flower hears all and sees all. If I want to know what's happening in Bengarath, Nimsah is the one I ask. She knows how to pay attention to the important things."

Jandral nodded, dark eyes boring into Nimsah. "How old are you, child?"

Nimsah felt a prickle of heat rise up her neck and face. "I don't know, sir. I was brought here as a small child and I've worked for Farooq for the past ten years."

"And what of your parents?"

"I don't know what happened to them, sir."

Jandral turned to Farooq, who shrugged. "The girl only knew her first name when she arrived. It's a sadly familiar tale here. Are her parents important?"

"That depends who they are," Jandral replied. "Are they important to you, Nimsah?"

Nimsah thought for a moment, trying to sort through her feelings. She was good at finding out secrets and people. Why hadn't she ever thought of looking for her parents? Her insides churned at the hazy memory of being led through the tent city by the hand. It had been a warm spring day, her mother crying as they weaved their way through the town. She tried to recall the sound of her mother's voice, or even her name. There was nothing. Too long ago. Too far away.

"I live here now," Nimsah told Jandral, who raised an eyebrow at her answer.

"Farooq tells me you have a good memory and can be relied upon. I have a task for you, one to which you should be well-suited. I have business here in Bengarath, and I'm staying as a guest at the Royal Palace of Emir Haraq-Al-Souk. Do you know where that is?"

Nimsah nodded and Jandral continued. "A few days ago, someone went to great lengths to try and kill the emir and his family. A group loyal to the Bel-Deem house, those who ruled here before Haraq usurped them, has been blamed. It may be true, of course. However, I have business to conduct with the emir and I have wondered if these events are connected."

"Jandral has asked for our assistance in getting to the truth," explained Farooq. "He needs a go-between whilst he's staying at the palace."

Jandral nodded. "Coming here today was a risk – worth it, as I wanted to conduct my business with Farooq in person. However, it won't be possible for me to return for the remainder of my stay. I need you to travel between the palace and the tent city so we can communicate."

"And if Farooq helps you in this way, you'll forgive him for what happened to the merchant Denek and Kamjah's Krakens?" said Nimsah. Farooq and Jandral exchanged a look, a smirk on Farooq's face.

"I told you, Jandral. My little flower misses nothing."

Jandral paused, dark eyes regarding Nimsah intently. "All I need is someone who can be relied upon to carry a message, tell it accurately and be trusted to keep my affairs secret. Be careful, Nimsah, about how far you pry into matters that don't concern you."

Nimsah swallowed. "I'll remember that, sir. I promise."

"Good – make sure that you do. Farooq, thank you for your hospitality. Send the girl to me at dusk in two days' time with a report on what you have found."

Farooq bowed his head. "It has been a pleasure to receive you. I look forward to our new business relationship being profitable for both of us."

Jandral rose, offering Farooq a cold smile. "Prove your worth and I'm sure that will be the case."

CHAPTER 16

Summer 213 – Kandarah, Shekh Birizal's Palace

While Dojan settled into his chambers in Birizal's palace, the rest of his party were accommodated on its various levels. As the most important members of their delegation, Dojan's chambers were shared with Pasha Ulan, Tormindah and Arak, together with Quizar, Shinva and Yanzin. Six of Hadir's Mighty Spears, led by a man called Khalid, were assigned the night shift for the duration of Dojan's stay and given lodgings on the fifth floor of the spire, the score of Blessed Swords stationed with them. Hadir assigned himself the duty of guarding Dojan during the day with his five remaining warriors, although Dojan could tell he wanted more. Khanir Shinva overruled Hadir, anxious not to give the impression that they were overly concerned for their safety whilst under Birizal's protection. Dojan was forced to support her to break the deadlock and, whilst it was clear Hadir disagreed, he accepted the ruling of the crown prince without complaint.

After a time it became obvious Nimsah wasn't going to return before the feast, much to Dojan's disappointment. When Quizar asked one of the servants whether she would be staying with them the man shrugged.

"She's not part of our delegation," Quizar reflected as he took tea with Dojan on the balcony overlooking Kandarah. "Her task was to bring us here and ensure we took part in these negotiations. Ultimately, she speaks for Illesh, not Fujareen."

"Illesh or Kandarah?" mused Dojan.

"Illesh – of that I have no doubt. Birizal is a powerful Kandaran shekh in his own right. Whilst he's profited from a close relationship with the banking clans, the two remain distinct."

"Like Fujareen and Illesh? I know you studied the terms of our banking facility with Illesh. I'll confess, Quizar, it makes me uneasy to see the fate of our emirate placed in the hands of an unaccountable foreign power."

"The agreement is sealed," Quizar replied. "We have pledged our cause to Illesh and their allies. Crown Prince, I'd urge you to banish such thoughts from your mind, especially while we enjoy the hospitality of Kandarah."

Dojan grimaced. "Let's see what Birizal has to say this evening. I don't like how we're the ones left here waiting, when we should be taking charge of matters. There are too many questions to which we need answers before we can decide on the right course of action."

Quizar leaned back, sipping his tea with a satisfied smile on his face. The expression irritated Dojan, and he didn't bother to disguise it when he spoke. "What's that look for?"

Quizar continued to smile. "I meant no impertinence, Crown Prince. I was merely thinking that your father was right. This trip has been good for you. I've not seen you so engaged in Fujareen politics for … Well, for as long as I can remember."

Dojan opened his mouth to say something more, closing it when he realised his katib was correct. He occupied himself with his own tea, waving a servant over to pour him another cup. It eased his nerves – sitting around here wasn't good for them.

Pasha Ulan appeared at the entrance and cleared his throat. "Crown Prince, you have a visitor. A man called Fasil, a member of the Abitek tribe."

"The Abitek leader?" Dojan asked.

"The same. His delegation is already here in the shekh's palace, along with the Edeen tribe, both waiting to conduct the next round of negotiations. It could be useful to have a brief audience with this man, and it will be some time before we join Shekh Birizal."

"Show him in," Dojan said with a lazy wave of his hand.

Ulan hesitated. "You need to know that Fasil is a Sightwielder, so Tormindah should be with us during this discussion. To prevent unwanted intrusions, you understand."

Ulan returned with Fasil, who was escorted between two of Hadir's guards with Arak and Tormindah following closely behind. Their visitor was smiling, revealing a perfect set of teeth framed within a short grey beard. His head was uncovered, revealing more grey hair, closely cropped. Dojan would have guessed the Naroque man to be somewhere in his early sixties, though he looked trim and fit. He noticed that one of the guards was holding a Samarak fighting spear, which he passed over to Hadir. The mubarizun inspected the weapon closely, admiration on his face as he examined the black polished wood and the decorative etching on the blade.

"A fine weapon," Hadir announced as Fasil sat down with the others, servants offering the visitors more tea and coffee.

"Thank you," Fasil replied. "The fighting spear was a Naroque invention, after all. I see it is one you favour as well. I thought in the emirates the sword and shield were preferred."

Hadir smiled, carefully placing the spear in a corner of the balcony, well out of Fasil's reach. "I'm proud to serve the Mighty Spears. In the Emirate of Fujareen we pride ourselves on mastering all the military disciplines and styles of fighting."

Fasil's smile broadened. "I see the crown prince is in good hands with you to guard him, Hadir. I'm pleased to make your acquaintance."

Pasha Ulan completed the introductions as Hadir looked on, a smile playing on the corner of his lips. Dojan decided he would have to remember to pay his mubarizun more compliments in the future.

Fasil glanced at Tormindah. "Please, my lady, you can relax. I'm here to speak to your prince, not practise the art of magic on him."

Tormindah inclined her head, offering the smallest of bows. "I don't doubt your sincerity. However, we must insist that the crown prince is accompanied by one of the Magi of the Farseeing whenever a Sightwielder is present here in Kandarah. It is a sensible precaution when meeting strangers for the first time, an arrangement that I would be most grateful for you to respect during our stay."

"I understand perfectly," Fasil replied, thanking the servant who had poured him a cup of steaming black coffee. He took a moment to sit back and breathe in the steam with a sigh. "The pleasure of this drink is all in the smell, don't you find? I spent a number of years living far away, in northern Beria in Valistria. Tea leaves were imported from time to time by Oomrhani merchants. Sadly, though, a decent pot of coffee was unheard of in those lands. It was the thing I enjoyed most on my return."

"Presumably your tribe has a pressing desire to speak to our crown prince on matters other than the merits of good coffee," Ulan observed. "We haven't even met our host and been formally introduced before you came knocking on the door."

Fasil smiled. "Forgive my eagerness. It was my intention to speak with you candidly before your formal dinner with the shekh. I understand why you are here – military might designed to break the deadlock of these negotiations. However, I would urge you to listen to all the sides in this matter before making your decision about who to support."

"And what possible advantage could we gain by supporting the dragon tribe?" asked Ulan with a sour look.

Fasil drank from his coffee cup, appearing more interested in the beverage than Ulan's words. He set the cup down on the table. "That *is* good. Shekh Birizal isn't scrimping on his duties as a host for those in his favour. The servants in my quarters see to my needs, of course, but I think they have reserved the best coffee beans for your own enjoyment."

Dojan laughed. "Is this your masterful strategy, Fasil of the Abitek? Are you here to sample our coffee or do you have a more meaningful purpose in visiting my quarters?"

Fasil looked around, gesturing towards the magnificent view across Kandarah. "This is all very fine, is it not? Shekh Birizal has placed you in luxurious quarters, provided servants to cater for your every need and, I can promise you, you will never enjoy a finer meal when you dine in his company this evening. Kandarah reeks with money and magic, and how can you have failed to be impressed by the City of a Thousand Spires? One of Amuran's marvels, an echo from the Enlightened Age before the avatars visited this world with war and fire. Together with Kandarah, Fujareen could rise to even greater things – perhaps even one day uniting the emirates once more. Imagine that, the Emirate of Murtak made anew, with Haraq Al-Souk as its all-powerful emir. Perhaps even Haraq Bel-Doshok, when all this is over?"

Dojan had to concentrate hard not to look at Quizar, uncomfortable at how close Fasil was to the mark. It was as if he'd been listening to the private conversation he'd shared with his father before the voyage. Dojan realised he'd underestimated the Abitek tribe.

"I think you'll find you've summarised the benefits of our proposed alliance with *Kandarah*," Ulan said in clipped tones. "Weren't you here to speak on behalf of your tribe?"

Fasil smiled. "Think on this. If all that I have described is on offer for the simple task of lending your army to the Kandaran cause, what must Amonduras be worth to them?"

Dojan thought on Fasil's words, cutting across Ulan as he began to speak. "People will do surprising things for sites of religious or national importance. Who knows what secrets are hidden within this lost city of the dragons? There is a saying – knowledge is prized more highly than gold."

"Nimsah told you that. Be careful with that one, and ask yourself who really pulls Birizal's strings. Look around at the wonders you see in this city. What could Kandarah possibly want with a ruined city, when you consider everything they have built here?"

"What indeed?" asked Arak. "Yet I fail to see how that matters. The fact is, they are interested in the fate of Amonduras and we will be handsomely rewarded for assisting them. You're offering us nothing."

Fasil took another sip of coffee, breathing in deeply, eyes closed. "You don't know the best part, do you? I'm offering you *everything*. There's a reason these negotiations have dragged on for so long. Shekh Birizal needs the dragon tribe in order to access the lost city. He may have found safe passage to the gates, but only those of our bloodline can open them."

"The Edeen share your history," Ulan said, sitting forwards in his chair, tea forgotten. "Could it be that the same blood runs in their veins? Is that what these negotiations have really been about? Which tribe gets to share in Shekh Birizal's discovery?"

Fasil nodded. "Just so, Pasha Ulan. I see your reputation as the most promising member of the emir's government is well-deserved."

Once again Dojan noted that Fasil was singularly well-informed. He leaned in closer, speaking in a lower tone. "You're telling me we need you, or the Edeen, to take control of Amonduras. Unfortunately, you're forgetting one crucial thing – only Shekh Birizal knows the safe route through the poisonous lands surrounding your sacred city. That is a secret he must have kept from you, even with your Sight magic. Your offer is worthless without that knowledge. We need the Kandarans – you would be better placed negotiating your own position with Birizal to share in the spoils, otherwise he may turn to the Edeen, leaving you with nothing."

"When all this plays out, Birizal must share his secret in order to make use of your army to secure Amonduras," Fasil told them, rising from his seat. "Think carefully on the terms you have been offered by Illesh and Kandarah. They will tell you there is only one way, the easy way, for you to profit from this situation. Of course, that's not true – you have other options, if you choose your allies carefully."

Tormindah stood up hurriedly after Fasil left, hugging herself as if chilled. "Tormindah? What's wrong?" Arak asked her, sounding concerned.

The woman shuddered and paced the floor. "I've rarely met one with his abilities. I probed his mind, only to be met by a solid wall – no way through. As far as I'm aware, he didn't reach out with the Sight. If he had done, I'm not certain I could have held him back for long."

"As far as you're *aware*?" hissed Ulan.

Tormindah shook her head. "I told you. He's skilled. We all need to be careful around him, Pasha Ulan. I warned you we should have brought more members of my order with me."

Ulan sat back in his chair, looking worried. "You said your order can work together effectively, even at a distance."

Tormindah sighed. "Fasil is working with his own Sight Fellowship and their power will be enhanced if they are working in close proximity. If they use their combined abilities to the full, we might find ourselves outmatched."

"Wonderful," Ulan muttered, getting up and walking to the edge of the balcony.

"Tormindah must speak the truth if she's to serve you," said Arak. "The power of the Veiled Magi is also at your disposal. We are versed in various ways to defend ourselves against these Sightwielders, and I would be happy to assist Tormindah so that our delegation is protected."

"Do it," Ulan replied, waving the pair away.

"Hadir," said Dojan. "Please can you give me, Quizar and Ulan a moment's privacy?" Hadir nodded, stepping inside and closing the enormous glass doors behind him.

"What is it?" asked Ulan, glancing at Quizar. "Is this something we should really discuss in front of your katib,

Crown Prince?"

Dojan smiled. "I trust Quizar completely, Ulan, and you'd do well to do the same. I'd like to know what he made of our encounter with Fasil."

It took a moment for Quizar to recover his poise after Dojan put him on the spot. "I think there are things that your good friend Nimsah has neglected to tell us, Crown Prince. Fasil is presenting us with an opportunity to seize Amonduras and cut out the Kandarans in the process."

"Breaking a *binding* legal agreement," interjected Ulan. "Crown Prince, surely you understand, sire, that there would be severe consequences if we were to side with the Abitek in this dispute? That's not why we're here."

"Remind me, who's the representative of the Edeen tribe?" Dojan asked.

"Their elder is a woman called Narinda, Crown Prince," Ulan replied, looking horrified at the prospect of his prince taking such an active interest in their diplomatic mission.

Dojan smiled, enjoying how it made his prospective brother-in-law squirm. "Perhaps it would be wise to speak with her privately as well? If you would be so good as to make the arrangements?"

CHAPTER 17

Summer 199 – Bengarath Palace

Nimsah slipped through the palace gates at the rear of the building, the four spear carrying warriors watching the entrance not sparing her a second glance. Dressed as a servant girl, she walked with the assurance that came from belonging to the household. It was a sufficient half-truth, as she was there on Jandral's authority, giving her the confidence to move about the palace with ease. Farooq had been quick to see the wider advantages of the arrangement, encouraging her to learn what she could on these visits. This was easier said than done on her first trip – having only been as far as the gates when she brought Dojan home a little over a week ago.

Nimsah concentrated on finding her way to Jandral's chambers. Before leaving, he'd given directions, making sure she'd memorised them before leaving the City of Tents. Nimsah found the entrance exactly as described, a tall cedar door with a relief showing a victory of the Fujareen navy against one of their rival emirates. Nimsah knocked and stepped inside when she heard Jandral's voice.

"Leave us," the banker said to two servants in attendance. The men bowed, one of them frowning at Nimsah as he passed.

"You're on time, which is a good start," said Jandral with a smile, fingers playing with the tip of his beard as he lounged in a chair by the window. "Are you hungry? Thirsty?" He gestured at a table, set with fresh fruit next to a silver pot of coffee.

Nimsah shook her head and politely declined. She was nervous at this first meeting, which suppressed the typical appetite of an opportunistic street child. This was the most important task Farooq had given her and she was worried about the consequences if she let him down.

Jandral shrugged, raising a china cup to his lips. "As you wish. Tell me, what word from your master Farooq?"

Before leaving that morning Farooq had summoned Nimsah to his tent, where Raqqath and Kandilla were already waiting. Farooq looked Nimsah in the eye, explaining how crucial this day was.

"Things have worked well for us up until now, Little Flower. We've landed on the right side of this matter with the bank. Now you must play your part to perfection."

"This is what it's come to?" muttered Kandilla, scowling. "Our future depends on the wits of this child?"

Farooq rounded on her, eyes flashing. "Careful, Kandilla – remember, this is at Jandral's request. Will you be the one to tell him we'd prefer alternative arrangements?"

Kandilla gave him a haughty look. "You should never have killed Denek. We should have walked away the moment he mentioned any involvement with the banking clans."

Farooq's face twisted, no longer concealing his anger. "And who was it who wielded the knife, my love? I've kept that important fact from Jandral, up to now."

"Are you threatening me?" Kandilla hissed, rising from her seat, hand moving towards the knife on her belt. Farooq saw the movement and caught her about the wrist with a sharp slap of flesh on flesh.

"This isn't helping," Raqqath stated, remaining in his seat.

Kandilla glanced from her wrist up into Farooq's eyes. "I don't like it."

"Sticking me with *that* won't help things."

Kandilla let go of the hilt as he released her hand. "I

don't know. It might make me feel better."

Farooq threw back his head and laughed. "This is why I love you, Kandilla – the fire in your spirit. Who else would I allow to speak to me in such a way?"

Nimsah watched as Kandilla relaxed, turning her back on Farooq so he wouldn't see her rub her wrist, the marks left by his fingers standing out darkly on her olive skin. She glared at Nimsah, who quickly turned her attention back to Farooq.

"This is very important, Nimsah," he told her, squatting down low so they were eye to eye. "These bankers are magi of coin, possessing arts and powers us ordinary folk don't understand. When you speak to Jandral only answer the questions he asks you and *always* answer honestly. Hold nothing back – he'll know if you do and that will reflect badly on me. We want to come out of this with the bankers on our side. Give them a reason to be offended and things could become … uncomfortable for us here."

"You mean he'll send more men to kill you?" Nimsah asked.

Farooq gave her a wry grin. "Yes. That's exactly what I mean. These people only deal on their own terms, so we have to respect that and work with it."

Standing before Jandral, Nimsah remembered Farooq's words, swallowing down her nerves as she recounted their progress carefully and honestly, as she'd been told. Raqqath had been talking to his network of acquaintances for the past few days, drawing out the circulating rumours following the attack on the docks. Plenty of people believed the story that Bel-Deem loyalists were behind the assassination attempt, looking to avenge the murder of the last emir and the fall of their house. However, most folk were sceptical. After all, Godan Bel-Deem had been dead for thirteen years, his household exterminated. The manner in which Haraq Al-Souk consolidated power had outraged many of the old houses, yet were their objections strong enough for them to take up arms against their new ruler? And why wait more than a decade to do so? Despite the cries of the assassins on the docks, declaring they fought for Bel-Deem, many thought this nothing more than a ruse.

None of the attackers had been caught alive, so they couldn't be put to the question. Five of them were dead, whilst the rest had melted away into the crowd during the confusion afterwards. Their black robes had been abandoned in nearby alleyways, suggesting fifteen men were involved in the plot. Then there was the use of fire powder – five barrels amounted to a small fortune, and would have been difficult to acquire. With such a well-financed and organised plot, most people believed that one of the neighbouring emirates was behind the attack and they were trying to cover their tracks.

Jandral listened carefully as Nimsah told him what Raqqath had uncovered. He put a fresh fig in his mouth, biting into the purple flesh with a satisfied sigh. "These really are very good. You should try some."

Nimsah didn't want to offend the man but she wasn't hungry, so instead she offered him a bright smile. "I've not long broken my fast, master Jandral. Perhaps I could take some for later?"

Jandral waived his hand at the bowl. "Feel free to help yourself."

Nimsah took three ripe figs and put them in her bag, intending to share them with Chandra and Rogesh. "You're very kind, master."

"It's not me who's feeding you," Jandral chuckled. "These come courtesy of the emir. Now, have you anything more to tell me?" Nimsah shook her head as Jandral sat in his chair, pondering on what she'd said. "The use of fire powder sets this attack apart. Tell Farooq that's where he needs to focus his efforts. Who supplied those barrels? Did they arrive by ship or over land? Was the powder made in Fujareen or from outside the emirate? Someone knows something, you can be sure of that."

"I'll pass that message on to Farooq," said Nimsah with a

bow.

Jandral nodded. "You're bright for someone so young and you have a good memory. Tell me, can you read your letters?"

Nimsah chewed on her bottom lip. "I came to the City of Tents when I was very young."

"It's nothing to be ashamed of," Jandral told her. "You can't help where you came from, can you? I'm going to be in Fujareen on business for some time, based here at the palace. Bring your next report to me in five days' time, and I will set aside an hour to show you the Samarak script. Would you like that?"

"That's very kind of you," Nimsah replied, opening her mouth to say more before hesitating.

"What is it?"

"I was wondering ... Why would you do such a thing? For someone ..."

"Like you?" asked Jandral, dark eyes boring into her. "For a parentless street child? Do I need to justify myself to you, Nimsah?"

She shook her head, heart beating fast. "No, master. I was surprised, that's all."

Jandral chuckled. "Farooq sees your potential and has you where he wants you. Think about this on your way home, Nimsah – what do *you* want from life?"

Nimsah felt giddy with excitement as she closed the door behind her, knowing things had gone better than she could possibly have hoped. Now her appetite had returned she was feeling famished, deciding to use her new-found freedom to locate the kitchens and see what she could pilfer. She would save the figs for later. Besides, Farooq had told her to keep her eyes and ears open in the palace and there was always the chance of hearing some useful gossip.

The first two servants ignored her questions but the third, a greybeard with a pronounced limp, was more helpful and went out of his way to accompany her to the kitchens.

Inside it was noisy and hot – a hive of well-ordered activity supervised by a haughty-looking head chef in black robes wearing a white handari on his head. Nimsah didn't like the look of him and kept to the edges of the room, sauntering over to the table where she spied flatbreads piled high inside a wicker basket. She wondered if this was Fenara's handiwork – the woman would be so proud at the thought of her wares gracing the emir's palace.

"What are you doing here, girl?" asked a woman working nearby, giving Nimsah a suspicious look.

"Master Jandral of the Bank of Illesh sent me. He's hungry."

The servant frowned. "Why hasn't he sent one of the palace staff attending him?"

"I'm attending him," Nimsah lied. "He asked me to fetch it."

The woman didn't look convinced as she passed Nimsah a tray, putting on some of the bread, a bowl of black olives, some white salted cheese and, with Nimsah's encouragement, an assortment of fresh fruits. "Clearly master Jandral has an appetite."

Nimsah smiled as she carried the tray out of the kitchen. She might not have gleaned any useful gossip from her brief visit but she had still learned more about the layout of the palace. Rogesh was fond of fresh fruit and would appreciate her bringing him something extra when she returned. She looked for somewhere private, where she could inconspicuously empty the contents of the tray into her bag before making her return to the City of Tents. Perhaps she would treat herself to the ripest of the figs whilst she was walking.

"It really is you."

The voice made her jump. Nimsah glanced around to find a young boy with a grin on his face, wearing a white tunic and trousers, standing at the entrance to a chamber. He was handsome, his hair jet black and long for a Fujareen, worn swept back. Nimsah noticed some bruising, fading now, around one of his eyes and running down his jaw.

"Nimsah?"

Her eyes widened. "Dojan?"

The boy laughed. "Yes, it's me. I almost didn't recognise you at first. What are you wearing?"

"I work here now," Nimsah told him with a coy smile.

"*Really?*" Dojan looked excited. "Are you living in the palace with the other servants?"

Nimsah hesitated, realising she didn't have a clue where the servants' quarters lay. Best not to fashion a lie out of pure guesswork. "No. I've been taken on to run some errands for one of your father's guests. How are you feeling?" she asked, keen to move off the subject.

Dojan shrugged. "I'm fine. Mother's more concerned about Adina, who hasn't left her bed in over a week. If you want to know the truth, my sister enjoys all the attention. I saw her sneaking out when she thought no one was looking. Father keeps fussing over me – I don't know which is worse. I've had guards following my every move since the attack."

Nimsah glanced around, half-expecting to be pounced on by a horde of warriors hidden in the shadows. Peering over his shoulder into the chamber, she could see the room was larger than Fenara's whole house, with an assortment of chairs, couches and cushions scattered about on top of a thick Oomrhani rug. However, it appeared they were alone.

"I gave my guards the slip," Dojan told her, looking pleased with himself. "I was being schooled by Vizier Haman until he was called away on urgent business. I was told to stay in the study, but the windows open onto a veranda above this room. I climbed down into here."

Dojan looked disappointed when Nimsah shrugged, unimpressed. "You didn't get very far then, did you?" she told him with a giggle.

"I've only *just* made my escape," he told her, pride wounded. "Ever since the attack I've not been able to do *anything* on my own. Father had me surrounded by guards day and night. I told him they were putting me off my studies when they were standing over my shoulder, so he eventually agreed to station them outside in the corridor. I've been cooped up in the palace for so long I'm dying of boredom. I want to see more of the city, like when you and I went exploring that time."

"We were hardly exploring – we were running for our lives," Nimsah said with a laugh.

A mischievous grin spread over Dojan's face. "And it was fun. Where are you going? Can I come with you?" Nimsah stared at the boy, realising he was completely serious. The words were out of her mouth before she knew she'd said them.

"I've finished my work here and I'm heading back to the City of Tents."

"I've never seen the Bridge of Steel – at least, not up close," Dojan replied. "Would that be more impressive than just climbing down from the veranda?"

CHAPTER 18

Summer 213 – Kandarah, Shekh Birizal's Palace

The evening meal on the topmost floor of Birizal's spire was every bit as sumptuous as Fasil had predicted. An open air space had been created on this level, offering an uninterrupted panorama of Kandarah, lights glittering in the neighbouring spires like jewelled sceptres as darkness fell and a thin crescent moon rose above the horizon. More of the extraordinary glass, fashioned in a single flowing sheet, created a barrier around the edge that prevented the most curious from plummeting to their deaths far below. It also acted as a windbreak, with canopies erected above the three long tables upon which the feast was served providing further shelter from the elements. Musicians performed to one side, creating relaxing strains on instruments Dojan didn't recognise. Arak sat across the table, deep in conversation with Tormindah. He had removed his veil to eat, revealing a smooth clean-shaven face with rounded cheeks and heavy jowls – clearly Arak enjoyed his food.

Birizal was a small man with a long, pointed moustache, dressed in robes of the emirate style that were fashionable amongst the Naroque city states. Quizar had told Dojan that the shekh was widowed and childless. Since he was still in his early forties, that made Birizal the most eligible man in all of Kandarah. However, he remained unmarried, which meant that on his death the title of shekh would pass to whoever he decided to nominate in his will. This explained the throng of people at his dining table that evening, each representing a faction of Kandaran high society keen to curry favour and improve their position. All five major tribes of Naroque were present. In addition to the red-robed delegation of the Abitek, he saw smaller numbers of Halak, the seafaring serpent tribe of southern Naroque wearing their traditional green. A group of Culah warriors from the east were sat on the table furthest from the Halak delegation – a sensible move, as the two were great rivals. They were engaged in a noisy game of dice, frantically gesticulating to each other as they placed their wagers, whilst the odds and stakes changed at breathtaking speed. In one far corner sat a couple of yellow-clad Kaal, the nomadic scorpion tribe who tended their flocks in western Naroque. They were scowling as they looked on, perhaps nursing some disappointment at their treatment at the hands of the shekh. Quizar pointed out that there were also representatives here from the other emirates as well as a minor prince of one of the southern Kingdoms of Kalat – the youngest son of Beghani, Sultan of Urumesh. Ulan clearly knew the man from the time he had spent in that country, the pair of them embracing warmly on their unexpected reunion.

The evening also gave Dojan the opportunity to see Narinda for the first time. The Edeen wore robes of either black or white, decorated with patterns of stars in silver and gold. Narinda was younger than Dojan expected, a round woman in her mid to late thirties. Her head was shaved, and a circlet of golden stars had been tattooed onto her jet-black skin, the largest of these prominent as it sat in the centre of her forehead. Dojan, who was more familiar with the tattooed faces of Zirhidan ladies, thought the artwork that adorned Narinda showed exquisite skill. As night fell they made her look more extraordinary, the stars glittering with their own lustrous hue, as if illuminated from within.

Quizar caught Dojan staring. "We can arrange a private audience, Crown Prince. However, I would recommend spending some time with our host first of all. It would have been rude to refuse Fasil access to your chambers earlier, but

I would not recommend giving Birizal cause to take offence by snubbing him in his own palace and speaking to the Edeen before him."

Dojan nodded. "I'll take your advice. However, we've been here for hours and still Birizal makes us wait before he formally introduces himself. I swear, he's spent longer talking to that gangly prince from Urumesh."

"The feast is almost over," Quizar replied. "Once the food has been cleared away the formal business will begin."

Dojan waited patiently as servants appeared and tidied the table, leaving only jugs of water and wine. He'd planned to leave a clear head for negotiations with the shekh, but the red served that evening was fabulous and Dojan was unable to restrain himself from asking a servant to fill his goblet. Pasha Ulan, who drank nothing stronger than tea, cast Dojan a warning look, which the crown prince ignored as he raised his goblet and toasted his good health.

Shekh Birizal rose from his chair. The man was so short it made little difference, and he had to walk over and stand on the musicians' stage before most people noticed.

"My friends," Birizal's voice boomed out despite his diminutive stature, the crowd turning to look at him, conversations dying on their lips as silence fell over the feast. "My friends, thank you for your company this evening. I regret I have urgent business I must attend to, for our honoured guest, Crown Prince Dojan Al-Haraq of the Emirate of Fujareen, has joined us after his sea voyage across the Strait of Bezeen." He turned to Dojan and bowed his head. "Crown Prince, welcome to Kandarah. If you and your companions could remain behind I have matters to discuss with our Abitek and Edeen friends, which I'm sure you will find of interest."

Dojan rose and gracefully accepted the invitation before being ushered to a circular table where he took his place with his advisors arranged about him, Tormindah sitting on his left side to protect him against any underhand use of the Sight. Hadir stood guard at Dojan's back, eyeing Khan Lemarr, who had taken up the equivalent position behind his shekh. In contrast, Fasil and Narinda joined them alone, their warriors only permitted to watch from a distance. Nimsah was accompanied by a man Dojan presumed to be another member of the Illesh bank, since he had worn a veil covering his face before the feast. When he removed it to eat it revealed a man with a long black beard, shot through with grey, and dark, piercing eyes. It was only as Birizal began the introductions that Dojan realised this man was Jandral, the senior banker to whom Nimsah reported.

"These meetings are usually smaller, more intimate affairs, Birizal," said Narinda in a soft, cultured voice. The stars encircling her head created a diffused halo of light that shone on her face whilst casting her eyes into shadow.

"Things have changed," Birizal told her with a smile. "Pasha Ulan Bel-Naraar speaks on behalf of foreign matters for the Fujareen Emirate. Our friends here from the Bank of Illesh have been in discussions with his emir for some time. Perhaps you would like to enlighten our companions concerning the outcome of those negotiations?"

Ulan smiled as he began to outline the nature of the agreement between Fujareen and Illesh. "I am pleased to say that Fujareen now includes the Illesh bankers amongst our closest friends. At the request of Nimsah, we have journeyed to Kandarah to assist Shekh Birizal in this ongoing dispute concerning the future of Amonduras. The time has come to resolve things, once and for all."

Shekh Birizal sat back in his chair, pleased with himself, watching the reactions of Fasil and Narinda. "My patience has worn thin this past year," he told them. "The Bank of Illesh did not finance my expedition to Amonduras for its own amusement. They expect to see a return on that investment."

Jandral leaned forward, elbows on the table as he rested his chin on his hands. "Illesh's arrangement with Fujareen places their army at our disposal. We have decided enough time has been spent in endless, fruitless discussions. We have tried, always acting reasonably throughout, to deal fairly with both your tribes. If you continue to refuse to cooperate, we must look at other options."

Khanir Shinva nodded, Mubarizun Yanzin also standing on watch at her back. "An advance unit of the Blessed Swords and warriors of the Regiment of the Tireless Shields disembarked at the docks this morning. They are now setting up camp beyond Kandarah's city walls, and in the coming days more of our ships will land, swelling our numbers as we build our army base here in Naroque. We are not looking for conflict, although you'll find us more than ready if it should come to that."

Fasil flashed his familiar smile, which Dojan was already finding infuriating after a single day. "A significant undertaking, I would imagine, transporting so many of your warriors across the sea. And expensive too, I don't doubt. I hope all goes well and your army travels here safely, although I fail to see the relevance to the situation here."

"Fail to see the relevance?" Birizal snorted. "Fujareen is the most powerful military power in the northern emirates. Whilst your people invented the Samarak fighting spear, Fasil, you'll find the Fujareen army perfected the art of wielding it. The time has come for me to claim my prize and you or your friend Narinda will help us or face the consequences."

"You need the help of the Edeen or my people to open the gateways of Amonduras," replied Fasil. "We cannot help you if we are slain at the … How did you put it? The *artful* hands of the Fujareen army."

Shekh Birizal played with the corner of his moustache. "I only need one of you to open the gates."

"Seize one of us, and bloodshed and war will be your reward," Narinda told him. Silence followed her remark, during which Dojan found the cuffs of his tunic very interesting. He felt heat creeping up his neck, his throat dry and tight. He glanced at Nimsah, whose company he had enjoyed so much during her visit to Bengarath. She sat listening to the discussions, an intense expression of concentration on her face, thoughts inscrutable.

"If this city was so important to the Edeen, how is it that you managed to misplace it for two centuries?" Birizal finally snapped. "I thought your tribe valued knowledge above all else?"

Narinda looked annoyed. "Please, Shekh Birizal, do not treat us as if we're ignorant fools. It's unbecoming of you and shows us the utmost disrespect. If the task of crossing the Shimmering Way was easy, you would not have wasted a fortune on doomed expeditions before Khan Lemarr's unlikely success."

Dojan cleared his throat. "You must forgive me. I am a poor student of geography. This thing you speak of – the Shimmering Way. What is it?"

"It is the name those living in Naroque have given to the poisoned lands surrounding Amonduras, Crown Prince," Ulan explained.

Narinda leaned forwards. "During the War of the Avatars fearsome and terrible weapons were used by both sides, in increasingly desperate attempts to end the conflict. The dragon race was massed at Amonduras, preparing to fight alongside Vellandir's avatars and put an end to the uprising of Morvanos and his followers. Morvanos learned of their plans and unleashed a dreadful weapon in the skies above Amonduras. It cast a bright light, a second terrible sun, that killed every living thing whose skin it touched. Many thousands of Edeen and Abitek died that day as the might of the dragon race was broken. The land for fifty miles around the city was ... transformed and poisoned, discernible only by a strange alteration in the air. Cross into that space, where the air moves of its own volition and the light plays strange tricks on the eyes, and you will never return. No one can venture into the land around Amonduras without their flesh corrupting, their mind turning on itself. All wholesome things that move died, and the great jungle took Amonduras to its heart, wrapping it in an impenetrable forest of stillness. Since that awful day we thought the ancient seat of the dragons, the race we served for centuries, had been lost forever."

Dojan swallowed as he listened to Narinda's story. The uncomfortable truth was the emirates had supported Morvanos' cause, with the Abitek and Edeen on the opposing side in the conflict. Their worship of the dragons had blinded them to the fact they were upholding the Tyranny that kept humanity in servitude to that older race. Such divisions ran deep, even after two hundred years, so the fact Fasil had appealed directly for Fujareen to help the Abitek showed how important this was to them.

Birizal smiled. "Over the years, people living on the edges of the Shimmering Way noticed a gradual lessening of its potency. They risked grazing their animals closer to those forbidden lands. Some fared well. Others ... less so. When news of this reached me, I began to wonder if the ways that had been closed for hundreds of years could now be crossed. Over ten years I paid for four separate expeditions, all of which met with failure. It was then that a further venture was discussed, with the Bank of Illesh. Together, despite a great cost in coin and lives, Khan Lemarr led the expedition that proved there is a route through the Shimmering Way, one that leads to Amonduras' gates."

"You have no way of knowing if the path your men used remains safe," pointed out Fasil.

"The city can be regained," Birizal argued. "Think about it. This is your sacred site, and I'm offering it to you."

Narinda rose sharply from her seat. "I'll hear nothing more of this. Amonduras is not yours to give, Birizal. It is our birthright and we will never help you lay a finger on its riches, no matter what you threaten us with." She cast a scornful glance in Dojan's direction before stalking away towards a knot of white and black-clad Edeen.

Fasil spread out his hands, palms open. "The lady Narinda is not afraid to speak candidly. I must also make clear to all those around this table that the Abitek tribe will not help you, Shekh Birizal, whilst you maintain your claim to what lies inside Amonduras. A share of the spoils – well, that's something else entirely. Grant the Abitek free passage to Amonduras and accept our right to reclaim the city, and we can come to an accommodation. Your new army doesn't frighten us, Birizal. I'm only disappointed your banker friends have advised you so poorly."

Shekh Birizal slumped back in his chair, disconsolate, as Fasil left his table. "You see, Crown Prince – *this* is what I have had to endure. The help of your people will never be forgotten by Kandarah, if you can bring this whole wretched dispute to an end."

Both Nimsah and Jandral stood, replacing their veils as they did so. "Please excuse us, Shekh Birizal," Jandral said. "We have other duties to attend to this evening. We will reconvene in a week, when the Fujareen army has had time to mass its forces."

Khanir Shinva looked up, shocked. "A week?"

"Ample time, I'm sure," Jandral replied, extending his hand to invite Nimsah to lead the way.

Birizal leaned towards Shinva, speaking in a low voice. "They will expect significant progress by the end of the week – have your Sight user reach out to pass on the message to your andral without delay. If the Edeen and Abitek continue to defy us, we must be ready to persuade them to change their current course – with more than just a show of force, if necessary."

Shinva looked at Tormindah, who nodded. "I can send a message to my Fellowship. Our ships will be here as instructed."

As instructed, thought Dojan. That was about right. This was no alliance of equal partners.

"Good," Birizal sighed with relief. "Crown Prince, I thank you for your help in this matter – it will never be forgotten. Welcome to Kandarah, and all it has to offer."

CHAPTER 19

Summer 199 – Bengarath

Nimsah found it difficult to believe how easy it was to leave Bengarath Palace with the crown prince in tow. People saw what they expected rather than what was in front of them. All it took was a pilfered set of nondescript brown robes and Nimsah's servant girl outfit and they melted away, the warriors seeing through them as they left the palace via the staff entrance at the rear. It was accessed through a narrow, twisting tunnel, protected by a portcullis at either end. Nimsah felt a tightening in her guts at the thought of them closing those defences, trapping her in the tunnel with the prince. For the first time, the seriousness of what they were doing hit her. Farooq had put his trust in her and she was putting everything in danger, acting on Dojan's whim. Yet part of her thrilled at the risk they were taking and there was something about this naïve young boy. Everything in the City of Tents turned on who benefitted from each and every action, each favour owed or given carefully weighed and measured, waiting for the time when payment would be due. In contrast, Dojan wanted nothing in return, the time they were spending together its own reward. He was breathing fast as he gave her a conspiratorial glance, eyes twinkling with excitement. Nimsah sighed as they passed through the outer gate – no going back now. She finally relaxed once they'd wended their way through the streets and the palace was out of sight.

Dojan laughed out loud. "That was too easy. How far is

it to the City of Tents?"

"A little way," Nimsah told him. "We could be there by late morning, if we hurry."

Dojan gave her an elaborate bow. "Lead on."

***

The pair sat under a rickety canopy, its thin bleached wooden poles so old they bent under the insubstantial weight of the threadbare cloth shielding them from the bright sun. The Namja River was busy with boats, a group of women and children washing clothes in the shallows. Arching overhead was the Bridge of Sorrows, its weight suspended via an elaborate arrangement of steel wires fixed to slender metal columns. In several places the wires were broken, creating a gap in the regular, pleasing pattern of interlaced steel. Nimsah could see carts crossing the bridge, led by horse, pony or in a couple of cases pushed by hand. Raqqath once told her no one knew how the bridge had been constructed, yet people placed their faith in this mystery from the Enlightened Age every day to cross the Namja. Only the most superstitious refused to go near the rusting metal edifice, placing their trust in the ferrymen who scratched a living in the bridge's shadow.

"Do you know the story of the Bridge of Sorrows?" asked Dojan in a sleepy voice, rocking back on one leg of his stool.

Nimsah nodded. "The emir hung his enemies over the river from the bridge, as a warning. Their bodies stayed there for days – or so I'm told. It happened before I was born."

"Yet they still talk about it. I suppose that's what my father wanted. Those men, down at the docks, attacked us to avenge the destruction of the Bel-Deem house, or at least that's the rumour amongst the Mighty Spears. There's ... a connection, I suppose, between this place and what happened to me all those years later."

Nimsah kept tight-lipped, choosing not to argue against the tales the prince had been told. His words reminded her that she still hadn't sought out Farooq to give him Jandral's instructions. They hadn't been on the outskirts of the tent city for long. She glanced at Dojan, the boy looking thoughtful as he stared at the bridge above the glittering river. Could she trust him not to get into trouble if she left him alone?

"Could we explore the place where you live?" Dojan asked, nodding towards the maze of tents spread out on the Namja's eastern bank as the Bridge of Sorrows soared overhead.

"It's not a good idea," Nimsah told him. "If people look too closely and see a rich boy, things could turn … nasty."

Dojan looked disappointed. "We've only just got here."

"And now you've seen the Bridge of Sorrows as we see it, here in the tent city," Nimsah pointed out.

Dojan shrugged, mollified by her words. "I suppose. Why do you think I stand out? What could I change so I could come with you?" He pointed to the brown robe he was wearing. "I could get a better disguise."

"I stand out wearing servant's clothes," Nimsah explained. "Hearing you speak is all it would take. They'd be on you like a pack of jackals."

"Is that what you are? A jackal?"

Nimsah giggled, although in her mind's eye she saw a merchant cowering in a cargo hold, his killers led there by a little street rat. "No. I'm no jackal. I'm a … a lioness."

"You're a very *small* lioness," Dojan told her with a grin. He looked handsome when he smiled, despite his bruises. A pretty rich boy, grown soft in his palace until the real world intruded with violence, blood and murder. Now he craved a taste of freedom, latching onto Nimsah as the only person in his circle who wasn't bound to follow the emir's every command. He owed her his life, yet Nimsah hadn't worked out a way to use this to her advantage. Those innocent dark eyes stared at her, unaware of the thoughts racing through her mind.

"One day you'll see that I'm right," she replied. "One day, I'll rule all this."

"Does Farooq know?"

"Farooq won't be around forever."

Dojan's smile faltered as he sat there, trying to work out if Nimsah was joking. "This has been fun, little lioness. I can't remember another time when I've just done whatever I wanted, when I wanted." Dojan sighed, looking up at the sun. "I need to head back to the palace. They'll have noticed I'm gone soon, if they haven't already."

Nimsah thought of Dojan's bodyguards, frantically looking for their charge just over a week since his attempted assassination. The emir had hung hundreds of his enemies from the Bridge of Sorrows – what would he do to the warriors who'd failed to protect his eldest son? Dojan was sitting on the stool with a self-satisfied smile, blissfully unaware of the possible ramifications of his actions.

"Farooq will be expecting me," Nimsah began, wondering if she had time to return Dojan to the palace or whether she should risk leaving him here.

"I'll make my own way back," he said, making the decision for her. "I can remember the route and I like the idea of walking my own streets."

"Take care," Nimsah replied, surprised at the pang of worry she felt at the notion of Dojan walking home alone. "There are people in Bengarath who wish you and your family ill. I wouldn't want my efforts to save you to have been in vain."

Dojan rose and pulled the brown robe tighter around his pristine white clothes. "I'll be careful, I promise. Listen, you said you're working for the banker, Jandral? We could meet, in the palace, if you like. I could arrange to be around if you know when you're going to be back." Dojan's face fell when Nimsah told him Jandral was expecting her in five days' time.

"It's in less than a week," she said. "We've only met twice in all our lives."

"Yes … but …" Dojan's voice trailed off and he refused to meet her gaze.

Nimsah turned as she heard the chattering of excited

voices and saw a group of children running towards the tent city. They were clamouring for the attention of Kandilla, who had appeared nearby, seeking an errand that would earn them a copper or two.

"I have to go, and so do you. You don't want to get to know this one better," Nimsah told him, the urgency in her voice making Dojan stand up straight.

"I'll see you in five days, Nimsah my lioness," he said, moving off in the direction of the palace. "Promise?"

"I promise," she threw over her shoulder as she walked towards Kandilla, who's face brightened when she saw her.

"Farooq's asking after you, girl. We were wondering if you'd got lost in the palace."

Nimsah couldn't help herself, looking back towards where Dojan had been standing. She was relieved to find he'd already disappeared into the flow of people moving along the street.

"Nimsah?" Kandilla gave her a thoughtful glance, eyes narrowed above her tattooed cheeks.

Nimsah arranged her face into a bright smile. "All went well, Kandilla. I have a message for Farooq from Jandral."

"Let's not keep him waiting," Kandilla replied.

***

Jandral surprised Nimsah by showing as much interest in her education as the results of Raqqath's investigations. The latter progressed well, and Jandral's suspicions about the origin of the fire powder proved useful. Several dockers had seen those barrels being unloaded from an Amjahran dhow and placed on the dockside that morning. The ship, called the *Sea Spirit*, left before the emir's baghlah arrived. Raqqath was seeking more information on the owner of the *Sea Spirit*, whilst further questions were posed about who knew where the emir's ship was due to land. The investigations in Amjahran meant a voyage north, and Jandral gave Nimsah a purse heavy with coin to meet the costs of the trip. She placed the purse in her bag, knowing better than to open it – no one willingly crossed the Bank of Illesh.

Afterwards, Jandral spared her half an hour to show her the basics of Samarak script and test her knowledge of mathematics. Nimsah couldn't understand the symbols that represented each number, although she was pleased at how quickly she could work out the sums Jandral posed. She understood how many coppers amounted to a silver shekel, and the value of silver shekels that could be exchanged for a single gold coin. Anyone at the markets could do that, although Jandral seemed impressed by her efforts.

"You've a good head for numbers, Nimsah. Tell me, would you like to learn more on your next visit?"

Nimsah shrugged, still bemused at the interest Jandral was showing in her. "If it pleases you, my lord."

"No titles here," Jandral told her with a benevolent smile. "All in the bank are employed as equals, distinguished only by our experience and length of service. I am Jandral, of the Bank of Illesh."

"If you're all equals, who's in charge?" Nimsah asked.

"A council of the bank's elders direct our affairs and purpose," Jandral explained. "To serve on the council is a great honour, one I am pleased to say has been bestowed on me. It is a great responsibility."

"And the council sent you here?"

"Indeed. They thought I was best suited to the task of opening up negotiations with Fujareen. In the years to come, I hope our interests will become more closely entwined."

"So that's why you're interested in what the Amjahrans are up to? Because they're working against Fujareen?"

Jandral paused, looking at Nimsah for a long time as he stroked his oiled beard. "I thought I was the one asking questions."

Nimsah stiffened, wondering if she had caused offence. "Forgive me, my lord ... Jandral. I was merely curious. I have to memorise the messages and I can only do that if I understand them."

Jandral sighed. "It's a good question, one that I refuse to answer as much for your protection as anything else. Be careful who you confide in, Nimsah. You're wiser than your years, something Farooq has exploited. However, there are those in this city who would wish you harm if they knew who you were helping. Do you understand?"

Nimsah nodded, so wrapped up in her thoughts whilst leaving Jandral's chamber she almost bowled over the young servant boy in smart robes standing outside. In the exchange of apologies that followed, she was surprised to find the boy was waiting for her.

"I'm Quizar Bel-Khandir," he explained. "Crown Prince Dojan Al-Haraq said you would be here. He'd like to speak to you."

Quizar looked Nimsah up and down as he spoke, taking in her ordinary servant's clothes and frayed sandals. If the boy was of the Bel-Khandir house it was obvious, even to Nimsah's rudimentary understanding of the Fujareen class system, that he was no mere servant.

"Follow me," Quizar told her. Nimsah obeyed without question and she was led to Dojan's chambers. The doors were well-guarded, although the spear-carrying warriors only gave the young servants a passing glance as they entered.

Nimsah had to clamp her mouth shut as she took in the opulent chambers in which Dojan lived. Thick carpets covered the floor, fine silks curtained the windows, shutters opened wide to let in a cool breeze that rippled through the fabrics. The large room accommodated an assortment of tables, chairs, cupboards and cabinets filled with a variety of ornaments.

Dojan was reading a book, idly leafing through the pages. He looked up and a broad smile spread across his face when he saw Nimsah. The bruises on his face were almost gone – a faint shadow around one eye all that remained.

"Leave us, Quizar," Dojan commanded. The young boy bowed low, backing out of the chamber and closing the door on Nimsah with a suspicious frown.

"These … these are your rooms." Nimsah tried and failed to keep a note of awe out of her voice.

Dojan glanced up, as if seeing them properly for the first time. "Yes, this is where I spend most of my time. Haman's left me reading through this," he tossed the leather-bound book onto a mahogany table where it landed with a heavy thud. "Now you're here we can do something more interesting."

"I can't stay for long," Nimsah told him. "Farooq will be expecting me."

Dojan grinned, walking over to one of his cabinets and fetching a small black box from a drawer. "Surely there's time for a game of Naroque tiles before you head back?" he asked, pouring the black and white bone pieces over the table with a clatter. He began sorting them into two piles.

Nimsah sighed. "*One* game?"

"I've been waiting five days for your visit," Dojan replied. "You don't begrudge me one game of tiles, do you?"

CHAPTER 20

Summer 213 – Kandarah, Shekh Birizal's Palace

Dojan took breakfast with Quizar on the balcony overlooking Kandarah. Despite the early hour it was already stifling, with little breeze from the sea to offer relief. The temperature did little to improve Dojan's mood as he reflected on the events of last night. He was glad he wasn't a member of the Blessed Swords and Tireless Shields, working nearby to build the camp that would receive the might of the Fujareen army in six days' time. By late morning the workers would have to take shelter from the scorching sun that was steadily rising in the clear blue sky, glinting off Kandarah's spires.

Pasha Ulan arrived with Khanir Shinva, Arak and Tormindah. Servants poured them tea as Tormindah fanned herself, suffering from the heat, sweat beading on her forehead under her black headscarf. Ulan informed Dojan that Tormindah had sent word using the Sight, requesting Andral Illana to ready her army for the crossing to Kandarah.

"That's all very good," Dojan replied with a wave of his hand. "What I want to know is what you thought of our meeting with Birizal last night?"

Ulan cleared his throat. "Forgive me, Crown Prince, I'm not sure I follow? Our attendance at the feast was expected, since Birizal is our host. To refuse such an audience –"

"It wasn't really an audience, was it? After keeping us waiting all day Birizal summoned us to his table merely as a show of strength. We weren't there to take part in the

149

negotiations in any meaningful way. How do you think it felt, having to sit there and agree to issue the order for war at a snap of Jandral's fingers?"

Ulan looked aghast, taken aback by Dojan's ire. "Crown Prince, if this situation has left you feeling discomforted, I can only apologise. However, if you will permit me to say so, I think you are reading too much into the events of last night. We have a clearly defined part to play here in Kandarah and such things have already been settled."

Dojan gave Ulan a poisonous glare. "Discomforted? Is that the word we use when we ask our troops to die on foreign soil and can't even tell them what they died fighting for?"

"War can still be avoided," interjected Arak, inscrutable behind his veil. "The mere arrival of our army is likely to be enough to settle matters."

"Settle it for *whom*?" asked Dojan. His question was met with silence as he continued. "I thought we were coming here to aid Sheik Birizal in the negotiations – only to find they have been concluded in our absence. We've been drawn into the final moves of this game, our spears and swords used to bring the Edeen and their cousins the Abitek into line. We're nothing more than mercenaries, hired by the highest bidder. And how could we not know the importance of the tribes' bloodline to Birizal's ambitions? Unless this was something you didn't feel the need to tell me, Pasha Ulan?"

Ulan sat up a little straighter at the reprimand, placing his teacup on the table with the faintest tremor in his hand. "I can assure you, Crown Prince, that news came as much of a surprise to me as to anyone. I have studied long and hard to become the pasha dedicated to foreign affairs and, whilst I knew of Amonduras' *symbolic* importance to the Abitek and Edeen, this linking of access to their blood was never mentioned."

Arak leaned forwards to intervene. "Begging your forgiveness, Crown Prince, does any of this matter?"

"Matter? Of course it matters. How could it not?"

"As Pasha Ulan has explained, the nature of our arrangement is the alliance with Illesh. Illesh supports the Kandaran cause and Shekh Birizal desires Amonduras. If the Abitek or the Edeen attempt to oppose us, we are honour-bound to stop them, with force if necessary. We are not here to debate whether Fasil or Narinda has the better claim to Amonduras – this is irrelevant. The exact means Shekh Birizal uses to gain access to Amonduras is also none of our concern. Our presence is to do the job of enforcing the shekh's will, as directed by the Illesh bankers. Nothing more."

Dojan sat back in his chair, debating the merits of the Veiled Magus' argument. He hadn't enjoyed how exposed he'd felt at the feast, trying to keep up with the conversations between Birizal, Narinda and Fasil, realising he was ignorant of so much of the history behind the dispute. Worse had been that look of command when Jandral spoke, talking to them as if they were servants rather than partners in this new arrangement.

"Arak has a point," Quizar added. "We need to be clear about our objective, Crown Prince. If we aren't careful, we will find ourselves mired here – Shekh Birizal has already presided over this dispute for eighteen months. Do you really wish to establish a more permanent residence here and allow things to drag on?"

Dojan turned to Shinva. She'd removed her helmet, her only concession to the sweltering heat, revealing short dark hair, greying at the temples. Now into early middle age she was still an attractive woman, although the regular features of her face were marred by a crooked nose. Dojan winced, remembering how she'd broken it.

"And you, Shinva? Are you happy with this?"

The khanir of the Blessed Swords inclined her head. "My orders are clear, Crown Prince. If the Fujareen army is required to fight for Kandarah against the Abitek, Edeen or both if necessary, then that is what we will do."

Dojan pursed his lips, annoyed that no one was

supporting him. As he glanced around the advisors at his table he understood what Arak was saying. None of them wanted to be here a moment longer than necessary. The Illesh bankers had paid handsomely for swift military action. Although he had relished the responsibility to lead the Fujareen delegation, Dojan now realised he was only here because no decisions needed to be made. Pasha Ulan's task was to make sure the status quo remained unchanged.

"I admire your confidence, Khanir Shinva," Dojan replied before turning to Tormindah. "I've one more question, if you'll indulge me. Khan Lemarr led the party that made its way through the Shimmering Way, so why doesn't Fasil use his Sight magic to pluck that knowledge from his mind? Wouldn't that have been the simplest way to resolve matters?"

"Shekh Birizal chose his party carefully," Tormindah explained in a voice edged with exhaustion, eyes ringed with dark shadows. If Tormindah was the last bulwark against Kandaran Sightwielders prising open his own mind with their magics, this didn't bode well.

"Careful in what way?"

"Not all people can be touched with the Sight. Some minds are naturally closed, whilst others can learn to close off their thoughts to unwanted intrusions. Lemarr's mind is like a smooth stone, revealing nothing. Shekh Birizal is also skilled in shielding himself from the Sight, although if it was possible to break down his defences he will have taken other precautions. Were I advising him, I would have counselled Lemarr to only confirm to the shekh he had reached Amonduras and nothing more. Shekh Birizal will never dare cross the Shimmering Way, so why place such crucial knowledge at risk if he doesn't even need it? Lemarr's mind is his strongbox, into which the shekh can place his most closely-guarded secrets."

"That's placing a lot of faith in one man," Dojan observed.

"We all have to place our faith in someone," Tormindah

replied, rising with a sigh. "Crown Prince, you will have to forgive me. I need to take some rest. Arak?"

The Veiled Magus nodded. "I will take care of the prince as we have discussed. You need to look after yourself. There's a powerful Fellowship of Sightwielders in this city," Arak went on to explain as Dojan watched with concern as his farseeing magus weaved her way inside with the assistance of Yanzin. "They have been trying to worm their way through our defences all night and Tormindah has spent her strength shielding you. I have enough skill to take her place for a few hours while she rests. We have summoned the rest of her Fellowship to Kandarah, Crown Prince, so they can better protect you. They will arrive with the first ships of the Fujareen army in a few short days."

"Is this Fasil's Fellowship that Tormindah mentioned, or someone else?" Dojan asked.

Arak spread his hands wide by way of apology. "We cannot say, Crown Prince. This land proves to be full of surprises."

"Yes, that seems to be the case," said Dojan, casting a dark glance in Arak's direction.

***

Dojan and Quizar remained on the balcony, taking more tea and watching the sun creeping across the sky, servants moving their table and chairs so they could remain shaded and comfortable.

"Shouldn't we be *doing* something?" Dojan mused.

Quizar sipped his tea. "Like what?"

"We're the Fujareen delegation. Shouldn't we be … delegating somewhere?"

"Pasha Ulan is attending to such matters," Quizar told him. "Now the Fujareen army has been summoned there's very little for us to do except wait. The next move lies with how the Edeen and Abitek decide to respond. Each of them has six days to broker a deal with Birizal regarding who shares in the spoils of Amonduras – we're playing our part simply by being here.

If all this works out as intended we'll return to Bengarath and be feted as heroes, as well as improving our standing with the Bank of Illesh."

"Which of those is more important, I wonder?" said Dojan, a sour taste in his mouth.

"Ulan and Arak are both right. You knew the nature of the bargain," Quizar pointed out. "I know you spoke at length with your father about such matters, so I don't understand why this melancholy mood has descended on you."

"Are you telling me that as an ambitious katib or my friend?"

"Both. Let Ulan and Shinva do their jobs. This deal is done, so if you want my advice you shouldn't go picking at the threads of this tangled argument between a covetous shekh and the local tribes. No good will come of it – our role is simple, and we need to keep it that way."

"And what am I here to do?"

"Stick with me and look devastatingly handsome," Quizar told him with a wry grin. "There were plenty of ladies at Birizal's feast last night and a handsome young Halak man caught my eye. We're here for a week with nothing to do. Why not get better acquainted with some of the locals?"

"*That's* your suggestion?" Dojan felt the heat of his anger rise up from his stomach, in part because he knew that until recently he'd have liked nothing better than to spend his days as Quizar was suggesting. Ever since meeting Nimsah, he'd felt … unsettled, less sure of himself, full of questions. What made matters worse was the fact she'd more or less ignored him since they'd arrived in Kandarah.

Quizar looked unruffled by Dojan's tone. "You've a better idea?"

Dojan pursed his lips, taking a moment to master his ire. "Perhaps you're right. Why come all this way and not spend it in the company of the people of Naroque? We need to understand this place better. I'm sure Narinda's company would prove illuminating."

Quizar rolled his eyes. "If you insist, although you know that wasn't what I meant. I'm sure Pasha Ulan can arrange a meeting."

"No. I don't want him involved. I've already asked him once, and it seems our pasha has conveniently forgotten that conversation. Your task is to keep me entertained, and Narinda is the woman whose company I most desire. I'm sure that's something you can deal with. After all, there isn't anything else I should be doing whilst I'm here, is there?"

CHAPTER 21

Summer 199 – Bengarath, the City of Tents

"You're late," said Rogesh, when Nimsah reached the edge of the tent city. "Farooq's been asking after you all morning."

"I got delayed," Nimsah explained, wiping stray strands of hair off her sweaty forehead. She'd run back, insisting she left Dojan's chambers after the third game of tiles. She'd won that last game, an event that left the crown prince dumbstruck.

"Delayed?" Rogesh frowned, squinting at Nimsah as they walked.

Nimsah paused, knowing that her burgeoning friendship with the young prince had a value all of its own. She didn't want to share that secret with Rogesh and she wasn't sure whether she should mention it to Farooq. When the time was right, perhaps – not now. You only played your best cards at the right time and Nimsah didn't want to squander this opportunity without making sure she got something in return.

"Not talking to me?" pressed Rogesh.

"Being disguised as a servant girl has its drawbacks," Nimsah lied. "People kept finding me things to do."

Rogesh laughed, putting his arms around her shoulders. Her bag swung into his hip, the weight of Jandral's silver making him yelp.

"Don't make a fuss – I didn't hit you that hard."

"What's in there?" Rogesh peered into her bag, fingers

trying to snake inside.

"Get off. It's nothing to do with you." She pulled the bag out of reach, the sharp movement resulting in an unmistakable clink of coins. Rogesh's eyes widened.

"How much have you got in there?"

Nimsah took a step back. "It's not mine."

"It's in *your* bag," said Rogesh. He looked tired, his clothes more threadbare than ever, the widening hole in his trousers flapping around his knee. Nimsah knew Rogesh had nothing in his pockets to earn him a place at Farooq's table that evening.

"That doesn't make it mine –" Nimsah stepped back and slipped on something wet on the ground, falling over onto her backside. Several onlookers burst into laughter as the smell hit her.

"Rogesh!" Nimsah yelled, peering over her shoulder. Despite the heat the round camel dung pellets were still fresh, leaving a dark stain and an unmistakable odour. Nimsah threw a curse at Rogesh. "Idiot. Look what you've done. Now I need to change and I'm already late."

She turned her back on Rogesh and hurried to their tent, the boy following a pace or two behind, making various apologies – all of which she ignored. She snapped the tent flap shut in front of his face, threw down her bag and rummaged around in a chest for something else to wear.

"Ugh. You stink." It was Chandra, sitting with a group of her friends inside. The others giggled.

"I'll wash my clothes later," Nimsah replied. "Right now I need to get changed."

"You can't leave those smelly things in here," Chandra objected.

Nimsah whipped round, half-undressed. "Shall I tell Farooq you're the reason why I'm late?"

Chandra spread out her hands placatingly. "Er, no. Don't worry about it. Just don't leave them there too long."

Nimsah finished getting changed, choosing a pretty

green silk dress she knew Farooq liked. Flustered, she took three attempts to get the thing on over her head, jumping when she turned and found Rogesh standing there, holding her bag. He looked like a whipped dog, cowering under her glare.

"What do you think you're doing?"

Rogesh jumped back. "Nothing. I'm not doing anything. I just came in to say I'm sorry, that's all." Shamefaced, he handed her the bag. She snatched it, not bothering to hide her suspicions as she checked that Jandral's purse was still inside. Her heart steadied when she saw it sitting in the bottom of her bag.

"Don't ever touch my stuff. Do you hear me? Rather than standing there like an idiot, why don't you go and earn your keep? The day's still young and I'm not going to filch scraps for you tonight, do you understand?"

Everyone was looking at the pair of them, Rogesh close to tears as he stood there. Without waiting for an answer, Nimsah pushed past him and hurried to Farooq's tent.

***

Nimsah ate well that evening, served by Farooq himself, Kandilla watching as she lounged on a cushion. After a while Rogesh appeared, not meeting her gaze as he slunk towards Farooq, feet dragging on the dusty cobbles. He mumbled something about cheating a merchant down by the markets, dropping a single silver shekel into the pot at Raqqath's feet with a dull clink. Raqqath raised an eyebrow, turning those icy blue eyes towards Farooq.

"Let the boy eat," Farooq said with a lazy wave of his hand. Rogesh took his seat as far away from Nimsah as he could, heaping food into his bowl. She smiled to herself, pleased that her advice hadn't gone unheeded. She'd make peace with him later this evening.

Farooq conducted business with a number of visitors as he finished his meal. At the end he rose and retired to his tent with Raqqath and Kandilla, Bizek taking his customary place at the entrance, arms folded across his enormous chest.

Nimsah toyed with the idea of speaking to Rogesh, only to find that Chandra had got there first. The pair of them were chattering in low tones, their eyes flicking in Nimsah's direction in unison. Realising she was the subject of their conversation, Nimsah began to walk away towards her tent, deciding to wait for a better time to bestow forgiveness on her old friend.

"Nimsah." Bizek's voice was like crushed gravel, harsh from infrequent use. She hesitated and turned towards Farooq's guard, trying not to stare at his left eye, which strayed off into the far distance as he focussed on her with his right.

"Farooq wants you," he told her, holding the tent flap open, blue cloth draped over his massive hairy arm.

A hush fell on the crowd as Nimsah hurried inside, wondering what Farooq wanted to speak to her about. She'd already reported Jandral's instructions that morning and assumed she wouldn't be back in the palace until after Raqqath had returned from Amjahran. She could see him sitting next to Farooq in the half-light of the tent, a few oil lamps scattered around casting their warm glow as evening stole across Bengarath. Kandilla stood and walked behind her, blocking the entrance to the tent with a cold smile and Nimsah felt a twist of worry in her guts.

"Do you understand what this purse is for?" Farooq asked her, holding it out towards her in his palm.

Nimsah nodded, mouth dry. "Jandral asked me to take this to you. It's to pay for the cost of sending some men to Amjahran, to find the *Sea Spirit*."

"Turn out your pockets and your bag, you thieving little bitch," hissed Kandilla, placing a firm hand on her shoulder, fingers digging into her flesh.

Nimsah bit her lip to avoid crying out in pain as she reached out and opened her bag. Kandilla's hands shot inside and Nimsah felt a moment of relief she hadn't taken food for Rogesh that evening. She suspected this wasn't what interested Kandilla, who gave a frustrated cry and dropped the empty bag onto the floor.

"Nothing. She'll have hidden it somewhere."

A chill crept down Nimsah's spine, her eyes drawn to the purse in Farooq's hand. How could she have been so stupid?

"I was expecting a precise amount from our banking friend," Farooq explained. "The price of a passage to Amjahran is well-known, as is the amount I agreed that Jandral would pay me for my services each month. Imagine my surprise, my precious Little Flower, when I discovered I had been short-changed. The word of the banking clans is their bond – their price sometimes reckoned in blood. Savage, yet always fair. Jandral would never have tried to cheat me, so what am I to think?"

"Did you imagine we wouldn't miss the money?" Kandilla hissed. "Did you have your eye on some more pretty silks, perhaps?"

"No," Nimsah stammered.

Kandilla's breath was hot on her neck. "No? Are you saying Farooq is wrong? Are you calling him a *liar*?"

"No."

Kandilla's knife was in her hand – the same blade that had opened Denek's throat. The tip ran along the skin of Nimsah's cheek, the pressure a fraction less than needed to draw blood.

"I lost it, gambling," Nimsah told her, eyes downcast. It was the most believable of the lies that came to her mind as Farooq glared at her.

"Who in their right mind gambles away money belonging to the Illesh banking clan?" Farooq uttered the words with precision, underscoring her stupidity with each syllable. "Kandilla, let the girl step forward. I want to hear this properly."

Kandilla put away her knife, pushing Nimsah in front of her. She couldn't tell if she dropped to her knees out of deference or fright as she cowered in front of Farooq's chair. The Naroque man folded his arms, adorned by lustrous bracelets of gold and silver. Around his throat a golden torc was a new addition – something from a faraway land that had recently found its way into Farooq's possession.

"You were given this purse this morning. Is this why you were late returning to me? So you could steal a coin and place a wager in one of Bengarath's gambling dens?"

Nimsah shook her head. "Master, I didn't have any choice. I was summoned to see the crown prince and he insisted we placed a bet on the outcome of a game of tiles. I couldn't think how to say no and everyone knows better than to win a game against the emir's own son."

"*What?*" Farooq looked incredulous.

"Tell us where you've hidden the money and we might let you keep *some* of your fingers," hissed Kandilla, tattooed face split by a hungry, white-toothed smile.

"The crown prince is lonely and knew I was newly arrived at the palace, working for Jandral," Nimsah began, keeping her eyes fixed on Farooq. "He sent his servant, Quizar Bel-Khandir, to find me. I think he was bored and he wanted to play a game of Naroque tiles. When he saw Jandral's purse he assumed it was mine and suggested a bet on the outcome of the game to make it more interesting. I ... I didn't know how to say no. I only meant to bet a few coppers but I kept losing and by the time I was able to leave I had to hand over a whole silver shekel."

Even as she wove her lies Nimsah knew she was taking a risk. There was every chance that Rogesh had been greedy and taken more than the single coin he'd put in the pot at Farooq's table. She waited, heart hammering as Farooq considered her story. She'd played her most valuable card earlier than she'd intended – was its value worth more than a single silver coin?

"Quizar Bel-Khandir *is* the name of Crown Prince Dojan's companion at the palace," Raqqath observed, blue eyes appearing to radiate with an inner light in the shadowy tent.

Kandilla looked ready to claw Raqqath's face. "What did

you say? Are you suggesting we believe this nonsense?"

Raqqath looked unruffled as he returned her stare. "It's a very specific fact."

"It's the name of some palace lackey she could have heard anywhere. She's admitted to gambling ..." Kandilla's voice trailed off. "I don't believe her story but, even if it's true, that still means she's gambled your own money away, Farooq. You must see how we can't let this stand."

"Leave us." Farooq's voice contained the unmistakable note of command. Raqqath rose, bowed and left the tent without a word. Farooq scowled as Kandilla hesitated. "Wasn't I clear, my love? I want to talk to Nimsah alone. Leave us."

Kandilla stalked away, Nimsah kept staring straight ahead to avoid looking at her. When they were alone Farooq hooked a ringed finger under Nimsah's chin, gently lifting her face.

"Little Flower, what have you done?"

"I'm sorry, master. I should have told you what had happened. I never thought you would miss a single coin. I was wrong – please, forgive me."

Farooq smiled, the gesture reaching his eyes as he shook his head. "You didn't know the coin was missing from the purse, did you? You're an accomplished liar and there's truth woven into your tale, I've no doubt. It was your face that gave you away, Little Flower; you had no idea any money was missing until you were brought here. Am I right?"

Nimsah thought of Rogesh. She owed the boy nothing, yet they had grown up together and the idea of betraying him felt wrong. She stayed quiet and Farooq sighed.

"Did you steal from me?"

"No, Farooq I swear I never laid a finger on the coins in Jandral's purse. I promise you, that's the truth."

"So the story of the prince and you gambling away Jandral's money isn't true?"

Nimsah swallowed. "I played tiles with the prince. I

told you, he's lonely but he never asked his servant girl to bet on the winner of the game."

"Protecting someone else, then," Farooq deduced. "I think I can guess who. You think I haven't seen you putting food in your bag for the children you share your tent with? I miss nothing – not even your clever hands."

Nimsah stayed silent, watching Farooq carefully. After a while he shook his head. "Loyalty isn't always rewarded in the City of Tents. I hope the person is worthy of protection. Now, Little Flower, tell me more about the unlikely friendship you've struck up with this prince."

***

It was dark when Nimsah left Farooq's tent and headed home, her feet as heavy as lead. Rogesh was sitting outside their tent flap with Chandra and a few other smaller boys and girls, gathered around a cracked lamp. His face brightened when he saw her and he stood up, opening his mouth to speak. She threw a punch that landed with a crack on his jaw.

"Ow!" Rogesh sprawled on the ground, clutching his face. Nimsah felt anger course through her veins, her ears rushing with noise as she aimed a kick at his shins.

"Get off me," Rogesh howled as Chandra grabbed her by the waist.

"I've not finished with you," Nimsah spat, shaking off the smaller girl.

"I'm sorry." Rogesh cowered from her, not trying to rise. "I was hungry."

Nimsah took a long breath in through her nose. "Kandilla was going to cut my throat."

Tears welled up in Rogesh's eyes. "I never thought they'd miss one coin. I'm sorry – I just couldn't face going another night without food. You left your bag lying there while you were getting changed …"

"Keep away from me, Rogesh. Find somewhere else to live."

"Nimsah," Chandra cried. "You can't do that. This is his

home."

Nimsah rounded on the Naroque girl, who shrank away in the face of her anger. "You think I'm so stupid I don't realise you were in on it? You saw him steal from my bag and you let me hand that purse over to Raqqath. You're no better friend than he is. I want you both gone. Find somewhere else in the City of Tents, or the slums of Bengarath, or take a ship to another of the emirates. I don't care. You'll not spend another night under the same canvas as me."

By the time Nimsah settled down for the night, Rogesh and Chandra had packed their meagre belongings and gone. Nimsah curled up under her blankets and hugged the pillow tight to her face, making sure that the other children didn't hear her sobbing.

CHAPTER 22

Summer 213 – Kandarah, the Edeen embassy

Narinda's residence was less grand than Shekh Birizal's palatial spire, although it still rose some thirty levels into the air, suspended on steels woven into fantastical shapes by the mysterious arts of the Kandaran magi. The effect was a building that twisted upon itself as it rose, resembling an exotic fruit, not dissimilar to a pineapple.

Hadir led the way inside the building, Dojan following in his wake flanked by five other Mighty Spears and accompanied by Quizar. He'd felt a little guilty giving Arak the slip, telling him he was going to take some air on the top floor of the spire before leaving through the main entrance. Quizar had objected at first, worried by the warning about the Sightwielders, only finally conceding when Dojan threatened to leave him behind as well. Dojan was sure the Veiled Magus could protect him from a distance, although if he was being truthful he didn't really care. What possible use could the Kandaran Sightwielders have with him? There was nothing to learn they didn't already know. Probing the crown prince's mind was, frankly, a waste of their time and efforts, despite all Tormindah's worrying.

Inside Narinda's spire they were met by a sea of black and white robes, the Edeen people filling every available inch of space in the entrance as they chattered in their own staccato tongue. Smaller knots of green and yellow denoted the presence of the Halak and Kaal tribes. The colour red was notably absent.

"This place is an embassy for the Edeen in Kandarah?" Dojan asked Quizar.

"Exactly. Narinda has been living here for the past year, trying to persuade Birizal to part with his secrets. Whilst we're here, you're effectively on Edeen territory and technically beyond the laws of Kandarah."

"You are taking an unnecessary risk, Crown Prince," added Hadir, eyes scouring the crowded entrance with alarm. "You're no longer under Shekh Birizal's protection inside this building."

"That's why I have you at my side," Dojan told him, patting his armoured shoulder.

"You place too much faith in me, Crown Prince."

"Nonsense. You worry too much. I've had a revelation, Hadir – no one actually cares that I'm here. To be honest, you could take the afternoon off and enjoy a glass or two of something and I'd be fine."

"I'll respectfully decline your kind offer, Crown Prince."

"Of course you will."

Dojan's party was approached by two warriors, a man and a woman, wearing black robes decorated with swirling patterns of white stars, each carrying spears. The older of the two bowed low, listening patiently as Quizar explained they were seeking an audience with Narinda.

"Our elder has many demands upon her time," the warrior explained, looking apologetic.

"I'm sure for the Crown Prince of Fujareen she'd be prepared to make an exception," Dojan told the man with a guileless smile.

The two guards conferred in their own tongue before the younger woman left. The older warrior smiled at Hadir and directed them to some couches near the window. Some Halak tribesmen were already sitting there but after a quiet word from the Edeen warrior they moved away.

"It appears that the name of Dojan Al-Haraq carries

some weight, even this far away from Bengarath," Dojan whispered to Quizar.

"Indeed, my lord, as befits your station."

Hadir and his warriors remained standing as they waited for the female guard to return, leaving Quizar and Dojan to enjoy the comforts of their surroundings.

"Do we have an objective?" asked Quizar.

Dojan frowned, wishing he'd thought this through. "We're here for information, Quizar. There are pieces of this puzzle we still need to understand, which is where Narinda can help us." That sounded far better than admitting he was bored after less than two days in Kandarah.

"Is there something you particularly wish to know?"

"Is there something *you* would wish to learn, whilst we are on the subject?"

Quizar smiled. "I would ask Narinda why Shekh Birizal and the banking clans have spent so much coin locating an abandoned ruin. This part makes so little sense to me. The site is revered by the Edeen and Abitek, so why the sudden interest by the Kandarans?"

Dojan nodded at his friend. "My thoughts exactly."

A servant brought them fresh coffee and tea as they continued to wait, Hadir prowling around them like a she-wolf protecting her cubs. After a time a hush fell over the receiving chamber as Narinda appeared, dressed in white robes, the circlet of golden stars above her brow recognisable even at a distance. Accompanied by more black-clad guards, the Edeen elder approached Dojan, bowing low.

"Crown Prince. An unexpected surprise."

"A pleasant one, I trust?"

Narinda beamed. "Oh, of course. Please, let me escort you to my private chambers where we can speak more freely. Ramdha, please lead the way."

The older warrior who had first greeted them at the entrance bowed, stretching out his arm to invite Dojan to follow him. Ramdha led them to the elevator. Dojan smiled to himself as he realised after two days in this city he was already growing used to its comforts. Narinda's residence on the top level of the spire was laid out with an ornate garden, fountains tinkling, droplets of water catching the light as they fell, the lawns lush and green, flowers of every colour combination bursting from glazed stone pots. On three sides, more of the wonderous flowing glass had been used to create an invisible screen through which the beauty of Kandarah could be safely admired. At the far end a section had been walled off, creating the private chambers of the Edeen's elder. Ramdha led them inside, standing at a discreet distance as Dojan took one of the high-backed chairs set around a rough wooden table, which had been fashioned from the upturned roots of a tree. Were it not for the parched, bleached white colour of the table, Dojan might have thought the whole thing looked alive, like a pit of writhing snakes frozen in motion.

"The table belonged to my mother, many years ago," Narinda explained as she caught Dojan staring. "The tree in the centre of our village came down in a storm and my father fashioned this for her as a gift, so they would always remember the place where they first met."

"How … romantic," said Dojan, thinking he'd rarely seen such an ugly piece of furniture.

Servants brought them cold water and crystal glasses, setting a tray on the undulating table in such a way that it didn't wobble. Clearly this was something that took practice, for when Dojan tried to place his glass down it refused to stay balanced, forcing him to hold it.

"Crown Prince," said Narinda. "It is an honour to receive you. I hope the view was sufficient reward after your journey here in the heat of the day."

"The setting is spectacular," Dojan admitted.

Narinda shrugged. "After living here for a year it does feel like home. It's also safer, for who would be foolish enough to try and attack me up here, when many citadels and castle walls are easier to scale?"

Quizar took a sip of water. "A remote possibility, surely?"

"Nothing is beneath Shekh Birizal – remember that little man cannot be trusted," Narinda replied before turning and looking hard at Dojan. "Now, why don't you tell me why you're here?"

Dojan shifted in his seat. "I've every reason to spend time understanding this conflict. A fresh perspective might provide a solution to the intractable problems of this dispute."

Narinda gave a short, scornful, laugh. "I don't believe that and neither do you. You're Jandral's lackey – the figurehead of a hired army, here to trample over centuries of tradition, dating back to a time when our tribe walked side by side with the dragons. What do you know, with your crude fire powder weapons and your naked avarice for silver and gold?"

"Some of us aspire to something more ... worthy," Hadir observed.

Dojan gave him an incredulous look. "I think my mubarizun is forgetting his place."

"I think your loyal mubarizun is one of the few people speaking honestly," Narinda replied with a smile. "It's obvious this isn't an official visit, otherwise you'd have brought your pasha and khanir." She cocked her head on one side, eying Dojan shrewdly. "They don't know you're here, do they? What will poor Tormindah and Arak think when they learn you've gone missing?"

Dojan leaned forwards. "I'll speak plainly, if that's what you desire. I find our position here ... Well, let's say things are far more delicate than I was expecting. If you and your Abitek friends don't find a way to reach agreement with Shekh Birizal things could quickly escalate. Are the lives of your people really worth this claim to a city that hasn't been occupied for two centuries?"

"The lives of my people wouldn't be at risk at all if you weren't landing an army on the shores of Naroque," Narinda countered.

"If it wasn't Fujareen, someone else would have come to the aid of the shekh," Quizar pointed out.

"True. Mercenaries willing to shed blood in return for a bag of shekels are all too easy to buy."

Quizar pursed his lips. "I think the comparison a little unfair. We're entreating you to find another way so we can avoid that outcome."

Narinda set her empty glass on the table and a servant refilled it. "Nimsah and Jandral have snared you so well you don't even know it. They *want* to see the Edeen and Abitek crushed, settling once and for all who has the right to claim Amonduras."

Quizar sighed. "If you're correct, then you must remove any possible excuse for war. Offer to help them in return for a share of the spoils. The price of your stubbornness will be the death of your own people, with Birizal bringing the survivors with him in chains to open the gates by force. This can't be what you or Fasil want."

"We swore an oath," Narinda told them in a low voice. "There's a reason why the blood of our ancestors is required to open the way into Amonduras. We and the Abitek are both bound to protect the city and serve our long-dead masters, though we took very different paths in living out that promise. I'll not break the binding vow our forefathers made and willingly hand over the keys of Amonduras to someone so unworthy as Birizal. He's a slave to coin and the Bank of Illesh controls him utterly."

"What good is an oath that results in your people being enslaved – or worse?" remarked Quizar. "Forgive my impertinence – I understand the importance of this for both you and the Abitek. However, you're talking here of events that took place beyond living memory. The dragons were defeated – doesn't that mean you're released from your ancient vow?"

Dojan expected Quizar's comments to provoke the same fierce reaction he'd witnessed at the shekh's palace. Narinda surprised him, looking thoughtful as she pondered Quizar's words before replying. "You don't understand, Quizar Bel-Khandir. The Edeen are defined by their past. We cannot simply walk away from our history and act as if those promises were never made."

"Even when your masters are long dead?" Quizar pressed.

"We honour their memory still and are sworn to protect and preserve their secrets."

"You can't do that if your people are crushed on the orders of Shekh Birizal."

Narinda smiled at Quizar. "I see what you're trying to do with your clever words. They're not going to undermine centuries of tradition and service."

Quizar bowed his head. "With respect, I'm not trying to undermine anything. I'm trying to find a path that would preserve your traditions for the centuries to come."

Dojan sighed. "I still don't understand. What can possibly be in this lost city that Birizal would be prepared to wage war and you would be willing to sacrifice your people for?"

"The dragons were the firstborn of the avatars, steeped in their knowledge and secrets from the very beginning," Narinda explained, a frown creasing her tattooed forehead as she still pondered on Quizar's words. "You must know from the old legends how the dragons despised the human race. Only the Abitek, the tribe from which the Edeen were later to sprout, proved themselves worthy to serve them. It was here in Naroque that the Abitek learned the dragon tongue and first picked up the fighting spear. It began in Amonduras, thousands of years ago. That single city represents the foundations upon which the Enlightened Age was built. The Age of Glory, when lifespans were measured in centuries and anything was possible through the harnessing of magic. Don't you understand what Kandarah represents? Its wonders are but the faintest echo of that lost age. Why do you think Birizal builds his spires, reaching towards the heavens? He's trying to recapture those times, with his palace at the centre of this renaissance. Once, all of Amuran's cities resembled Kandarah." Narinda paused, letting that statement sink in before she continued.

"Birizal's ancestors were able to fashion their liquid steels, deep within the hidden forges of Kandarah. After it was destroyed in the War of the Avatars they recreated this city as best they could from memory, old drawings and long-forgotten plans."

"An incredible feat of … masonry?" Quizar frowned, realising he was using the wrong word.

"The ancients called it engineering," Narinda supplied. "These new Magi of the Order of Engineers devoted themselves to studying this lost art, trying to piece together enough knowledge to fashion Kandarah anew. Many people died constructing these spires, some even collapsed under their own weight. Yet such was the vanity of the Kandaran shekhs they called it progress and emptied their vaults on this venture."

"And the Bank of Illesh saw an opportunity?" guessed Quizar.

"Exactly. Before long, Kandarah had borrowed so much coin it would take a hundred years to pay back every shekel they now owe. Perhaps the Kandarans were right, because in time they wrought mighty wonders. However, there was one thing they were unable to master. The secrets of what power fires their forges and supplies heat and light to their spires remains lost."

Dojan glanced around the chamber, noting the soft smokeless glow emanating from sconces set into the walls. "Yet here we are, bathed in the light of this lost art."

"For now," said Narinda. "The avatars revealed secrets to the dragons concerning many things. The true nature of consciousness, the division of the Real from the other Realms and how they can be accessed, shaping time, harnessing magic and capturing it in caskets from which it can be drawn at will. Those caskets are what Birizal craves above all else. Kandarah is powered by a single one of these, found long ago, hidden deep beneath the ground. Our spies tell us the light within is fading, growing fainter each year. Without the power of its magic the spires will darken and the secret forges fall silent. The sun will set on the second glorious age of Kandarah if the Magi of the Order of Engineers cannot find a way to rekindle the fire in the heart of this casket."

"And Amonduras was where it all started," said Quizar. "This is what Birizal and the banking clans are so interested in. There's a chance, however small, that within those ruins something survived."

"A single casket could power Kandarah for a hundred years, perhaps longer – a sufficient prize of itself. The person who learns how to fashion more would be heir to an even greater legacy."

"Fasil knows this too?" asked Dojan, Narinda nodding to confirm his suspicions. "This is what he meant when he came to visit us, telling us there were other ways to profit from this situation."

Narinda smiled, the golden tattoos on her brow glowing. "Are you any more worthy to claim this prize than Birizal or Jandral? Your friends kept you blind to the facts, dangling gold before your nose to entice you into an agreement signed by the emir himself. What kind of man breaks the word of his father? Can such a man ever be trusted with so great a secret?"

A servant appeared and whispered something into Ramdha's ear. The wiry old warrior approached Narinda apologetically, bowing low to Dojan.

"Crown Prince, some of your companions have arrived downstairs and are requesting that they speak with you, urgently."

Dojan cursed silently. "Ah. Who is it?"

"Pasha Ulan Bel-Naraar, Khanir Shinva Bel-Kamil,

Mubarizun Yanzin El-Tebir, Arak Bel-Yangash of the Veiled Magi and Tormindah El-Shan, Magus of the Farseeing," Ramdha replied. "Oh, and twenty of the Blessed Swords."

"All of them, then," said Dojan, crestfallen.

Narinda smiled. "It appears our audience is at an end, Crown Prince. Did you learn what you hoped?"

Dojan rose from his seat. "I found our conversation most illuminating, Narinda, Elder of the Edeen. Perhaps there is some way we can work this situation to our mutual advantage?"

Narinda also stood, bowing to Dojan. "First you must give me a reason to trust you, Crown Prince. Then, perhaps, we can talk again."

CHAPTER 23

Autumn 199 – Bengarath

Nimsah's business at the palace kept her busy for several weeks while Raqqath was away in Amjahran, trying to locate the *Sea Spirit*, the days growing shorter and cooler as summer gave way to autumn in Bengarath. While she had relatively little to report, Jandral had a knack of sending her to and fro with a series of minor questions for Farooq, which always necessitated another trip to the palace to report his answer. Nimsah knew something was going on, as Jandral began to take a keener interest in her studies. They covered the rudiments of Samarak script and mathematics, and lately they'd begun storytelling. This was the one Nimsah enjoyed the most, where Jandral would tell her a story and she would have to memorise it on the spot and recite it back to him. Each time the tale got longer and more complicated and, whilst Jandral said very little as he sat there listening to her, she could tell he was impressed at how many of the details she remembered.

Farooq was happy for Nimsah to spend time at the palace, encouraging her to see the crown prince at every opportunity. Nimsah didn't mind playing games and chatting with Dojan, although she worried Farooq was plotting some scheme and fervently hoped it didn't involve the prince personally. She knew she couldn't warn him to be careful – after her last brush with Farooq and Kandilla, Nimsah didn't want to put a foot wrong.

When not busy running errands between the palace and the tent city, Nimsah spent more of her time working at Fenara's market stall. Fenara was always pleased to see her and it meant she could put off returning to the City of Tents, where Rogesh and Chandra were now part of another gang of street children. Each day Fenara invited her home to eat, and Nimsah accepted more often than not. On one such occasion, with the smell of baking fish wafting through her small home, Fenara stroked her hand through Nimsah's dark hair.

"Child, you've been so quiet lately. Is everything alright?"

Nimsah looked up at Fenara, trying to form an answer. Telling her everything would only give her cause to worry. Instead, Nimsah shared as much of the truth as she dared, without going into the details. Fenara listened patiently as Nimsah told her how one of her friends had stolen something from her belonging to someone else, for which she'd taken the blame.

"This person doesn't sound like much of a friend," Fenara said when Nimsah had finished. "They knew the coins in that purse were meant for somebody else and they stole from you anyway."

Nimsah shrugged. "I didn't want him, Rogesh, to get into trouble. He'd have … well, he'd have come off much worse than me if the truth had come out."

"Worse? Worse how?"

"Just worse."

Fenara paused. "Nimsah, I have to ask you. What were you doing with a purse full of silver in the City of Tents?"

"I told you, I was carrying it for someone else," Nimsah replied, hugging her knees to her chest and wondering how long it was before dinner was ready.

"Farooq?" Fenara guessed. Her brows knotted when Nimsah didn't reply. "Of course it was. Nimsah, please listen to me. I've told you before, I don't like you living there, mixing with people like Farooq. He's dangerous –"

"Do you think I don't know that?" Nimsah snapped. "I'm not stupid."

"No, you're not stupid, you're *young*," Fenara said in a soothing voice. "Farooq has a reputation in Bengarath – it's common knowledge he uses street children as his spies. You think I don't notice how you prick up your ears whenever people are talking to me? Child, I know you're listening for him."

"Farooq protects us," Nimsah argued.

"Farooq *uses* people. For now, you're his eyes and ears in the marketplace and wherever else you go in this city. You're getting older Nimsah. After a time, Farooq will find other uses for those young women under his protection. Is that what you want?"

When Nimsah didn't reply Fenara gave a heavy sigh and stirred the cooking pot. "I'm only trying to make you see your future doesn't have to be like this. You could stay here, with me, and help run the stall. My fingers get stiff these days after I've finished weaving. You could do the work in half the time, whilst making an honest living."

Nimsah glared at Fenara. "I'm not a thief," she lied, hating herself for it.

Fenara tucked a stray strand of greying hair back under her green shawl. "Don't tell me what you're not. Tell me what you want to be."

Nimsah hung her head, clasping her hands together. Her wrists might as well have been chained, invisible links leading back to the tent city under the Bridge of Sorrows, right to the entrance of Farooq's blue tent where Bizek stood guard. Farooq would never let his little flower escape the life he had mapped out for her, no matter what Fenara thought possible.

"The food's ready," Fenara announced. "Go and fetch those bowls and bring them over to me."

The two of them ate together, talking of other things, laughing over the ridiculous hat Ozmun the ironmonger was now sporting and complaining about the inflated prices at Surat's coffeehouse. Nimsah felt safe with Fenara and, although it was an illusion, she enjoyed those precious moments pretending to live an everyday life in the company of the kind-hearted basket weaver.

***

Mubarizun Hengesh looked down at Nimsah, standing there in her servant's outfit, barring the door to Dojan's chambers.

"Looking for your playmate?" he asked, his voice a low rumble. He shook his head when she nodded. "He's in the gardens with Her Royal Highness this morning. Mother and son, spending some time together with his sister and brothers. I'm afraid he won't be able to see you today, young lady."

"Shouldn't you be guarding him?" Nimsah asked, only realising after the words left her mouth the impertinence of the question.

Hengesh frowned. "Khanir Shinva and her Blessed Swords have that honour today, not that it's any of your business. Now run along."

Nimsah didn't wait to be asked a second time, scurrying through the palace and slipping out of the rear entrance. It was colder and it began to rain as she hurried home, dodging the puddles forming on the cobbled street. She was shivering by the time she reached her tent, a couple of girls inside giving her a wide berth after her treatment of Chandra and Rogesh. Once she'd changed, Nimsah went to find Farooq, only for Bizek to hold out his hand and tell her to wait.

"Farooq's busy."

"He'll want to see me," Nimsah insisted.

"He's *busy*," Bizek repeated, squinting hard to bring both eyes swivelling round to stare at her.

"Is that my little flower?" called Farooq from inside his tent. "Let her through, Bizek. She may as well hear this first hand."

Bizek shrugged and held the tent open so Nimsah could escape from the rain. Inside Kandilla was in her customary place at Farooq's side and with them was Raqqath, newly returned from Amjahran, several days earlier than Nimsah had been expecting. He smiled at her, blue eyes sharp and penetrating.

"I'm sorry, Nimsah. I've timed my arrival poorly. You'll have to return to the palace, because I'm sure Jandral will be interested to hear we've found the *Sea Spirit*."

***

Nimsah made the journey back to the palace later that afternoon, waiting outside Jandral's chambers while a servant found him, since he was conducting some business elsewhere with the emir. After a long while she heard him walking up the corridor towards her. His expression was difficult to read – somewhere between annoyed at being interrupted and intrigued that Nimsah had returned so quickly. Once they were alone inside his quarters his eyes widened with surprise as Nimsah explained what Raqqath had uncovered.

"There's nothing as dangerous as a slighted emir," Jandral remarked as he sat in his chair by the window, his brown robes spotted with six pointed stars of light where the sun poured through in precise beams, cut by the decorative patterns of the shutters.

Nimsah nodded, reflecting that Jandral had been right all along to follow the trail left by the fire powder. Raqqath had uncovered the merchant who chartered the *Sea Spirit* that transported the barrels to Bengarath. Under question, the merchant had revealed that servants working for Emir Cassim of Amjahran had paid him to have his dhow moored a short distance from the Bengarath port, where they were to await further instructions.

"The merchant said that after they had been waiting four days a boat rowed out to them," Nimsah explained. "The men inside told them to land at the docks that morning, which was the day Emir Haraq was due to return. They were told to unload their cargo at a specific quay and only hand the barrels of fire powder over to a particular man they called Benazar."

Jandral nodded. "They will have received intelligence as

to where the palace guards were stationed, to ensure the emir was protected on his arrival. They were careless deploying his bodyguards to the docks so early, unless someone in the palace leaked the information."

"Why would the emir of Amjahran want Haraq dead?"

"There could be any number of reasons," Jandral told her. "All four of the emirs want to reunite the kingdom into a single Emirate of Murtak, returning this region to its former glory before the War of the Avatars. Fujareen has been growing in power, and Haraq's continued rise represents a threat. It's also no coincidence that the Bank of Illesh has been strengthening its ties with Fujareen of late. Emir Cassim has also been trying to woo the banking clans, with limited success."

The mystery was intriguing – a story like the old legends, except this one was true and she was part of it, even though it was only on the very edges. A dozen questions bubbled up in Nimsah's mind and she tried to sort them out, not wanting to waste this time when Jandral was in a talkative mood.

"Who's Benazar?"

Jandral furrowed his brow. "That, child, is a very good question. It's not the first time his name has cropped up concerning plots against the Emir of Fujareen, although no one seems to know who he is, or whether Benazar is even his real name."

"Was he one of the men who died during the fight at the docks?" Nimsah asked.

"Perhaps, though I somehow doubt it. And if he did lose his life that day, how would we know? As I said, he guards his identity closely."

The sun disappeared behind a grey bank of clouds, the star-shaped patterns fading on Jandral as he stood, indicating their audience was at an end. "I have to leave. You've done well, Nimsah. Very well, in fact. When I return to Fujareen I'll seek you out, I promise. For now, I have business to attend to elsewhere."

"Are you going to Amjahran?"

Jandral glanced down at her. "This doesn't concern you, Nimsah. As I said, you've served me well. Right now, the less you know, the better."

"Won't you tell the emir first?" Nimsah asked.

Jandral looked surprised at the question. "Haraq? Why does he need to know?"

"Shouldn't he know who tried to kill him and his family?"

"I can see why you would think that," Jandral told her with a smile. "The trouble is, Haraq has been advised poorly. His own investigators reached the conclusion local Bel-Deem loyalists planned the whole thing before they even started looking, so naturally that is what they discovered. That these so-called Bel-Deem sympathisers mounted such an indiscriminate attack, which cost the lives of so many innocent people, helps paint Haraq in a better light. It proves he's more fit to rule than the dynasty he usurped – the fact the story isn't true is a minor inconvenience."

Nimsah knew she was pushing her luck as the next question escaped her lips. "If you're building closer ties with Fujareen, shouldn't you help the emir? You said you were working with him, but aren't you leaving him in danger if you don't tell him who his real enemy is?"

Jandral sighed and walked over to a dresser, unlocking a drawer with a small silver key kept on a chain around his neck.

"Here," he said, passing her a leather pouch, heavy with coin. "I must give my thanks to the emir for his hospitality before I take my leave. I want you to take this to Farooq and make sure that Raqqath gets a quarter share. They have done the Bank of Illesh a good service and I will ensure it's not forgotten."

"But –"

"Don't presume because you're privy to the secrets you learn as my errand girl that gives you the right to lecture me," Jandral told her in a cold voice. "The fate of Haraq Al-Souk is not a matter where I am interested in your opinion. Leave Emir Cassim's clumsy meddling to me and do the job I've asked of you." Nimsah stepped back several paces as Jandral's expression softened. "This is the way of things among the bankers of Illesh, where each plays their own part for the good of all. Remember the part I have asked you to play, please."

Nimsah nodded as she gave her apologies. She was turning the door handle when Jandral called out after her. "I meant what I said. You've done well. After my affairs are completed I will return to Fujareen and when I do I will seek you out, young Nimsah. You've shown great promise. Take care of yourself while I'm gone."

CHAPTER 24

Summer 213 – Kandarah, the Edeen embassy

Ulan didn't even wait until they were outside, rounding on Dojan in the receiving chamber on the ground floor of Narinda's spire. "How am I to explain this, Crown Prince? Your visit to Narinda will not have gone unnoticed, I can promise you. I had to leave a meeting with Shekh Birizal himself, make my excuses and come here to find you."

"A meeting to which I was not invited," Dojan remarked.

Ulan's face became taut, muscles playing in his jaw as he bit down on whatever words first came to mind. Dojan couldn't remember a time when he'd seen the pasha so angry. "Crown Prince, I am your loyal servant and your father entrusted me to handle the details on this visit. It would be tedious in the extreme if you had to concern yourself with each and every item of business on our daily agenda."

"Details, Ulan? You speak of details? What does Shekh Birizal hope to find within Amonduras? Is that a mere *detail*? Something I didn't need to concern myself with?"

"We can't do this here," hissed Arak, nodding his head in the direction of a group of yellow-clad Kaals, who were standing nearby and listening to the exchange with interest.

Dojan felt his anger rising. "And who are *you* to tell me what I can and can't do?"

"Crown Prince, he's right," said Quizar, laying a hand on his shoulder, which he quickly pulled away when he saw his expression. "Forgive me, padishah, for my over-familiarity. I was anxious to impress upon you that what we are discussing is not … common knowledge. Narinda placed her trust in us and we should repay her faith with discretion."

Dojan took a deep breath, glancing between Ulan, whose eyes blazed with barely contained anger, and Quizar, who was pleading with him to listen. He licked his lips. "Take me back to my chambers and we'll discuss this further."

Khanir Shinva bowed low. "Your carriage awaits you outside, Crown Prince. Please, allow us to escort you."

Hadir interposed himself between Dojan and the commander of the Blessed Swords. "With respect, Khanir Shinva Bel-Kamil, that duty rests with me and my men."

Shinva smiled as she stood aside. "Of course, Hadir. I had no intention of suggesting otherwise."

***

Dojan bounced on his heels in his private chamber back in Birizal's palatial spire – he felt energised by his act of defiance, although he had a sinking feeling that he would pay dearly later. Quizar sat in a chair nearby, head resting in his hands, deep in thought. He looked up as there was a knock at the door, Hadir announcing Ulan's arrival moments before the pasha pushed himself inside.

"Are you happy to speak to Pasha Ulan?" Hadir asked, looking the shorter man up and down. Dojan sighed and gave Hadir a weary wave to allow the three of them to speak in private.

"No cronies with you, Ulan?"

"Arak and Tormindah are hardly that. They're trying to help you. We all are."

"By keeping me in the dark? Is that how little you trust me?" Dojan spat the words at his advisor.

Ulan glanced at one of the couches in Dojan's room. "May I sit, Crown Prince? It's been a long day."

Dojan dropped into a chair opposite Ulan and waved at the pasha to do the same. The two glared at each other for a time before Ulan spoke.

"Dojan. One day in the not too distant future I'll be wedded to your sister and we'll be brothers-in-law. We're practically family, so you must believe I have only your best interests at heart. Your father has been conducting the negotiations with the Bank of Illesh for many years. The beginnings of this arrangement, upon which our latest agreement is founded, date back to a time when we were still children. I respectfully beg that you think upon this and how your rash actions could undo all of that in a few short days. Do you really wish to return to Bengarath and explain to your father how you broke the agreement with Illesh?"

"I've done no such thing," Dojan argued. "How do you excuse not telling me what we were walking into? This is no mere land dispute. We're here to wage war on the Abitek and Edeen, with the sole intent of crushing them completely. Do you know what the Edeen call us? An army for hire, here to kill at Shekh Birizal's bidding. How could you and Haman do this to our people?"

"With Illesh's backing we could unite the Emirate of Murtak once more," Ulan replied. "Every emir desires to rule the emirates as one. This could be *your* future – think on that."

"At what price, Ulan? You understand what Birizal believes may lie within the ruins of Amonduras? He's seeking magic and knowledge that, if it fell into his hands, would mean Kandarah became all-powerful. And that's if even a *tenth* of what Narinda imagines might be found there is true. This city is a monument to the might of the Bank of Illesh. They control the shekh as completely as they control us – ruling the Emirate of Murtak means nothing if we're beholden to them. Can't you see that?"

Quizar cleared his throat. "There is another way. If we could discover the route that Lemarr took to reach Amonduras in safety then other alliances become feasible. We could broker a deal with Narinda or Fasil, granting us access to the city and its secrets."

Ulan looked horrified at the suggestion. "A lowly katib

should know his place. Your words are nothing less than treason."

"Can the crown prince commit treason?" Dojan asked. "Quizar is only voicing my own thoughts."

Ulan paled, lips tight. "Anyone who works against the will of the emir is guilty of treason. Anyone, padishah."

Dojan paused, mind racing. Had his father really sent him all this way, acting as his representative, only to do what Pasha Ulan told him to? "How much does my father know?"

"He didn't ask," replied Ulan with a sigh. "Your father's not concerned with the affairs of state. He was born a warrior, never groomed to become emir. He knows this, as do you. This is why he has arranged his affairs so matters of state are discharged through his vizier and his pashas. The alliance with Illesh will ensure the future of Fujareen is bright. If it means killing the tribes who oppose our interests here in far-off Naroque, what of it? Who are these people to you? Before you came here two days ago you'd never even met them and now here you are, giving me a lecture on politics and the future of the emirate?"

Ulan turned his back on Dojan and walked to the door. "I have to take my leave, Crown Prince. There is much to do and I have to speak to the shekh in order to smooth over your ... over enthusiastic embracing of Naroque culture."

Dojan let out a long breath through his nose, watching as Ulan's hand reached for the door. "I haven't given you permission to leave, pasha."

"Are we really going to do this?" said Ulan, turning around, his voice tight, as he took several quick steps back towards Dojan.

"Your father wanted to give you the chance to be a man," Ulan hissed. "Do you know what they call you around the palace? The idle prince. What qualities do you possess, other than the happy accident of your birth, that places you as next in line? Adina is more charming, Saraj a promising warrior and Beneth a gifted student. Compared with your siblings, what are your notable qualities, Crown Prince?"

Dojan stared at him, completely disarmed, as Ulan continued. "No witty answer? It seems you're ill-equipped to deal with the freedom you think you have in this city. What do you think you're doing, engaging in secret diplomacy that undermines the work your father's advisors have spent *years* putting together? How would Adina feel, knowing you've compromised me and my office? For her sake as well as yours, we must act as one while we're in Kandarah."

Dojan drew in a deep breath, heart pounding, finding he was unable to meet Ulan's stare. "You will keep me informed, Ulan. Do you understand? You will advise me on all matters of diplomacy and military tactics while we are here."

"As you wish, Crown Prince," Ulan replied, lips pursed tight.

"And as the emir's representative, here in Kandarah, you will instruct Arak and Tormindah to discover the route to Amonduras. If we learn that, we have choices, Ulan. We might avert a war and come into possession of knowledge that will make the Bank of Illesh reconsider their bargain with us. We could strike a better deal, one that benefits everyone."

"Crown Prince ..."

"Am I my father's representative?"

Ulan spoke reluctantly. "Yes, padishah."

"Then you will do what the *idle prince* has commanded."

Ulan shot a poisonous glance at Quizar. "You should think carefully about the advice you're giving your master, Bel-Khandir. You're steering your friend into dangerous waters – a course that places all of us at risk."

Quizar sighed as Ulan slammed the door closed. "That ... That was ..."

"An unmitigated disaster?"

"Yes," said Quizar with a wry grin. "Precisely."

Dojan dropped back into his chair, exhausted. "Will he do it?"

"Follow your orders? Yes, Ulan is loyal to a fault.

Whether Arak and Tormindah carry them out with sufficient energy and enthusiasm – that's a different matter."

Dojan was silent for a time. "What Ulan said, about me being called the idle prince. Is it true?" His katib hesitated and Dojan laughed. "Stop torturing yourself, Quizar. I already have my answer. It's fitting, I suppose. A title I deserve."

"The idle prince wouldn't have stood up to Pasha Ulan like that," said Quizar. "It's far more exciting than courting the ladies flocking around your father's throne, isn't it?"

"You're enjoying this, aren't you?" Dojan said with a frown, seeing Quizar in a different light.

"Of course. There's something to play for in all of this, Dojan. We can shape events here in Naroque that will affect Fujareen's future."

"And the fact Ulan is annoyed by our interference only makes it all the more fun?"

Quizar laughed. "Precisely. Why should the house of Bel-Naraar be the only one to profit from our dealings here? Why not the dynasty of Bel-Khandir?"

"And the royal house of Al-Souk?" Dojan prompted.

"Of course, Crown Prince."

CHAPTER 25

Autumn 199 – Bengarath Market

Nimsah felt lost without her frequent trips to the palace. Farooq toyed with the idea of using her burgeoning friendship with the prince, reluctantly deciding against it. She had been Jandral's servant, and the last thing Farooq wanted was gossip as to why she had been left behind, drawing unwanted attention on the banker. Farooq played things safe and directed Nimsah back to the marketplace, where she could listen and watch for news.

Fenara was delighted Nimsah was spending more time with her, chattering away with a broad smile and at least once a week treating her with small paper parcels containing delicious baklawa. Nimsah worked hard with her weaving, spent several evenings eating with Fenara and tried to resume her old life. She found she couldn't shake the feeling there was something missing, although she enjoyed Fenara's company. Jandral had opened her mind to a wider world with his teaching, and she had seen enough of life at the palace to understand how mean and low her place in Fujareen society really was. She had her expensive clothes, gifts from Farooq, which in certain company might suggest she was the daughter of a merchant or a well to do craftsman. That illusion was dispelled the moment she opened her mouth, her accent telling a different story – of a life lived on Bengarath's streets, a world away from where Dojan was privately tutored by the vizier and slept in his luxurious chambers. Nimsah's head was so full of these thoughts she walked straight into Rogesh and Chandra on her way to the market that morning. Rogesh had the decency to look embarrassed, while the Naroque girl was all bright smiles and hellos. Nimsah didn't believe a word of it.

"What are you two doing here?" Nimsah asked, unable to keep a sullen note from creeping into her voice.

"Farooq's got a job for us," Rogesh explained. He'd grown bigger in the past few months, taller and broader.

"You still weaving baskets?" added Chandra. "I wish Farooq would reward us with a place at his table every night for doing so little."

Nimsah ignored the jibe, addressing Rogesh instead. "You'll be careful, won't you?"

"Of course," he replied. "I know how to look after myself, Nimsah. You taught me that."

Chandra looked annoyed. "Come on. We're going to be late."

"We've got a bit of time," Rogesh told her, looking at Nimsah. She waited, expecting him to say more, only for silence to stretch out between them.

"I have to go," Nimsah said finally. "Fenara will be waiting for me."

"Perhaps I'll see you tonight?" Rogesh asked. "If today goes well, we'll have earned our place at Farooq's table this evening. We could sit together, if you like ..."

That last remark stung and Nimsah wasn't able to hold back on her barbed reply. "No, we couldn't. You betrayed me, Rogesh. You stole from me and gave Kandilla the excuse she'd been looking for to slit my throat. Did you think I'd forget that – how you left me pleading for my life?"

Rogesh's face crumpled with misery. "I didn't know that would happen ... I thought, when you told me just now that I needed to be careful ... I thought ..."

"I don't want anything bad to happen to you," Nimsah snapped. "I miss you but I can't trust you anymore, Rogesh. Things are different and they can't go back to the way they used to be."

Chandra laid a hand on Rogesh's shoulder. "You don't need her any more. You have me now, and we're better off without Farooq's favourite pet. She always kept you in her shadow."

Rogesh looked at her, doubt in his eyes. "We do alright, don't we?"

"I meant what I said," Nimsah told him. "Take care of yourselves."

"We don't need you to lecture us," Chandra replied. "Come on, Rogesh, let's go."

Nimsah watched as the pair weaved their way through the crowd, Rogesh looking back at her once before disappearing into the throng.

***

Fenara donned her blue shawl and black woollen robes as the days shortened and winter crept over the city of Bengarath. Although trade in the market continued to be brisk, people were less inclined to stop and chat, so Nimsah's usual well of rumour and gossip dried up. She took to frequenting Surat's coffeehouse some days, helping out in his kitchens and serving at the tables for a few coppers so she could listen to the talk of his customers.

A group of three men, each with the tattoo of the kraken on their arms and daggers tucked into their belts, were frequent visitors. After a whisper in Farooq's ear later one evening, she never saw them again. Nimsah tried not to imagine what might have happened to them – that was down to Farooq. All she did was listen and tell him what she heard. At least, that was what she told herself.

Nimsah had been hopeful Jandral would return quickly from Amjahran. She smiled to herself as she carried pots of coffee to Surat's customers, remembering how she had coaxed him into letting slip that little piece of information. What had Jandral meant when he said he would deal with Emir Cassim's 'clumsy meddling'? She had no idea, unsure if Jandral would be back in days, weeks, months or years. If he was coming back at all. Keeping the smile fixed on her face as she talked to her customers, she had to believe he was.

"You look cheerful," Surat told her. A large man with a round belly and bent legs, he waddled around his coffeehouse, chatting with those inside, dark eyes nestled in crow's feet that resulted from the permanent smile he wore.

"Your patrons are tipping well this afternoon," said Nimsah, patting her pocket.

Surat's smile widened. "They're drinking the best coffee in Fujareen, after all."

The door opened and Fenara stepped inside, a chill gust of wind following her. Surat greeted her with a friendly wave. "Fenara, my dear. So good to see you."

"And you, Surat. It's good to see so many people braving the cold to spend their coin in here. My late Biwan always enjoyed your company."

Surat's face grew sombre. "Your loving husband is sorely missed. Can I offer you something, Fenara?"

"No, thank you," Fenara replied. "I was wondering if Nimsah was here and I see I've guessed right. Could I steal her from you for a moment?" Surat agreed and called Nimsah over, the pair taking a seat together in a darkened corner.

"What is it?" asked Nimsah, worried something must have happened.

"It's nothing …" Fenara trailed off, looking thoughtful.

"Nothing? You called me away from work to tell me nothing?"

"No, of course not. It was strange, that's all. I don't know what to make of it."

"Why don't you start at the beginning?" said Nimsah, intrigued.

"I was working at my stall when I was approached by a servant from the royal palace," Fenara explained in a low voice. "At first I thought he was there to purchase some of my wares. I was wrong – he was asking after you."

"Me?"

"He asked for you by name, Nimsah. He said he was part of the household of Crown Prince Dojan. The young prince was asking after you, saying he'd not seen you around the palace recently."

A chill ran through Nimsah's spine as Fenara regarded her shrewdly. Although she missed her errands at the palace it had never occurred to her that Dojan would miss her company as well. Drawing attention to her was the last thing she needed – it might even make it difficult to resume her duties when Jandral finally returned.

"What were you doing in the palace?" Fenara asked. "What have you gotten yourself mixed up in?"

Nimsah coughed and cleared her throat. "Nothing."

"Really?"

"I'm telling the truth," Nimsah protested. "Farooq had some business to attend to and I acted as his messenger, that's all."

"Where Farooq is concerned, that's never all there is to tell," Fenara replied, frowning hard. "Why would the palace be looking for you, Nimsah? What have you done? What's Farooq got you involved in?"

Nimsah put her finger to her lips. "Shush. Not so loud. Fenara, I promise you, there's nothing to worry about. I did some work at the palace and the prince took a shine to me, that's all. He asked me to play some games, nothing more."

Fenara looked unconvinced. "Are you asking me to believe that you're the crown prince's playmate? You've not gotten yourself into … anything … more serious than that?"

"Like what?" Nimsah replied, an icy edge to her voice.

"The sorts of things Farooq is involved in, that could be quite a list," said Fenara, returning Nimsah's hard stare. "This is no joke, child. I'm worried about you."

Nimsah reached out, taking Fenara's hand and giving it a squeeze. "Fenara, I promise, you don't have to worry. The boy was lonely and I played with him, that's all."

Fenara sat back on her stool, resting her back on the wall, and sighed deeply. "Well, look at you, Nimsah. Always full of surprises."

"I don't know how many people in the palace knew I was spending time with the prince. This servant ..."

"The man was very discreet," said Fenara, guessing at what was worrying her. "He knew you weaved baskets at the market and he came there, alone, to ask after you."

Nimsah nodded. "I mentioned that to Dojan. What did you tell him?"

Fenara looked uncomfortable. "I don't like telling lies, Nimsah. You put me in a difficult position."

"I'm sorry. I didn't think he'd send anyone after me."

Fenara's face softened. "Oh, it's impossible to stay angry at you, child, even for a moment. I didn't know what this man wanted and why he was so interested in you, so I lied to his face, telling him I'd never heard of you. He seemed satisfied with my answer and he was even polite enough to buy a basket from me before he left. Imagine that, one of my baskets, gracing Bengarath Palace. Biwan would never have believed such a thing."

Nimsah closed her eyes, relief washing over her. She was touched Dojan was concerned but if word got round the city that the prince was interested in her things could become ... complicated. She certainly didn't want Farooq or Kandilla finding out – it might renew their interest in using her in some plot concerning the prince. Something she was keen to avoid.

"Did I do the right thing?" Fenara asked, stirring Nimsah from her thoughts.

"Yes," Nimsah squeezed Fenara's hand again. "It's for the best. My work at the palace is finished, at least for now."

Fenara laughed, eyes twinkling. "Well, that decides things."

"What?"

"You're coming to my house for dinner this evening. I want to hear every detail about this prince and the palace he lives in. I've covered for you today and you owe me a good story."

Surat wandered over. "Forgive the intrusion. I was only wondering whether you've finished with my waitress? There are tables waiting to be served."

Nimsah rose and ran to fetch a tray, serving drinks to some more patrons. Fenara patted her lightly on the shoulder before she left the coffeehouse.

"I'll see you later tonight?"

"You will," Nimsah replied, giving her a smile. "I promise."

CHAPTER 26

Summer 213 – Kandarah, Shekh Birizal's Palace

On the evening after his unscheduled visit to Narinda's embassy, Dojan found himself the centre of attention at a feast organised by Shekh Birizal. Shinva and Ulan never left his side, preventing any further impromptu negotiations as they mingled with the crowd, waiting for the first course to be served. Fasil and Narinda spoke to him in turn, exchanging nothing more than pleasantries. At Dojan's prompting, Ulan did arrange a private audience between Dojan and Fasil for the following morning, recognising that it was important to treat both Naroque tribes equally. As dusk fell across the city, music played softly on the open top floor of the spire, though it and the cooling air did nothing to soothe Ulan's ragged nerves.

"You're raising their expectations," Ulan said afterwards as Fasil moved off.

"I'm being polite, nothing more," Dojan replied.

"Crown Prince," Shinva began, the khanir looking embarrassed at having to speak to him so directly. "As your military advisor, I have to counsel you against doing anything that undermines our alliance with the Kandarans. Shekh Birizal is asking to speak to us privately this evening – how are we to explain all of this?"

"Let me handle the shekh," said Ulan. "Ahh, that didn't take long – here he comes now."

The diminutive shekh walked towards them, surrounded by several Kandaran military officers, including

Khan Lemarr, and a gaggle of advisors. Dojan greeted his host with all the enthusiasm he could muster, thanking him for his hospitality and entertainment. Birizal smiled, moustache twitching, as he cut straight to business.

"I understand you have been exploring our fine city this morning, making yourself acquainted with the Edeen. I hope I'm not failing in my duties as your host to keep you comfortable and entertained during your stay."

Ulan bowed low. "Whilst we want for nothing in your exquisite palace, Shekh Birizal, Kandarah is an amazing city – one that begs closer inspection. I hope you understand the enthusiasm of Crown Prince Dojan to explore what you have built here is a mark of nothing other than his great respect for all your achievements."

The shekh raised an eyebrow. "And this closer inspection brought his majesty directly to the Edeen embassy, for a private audience with Narinda? What am I to make of such a thing? I saw you discussing matters with Fasil earlier tonight, conversations that give me cause to wonder whether the focus of the Fujareen delegation is entirely where it should be."

"We have a saying in Fujareen, know your friends well and your enemies better," Ulan told Birizal. "If we are to fight for you, we must learn all we can concerning your foes – assuming that these negotiations do not broker a peaceful outcome."

"A result we all hope for," added Dojan.

"Indeed," Shekh Birizal replied without enthusiasm.

"The sentiment is a wise one," added Lemarr. "However, I can assure you that the Kandaran army knows these tribes extremely well. If war is unavoidable we can instruct your forces in how best to engage and defeat them."

Ulan smiled. "Whilst I've no doubt you're correct, I'm sure you will indulge us in learning all we can. That way, we can better serve you and secure the prize of Amonduras for the glory of Kandarah."

Shekh Birizal clapped his hands, silencing his musicians as he called for the feast to be served. "It's good to see our new allies take such a keen interest. I'm sure we'll speak on this further. For now, it's time to eat."

"Is that *really* a saying in Fujareen?" muttered Quizar as they walked to their table to begin their meal.

"It is now," hissed Ulan, taking a seat next to Dojan.

***

While Narinda lived in the Edeen embassy, Fasil had quarters within the shekh's palace. The Edeen were a peaceful tribe, their warriors few in number, whereas the Abitek were more numerous and better equipped for battle. Over their drinks in Fasil's quarters Ulan explained to Dojan that Shekh Birizal had closed their embassy when the dispute over Amonduras first arose last year, only allowing the Abitek into Kandarah in small numbers to trade and, in the case of Fasil, negotiate.

Fasil sat opposite Dojan, back straight, eyes alert, agreeing with everything Ulan was saying. They were sitting in the open balcony of Fasil's chambers, Hadir at Dojan's side and the rest of his Mighty Spears watching by the entrance. The air was hot and humid, iron-grey clouds slowly rolling in from the bay and trapping the heat. Dojan was sweating and he dabbed at his brow, trying to concentrate on Ulan's words. Tormindah sat in the chair next to him, shielding him from Fasil's dark Sight magic, although his mild-mannered expression made Dojan wonder if the threat came from elsewhere. Arak was absent – carrying out his investigations into the location of Amonduras in accordance with Dojan's instructions. Dojan met Fasil's eyes and he pushed the thought to the back of his mind, wondering how much this Naroque Sightwielder could see. He cast a glance at Tormindah, who looked tired, although they'd been in Fasil's company for less than a quarter hour. The farseeing magi on his father's ships couldn't come soon enough so that she could bolster his defences.

Fasil waved an impatient hand at Khanir Shinva as she

was in mid-flow, telling him precisely how outmatched the Abitek warriors would be against the might of the Fujareen army. "You can save your breath, khanir. You don't have to convince me that the Abitek would suffer a defeat on the field of battle – I already know this. Shekh Birizal has chosen Fujareen as his ally – or rather, he's been *instructed* to choose you, for precisely this reason. You have the military advantage; this isn't in dispute, nor would I insult your intelligence by pretending otherwise."

Shinva sat back in her chair, unsure how to take Fasil's words. "Then why won't you agree to Birizal's demands? If you can't win by military means, why try and fight against the outcome?"

Fasil leaned forwards in his chair. "If an army twice the size of yours laid siege to Bengarath, what would you do? Would you throw open the doors of your city and spare yourselves, or fight for every foot of city wall and bleed to protect every street corner?"

"Fair point," Shinva conceded. "Surely, though, the difference is Bengarath is a living city, whereas Amonduras is an abandoned ruin."

Fasil turned to Dojan. "You've spoken already with Narinda, so you know it's more important to our tribes and the Bank of Illesh than that. With Amonduras, we could fashion new wonders, rather than this crude copy of the past Birizal and his ancestors have created. A new age, with all the glory and riches of the Age of Enlightenment at our disposal. We are the tribe of the dragon and our ancestors swore an oath to protect that race and their knowledge. The Edeen chose the way of study, we chose the way of the spear. Though we are rivals in many things, our oaths bind us and we will stand, and fall, together. If that means I must walk in chains with an axe held to my neck because Birizal thinks I will open the gates of Amonduras then so be it. He'll be sorely disappointed."

"You understand the Crown Prince is trying to help you and Narinda?" Pasha Ulan replied. "We could avoid this war."

Fasil shook his head. "No. War is already inevitable. The only choice you face is whether you stand in service to the Bank of Illesh or join the side of the rightful heirs of Amonduras."

"You speak of honouring oaths, whilst encouraging us to break our agreement with Illesh," said Shinva. "Can't you see the irony?"

Fasil fixed her with a fierce stare. "Since when were the Blessed Swords the lapdog of a foreign city, paid to do the bidding of bankers and shekhs who care nothing for your history and heritage? Every day since you fell from grace and bought the silence of others to maintain your position, you've felt guilty as you strive to live up to being khanir. Was it worth it to become a common mercenary?"

Shinva looked stunned. "What? What did you say to me?"

"The truth," Fasil replied with a grin. "Uncomfortable, isn't it?"

Dojan's mouth was dry. What was Fasil referring to? Surely, he couldn't know about that afternoon, the baking hot stones standing as their accusers, Shinva wiping blood from her face and broken nose. Dojan closed his eyes, forcing the memory away, afraid that Tormindah's protective spells would weaken and the whole, sordid, horrible truth would spill out from him right there on the balcony.

"I don't know what you're talking about." Khanir Shinva stammered, a deep frown gathering above the broken nose marring her attractive features.

Fasil bowed his head, a smirk playing on his lips. "As you wish."

An uncomfortable silence fell over the group as they sat together on the balcony, sipping tea and coffee as the humidity built under iron grey clouds.

"Why you?" Dojan asked. "Why should we side with the Abitek? What do your centuries of tradition and your dusty oaths mean to us? Why should I even consider breaking the promises made to the Bank of Illesh to help a group of strangers on the wrong side of the Strait of Bezeen?"

"Why are you here in my chambers?" Fasil asked.

Dojan hesitated. "My father is an honourable man, served by loyal people like Pasha Ulan and Khanir Shinva. He's asked me to represent him in Kandarah and my legacy isn't going to be one where I blindly lead our people into a war they don't understand or care about. I want to protect his interests and do what's best for Fujareen. I want to avoid war but, if as you say, war is inevitable, then I want to be fighting on the right side."

Fasil sat back in his chair, sipping hot black coffee from a china cup. "And which is the right side?"

"I'm still making up my mind," Dojan told him.

***

As they walked back to Dojan's chambers after their inconclusive audience with Fasil, Ulan leaned in close to Shinva, his words still carrying in the narrow corridor. "What did Fasil mean? What was this 'fall from grace' he was talking about?"

"Nothing that needs concern you," Shinva replied, her back stiff, staring straight ahead as she walked. "He was toying with us, that's all. You can't believe anything a Sightwielder says."

"If you're holding anything back from me, Khanir Shinva, I swear ..."

The woman stopped, bringing their group to a sudden halt. "You swear what, Pasha Ulan? Choose your words carefully. What is it you'd do?"

Ulan took a few steps back, diminishing under Khanir Shinva's glare. Shinva grinned and shook her head.

"I thought so. Come, Crown Prince, we should return to your chambers."

Dojan followed as Shinva led the way, wishing he could go back to that summer in Bengarath and change things. Knowing there was nothing he could do he trudged, disconsolate, back to his rooms, Hadir walking next to him, closely watching his ward.

**

Dojan decided to change out of his sweaty clothes once they were back in his chambers, Quizar helping him to pick out a fresh white outfit, which he laid on the bed. After Dojan had dismissed his katib he dressed and called Hadir inside. The mubarizun of the Mighty Spears towered over him, overlarge in his armour with his Samarak fighting spear strapped to his back.

"You've been at my side every step while I've been in Kandarah," Dojan began. "While you're a quiet man, Hadir Al-Nadim, I know you're not stupid. I'd really value your advice."

Hadir stood tall and straight before his prince. "If I can offer any assistance, Crown Prince, you need only ask and I will serve you as best I can."

Dojan cleared his throat, trying to sort his own thoughts. "My father has placed me in an impossible position. Did he really intend to make Fujareen the vassal of Kandarah and the Illesh banking clan? Is it right for the Blessed Swords, Mighty Spears and Tireless Shields to fight and die for their cause on a distant land, ending the tradition of the Abitek and Edeen tribes on their spears and forcing them to cede their claim?"

Hadir looked at Dojan for a time. "These are questions best addressed to your pasha or katib. My only concern is to protect you from harm, Crown Prince."

"What if I were to say good advice offers the best protection?"

"Then I would defer to the judgement of Pasha Ulan or Arak of the Veiled Magi, or Tormindah of the Farseeing," Hadir replied, giving Dojan a small bow.

Dojan gave a short, bitter, laugh. "You think so? Their advice, and that of Vizier Haman, is why I'm in this situation in the first place. They think filling Fujareen's coffers means they are serving their kingdom well. I find myself asking if the price of our loyalty to our new friends isn't too high."

Hadir frowned and removed his helmet, revealing a shock of spiky black hair. "Crown Prince, I fear I'm poorly qualified to give my opinion."

Dojan gestured to one of the chairs in his room. "Yet it's obvious you have one, Hadir. Please, sit. I want to hear what you have to say."

Hadir took a seat and sighed. "I don't wish what I say to be considered as a disagreement with our vizier or pasha. That's not my place."

"No, of course not," Dojan replied, shaking his head. "I'm asking for a different perspective, that's all. I keep trying to work my way through this and everyone's position is so … fixed. The Abitek, Edeen, Kandarans, Fujareen, the Illesh bankers – all of them are entrenched, no one willing to give ground to the other. I'm worried Fasil is right, and blood will be spilled before this is over. The question I keep coming back to is whose blood do we shed? What's the right thing to do, Hadir?"

His mubarizun sat there, thinking for a time. "Do you wish me to answer you honestly, Crown Prince?"

"Of course."

"If war is coming and there's nothing we can do to avoid it, then I would fight on the side of the Abitek and Edeen. Their claim is old and no one disputes its validity. Shekh Birizal is only involved because he has the coin and the might of our army to enforce his desire to take something that was never his by right. This dispute concerns something rooted in a time long before the Fallen Age. Shekh Birizal's desire to secure the future of Kandarah is understandable, even honourable. However, should he be entrusted with the knowledge of the lost race of the dragons? There are things that Narinda and Fasil aren't telling us and there's a reason they are willing to die rather than share their secrets. If I was to prepare for battle all I know is I would rather have them at my side, rather than Shekh Birizal and the banking clans."

Dojan felt a weight lift from his shoulders at Hadir's words. His mubarizun had managed to articulate the unease he'd felt from the first moment he'd arrived in Kandarah. The only question left was what he should do about it.

"Do you think your father thought about the consequences when he declared war on Godan Bel-Deem?" Hadir continued. "Haraq did what he thought was right, and he won the emirate. If he'd been defeated in battle, would he have felt any differently before he died at Emir Godan's hand? Would that have changed what he thought was the right thing to do? I think, with the greatest respect, Crown Prince, this is the dilemma you are wrestling with."

Dojan sighed. "Hadir, have you ever considered a position as my katib once your fighting days are over?"

Hadir smiled, an expression Dojan was unsure if he'd ever seen before. "Crown Prince, I trust I have served you well. There are times when you remind me of your father and this is one of them. I hope I have been of service."

"You have," Dojan told him as Hadir stood and donned his helmet. "Thank you."

CHAPTER 27

Winter 199 – Bengarath

Snow fell over Bengarath as the shortest day of the year approached and the city made ready to mark the second century since the War of the Avatars first began. Nimsah thought it was strange that people would want to celebrate the 200th Year of the Fallen Age. Surat told her it was because people loved round numbers and two hundred was more pleasing than one hundred and ninety-nine. Fenara explained it was all about looking forwards, and people wanted to imagine the new year would be prosperous.

"It doesn't matter what sort of year you've had," Fenara told her over dinner one evening, as the wind outside rattled the shutters of her small house. "The poor will offer up prayers to Dinuvillan for better times, whilst the rich will desire to ward off the misfortunes of Myshall. Everyone in Fujareen is looking forward to something."

"But don't the legends tell us what we had before was so much better?" Nimsah asked.

"Even if that's true, child, there's no one alive today to remember those times. All we can do is look to the future with hope."

Nimsah knew Fenara was right, although that winter in the City of Tents was hard. The faces of those children she shared her tent with changed each month as they came and went without warning or explanation. On one particularly cold winter night a small Bengarath boy went to sleep under his blanket and never woke the following morning. Afterwards, Nimsah found herself in tears at Fenara's stall, missing Rogesh and Chandra more than ever. She quickly dried her face, although she thought Fenara noticed out of the corner of her eye.

On some days Nimsah thought of returning to the palace. She still had her servant's outfit, although the trousers had become a little short since the summer. While she was sure she could charm her way inside, even if Jandral was no longer there, she knew it was a risk. Farooq wouldn't be happy with her if she got in trouble and he had to find someone else to act as his go-between with the banker. Instead, Nimsah did what Farooq asked of her, keeping watch over the markets, docks and coffeehouses, bringing him the news he craved and sharing his food in return. Kandilla watched over the pair of them, saying nothing, as Farooq fussed over his little flower.

People hung lanterns outside their houses, shops and stalls in Bengarath to mark the last day of the old year. They stayed up late, lighting braziers in the central square to keep warm, cooking food on open fires, some drinking beer from Medan as a group of palace katibs looked on with disapproval. There were performers entertaining the crowd with jokes, tricks and songs, earning a few shekels for their trouble. Fenara stayed out late with Nimsah and she saw Rogesh with Chandra watching them from a distance. Rogesh offered her a half-hearted wave before Chandra snatched at his hand and led him off into the darkened crowd.

Farooq ventured out from the tent city that night, accompanied by Bizek and Raqqath, Kandilla hanging off his arm. Nimsah steered Fenara away from them towards a noisy puppet show where a gaggle of children, including a couple she lived with, were laughing hard at the crude jokes. Fenara's hand rested on Nimsah's shoulder and the pair stood there, the warm orange glow of the firelight on their smiling faces as they watched the performance together.

A loud bang made Nimsah jump as a brilliant light

appeared in the sky overheard. Several people screamed while others laughed and she caught a glimpse of Farooq, head upturned, eyes wide as a flurry of small flashes, each a different colour, hissed through the air.

"The emir marks the new century with a display from his palace," Fenara shouted to be overheard above the crowd. "Look." Nimsah followed Fenara's pointed finger and saw the palace walls, where darkened figures were moving around, carrying torches and letting off streaks of fire into the air as they passed.

"Fireworks," Nimsah said, trying to imagine the cost in fire powder to put on such a lavish display. No sooner had the thought occurred to her, there was a deafening crash as dozens of flaming fireworks were launched into the air at once, gathering overhead in an increasingly noisy and colourful display. The crowd gasped and even Kandilla was smiling, wrapped around Farooq's strong body as they laughed together. Bizek stood behind them protectively, though whether he was watching the fireworks or keeping his eye on Farooq was impossible to say.

Fenara crouched down next to Nimsah. "A new century has begun," she told her. "I pray to Dinuvillan it brings you everything you wish for, Nimsah."

Nimsah leaned in close, giving Fenara a brief kiss on her cheek. "And you too, Fenara. May Dinuvillan smile upon you."

Fenara beamed, eyes bright. "She's already given me everything I could ever want."

***

The first few months of the Year 200 were unremarkable. Nimsah found herself walking past Bengarath Palace one chilly spring morning and stopped, leaning against an olive tree. She counted the windows, smiling as she remembered Jandral's teaching, trying to work out which room belonged to Dojan. The shutters of the palace were closed, although she could see a few guards patrolling the wall. When she glanced back Nimsah saw one of the shutters had been opened, a small dark-haired figure peering out, face pale in the weak sunlight. Was it Dojan? Nimsah was too far away to be able to tell, although she thought the figure at the window was looking straight at her before moving away. Shivering, Nimsah realised she was late and, wrapping her arms around her chest for warmth, she hurried on into the merchant quarter.

Nimsah found Odilla's house easily – the gold merchant had one of the grandest dwellings in Bengarath, orange and lemon trees filling the garden that led to her front door. Nimsah knew better than to knock on it, skirting around the building towards the servants' entrance at the back. She knocked smartly three times and waited until an elderly woman answered.

"I'm here to see Odilla," Nimsah told her, speaking louder as the crone bent low to hear her better. "Master Farooq sent me. You're to mention his name and tell your mistress she needs to speak to me in person."

"You're a bit young to be giving orders in this house," the old woman complained.

Nimsah shrugged. "Master Farooq was very clear. He told me to wait here all day if Odilla isn't around."

The servant sighed and shuffled inside the house, leaving the door ajar. Nimsah decided it was too cold to stand in the garden and followed her into a large kitchen. Several cooks were busy preparing food – the evening meal by the looks of things, a whole lamb lying on the table where it was being glazed with honey and spices. Nimsah folded her hands behind her back and tried to ignore the smell of flatbreads cooking in the oven.

Odilla appeared in the kitchen a few minutes later, looking flustered. A round lady in early middle age, she was instantly recognisable, a dark birthmark like a crescent moon under her right eye and a large gold nose stud on the left side of her face. Odilla was fussing with her black headscarf, the thin gold thread in the fabric making a diamond pattern.

"Outside," the merchant muttered, placing a hand on

Nimsah's shoulder and steering her with a firm grip back into the garden. She closed the door behind her with a sharp tug and bent low, whispering in Nimsah's ear. "Farooq doesn't have to make a scene. Everything's going to plan."

"Farooq's not making a scene," Nimsah replied. "He sent me here to check all was in order."

"I can assure you it is," Odilla hissed, nostrils flaring, her breath hot on Nimsah's face.

"Farooq said you'd have the first payment ready," Nimsah said, taking a step back and holding out her hand.

Odilla shook her head. "You think I'll just hand something like that over to you?"

"Farooq said you'd say that and I was to tell you that if you don't do as I ask he'll send Bizek round to visit you tomorrow. Would you prefer to deal with me or Bizek?"

"Tsk," Odilla hesitated before plunging her hand into her red robes and pulling out a small felt purse. When she placed it in Nimsah's hand she was surprised by the weight of it.

"Thank you," Nimsah said with a smile. "I'll tell Farooq all goes well and I'll be back next month for the rest." She gave the woman a short bow and skipped away, dropping the purse into her bag as she left.

"Finding that coin wasn't easy," Odilla called out after Nimsah. "With all the trouble in Amjahran, Farooq should be grateful I've got the connections to keep things running smoothly."

Nimsah stopped and turned around. "What's happened?"

"What business is it of yours?" Odilla said tartly, raising an eyebrow as Nimsah retraced her steps. "Just pass on the message that his investments are safe with me."

"No, I mean, what's happened in Amjahran?"

Odilla stared at Nimsah and when it became obvious the girl wasn't going to go away she sighed, talking in a lower tone. "You haven't heard the news? Emir Cassim has been deposed in a bloody coup. Half of Amjahran is in uproar, some siding with Cassim's family, others backing the pretender to his throne, the so-called Emira Ledana. I heard a whisper about the coming change and made sure I moved my gold out of the capital – just in time as things turned out. Farooq's in business with the right merchant – you can tell him that from me."

"Cassim is overthrown?" Nimsah asked, wanting to make sure she had understood correctly.

"What's he to you? A personal friend?"

Nimsah ignored the jibe. "I'll make sure I pass on the message, Odilla, thank you."

"I don't want your thanks. Just look after that coin," Odilla hissed, looking around her garden as if it were full of cutpurses and robbers.

Nimsah headed away from the merchant quarter, head down, mind full of questions. Could Emir Cassim's downfall have anything to do with Jandral? He'd spoken of taking care of the emir and now he was gone, replaced by someone else less than a year later. Nimsah had always thought of Farooq as being powerful, the shekh of the City of Tents, influencing events around Bengarath far more than the authorities ever really knew. Yet here was Jandral, a member of the Council of the Bank of Illesh, wielding enough power to decide who sat on the emir's throne.

Another thought occurred to Nimsah as she walked through the market square, taking care to give Fenara's stall a wide berth so she wasn't delayed. With Cassim gone Jandral might return to Fujareen. Perhaps her trips to the palace would resume and she could pick up her lessons once more. A smile crept over her face and as Nimsah followed the winding streets towards the City of Tents her heart felt warm, her steps lighter.

CHAPTER 28

**Summer 213 – The Fujareen army camp
outside Kandarah's walls**

Dojan squinted in the bright sunlight, grateful for the handari headscarf protecting him from the sun's glare. Despite it being early morning he was already hot in the loose-fitting white cotton robes Quizar had selected for their visit. His katib was similarly attired, while Shinva, Yanzin and Hadir all wore their polished silver ceremonial armour and chainmail, resplendent as they gleamed in the sunlight. Dojan couldn't imagine how they could stand there in the baking heat as Shinva pointed out various uninteresting features of their camp to Khan Lemarr.

Shinva had put the advance guard of Tireless Shields to work under the supervision of her Blessed Swords for the past week, erecting tents, latrines and wooden fortifications to protect the military camp. Earlier that morning the Fujareen fleet had returned, disgorging over two thousand warriors, who now formed a line that snaked all the way back to the docks. Dojan could see the pennants of the Tireless Shields with their commander, Khan Gerber Al-Jalal, at their head, leading a regiment of one thousand five hundred warriors, spears pointing at the sky. The emir's Royal Arquebusiers followed close behind, carrying their deadly arquebuses, ranged weapons that used fire powder to propel lead shot several hundred yards. The banner of the Stooping Falcon, the archers of Fujareen's army, could also be seen in the distance.

"Two hundred archers and two hundred arquebusiers,

as agreed," Shinva told Lemarr.

Dojan stared at the back of the Kandaran officer's head as he nodded, wishing he was able to prise free the secret route through the Shimmering Way that led safely to Amonduras. Instead, they were standing here watching the Fujareen army file slowly into their newly-constructed camp. Dojan had to admit it was an impressive sight, although this was only the first of several landings that were planned in the coming days. By the end of next week there would be eight thousand Fujareen soldiers on Kandaran soil. Al-Jalal's Tireless Shields would be set to work immediately, expanding the camp and extending its defences.

"The shekh's investment has been well-rewarded," Lemarr observed, shielding his eyes from the sun as he watched the column inch forwards. The troops were directed to their tents by members of the Blessed Swords, who greeted them at the gates set in the wall of stakes surrounding the camp. It was all proceeding in an orderly fashion, although it was going to take hours before everyone was stationed and the army's goods and gear stowed away.

Dojan silently cursed Ulan. While the pasha conducted further negotiations with Birizal and Jandral, Dojan was going to have to stand here as the official representative of the emir and greet his father's troops. At least they had erected a pavilion nearby, its canvas rippling in the faint breeze, where he would be able to take shelter and some food at noon. He'd already exhausted his scant stock of military observations making small talk with Lemarr. What was the range of an arquebus? Two hundred yards? Four hundred? Quizar would know – his katib had an uncanny ability to remember facts and figures.

"What's that in the distance?" asked Yanzin, pointing a gloved hand in the direction of the hills that rose gently behind Kandarah.

Dojan turned and saw a faint dark smudge standing out against the baked yellow and orange dusty soil of the

Kandaran countryside. A haze of dust was rising up into the sky, an indistinct shape that grew larger as they watched.

"The Abitek warriors are here," Lemarr explained. "Word will have reached them that the negotiations are coming to a close and matters will have to be settled using sword and spear. They'll position themselves in the hills to take command of the higher ground."

"They finally show themselves," Shinva said with a smile. "Now we'll see what kind of numbers the dragon tribe can muster."

Lemarr nodded. "I'll dispatch some scouts so we can take a closer look. If I were to guess, they'll number three or four thousand at the outside, if everyone has heeded Fasil's call to battle. They will be no match for a disciplined and well-trained army."

"Take my mubarizun and a dozen of my Blessed Swords," Shinva said, placing a hand on Yanzin's shoulder. "Whilst your scouts know the country better we still need to see things for ourselves."

As the day grew hotter Dojan took shelter in the pavilion. He invited Lemarr to join him, only for the khan to politely decline, clearly more interested in talking to Yanzin about the deployment of their scouts. Shinva headed into the camp, leaving Dojan alone with Quizar, his dozen bodyguards arranged in a loose ring around them. Tormindah was with them, protecting the prince from unwanted intrusion by Fasil and his Sightwielders.

"This is going to be a long day," Dojan observed, taking a sip of water.

"It heartens your troops to see their crown prince has come out to greet them in person," Tormindah replied.

"Hmm. Ulan's managed to get me out of the way very cleverly, hasn't he? Now I'll have to come here every single day for the rest of the week, otherwise I'll risk giving offence to some khan or mubarizun who'll think I've favoured one regiment over another."

Quizar sat back in his chair, hands folded over his trim stomach. "The burdens of office. I think it's preferable to building an army camp under the scorching Naroque summer sun."

Dojan watched the tiny figures below unloading sacks, crates and barrels from carts, others carrying wooden stakes about the camp, making ready to build their fortifications. Back-breaking work, which made an idle day in the sunshine, sipping cool water and eating Kandaran delicacies less of a chore than he'd first thought.

"This plan of Arak's isn't going to be easy," Dojan said in a low voice.

"If it was, I think our Edeen and Abitek friends would have already uncovered Lemarr's secrets," Quizar replied.

Dojan sighed, wondering if Arak's heart was really in the task he'd been given. Arak's plan had been to use the inspection of Fujareen's arriving warriors to get closer to Lemarr. One of the water jugs in their pavilion was laced with a concoction Arak had prepared which would, he assured Dojan, have the effect of loosening Lemarr's lips and make it easy to interrogate him into revealing the safe route to Amonduras. Unfortunately, the arrival of the Abitek warriors gave Lemarr the perfect excuse to leave Dojan and Quizar to their own devices.

"He's not going to be allowed to scout out the enemy in person," Quizar pointed out. "He's too valuable to Birizal. Sooner or later, he'll have to pay a visit to his dignitaries or risk giving us offence."

Dojan pursed his lips, unconvinced. "He never goes anywhere without a dozen guards at his back. We can hardly put him to the question out here in the open air in full view of everyone. We need to find a different way to get to him in private, when he's back at Birizal's palace. Arak's plan is never going to work."

Quizar chuckled. "We've been here for one morning. You need to be patient – there'll be other opportunities."

"No, time's already running short. When the last of our troops land Shinva's going to want to force things to a conclusion as quickly as possible. Once battle is joined the Naroque tribes will never ally themselves with us."

"The worst that happens is we follow your father's original intentions and give Birizal exactly what he wants. Your father can hardly complain about that, can he?"

Quizar's reasonable observation annoyed Dojan, although he quickly changed his expression when he saw a horse-drawn carriage approaching them on the dusty road to their pavilion. Its driver drew up nearby and Hadir opened the door. A veiled woman dressed in flowing red silks emerged, taking his hand to steady herself as she stepped to the ground. Even with her face covered, Dojan recognised Nimsah's confident walk as Hadir led her towards them. Dojan and Quizar both stood to greet her.

"I hope your journey wasn't inconvenienced too greatly by the Fujareen warriors on the road," said Quizar, offering Nimsah a seat.

Nimsah's eyes twinkled behind her red veil. "Not at all. They kindly made way for my carriage and allowed us to pass. Displaying good manners so far from home is a mark of their quality."

"Fujareen's army is the finest in the world," Dojan replied.

Nimsah nodded. "As the Abitek will discover in a few short days."

"Must it come to war?" Dojan asked. "Fujareen is at your service, Nimsah, of course. Yet I can't help wonder if another way could be found to spare us all from bloodshed?"

Nimsah's eyes hardened. Dojan swallowed, trying not to appear guilty as he deliberately avoided looking at the water jug laced with Arak's potion, sitting on a table next to Quizar. The thought occurred to him that all he had to do was offer Nimsah a drink and her secrets would be his. Perhaps Lemarr had confided something in her? She had a way of making people tell them what was closest to their hearts.

"Forgive me, Crown Prince. Isn't that the reason why you're here?" Her voice was cold, the stare across their low table defiant.

"What?" It took Dojan a moment to realise she was replying to his earlier question.

"Fujareen is at your disposal, my lady," Quizar interjected.

"So you keep saying. However, I wonder if your prince has been paying too much attention to the opinions of Narinda and Fasil? Imagine my surprise when I heard you had requested private audiences with each of them."

"Know your enemy," Dojan said, feeling heat rising up his face.

"Indeed."

Quizar cleared his throat and offered Nimsah some refreshment, his hand hovering over the water jug. Dojan sat there, trying to decide whether to interfere or let things play out as Myshall and Dinuvillan determined. The moment of indecision felt like a lifetime, whilst in reality only lasting mere moments before Nimsah declined. Quizar's hand dropped away, the tainted water jug remained untouched and Dojan released his breath.

"Fujareen will be well rewarded once all this is done," said Nimsah, looking out on the busy camp below. "Sometimes we have to undertake an unpleasant task for the greater good. Perhaps all it will take is the sight of Fujareen's army to finally break the spirit of the Edeen and Abitek. As you say, if bloodshed could be avoided, that would be best. I hope you've made this clear to Narinda and Fasil in your discussions."

"I made that very point," Dojan replied.

"Although the massing army of the Abitek in the hills suggests they may not come to the same happy conclusion," added Quizar unhelpfully.

Nimsah adjusted her position, turning away from the camp and looking directly at Dojan. "If Quizar is right, then

I trust you will prove your loyalty. It would be unfortunate if the years of negotiations between Illesh and Fujareen foundered on the squeamishness of a young prince, far from home. One who should be listening to the counsel of his father's chosen advisors."

"My lady, please have no concerns on that account," Dojan reassured her, his throat dry. He coughed and took a little water. "Fujareen stands ready to do what is required."

Nimsah smiled behind her veil, the gesture visible through her eyes as her hard look melted away. "That's good to know, Dojan. I'm sure I can count on you."

Dojan stayed silent until Nimsah's carriage was several hundred yards down the road, the ranks of Tireless Shields parting to make way as she returned to Kandarah. When he spoke there was a tremor in his voice.

"She *knows*. Somehow she knows exactly what we've been discussing with Narinda and Fasil."

"That was a warning – no doubt about that," agreed Quizar. "The question is, has someone said something or is she just making sure we hold our nerve with war approaching?"

"I want to believe it was the latter, although I have my doubts. Perhaps we've overplayed our hand."

Quizar shook his head. "What is it about this young woman that riles you so? Whenever she speaks to you for longer than a minute it's as though you're unmanned."

Dojan stood and stepped outside the pavilion, turning to face the breeze, eyes closed. "I did something terrible."

Quizar joined him, a hand placed gently on his shoulder, his voice soft as he spoke. "Dojan, what do you mean?"

"I should have told you when she first arrived in Bengarath. I didn't think it would matter."

"Dojan?" There was worry in Quizar's voice.

"Me being here. All of this, I don't think it's an accident. I think Nimsah wanted me to come to Kandarah, to see all of this. To understand what she has become, partly because of me."

Tormindah's round face was full of concern as she joined them. "Crown Prince, we can't help or protect you if you don't tell us what's going on."

Dojan sighed, shoulders slumping, as he told them everything.

CHAPTER 29

Summer 200 – Bengarath Market

The baking sun filled the market square with an intense, dry heat which hung in the still air, the windless day offering no relief. The light was bright even under the canopy of Fenara's stall and Nimsah squinted as she wove, her fingers finding the task more difficult than usual. Fenara sighed, complaining that it was going to be a slow day for business.

"I might close up early," she told Nimsah, adjusting her green headscarf. "Only a fool would venture out in this heat."

Nimsah glanced at the other stalls, where a few people were examining the wares of the bakers and spice sellers. The cloth merchant had already closed, and Surat waved at them from the door of his coffeehouse, tucking his hands into the pockets of his apron and trying to entice a few passers-by inside.

A shout from the other side of the market drew Nimsah's attention. Fenara stood, trying to get a better view and Nimsah felt a pang of worry as she saw two female warriors wearing the armour of the palace guards approach Surat. He shrank before them, empty palms held out as they began to question him. After a moment he cast a guilty look in the direction of Fenara.

"What could they want with Surat?" Fenara asked, eyes wide as she saw more warriors fanning out through the market. The few customers began to move away, only to find themselves caught up in the raid. One man was shoved to the ground, knocking over a fruit stall as the owner protested to a nearby guard.

"They're looking for someone," Nimsah replied, a knot of worry settling in her stomach as the woman in chainmail who had spoken to Surat approached them. She knew enough from her time at the palace to recognise this was a high-ranking member of the Blessed Swords, the queen's personal regiment. Whatever this was, it was serious.

"Are you Nimsah?" said the warrior, staring straight at her. She had a pretty oval face and delicate features under her helmet, although the expression she wore made her look hard and unforgiving. Nimsah nodded, too frightened to speak.

Fenara looked alarmed. "She's not in trouble, is she?"

The woman glared back. "What's it to you if she is? Is this your daughter?"

"We're not related but she's under my protection," Fenara told her, putting a hand on Nimsah's shoulder. "Who are you and what do you want with her?"

"I'm not in the habit of accounting for my actions to a market stall holder. The child needs to come with us."

Several more warriors were now gathered around Fenara's stall and Nimsah had to fight the urge to run away. Fenara's grip on her shoulder tightened as she replied. "If you think I'm going to hand her over without you giving me so much as your name, you're gravely mistaken."

A heavy-set warrior carrying a long spear and wearing the decorative armour of a mubarizun in the emir's service jogged up, sweat running down his face. With a start Nimsah recognised it was Mubarizun Hengesh. "Khanir, he's not in the market and no one's seen him. Is this the child?"

The woman nodded. "I'm Khanir Shinva Bel-Kamil, commander of the Regiment of Blessed Swords, in service to Her Royal Highness Princess Tanah Bel-Doshok, wife of Emir Haraq Al-Souk. And you are?"

As more guards gathered, the seriousness of their situation sank in and Fenara bowed low. "Fenara, Biwan's widow."

"Well, Fenara, widow of Biwan, the crown prince has slipped away during a royal visit to the city gardens –"

"He's not here," Fenara blurted out.

Shinva's eyes narrowed. "I can see that. One of his friends mentioned that in recent weeks he'd been asking frequently about a young girl called Nimsah. Apparently, they were friends, though no one seems to have heard about her before today."

Nimsah guessed at once it must have been Quizar, the boy in Dojan's service, who had mentioned her name. Fenara was busy arguing there must have been some mistake and Nimsah was forced to shout to make herself heard.

"It's me. I'm Nimsah, the one you're looking for. I ran some errands for Farooq in the palace," she explained as Fenara stared at her in surprise. "That's when I met Dojan."

A murmur ran through the guards and Shinva bent down low, trying to arrange her face to appear more friendly. "That's *crown prince* to you, child. Why would a prince be looking for … you?"

"We're friends," Nimsah replied, frowning at the laughter from some of the warriors. "We are! I didn't think he'd come looking for me, though. I finished working at the palace and I haven't seen him in almost half a year."

Shinva shook her head. "Well, you must have made an impression on him. Why hasn't he come to the market to find you?"

A horrible thought wormed its way into Nimsah's mind as she remembered the last time she'd seen Dojan outside the palace. "I think I know where he might have gone," she told the khanir in a small voice.

***

Nimsah led two score warriors through the winding streets of Bengarath towards the City of Tents, Fenara refusing to leave her side. Could Dojan really have been that stupid? What would happen if Farooq found him and realised who he was?

Her legs felt weak and only Fenara's strong grip on her arm stopped her from stumbling.

"If anything's happened to the boy, Hengesh, I'll ask the andral's permission to flay you myself," Shinva muttered, her comment directed at the well-built mubarizun jogging along next to her. Despite being twice her size, her quiet words were enough to make him hang his head in shame.

"It won't come to that, khanir," he said, trying to persuade himself as much as her.

"Pray to Dinuvillan it doesn't."

Before long the Bridge of Sorrows was in view, the few people on the streets hurrying out of the way of Shinva's armoured column as they reached the City of Tents.

"Search every dwelling," Shinva ordered, frowning as Nimsah held up her hand. "What is it?"

"There's a quicker way," Nimsah told her. "Please, khanir, follow me."

Hengesh and the other warriors hesitated, waiting for Shinva's decision. After a moment the khanir nodded. "Let's see if she's right. The less fuss we make, the better."

"Do you know what you're doing?" Fenara whispered in Nimsah's ear as they headed for the centre of the tent city.

"If the soldiers search the tents there'll be panic and people could get hurt. Farooq will be able to find the prince much more easily, if he's here."

"You're leading them straight to that criminal? What are you thinking?"

Nimsah squeezed Fenara's hand. "This is safer for all of us. Trust me, this is my home."

Fenara said nothing in reply, holding on tightly to Nimsah as they reached the courtyard outside Farooq's tent. He was sitting in his usual place at the head of his low table, eating with a few of his friends under a dark blue canopy in the colours of Farooq's native Naroque. It took Nimsah a moment to register that Dojan was sitting between him and Kandilla, the Zirhidan woman offering him some dried dates from a bowl. Dojan's hand froze as he saw Nimsah and his face brightened, although his words of greeting died on his lips as he saw the palace guards flanking her.

Bizek and Raqqath blocked Shinva's path and her hand moved to the scimitar hanging from her belt. "Move out of the way."

"No," said Bizek, slowly shaking his head.

"No?" Shinva began to draw her blade. "How *dare* you."

Bizek drew his own sword, which looked tiny in his giant hands. Shinva cursed as she backed off, holding her scimitar in a protective stance as the warriors around her raised their fighting spears, Hengesh moving to her side. More of Farooq's gang appeared around the edges of the courtyard and Nimsah glanced behind her, her fears confirmed as she saw a knot of armed men blocking their retreat.

"Bizek, that's enough," Farooq's calm voice cut through the air and everyone stopped moving. He remained in his seat next to Dojan, looking completely unruffled. "We're not going to duel with the palace guard, are we? It's obvious why they're here." Bizek and Raqqath sheathed their weapons and stood aside, looking unashamed as Shinva glared at them.

"It's also obvious who brought them here," added Kandilla, giving Nimsah a poisonous stare.

Farooq smiled. "Nimsah did the right thing. Better to bring this matter to me."

"You're not in charge here," snapped Shinva.

Farooq raised an eyebrow. "And you are?"

"Khanir Shinva Bel-Kamil, commander of the Regiment of Blessed Swords, in service to Her Royal Highness –"

Farooq held out his hand and cut her off. "Khanir Shinva will do. I am Farooq, and while you may be the servant of the emir you would do well to remember that I rule here."

Shinva stiffened, noticing for the first time that although Farooq's gang members had sheathed their weapons her warriors were surrounded, their escape route blocked off.

"Now, Khanir Shinva," Farooq continued with a wide

grin. "I imagine you're here to recover your lost prince. As you can see, he's here, safe and sound under my protection. I believe some thanks are due?"

Dojan was staring open mouthed at the exchange, beginning to understand quite how dangerous a situation he had created. "Hengesh, I'm sorry. I didn't mean to cause all this trouble."

"It's alright, Crown Prince," his mubarizun replied. "We're here for you now. Quite a scare you gave us, running off like that."

"I just wanted to see Nimsah," Dojan said, glancing in her direction. "I thought I'd find her here and then this lady said she could help," he nodded at Kandilla. "I thought she was taking me to Nimsah."

"I thought it best to give him shelter from the sun," Kandilla explained, her voice a soft purr as she ruffled the boy's hair. "He was hungry and thirsty after his little adventure."

"Don't touch him," Shinva replied, biting the words off as the muscles played in her jaw.

Farooq shook his head. "That wasn't the thanks I was expecting. Don't they teach you manners in the palace?"

The guards muttered with discontent at Farooq's goading and a few of them began to advance.

"Hold still until we have the boy," barked Shinva, stopping them in their tracks.

"Dojan," Hengesh held out his gloved hand towards the prince. "It's time to go. Thank the kind people for their hospitality and take your leave. It's time we were heading back to the palace."

Dojan looked really frightened and Nimsah could feel her own heart hammering in her chest. Fenara's grip on her hand was so tight it hurt, although Nimsah didn't want her to let go. Dojan offered Kandilla a weak smile and began to rise, only for the woman to push him back into his seat.

"I still haven't heard you say thank you," observed Farooq, arms crossed in front of his chest, a smirk on his face.

"Thank you, Farooq," said Dojan. "I really have to go now."

Farooq smiled. "You're welcome, young prince. However, it was Khanir Shinva I was speaking to."

Shinva growled, her scimitar still in her hand. "Farooq. You have my sincere thanks for looking after the crown prince. You've made your point. Now please let the boy go."

Farooq nodded to Kandilla, who took Dojan by the arm and helped him to his feet. Farooq took a sip of coffee and watched as Dojan trotted to Hengesh. "You see, manners cost nothing. I hope you'll remember how I was a loyal servant to the emir and protected his son. Not everyone in the less desirable parts of this city would have been so kind."

Swallowing her pride, Shinva gave Farooq a brief bow as Hengesh ushered Dojan into the centre of the group of warriors. Dojan met Nimsah's gaze and blinked back tears.

"I'm sorry, Nimsah. I didn't mean for all this to happen."

Shinva stood in front of them before Nimsah could reply. She jabbed a finger into Nimsah's chest as she spoke. "I don't want you coming anywhere near the prince ever again. Do you hear me? If I even see you near the palace –"

"Don't talk to her like that," protested Fenara, pulling Nimsah away from Shinva. "She's just helped you get the boy back, safe and sound. None of this is her fault."

Shinva's face darkened and she shoved Fenara out of her way. Fenara gave a cry as she stumbled and fell backwards, her head hitting the cobbled courtyard with a hard crack.

"Get up," said Shinva, an edge to her voice. Fenara lay on the ground in front of her, unmoving. Nimsah dropped to her knees and reached for Fenara's hand.

"Fenara," Nimsah cried, trying to help her sit up. Fenara lay still and Nimsah gave a strangled cry as she saw blood pooling on the hot cobbles, seeping out from the back of Fenara's head, soaking into the green material of her headscarf.

"Get out of the way ..." Shinva shoved Nimsah to one side and put her hand to Fenara's neck, feeling for a pulse.

Her head dropped as she saw Fenara's sightless eyes, fixed on nothing. Blood flowed through the small channels between the stones, the dark pool spreading wider.

"You've killed her," Hengesh breathed the words, shock on his face.

"I only wanted her to move," said Shinva. "That's all. I only wanted her out of my way."

"Who was she?" asked Hengesh.

"A widow." Shinva turned to Nimsah. "Did she have any family?"

Shinva's question sounded to Nimsah as if it was coming from a long way off. "What?"

"Did she have any family? Any living relatives? She said the pair of you weren't related, didn't she? You've worked for her so you must know – is there anyone else?"

Nimsah shook her head, still on her knees next to Fenara's body. A choking cry rose up from her stomach and forced its way through her lungs. It felt like a knife had been sunk deep into her guts, Shinva's words a distant noise as she spoke to Farooq.

"I'm sorry. I'm so sorry, Nimsah," Dojan kept repeating the words as he stared at her, helpless. Nimsah couldn't reply, her words stolen by grief.

"We can deal with this quietly," Shinva was saying to Farooq. "If there's no family involved you can make this disappear. No good will come of people hearing about this – it was an accident. You all saw – she fell over as I was talking to her. She didn't watch her step. It was a tragic accident."

"Accidents happen," agreed Farooq. "For a fair price, Khanir Shinva, we can draw a veil over this unfortunate incident. Perhaps Fenara had some distant relatives after all. If I were to spread the rumour that she sold up her business before leaving for Al-Narah, far to the north, that would be better for all concerned."

"Khanir Shinva," Hengesh protested. "We have to report this. You can't seriously be considering handing over coin to this man to cover this up."

Shinva silenced him with a glare. "I have my position to think of and the good name of Her Royal Highness. I'll not see that blackened because some ignorant weaver didn't watch where she was walking. You were here too, Hengesh. Do you think taking this to the andral will help you become khan of the Mighty Spears? Don't forget, the prince slipped away on your watch."

"You *pushed* her," Nimsah shouted, forcing the words out as she sobbed. "You pushed her over." With a cry she sprang forwards, her fist connecting hard with the bridge of Shinva's delicate nose, which broke with a sharp crack. Shinva cried out in pain, shoving Nimsah down onto the ground.

"Nimsah! Enough," shouted Farooq. His words cut through her, the fight leaving her as grief became a crushing weight on her chest.

Shinva glowered, wincing as she wiped blood from her face with the back of her hand and passed over some coins to Farooq. "There'll be more when I have assurance this matter has been handled quietly. If word of this gets out, I'll know where it came from. Make sure the feral child stays silent as well. I understand she's part of your … circle."

Farooq's hand closed around the silver shekels. "I'll show the utmost discretion. It's been a pleasure doing business with you, Khanir Shinva. I'm glad I could be of service."

"Thank you," Shinva replied in a thick voice through her broken nose, which was still bleeding freely. She turned and walked away with Dojan, leaving Nimsah weeping next to Fenara's body.

CHAPTER 30

Summer 213 – Kandarah

Quizar leaned back in the carriage they were sharing with Tormindah and Hadir, his expression hard to read as Dojan finished his tale. Dojan found tears were welling in his eyes and he looked out of the window at the busy Kandaran streets, the citizens kept at bay by his honour guard of Mighty Spears and Blessed Swords. He wiped his face, trying to compose himself and glanced at Tormindah, who bowed her head.

"I suppose you could have prised that little secret from my mind without me putting myself through that," he remarked.

Tormindah smiled, looking at him kindly. "Whilst that may be true, Crown Prince, a secret gained through the practise of the Sight is worth far less than one freely shared with the people you trust."

Dojan sighed, wondering how much he really did trust Tormindah. Ulan had chosen her, after all, which didn't exactly count in her favour. However, if he couldn't place his faith in the woman protecting his mind from intrusion by enemy Sightwielders, there wasn't much hope for him.

"You never said a thing," said Quizar. "I remember your father being furious with you when Shinva brought you back to the palace. I thought you were upset because he punished you."

Dojan shook his head. "Father never knew the whole story. It was a secret that stayed between me, Shinva and

Hengesh all these years. I considered telling him, yet somehow the right moment never arose and gradually I thought about it less often."

"Until Nimsah returned to Bengarath Palace. Now I understand why you're so nervous around her. It all makes sense."

"I didn't realise who she was at first," Dojan explained. "Nimsah is a common enough name and she was so much older, although she seemed familiar from the moment we met. It was little things, like the shape of her mouth and face. When she mentioned we'd known each other as children I instantly knew who she was."

"You might not have remembered her, but I find it hard to imagine Nimsah will have forgotten the part you played in this woman's death," said Tormindah. "What does that say about her? Did she accept the delegation to Bengarath despite or because of what had happened to her as a child?"

"She told me she'd forgiven me," Dojan replied.

"Do you believe her? From what you've said, this Fenara was like a mother to her."

Dojan swallowed, his throat dry. "I want to believe her."

"Does she know about my part in this?" asked Quizar. Dojan frowned, confused by the question until his katib explained. "I was the one who gave Shinva Nimsah's name and told her you might have gone looking for her. If I hadn't said anything ..."

"You did what you thought was right," Dojan said, patting Quizar's shoulder.

"Is that how Nimsah will see things?" Dojan didn't have an answer for that and they rode on in silence towards Shekh Birizal's spire.

"You're very quiet, Hadir," Dojan said to his mubarizun at last.

The warrior sighed. "I'm disappointed, Crown Prince."

"I was only a boy," Dojan protested. "I was lonely, and worried about Nimsah. I thought I might get in trouble sneaking off but I never could have known … Well, what happened – no one could have predicted that."

Hadir shook his head. "You misunderstand me, Crown Prince. I meant I was disappointed in the actions of Khanir Shinva. What she did, paying a criminal like Farooq for his silence, lacked honour and compromised her position. The Blessed Swords and Mighty Spears are regiments with a higher calling, where we must be beyond reproach. Better she had admitted her crime and accepted the consequences, even if it meant her demotion."

"Your own khan was there too," Dojan pointed out.

Hadir sighed. "Yes, although Hengesh was only the mubarizun of the Mighty Spears at the time, so he was honour-bound to obey Shinva's orders as his senior officer. From what you told us, Hengesh tried to do the right thing. No, it was Shinva's decision and she must take responsibility for that."

A knot of worry twisted in Dojan's stomach. "Listen, Hadir, I told you this in confidence. You can't say anything. I forbid it. Think how this might affect you. Remember, your own khan was there. Once these things are out in the open, who knows where it could lead?"

Hadir looked at Dojan, unconvinced. He was a huge man and the way he sat there, with his hands resting on his knees, made him resemble pictures of the legendary warrior emirs of Murtak that Dojan had seen in books and paintings. Hadir could easily pick Dojan up and snap his spine in two, were it not for the obedience to the throne drilled into every Mighty Spear. Dojan had only ever known unquestioning loyalty from his mubarizun until this afternoon. Yet it seemed every man had his limits and they'd found Hadir's.

"As you command, Crown Prince." Hadir's face became blank, eyes distant. Dojan released a breath, relief washing over him.

When they arrived at the palace Tormindah took her leave, going to meet the new members of the Magi of the Farseeing who had arrived with the Fujareen army. As discussed, Tormindah's Fellowship had arrived in person to help her with the task of protecting the crown prince and his delegation.

Hadir led the rest of them to the elevator in the spire, only to be met by two apologetic Kandaran guards. Dojan listened with growing irritation as they explained the elevator was currently undergoing repairs.

"Are you telling me that Crown Prince Dojan Al-Haraq will have to ascend the stairs to his quarters?" growled Hadir, provoking a murmur of displeasure from the warriors of the Blessed Swords and Mighty Spears.

The Kandaran soldier had the good grace to look embarrassed. "A thousand apologies, Crown Prince. You could, of course, wait here in the reception chambers on the ground floor until the repairs are completed."

Dojan glanced at the crowded room, filled with Naroque tribesmen wearing robes in a variety of colours, Kalat merchants and various Kandaran katibs and officials. It had been a tiring, emotional day. All he wanted to do was get to his chambers, wash, and ensure he was refreshed before the evening banquet hosted by Birizal. He wouldn't be able to relax downstairs and he wanted to think of what to say to Nimsah. There was unfinished business between the two of them.

"We'll take the stairs," Dojan said, ignoring the groan that escaped from a couple of his guards, quickly silenced as Hadir glowered at them. "It will be fascinating to see how such things are built in a spire."

The guard led them to a small doorway and the group filed inside. The stairway was entirely independent of the elevator, which rose and fell within its own specially constructed shaft. The wide stairs were polished white marble, set into clean whitewashed walls, rising in an elegant spiral that was punctuated at regular intervals by doorways leading to each floor. The space was quiet, like a place of worship, illuminated by a bright light in the distant roof and evenly spaced magical lights set in the walls that emitted a pearlescent white glow. Dojan wandered into the centre of the stairway, where he was able to look at the staircase directly from below, its spiral forming shell-like patterns as it rose above him. A solid metal balustrade snaked around the outside of the staircase, protecting those ascending from toppling off the edge onto the smooth black marble floor, which was veined with white and the odd fleck of red.

"Why does everything in Kandarah have to be so tall?" mused Quizar.

"It's beautiful, though," Dojan replied. "This is no different to the climb to my father's private office in the palace. It's just more … open."

Quizar pursed his lips. "You could fit your father's entire palace in this stairwell."

Although part of him was already regretting his decision, Dojan turned to Hadir and invited him to lead the way. Together with his guards they began the ascent, the Kandaran soldier offering them more apologies for the inconvenience as he receded into the distance.

"Not so much city of a thousand spires as spire of a thousand steps," Quizar complained breathlessly once they reached the fifth floor, where the Blessed Swords were quartered for their stay.

Dojan peered up the spiralling stairwell, his thighs already burning. His own quarters lay on the forty-fifth floor, a fact enjoyed by the departing Blessed Swords. They made various barbed comments to the Mighty Spears as they headed through the doorway to find their chambers, leaving Dojan, Quizar and his six guards to face the rest of the climb.

"Do you wish to take a moment, Crown Prince?" asked Hadir. Dojan frowned as he realised the mubarizun wasn't even sweating, despite wearing armour. It *was* cool on the stairway, a faint breeze circulating around them. Dojan wandered to the edge, leaning on the metal rail that came comfortingly a third of the way up his chest. The dark marble floor with its swirls and patterns could still be made out below them. He glanced up, trying to gauge where his own floor lay, soon wishing he hadn't.

"Lead on, Hadir," said Dojan with more conviction than he felt.

Hadir kept a steady pace as they continued their ascent, knowing exactly when to order a brief rest to avoid Dojan and Quizar the embarrassment of having to ask for one. As they took a break at somewhere around the thirtieth floor, Dojan risked peering down the stairwell once more. The floor was lost in the distance, vanishingly small as it was swallowed up by the spirals.

"I mean," Quizar gasped and had to gulp down air before he could continue, "the sheer cost. No one even *uses* this part of the building normally. Why choose marble for the stairs when ordinary stone would have done? The balustrade is fashioned from pure steel – this would make a thousand swords if it was melted down. Probably more."

Dojan shook his head as he thought of the wealth of their new allies. The only thing Shekh Birizal's city state lacked was people, until Fujareen's army had arrived, their camp swelling with each passing day outside the walls of Kandarah. Dojan's mind reeled as he realised the Bank of Illesh *owned* Kandarah, their shekh beholden to them until such time as their debts were repaid. Feeling dizzy, he stepped away from the edge of the stairwell and looked upwards, gathering himself for the next climb. He paused as he saw a group of servants walking down towards them.

"We're not the only ones foolish enough to climb the spire," he remarked as they drew closer.

"We're the only ones climbing *up*," Quizar pointed out, which Dojan acknowledged with a weary nod.

Hadir became tense, realising that the servants were going to have to pass much closer to his charge than he would have preferred. He gently steered Dojan towards the wall to allow as much space on the wide staircase as they could as the servants approached. His eyes narrowed and when Dojan followed his gaze he saw another group of men climbing the stairs beneath them. They were still several floors down but what drew Dojan's attention was how they were hurrying upwards.

"Perhaps they're here to prepare Birizal's feast," mused Quizar.

"Perhaps," said Hadir in such a way that it was obvious he thought nothing of the sort. Quizar picked up on his tone and exchanged a look with Dojan. The five other warriors reached towards the spears strapped to their backs, holding just short of drawing their weapons.

Dojan's heart hammered in his chest and he prayed to Dinuvillan that Hadir's suspicions were misplaced. He made a quick count of the group of men below them – a dozen in total, some four floors down but getting closer all the time. Another dozen were closing in from above, each in servant's garb, a variety of nondescript browns, tans and beige colours. Out on the streets they would have looked unremarkable. Here, as they narrowed the distance between them, they acquired a sense of menace.

Hadir and two of his men stepped forwards to bar the way as the descending servants drew nearer. The group slowed, one of them stepping closer and bowing low.

"I am Mubarizun Hadir Al-Nadim of the Regiment of the Mighty Spears. You will stand aside and allow us to pass."

The leader of the group, a grey-bearded man with a lined face, gave a smile. "I'm afraid that will not be possible."

Hadir growled, pulling out his fighting spear and his two companions followed his lead, raising the bladed points of their weapons at the older man. To their rear, the three remaining warriors also drew their spears, watching with wide eyes as the group of men continued to race up the stairs, now only about three floors down.

"Stand aside," Hadir repeated, taking a step forwards. The older man fell back as his companions surged around him, drawing hatchets and long knives concealed in their robes.

"Oh no," breathed Quizar next to Dojan, seizing his arm.

Hadir swung his bladed spear, taking the first attacker in the stomach and opening him from groin to sternum. He planted his feet firmly, hurling the man's body into the path of his companions, slowing their advance. The other Mighty Spears also felled their first assailants with sweeping moves of their spears, somehow avoiding each other and the walls of the confined space as two more of the assassins died on their blades.

"Yes," Quizar cried, his voice becoming strangled as one of the hatchet-wielding men buried his axe in the head of the man to Hadir's left. Blood sprayed the white walls of the staircase as the momentum of the strike took the man over the top of the balustrade. Dojan watched as the warrior of the Mighty Spears dropped like a stone, vanishing from sight an instant later, falling silently, already dead. He waited for the sound of him hitting the ground, some thirty floors below where they were fighting. The noise, when it came several seconds later, was a distant, dull, spattering thud, barely audible over the noise of battle.

CHAPTER 31

Autumn 200 – Bengarath Market

Nimsah sat quietly in a dark corner of Surat's coffeehouse, ignoring the customers, wrapped up in her thoughts. Surat would once have scolded her for neglecting her duties. Nowadays he turned a blind eye to her brooding.

Farooq spread the rumour that Fenara had sold her business and travelled north to live with her cousin in Al-Narah. Her spot in the marketplace was quickly taken by a young woman selling necklaces, rings and other trinkets. Nimsah took pleasure in stealing from her a couple of times before losing interest. It wasn't the woman's fault Fenara was dead. Someone was going to take over the place where her stall had once stood – it just happened to be her. Farooq also sold Fenara's house, no doubt making a tidy profit from the transaction. Seeing the young family move into Fenara's former home felt like a punch to the guts as she remembered the meals they'd shared, the laughter in Fenara's face when she gave Nimsah treats like baklawa and honeyed cakes. What ate away at Nimsah the most, though, was the indifference with which Khanir Shinva had treated Fenara's death. It had been an inconvenience, an incident to be hushed up, swept away and forgotten – silence bought with a handful of silver shekels. Nimsah vowed never to forget the name of Khanir Shinva Bel-Kamil. She should have plunged a knife in her throat rather than swinging with her fists. She'd never get that close to the khanir again.

Surat waddled past and paused at Nimsah's table. "Rather than sit here and mope, child, why not finish early? Go and enjoy some sunshine, while we're still blessed with good weather."

With a start Nimsah remembered she was supposed to be waiting on tables. She looked up at Surat, who gave her a kindly smile. "Why not let me ask some questions and see if I can't find out where she's living?" he offered, not for the first time. "You and Fenara were so close. I'm sure if I wrote to her she'd consider taking you in. She wouldn't want you pining for her like this."

Nimsah shook her head, afraid that if Surat uncovered the truth it would place his own life in danger. She hadn't forgotten how Khanir Shinva looked long and hard at Nimsah's tear-stained face that day, weighing up whether she could trust an angry street child to hold her tongue. Nimsah was sure it was only the fact she was under Farooq's protection that stayed Shinva's hand from sealing her silence with more than just coin.

"I would speak with young Nimsah for a moment."

Surat and Nimsah both looked round in surprise. It took her a moment to place the man's voice as Jandral stepped forwards, veiled and dressed in his customary brown robes made of soft, rich cotton. He took a seat opposite Nimsah and ordered coffee from Surat, who pocketed the generous tip and hurried away.

"This is where you've been hiding yourself," said Jandral. Nimsah nodded, saying nothing.

Jandral waited until Surat returned with his coffee, watching as he poured the steaming dark liquid into his cup. He undid his veil to drink, offering Nimsah a rare smile, framed by his black beard.

"Do you want some?"

Nimsah shook her head. "I'm not thirsty."

"She speaks," chuckled Jandral. "There was a time when I couldn't stop your incessant chatter."

Nimsah tried to change the subject. "Why are you here?"

"My business in Amjahran is finished," he explained, taking a sip of his drink. "Emira Ledana is now installed as the new ruler. She understands the interests of the Bank of Illesh and the Emirate of Fujareen are closely entwined. The Emirate of Amjahran will now work towards building stronger ties with your country, rather than seeking to rival its power."

"That wasn't what I meant. I was asking why you're *here*, now, seeking me out?"

"What did I say to you before I left?" asked Jandral, eyes regarding her shrewdly.

Nimsah thought back to their last conversation. "You said you'd come back."

"I said I would return for you," Jandral told her. "Don't you remember?"

Nimsah shrugged. "People say all sorts of things they don't mean."

Jandral's eyes narrowed and he took his time answering her, taking another sip of his coffee. "It's important you understand this. When a banker gives his word on a matter, it is binding. It's the way of the banking clans and how we have conducted our business for centuries, long before the War of the Avatars. If I say I will do a thing, then it will be done." Nimsah nodded as Jandral continued. "I have returned to my quarters in Bengarath Palace and sent word to Farooq that I have need of my faithful servant once more. Raqqath came to the palace and gave me Farooq's sincere apologies, explaining it was no longer possible for you to serve me. Now, why would that be?"

Nimsah licked her lips, breaking Jandral's stare as she looked at the table and tried to think of what to say. "I can't work at the palace."

"That much I've been able to figure out for myself. I asked you why." Jandral's words were cold, flint-edged.

"I can't say," Nimsah whispered.

"Why not?"

Nimsah coughed and cleared her dry throat. "It's a secret, one Farooq was paid handsomely to keep. I can't breathe a word about it to anyone."

Jandral sat back on his chair, looking thoughtful. Nimsah stared at her lap, trying to hide the fact her eyes were swimming with tears.

"Your loyalty to Farooq is admirable."

Nimsah said nothing, loneliness gnawing at her, squeezing her heart tight and making it hard to breathe. Her world revolved around Farooq's table in the centre of the City of Tents, whispering secrets into his ear, acting as his eyes in Bengarath. There was always a seat for her at his side, a fact that stirred jealousy in the other children who flocked to Farooq's court. She thought back on how Rogesh had betrayed her, choosing to side with Chandra despite everything she'd done for them. What did she have to show for her life? A chest with some fine clothes, many of which were now too small, kept in a tent shared with a dozen other children who were all frightened of her. She remembered Fenara's warning of what happened to young women in Farooq's world. Fenara had offered her the chance of a different life, away from all of this. Nimsah curled up on her seat, drawing her knees up to her chest and hugging them tight, trying to stifle the sob that was rising up within her.

"It was my fault." Her voice was the shadow of a whisper.

"What was?" The harsh note of command was gone. Instead, his dark eyes were kind and inviting, drawing out her secrets more powerfully than by force of will.

Nimsah found herself compelled to tell her story through whispered words in the quiet corner of the coffeehouse. Sharing the secret acted as a salve, soothing the rawness of her insides, easing the ache of her heart. As she told Jandral everything he sat there, listening in silence, his coffee cup untouched. Surat and the other waiters hurried to serve the rest of his customers, the busy coffeehouse full of chatter and laughter. The noise didn't touch them, sat in a small pocket of stillness, silence settling over them as Nimsah finished speaking and Jandral considered everything she had said.

"More coffee perhaps?" Surat's question broke the spell and Jandral nodded. Surat paused when he returned with a fresh pot, looking at Nimsah's tear-stained face.

"Is everything … alright?" he asked, knowing full well it wasn't.

"Nimsah was telling me how much she missed Fenara," Jandral explained.

Surat's face softened, a pained look crossing his features. "Ach. I don't know how the woman could have done this to the child, leaving like that. I've told Nimsah I have some business contacts in Al-Narah who could help track her down. Only Nimsah's a stubborn one, aren't you? She won't hear of it."

Nimsah wiped her face with a corner of her apron. "I have my pride, Surat. If Fenara wanted to take me with her, she would have done. I'm not going to go chasing after her."

"Surat has a good heart," said Jandral as they watched him talking to other customers. "Your lie is perfect. As long as he believes you, he'll be safe."

"You can't tell anyone," Nimsah replied. Although she couldn't describe exactly how, she understood that in sharing the secret Jandral now had power over her. A chill ran up her spine as she waited to see how he would respond.

Those dark eyes hardened at her words. "Since when does a street child tell a member of the banking clans what to do?"

"They'll know I told you. You were asking for me, people have seen you talking to me in the coffeehouse. It'd be obvious."

"You're right. However, ask yourself – what would I have to gain from sharing your secret?"

Nimsah sat there, thinking hard. "I don't know," she said finally.

"Have you ever heard the saying that knowledge is prized more highly than gold by the Bank of Illesh?" Jandral asked. Nimsah shook her head as he continued. "Gossips love to hear a secret, because it makes them feel important when they share it with their friends. For them, the pleasure comes in showing off, proving they know what's going on and people confide in them. I'm no gossip, Nimsah. Knowledge has its own value and it should never be squandered."

"And what value is there for you in the secret of Fenara's death?" Nimsah replied, suspicious.

"Think about it. You've already seen the truth. Khanir Shinva is from the ancient Bel-Kamil dynasty. She's an ambitious woman, the commander of Her Royal Highness' Blessed Swords, with designs on becoming andral when the time comes for Illana Bel-Jedesh to step aside. Farooq understood this instinctively, knowing that taking her purse was the least useful part of the bargain that bought his silence. Farooq now owns Khanir Shinva's reputation and has leverage over a high-ranking official in the Fujareen army. This is an investment Farooq will ensure is paid back many times over in the future, irrespective of the coin he's made by selling off Fenara's worldly possessions. Do you understand what I'm telling you?"

Nimsah nodded, mulling over Jandral's words. "What will you do with what I've told you?"

Jandral shrugged. "Nothing. At least, not yet. A time will come when knowing about the secret dishonour of Khanir Shinva may become useful." He tapped his head, smiling. "Until then, such things are safely stored away in here."

"I should have traded something," Nimsah replied. "Rather than giving up my secret I should have bargained with you for something in return."

Jandral's smile widened. "Now you're learning. Though I think you did get something from our conversation. You look brighter and a little of your sorrow has lifted. Am I right?"

Nimsah pursed her lips. "Maybe. I still don't like how you're twisting this. Fenara's dead and no one's willing to do anything about it. All you talk about is how to profit from Shinva's actions."

"Old habits are hard to shake off," Jandral conceded with a bow of his head. "Forgive me if I appear mercenary. Perhaps some good can still come of this."

"What do you mean?" Nimsah replied, unconvinced.

"You've come to a fork in the road, Nimsah. Fenara's death has shown you the kind of man Farooq is. Perhaps it's time to think about whether you still want to serve him?"

Nimsah folded her arms and looked hard at Jandral. "From what I've heard, the pair of you aren't so different."

Jandral laughed at that, shaking his head. "You have me there. We're similar, yes. However, what can Farooq offer you? What are your plans for the future in the City of Tents? More importantly, what are Farooq's plans for you? Do you want to sit at his right hand side as his lover one day? Kandilla knows you are one of Farooq's favourites, and she sees you will rival her in the future. Are Farooq's affections really worth fighting over?"

"You've a better idea?" Nimsah asked.

"Yes. You're bright, Nimsah, and wise beyond your years. Don't you know how unusual it is to be able to remember the things in such detail that you see? You instinctively know what's important when you hear it, and you have a knack for discovering people's secrets without them even knowing you're there. I've schooled you enough to see how quickly you learned your letters and numbers. These skills shouldn't be squandered in the service of a common criminal."

"What are you offering me in return?"

"A chance to complete your schooling and take up a position in the Bank of Illesh, when you're old enough." Nimsah sat there, trying to work out if she'd heard Jandral correctly. He took her silence to mean she still had to be convinced. "Why are you in this situation? The answer is simple – you have no power. Those in authority will always oppress and use their inferiors to maintain their position. However, how powerful do you think an emir really is? Why was Emir Cassim executed, and why does Emira Ledana now sit on the throne of Amjahran? The concerns of Amuran's rulers are petty when compared with the quiet influence the banking clans exercise. The rule of an emir or a sultan is measured in years, while we orchestrate our affairs in spans measuring centuries."

Nimsah thought about her home in the tent city. She would never again knock on Fenara's door or sit with her, chattering about inconsequential things, weaving her baskets. Farooq didn't care about her – only what she could do for him. Kandilla's pretty tattooed face swam before her eyes, twisted and ugly with envy at the favouritism Farooq showed her. She closed her eyes, hearing again the sharp crack of Fenara's head hitting the stone cobbles in the courtyard, Farooq's hand reaching out for Shinva's purse.

Nimsah leaned towards Jandral. "Tell me more."

CHAPTER 32

Summer 213 – Kandarah, Shekh Birizal's Palace

A roaring noise filled the stairwell as Hadir's warriors fought to protect their prince, weapons clashing, men screaming. It was the smell that Dojan found most shocking. There was an iron tang to the air, mingled with the odour from the urine and excrement flowing down the pristine marble staircase: the stench of death when a man was disembowelled by a Samarak fighting spear. There had been nothing like this in the legends Vizier Haman had taught Dojan in childhood, he thought, trying not to gag. They were daydreams compared to this sudden nightmare. For the first time Dojan understood something of what it must had been like for his father when he fought Godan's guards and took control of Bengarath Palace. When a man died on a blade there was no honour or beauty, nothing like the stories would have you believe.

Hadir and his surviving companion were fighting back to back, the reach of their spears preventing the assassins from getting close to Dojan and Quizar, who clung, shaking, to his arm. Their matching white robes were already flecked with blood and Dojan pressed himself back into the wall as a dying man fell past him, his face sliced open by Hadir, jaw hanging loosely from one side. One of the warriors lower down the stairs turned and plunged the pointed end of his spear into the man's chest, drawing it back out with a shout. Only three Mighty Spears stood between Dojan and the dozen attackers coming up the stairs, now only fifty yards away, weapons drawn. He recognised the two guards they'd met at the elevator among them.

Dojan glanced back up the stairs to see a knife strike the armour protecting Hadir's ribs – the harsh scrape of metal on metal as the blade was turned aside. The mubarizun was holding his own against five assassins, while Hadir's companion wrestled with the older man who seemed to be leading the attack. As the two men struggled, another assassin darted in and plunged a knife into the throat of the Mighty Spear. With a choked cry, he staggered backwards, fighting spear whirling as it sliced through the neck of his attacker, dropping him as blood sluiced from the fatal wound. Now alone, Hadir grunted with effort as he forced another man over the edge of the stairs – he fell with a rapidly receding scream to his death, far below.

"Help your mubarizun," Dojan called out to the warriors fighting for him lower down. One of them turned and ran to Hadir's aid as the Mighty Spear who had been stabbed in the throat slid down the wall, hand trying to stem the flow of blood as his fighting spear clattered to the floor.

The remaining two warriors protecting Dojan's back fought off the attackers from the lower levels, combining effectively and making use of their reach and the advantage of being on higher ground. Clearly the attack had not been perfectly coordinated, because the dozen assassins who had rushed up the stairs had exhausted themselves with the effort. Already six of them lay dead or dying and the rest hung back, trying to find a way through the defences of the two warriors who defied them.

"We might make our way out of this –" Quizar's words were cut off as a hatchet whup-whup-whupped through the air and caught him in the head.

"Quizar!" Dojan cradled his katib in his arms, watching in horror as blood poured from the side of his head. He pressed his fingers to the wound, trying to staunch the bleeding as Quizar's eyes rolled. "Help us. Hadir – help us."

Hadir and the warrior Dojan had ordered to aid him were continuing to fight. The grey-bearded man brought his hatchet down into the small of Hadir's back, a series of vicious chops that had Hadir roaring in pain as he turned and used his spear to defend himself. His fellow warrior sliced another of the attackers with the bladed end of his spear, cutting him open from hip to hip. As he dropped, screaming, to the floor, the Mighty Spear's victory shout was ended as another thrown hatchet took off half his face. Hadir took another step upwards, stabbing the pointed end of his spear into the eye of the man who had thrown the axe, the force of his blow enough to pin the man's head to the wall. Hadir gave a grunt as his weapon lodged and the grey-bearded assassin swung his hatchet again, narrowly missing his head.

"Stand aside." Hadir spat the words as he managed to wrench his spear free, giving himself enough time to block the next swing with the shaft. He used his strength to push the man back, forcing him to lift his arms as the hatchet slid along the length of the spear. Dojan thought Hadir was about to lose some fingers, only for the spear to spin around in a wide circle, the bladed end taking the grey-bearded man's head from his shoulders. Dojan stared, unmoving, as the decapitated body of the man tumbled down the stairs.

Hadir turned to Dojan. "Up," he barked through teeth red with blood. Dojan glanced down at Quizar's still body, head nestled in his lap, the wound soaking into his now ruined white robes.

"Up," Hadir shouted again and Dojan felt himself lifted by the arm as one of the two warriors defending their rear reached him. The remaining Mighty Spear was fighting four men, moving carefully backwards one step at a time to guard their retreat.

As Dojan was lifted onto his feet he looked down at the body of his friend and tears filled his vision. His legs felt weak, lungs ragged as he tried to draw breath. The warrior at their rear lost his footing on the bloody stairs and slid back down into his assailants. One of them took off his foot with a hatchet, right above the ankle, his screams filling the air as they pinned him to the ground and wrestled the spear out of his grasp.

"Move." Hadir took Dojan's other arm and the two men dragged him up the stairs. Dojan tried to move his feet, his legs unwilling to follow the simplest of instructions.

"Try the door," Hadir gasped when they reached the next level on the staircase.

The other warrior turned the handle. "It's locked."

The man put his shoulder to the door and gave it a shove. Hadir let go of Dojan and joined him, the pair of them straining to force their way through. Down below the wounded Mighty Spear was screaming and pleading for mercy, his cries cut short as hatchet and dagger blows rained down on him, finding flesh through weak points in his armour. Dojan watched as one of the four assassins picked up the fallen warrior's fighting spear and they began to advance up the stairs.

"They're coming," Dojan whimpered.

"It won't budge," groaned the warrior to Hadir. It struck Dojan that he didn't know the names of any of the men who had fought for him beside Hadir. Now didn't seem the best time to begin introductions.

"We finish it here," Hadir replied, stepping back out to block the stairs as the four remaining attackers drew near. Blood was running from the wound in his back and he looked winded, struggling to draw breath as he spoke.

The man who had stolen the Samarak fighting spear was drenched with sweat and blood, a long scar running from the corner of his eye socket down the length of his jaw. His three companions kept close, using the reach of his spear for cover as they tried to find a way past Dojan's last two guards.

"You've fought well," the scarred man said, inching forwards. "Ask yourself, though – is this vain young prince worth dying for?"

Hadir didn't reply, instead raising his spear with a shout and rushing at the men. The other Mighty Spear hesitated for a fraction of a second, surprised by the speed of Hadir's attack. He raised his own weapon and yelled a challenge, only to drop to his knees, gasping. Dojan couldn't see what was wrong until he drew closer. A thrown dagger protruded from the man's eye, his shaking fingers trying to grasp the handle.

"I … It's …" the man's jaw twitched as he tried to speak, his hands shaking more.

"It's alright," Dojan lied. "It's going to be alright."

The warrior's whole body convulsed and he died, his one remaining eye fixed on Dojan, the light of life within fading to nothing. Dojan stared at the fallen man's spear as the clashes of weapons reached him from further down the staircase. He'd been trained by Khan Hengesh in how to wield a spear. It was something he'd never truly mastered but Hadir needed his help. Dojan's trembling fingers brushed the shaft of the spear, wet and sticky with blood. His hand tightened around the wood, his limbs heavy and sluggish as he rose, clutching the weapon awkwardly.

Hadir had already killed two of the assassins, although he was now pinned against the metal balustrade as the scarred man with the spear jabbed at him with the bladed end of the weapon. A dagger was buried up to the hilt under Hadir's ribs, having punched through his chainmail, and he was hunched over, hampered by his wound. The second man fighting him struck him with a hatchet on the side of his helmet, glancing off Hadir's head with a dull ring.

Dojan held out the spear and ran to Hadir's aid, screaming at the top of his lungs. He slipped on something wet as the hatchet-wielding man turned towards him in surprise. His eyes widened when the blade of the Samarak fighting spear slid between his ribs as Dojan clattered into him, both men tumbling down the stairs in a tangle of limbs. Dojan snarled, keeping a tight grip on his spear with one hand as the man thrashed under him. Dojan used his free hand to grasp the man's wrist, holding back the hatchet that was inches from his face. Underneath him the man grunted and choked, coughing blood onto the front of Dojan's robes. Dojan twisted the spear, feeling it grating against bone, driving it deeper, seeking out the man's heart. His opponent choked again, arm going limp in Dojan's grip as the hatchet slid out of his fingers and hit the stone, chipping a notch out of the perfect edge of one step. The man under him shook and coughed, gargling on thick black blood welling up from his throat. Dojan held him down, waiting until he was still before turning to see what had happened to Hadir.

The mubarizun of the Mighty Spears was leaning back against the wall, eyes tight shut, teeth bared as he grimaced in pain. Dojan struggled up the stairs, feeling dizzy, legs weak beneath him. He dropped down beside Hadir, half-afraid the man was already dead. He gave a cry of relief when Hadir opened his eyes.

"You fought well," Hadir told him, his voice a whisper. Blood was running down the side of his head where he'd been struck on his helmet.

Dojan laughed. "I think you deserve that accolade. Where's the man you were fighting?"

Hadir raised his head with an immense effort and nodded towards the balustrade. "He took the fastest route ... to the ground floor."

Dojan looked down at the dagger protruding from Hadir's body. The man was sitting in a pool of blood, his clothes soaked. Dojan took hold of Hadir's broad hands and placed them over the wound.

"Keep some pressure on," Dojan floundered, looking around for any signs of life on the staircase. Surely all the noise would have been heard by someone? "Help's on its way."

"No, it's not," Hadir's breath rattled in his chest.

Dojan choked back tears and realised he'd lost count of which floor they were on. He glanced upwards, trying to see where the next doorway was. He had to leave Hadir and get help before he bled to death.

"Stay there," Dojan told him. "I'm going to find someone."

"No," Hadir replied, his voice faint.

"No?"

"I don't want to die … alone," whispered Hadir, reaching out with his huge blood-soaked hands, enfolding Dojan's within them.

"You're not going to die," Dojan told him. "Let me go and get help."

"I served you … well … didn't I?"

Dojan blinked back tears. "You're the greatest mubarizun of the Mighty Spears. Of course you served me well. You're ten times the man I'll ever be."

Hadir nodded towards the mangled bodies, lying in twisted heaps strewn down the white staircase. "This … is … what war … looks like. Don't let the men and women of Fujareen … die like this. Find a way …" Hadir coughed and shook with the pain it sent through his body. "Find a way. Avoid the war with … the Abitek and Edeen. You're … an honourable man, Crown Prince. You'll … You need … find …"

Hadir was struggling to breathe and Dojan placed his free hand on his chest, above his heart. "I'll find a way," he promised. "And I swear to you, Hadir, that I'll discover who was behind this attempt on my life. You and your men will be avenged."

Hadir's head lolled forwards, chin resting on his chest as his breathing ceased. Dojan bowed his own head, tears falling freely as he wept, alone, on the silent staircase.

CHAPTER 33

Autumn 200 – Bengarath Docks

Nimsah sat watching the quays from her vantage point, high up in one of the wharfside buildings. Far below her, she could see the dockers and sailors working together to bring their cargo ashore. Sacks, crates, barrels and jars were carefully passed out of the hold and stacked on the dockside, the noise of the men and women far below drifting up, indistinct on the breeze. Nimsah sat on the ledge of the window, shutters pinned open, sagging on rusting hinges. She dangled her bare feet, enjoying the fresh air on her toes and shielded her eyes from the morning sun.

Somewhere out in the bay of Bengarath was the merchant dhow she was watching for, *The Seventh Son*, bound for Fujareen from Shaqran, one of the Three Kingdoms of Kalat to the far south. The people of Kalat were darker skinned than their northerly cousins in the Emirates, each kingdom aligned to one of the avatars who joined Morvanos' rebellion against the Tyranny. Shaqran worshipped Ceren, avatar of darkness. Like most inhabitants of the Emirates, Nimsah didn't tend to give the avatars much thought beyond offering up the occasional prayer to Dinuvillan for good fortune, whilst hoping to avoid the mischief wrought by Myshall. Raqqath told her that in the ports of Shaqran they held moonlit festivals to worship Ceren, drowning criminals and other wrongdoers in the waters as an offering to gain her favour. Nimsah shuddered, even though the sun was warm on her face; the kind of people who indulged in human sacrifice were not ones to cross. She hoped Farooq knew what he was doing.

She scoured the sails of the ships approaching port, looking for the symbols Raqqath had described. *The Seventh Son* flew under a banner of three waning crescent moons set in a triangular pattern above two crossed scimitars, the emblems white on black sailcloth. Unfortunately, most Shaqran traders favoured black sails. Nimsah squinted, trying to block out the sun reflecting on the rippling surface of the Bezeen Strait. The third Shaqran vessel she had spotted that morning was still too far away to make out its markings.

Her mind wandered as she thought again about Jandral's offer. Nimsah had lived in Bengarath her whole life, so the idea of crossing the sea to Kandarah was both exciting and terrifying. Part of her couldn't shake off the nagging doubt this was all some elaborate trick. Yet why would Jandral seek her out and suggest she worked for him if he wasn't serious? Life had taught Nimsah to be suspicious, but she couldn't see a reason why Jandral would lie to her. As soon as he finished his business with the emir at the palace he would be leaving Bengarath. All she had to do was board the ship with him and her life would change forever. It sounded so easy.

As the sun crept across the sky she glanced again at the approaching black-sailed ship. There were the three crescent moons, fluttering as the sail caught the wind and steered *The Seventh Son* towards Bengarath. Nimsah gave a small whoop of delight and waited until she was sure she knew which dock the dhow was headed towards. She scrambled back through the window, closed the shutters and hurried downstairs, sticking to the shadows in the building to avoid being seen by the dockworkers, before slipping out and heading over to where Raqqath and his men were waiting.

Nimsah had no intention of going with Raqqath to see exactly what business Farooq's gang had with *The Seventh Son*. Instead, her task complete, she hurried back to the City of

Tents, skirting the long way around the marketplace to avoid the place where Fenara used to keep her stall. She wasn't far from her tent when she found Chandra and Rogesh walking towards her. Chandra had grown tall over the summer, her hips and waist more curved, wearing a bright yellow dress. The Naroque girl was gone, now a young woman walking with a confident air. Next to her, Rogesh was also filling out, broadening rather than growing upwards. He offered Nimsah a shy smile as they drew near, unaware of Chandra's scowl.

"Nimsah," said Chandra with a bob of her head. She continued walking and had to turn around when she realised Rogesh had stopped to talk.

"How are you?" he asked, looking at his battered sandals, refusing to meet her gaze.

"Fine."

"That's good."

"Are you going to stand there all morning?" asked Chandra, hands on her hips. Rogesh became tongue-tied as he tried to answer, head sinking a little lower.

"What do you have planned?" Nimsah asked to try and spare his blushes.

"A trip to the marketplace," Chandra told her. "There are some merchants with heavy purses who need our attention."

Nimsah glanced at Rogesh, worry knotting in her stomach. She could guess the ruse Chandra had planned, where she would be all smiles and laughter as she distracted their target while Rogesh lifted his purse. Easy money, as long as you didn't get caught.

"What is it?" said Chandra, frowning. "We can't all wait on tables, serve coffee and have praises heaped on us for doing nothing. Farooq is pleased with the coin we bring back."

"Just be careful," Nimsah replied.

"We will," said Rogesh.

"Make sure you do. The emir will have your hand if they catch you."

"That's not going to happen," said Chandra, giving

Rogesh's shoulder a reassuring rub.

"I caught you once before," Nimsah answered. There – she'd said it and it was too late to call the words back. She'd reopened the wound that had ended their friendship, Rogesh looking anywhere other than at her.

Chandra bridled at the remark. "You think you're so much better than us, ever since you started paying your little trips to the palace. Well, those are over. How you avoided getting into more trouble with Farooq over that mess, I don't know."

As Nimsah turned to walk away Chandra grabbed her arm. "What? No witty comeback?"

"Get off me."

"Come on, Chandra, let's go," Rogesh pleaded.

Chandra's eyes narrowed, a calculating look crossing her face. "There's something going on, isn't there? I can see it in your expression."

"You're imagining things," Nimsah told her.

"You're up to something," said Chandra. "I don't know what it is, but I'll find out."

"Chandra, please," said Rogesh. "Leave it. It doesn't matter. We need to go."

Chandra sneered and released her grip, stalking away with Rogesh, who turned back once and gave an apologetic shrug. Nimsah rubbed her arm and watched them vanish into the crowd.

"Not like you to cause a scene," Kandilla remarked from behind her.

Nimsah spun round, trying to hide her surprise. "I was only reminding Rogesh to be careful. Chandra can be reckless sometimes."

"What's it to you?" asked Kandilla. "I'd heard you'd had a falling out with your little friends. You normally make things look so serene – arguing in the street isn't really your style, is it?" Kandilla looked Nimsah up and down, hand resting on the hilt of the dagger she carried on her hip. "Shouldn't you be somewhere?"

"I've done what I needed. Raqqath had me on lookout for *The Seventh Son* this morning. They landed earlier this morning."

"Making you a lady of leisure for the rest of the day?"

"If you say so."

"Hmm. You've nowhere to run off to now, have you?" Kandilla said with a smirk.

Nimsah crossed her arms, glaring back. "What's that supposed to mean?"

"That stupid woman from the market – the one who used to spoil you." Kandilla's mouth twisted into a mocking smile. "No more home cooked meals from a senile old woman you hoodwinked into thinking you were better than a street rat."

The air left Kandilla's mouth in a shocked O as she skidded onto her backside, provoking a few shouts of surprise and one or two laughs from nearby onlookers. Nimsah had no recollection of shoving her as she stared down at Kandilla, breathing hard, hands balled into fists.

"You little bitch." Kandilla was on her feet in an instant, catching hold of Nimsah's hair as she tried to dart away. "You'll pay for that."

Nimsah lashed out, catching Kandilla with the back of her hand across the mouth, drawing blood. Kandilla pulled her hair, bodily lifting Nimsah into the air although the two of them were almost the same height. There was a blur of motion and Nimsah felt the cold steel of Kandilla's dagger against her throat.

"You *dare* to strike me?" Kandilla hissed, licking her lip, tongue bloody.

"Now who's making a scene?" Nimsah said, aware of the blood pulsing through her neck, the edge of the knife pressing into her throat. The slightest increase in pressure would be enough to break the skin.

Kandilla glanced around, noticing for the first time the

circle of shocked faces in the watching crowd. She pulled the knife away and released her hold on Nimsah's hair, dropping her into a heap at her feet.

"Watch yourself," said Kandilla, looking down on Nimsah. "You're not as perfect as Farooq makes out. You've had your dalliance with the little prince and played happy families with Fenara. Now that's over and you're back here, where you belong. You're a child of the City of Tents and we've owned you ever since your parents abandoned you here. Don't forget that."

Kandilla stalked away, laughing, as Nimsah hurried to her tent. She sank down onto her bed and hugged her knees to her chest with shaking hands. She knew how close Kandilla had come to cutting her throat. On another day she might not have hesitated and that would have been the end, right there. Who would have missed her now Fenara was dead? Farooq would have been angry, of course, although he loved Kandilla and Nimsah was sure she would have found a way to earn his forgiveness. Rogesh was now tied in close with Chandra, their old partnership a thing of the past.

Nimsah made up her mind as she sat in her tent. When Jandral's call came, she'd be taking that ship to Kandarah. It was time to leave her old life behind and take the opportunity Jandral was giving her. She owed it to Fenara to make something of her life away from people like Kandilla and Chandra, who would only try and drag her down as they fought for Farooq's favour.

When she felt calmer, Nimsah opened her chest and sorted through her clothes. She wasn't sure what she would need in Kandarah, but she knew it could be cold at sea. She packed some of her warmer clothes into a bag and from the very bottom of the chest she pulled out a knife, dropping this into her shoulder bag. Nothing was going to stand in the way of her taking this chance.

CHAPTER 34

Summer 213 – Kandarah Cemetery

"Hasan Al-Saeed," intoned Khan Gerber Al-Jalar, taking the white cloth wrapped around the body of the fallen warrior and drawing the loose corner across the man's face. "You fought with honour and bravery, and will walk into Navan's Halls with your head held high."

The Khan of the Tireless Shields stepped back, bowing his head before the pyre on which the six bodies of the fallen Mighty Spears lay.

Khanir Shinva advanced, armour polished and glittering. She removed her helmet and stared down at the final body whose face remained uncovered. Hadir lay in front of her, white funeral cloth tightly covering his body. His face looked serene, peaceful in death. Dojan took a shuddering breath, trying to master his grief as he stood watching the ceremony with Tormindah and Arak. Ulan was a few steps away, looking sombre.

"Mubarizun Hadir Al-Nadim. You fought with honour and bravery, and will walk into Navan's Halls with your head held high." Shinva stared down at Hadir for a few moments, the wind in the cemetery rippling through her dark hair. She replaced her helmet and covered Hadir's face before walking back to join the Fujareen mourners.

"Hail, Hadir, mubarizun of the Mighty Spears," called out Khalid Al-Shah. As he repeated the words, his cry was joined over and over by the five remaining members of his regiment. As the most experienced member of the Mighty Spears left in Kandarah, Khalid had assumed Hadir's duties as Dojan's personal bodyguard, promoted from the night shift. He would remain at his side until such time as a new mubarizun was appointed by Khan Hengesh.

"Hail the Mighty Spears," called out Mubarizun Yanzin, drawing her scimitar and holding it in the air. The rest of the Blessed Swords did the same, pointing their weapons up towards the sun, the light sparkling off their blades.

Shekh Birizal was in attendance with Khan Lemarr, while all the Naroque tribes had sent representatives. In addition to Fasil and Narinda, Dojan had seen Kaal dressed in their traditional yellow robes, Culah wearing dark blue and a smattering of green mourning clothes denoting the Halak, their faces dusted with ash. While Fasil and his companions of the dragon tribe wore their reds, the mourning colours of the Edeen were pure white. Narinda had drawn white patterns across the dark skin of her face, framing the golden star on her forehead. When Ramdha of the Edeen Black Robes offered his condolences he explained Narinda was drawing upon the power of the stars, to better light the path in the Realm of Death for Hadir and his companions to find their way to Navan's Halls. Dojan had thanked the old warrior and shaken his calloused hand, unsure what else to say.

Quizar had miraculously survived the attack, although he had still to regain consciousness. He was being tended in the palace by some of Shekh Birizal's healing magi. The thought struck Dojan that on the day of the attack the two of them had been wearing matching white robes. There was every chance the assassins had mistaken Quizar for Dojan, although he was sure that their orders would have involved killing all of his party. The elevator had been in perfect working order, the bodies of Shekh Birizal's guards found hidden in a storeroom in the palace after the attack.

Khalid stepped forwards and lit the pyre with a burning torch, retreating quickly as the flames took hold, licking around the bodies of his fallen comrades.   Dojan bowed his head and offered up a prayer that Arkon would look favourably on his fallen mubarizun. The question gnawing at the back of his mind was who had been behind the attack? He really could do with Quizar right now to help him sort out the facts. Shekh Birizal's own guards had been killed, suggesting his innocence. Yet this could be misdirection, the attack aimed at curbing Dojan's interest in Amonduras, or as a warning against his private meetings with Fasil and Narinda. However with Dojan's army camped outside Kandarah's walls, it seemed unlikely the shekh would risk incurring the wrath of his new allies by murdering their prince.

The fact that war threatened with the Abitek and Edeen, with Fasil's army massing in the hill country, made them obvious suspects. But what would they have to gain from Dojan's death? Dojan had tried to find a peaceful route through his discussions, both tribes discouraging him from blindly following the terms of the agreement brokered by the Illesh bankers between Fujareen and Kandarah. Attacking him before those discussions were concluded made no sense.

Dojan looked up to where Jandral and Nimsah stood, staring into the fiercely burning pyre. Both were dressed in black, their faces veiled. Dojan remembered his last conversation with Nimsah, where she had warned him against becoming involved in matters that didn't concern him. Had she decided his investigations had gone too far? Again, it seemed far-fetched. He hadn't uncovered anything of significance, so why would the Illesh banking clan have moved against him? Such a strategy risked undoing their agreement with the Emirate of Fujareen and, with the Abitek army waiting to contest their right to Amonduras, they needed Dojan's soldiers now more than ever.

Whoever was behind the attack, they had come perilously close to succeeding. Hadir and his five warriors had fought off twenty four assailants, sacrificing themselves to save him. Dojan closed his eyes, trying to shut out the sound of battle. He felt a chill in his stomach, a tightening in his chest and he had to clasp his hands together to hide the fact that they were shaking. He missed Hadir, the lack of his quiet presence a hollow absence, sapping his spirit as the shock and fear of his encounter with death threatened to overwhelm him. Dojan couldn't stem the tears, wiping them away angrily with the back of his hand.

Find a way. Avoid the war. Dojan remembered Hadir's dying words. The man had been his personal guard for the past five years, ever-present at his side. Dojan had always thought Hadir disapproved of his feckless nature, failing to understand that the role of a prince was to enjoy himself for as long as possible before the heavy weight of office fell upon his shoulders. Hadir had always shown a level of deference and respect for the title of crown prince that Dojan didn't feel he deserved. Yet, at the last, Hadir had looked to Dojan to find a way to prevent Fujareen's soldiers dying on Kandaran soil. Eight thousand Fujareen warriors had now crossed the Bezeen Strait, outnumbering the dragon tribe two to one. Victory for Fujareen was assured, though it would come at a price, something Dojan properly understood for the first time.

As the mourners began to disperse Khalid joined the rest of the Mighty Spears at Dojan's side, bowing low as Jandral and Nimsah approached.

"Don't be so deferential," Jandral told him. "On this day the Mighty Spears bow to no one. I saw the aftermath of the battle on the staircase. I could hardly believe a handful of warriors could be so deadly."

"I should have been there," Khalid replied. "Had I been, our mubarizun might not be lying on a funeral pyre." Hadir had insisted on guarding Dojan during the daytime, which had left Khalid and his five men with the less attractive proposition of acting as the night guard. The young man was eager to prove himself in his new role.

Jandral's eyes smiled above his black veil. "He died a hero's death. If there was ever any doubt the Fujareen army is the best in all Samarakand, Hadir's actions dispelled such thoughts."

"The Mighty Spears should be leading the preparations for this war," Khalid told him.

"Your emir thought differently," said Jandral, nodding in Khanir Shinva's direction as she spoke to Ulan and Arak.

Khalid hesitated, unwilling to openly criticise Dojan's father in front of his eldest son. Dojan could see the widening smile on Jandral's face, crows' feet gathering around his eyes.

"Fujareen is blessed with experienced khans and a well-trained army," said Dojan, coming to Khalid's rescue. "Many commanders volunteered their regiments to support the Kandaran cause. Those who Father chose to stay by his side while our strength lies across the waters, they are the ones he truly trusts."

"Well said," Jandral replied.

"I'm sorry about Hadir," added Nimsah. "He was a good man and he and his men fought bravely. How is Quizar?"

Dojan sighed. "He's been unconscious for two days, and the healers were unable to save his ear. He's lucky he didn't lose an eye. Another inch and he'd probably be dead."

"I hope he recovers soon," Nimsah said, resting her hand lightly on Dojan's forearm for a moment. She seemed so genuinely full of concern, Dojan found it hard to believe he had considered that Nimsah could have been behind the plot for a moment.

"May I have a little of your time?" asked Jandral. "While I appreciate the timing is poor, Shekh Birizal will be keen to conclude matters now your army has been deployed. Respect for the dead is all well and good, but there is still the dispute to settle and two armies facing each other outside this city. Now the pyre has been lit, Birizal will insist on issuing Narinda and Fasil with a final ultimatum."

Dojan sighed. Any plans he'd had to try and play a bigger part in events now looked foolish and inconsequential. Arak's far-fetched plan to prise free Lemarr's secret no longer seemed important – without Quizar at his side he wasn't even sure he'd know what to do with the information. Time had run out once the Abitek army arrived and now he needed to play the part his father had assigned to him.

"Crown Prince?" Jandral's words stirred Dojan from his thoughts.

"I'm sorry, Jandral. What were you saying?"

Jandral's eyes flicked to Dojan's companions, Khalid and Tormindah. It took Dojan a few moments to understand the silent question.

"I trust them. The Mighty Spears are sworn to protect the emir and his heir, and Tormindah has been shielding my mind from Fasil's dark magic since I arrived here. If she wanted to harm me, she would already have done so."

Jandral leaned in close, speaking in a low voice. "If you are sure …"

"The Crown Prince will go nowhere without me and my men," Khalid said in a tone that brooked no argument.

Jandral looked hard at the young warrior. "What I am about to say requires complete discretion."

"The secrets of the Crown Prince belong to him and him alone."

Jandral turned to Dojan, who nodded that he was satisfied. "This is known only to myself, Nimsah and a couple of palace officials I trust completely. Even Shekh Birizal is unaware of this. One of the men who attacked you, Crown Prince, survived his injuries. He is being tended privately by healers in my employ. When he awakes, I will put him to the question."

"He's unconscious?" said Dojan, disappointed. "So he might not even survive long enough for you to interrogate him."

Jandral shrugged. "That remains to be seen. However, if he does recover I thought you'd like to join me."

Dojan tried to imagine what it would be like to face someone who had tried to kill him. "You'd be willing to involve me and not the shekh?"

"Crown Prince, you represent our investment. Our alliance with Fujareen has been years in the planning and execution … I'm sorry, that was a poor choice of words. What I'm trying to say is that the attack on you was also an attack on our interests. As I'm sure you've surmised, there are numerous possibilities as to its origins. I'll trust no one in Kandarah until I've discovered the truth for myself. I think I owe it to you and your father to share what we learn."

"Thank you, Jandral. Let me know when you're ready to proceed and I'll willingly join you."

"Do you believe them?" asked Tormindah as Jandral and Nimsah walked away.

"Do I believe what?"

"This man Jandral says he's captured – the one only *he* knows anything about. It's very convenient, wouldn't you say?"

Dojan frowned. "Are you suggesting Illesh was behind the attack? I'll confess, I thought about the possibility only to discount it. I can't see what they would have to gain."

"The Illesh are no different to the other banking clans," Tormindah told him. "They plan far ahead and only serve their own interests. Perhaps Jandral is speaking the truth and they are taking matters into their own hands to protect their investment. However, what they're doing breaks Kandaran law. The prisoner should be in Shekh Birizal's custody, not some private prison belonging to the bank."

"You're right to be careful," Dojan replied. "However, I can't ignore Jandral's offer. In fact, the more I think on what you've said, the more important it is that you join me."

"Crown Prince?"

Dojan smiled, explaining to Tormindah what he had in mind.

CHAPTER 35

Late Autumn 200 – Bengarath, the City of Tents

Nimsah waited patiently for Jandral to tell her he was ready to leave Bengarath, the days stretching on forever with no news from the palace. She joined Farooq's table every evening, sharing his food, watching how his followers curried favour, trying to maintain or improve their standing. Chandra was ambitious, and Nimsah saw for the first time a shadowy reflection of how she had been a year or two ago. Rogesh had firmly latched on to Chandra – the boy needed someone to follow and tell him what to do. Nimsah didn't like it because Chandra ensured Rogesh took all the risks, while she took most of the credit. Now the weather was colder he was wearing his old yellowed sheepskin jacket, although it was too small for him and could no longer be buttoned up at the front.

Whilst meals with Farooq filled her belly, they were far from relaxing. Kandilla wasted no opportunity to snipe at Nimsah whenever she could, drawing a satisfied smile from Chandra whenever she watched their exchanges. Their brief fight had been seen by so many people in the tent city word of it must have reached Farooq's ear. He continued to defend Nimsah, looking increasingly bored with how Kandilla was toying with her as the weeks went by and she showed no interest in relenting. Nimsah noticed Farooq had quietly dropped her nickname of Little Flower – using it always drew a barbed comment from Kandilla.

***

Nimsah wore warm robes over her working clothes for the walk to Surat's coffeehouse. While it didn't offer the same sense of home as Fenara's old house, the rich smells of roasted beans and the chatter of Surat's customers was familiar and comforting. The days she spent there were easy enough, although Nimsah never looked forward to the end of her shift and the walk back to the City of Tents. She hoped there would be some interesting gossip that would merit Farooq's attention – otherwise Kandilla would be gifted the perfect excuse to make life difficult.

Nimsah almost dropped her tray when she went to serve a customer in one of the booths late that morning, only to discover Jandral was waiting for her.

"Not often I see you lost for words."

"I've not heard from you for weeks," Nimsah replied as she took his order. "I thought you'd forgotten me."

Jandral spread out his hands. "My affairs at the palace have kept me fully occupied. However, I have been called back to Kandarah on urgent business and I must leave tonight. I've not forgotten my promise. If you can be ready to join me at the docks this afternoon we can leave together."

Nimsah had to catch her breath. She'd thought of little else since last talking to Jandral. Now the time had come she felt a moment of fear – was she really ready to leave her old life behind and trust this man?

"I'll be there," Nimsah replied, making the choice by forcing out the words before she had chance to change her mind.

"I have chartered a merchant baghlah called *Sumara*, which is waiting for me on the southernmost quay at the docks. The captain will be setting sail on the fourth hour after noon to catch the tide. Make sure you're there, or I'll have to leave without you."

Nimsah thought of her bag, packed and waiting in her tent. She wished Jandral had given her more warning but there was still plenty of time to retrieve her belongings and return to the docks.

"I won't be late," Nimsah told Jandral.

"Good. Your new life starts today, Nimsah. I will see you later on the *Sumara*."

Nimsah served Jandral his coffee, surprised that her hands were shaking as she poured the liquid into his cup. She walked back to the counter where Surat was sitting, folded her apron up and placed it neatly beside him.

Surat raised an eyebrow. "You haven't finished your shift."

Nimsah fluttered her eyelashes. "I'm sorry, Surat. Something's come up and I need to leave early."

"Is it something Farooq needs you to do?"

"Something like that. I won't expect you to pay me for a full shift."

Surat sighed. "You're right about that. I'll see you in a couple of days if you've more important things to do."

Nimsah nodded, hesitating as she was about to leave. "Surat."

He turned back to her, frowning. "What is it?"

"Thank you. You were good to me after Fenara died. I like working here."

"I'm sure you do," he said, his smile kind. "That still won't get you full pay for today."

Nimsah patted his hand and left the coffeehouse, her heart feeling lighter, as she set off towards the City of Tents.

***

Nimsah slipped into her deserted tent, picking up her bag and making sure the handful of coppers and her knife were still safely stowed inside. She changed out of the smock she wore at the coffeehouse and dressed in warmer clothes. Inside her bag were two further outfits, including the red one Farooq had gifted her that fitted her best. She had no idea what working for the Bank of Illesh would entail or what she was expected to wear. Nimsah sighed, deciding that if there was anything important she needed to bring, Jandral would have told her.

She had what she had and Jandral couldn't expect anything more after giving her less than a day's notice.

Nimsah glanced around her tent, a space she'd shared with so many different children over the years. Would she have her own rooms in Kandarah? She realised there were dozens of questions she should have asked Jandral that morning. Too late now. Although she knew she was making the right choice, Nimsah felt a pang of regret at leaving her old life and everything she'd ever known as she swept aside the tent flap and stepped outside. She set off for the docks, even though she would be waiting there for hours before the *Sumara* would be ready to set sail.

"Where are you going?"

Kandilla's cold voice behind her made the hairs on Nimsah's neck stand up and her heart felt like it was about to burst out of her chest. She hesitated, taking a deep breath before turning to face the older woman, trying to compose herself. Kandilla immediately sensed something was up.

"I asked you a question," Kandilla said, advancing on Nimsah, hips swaying. They were alone in the courtyard outside Farooq's tent except for Bizek, who was in his customary place guarding the entrance. He knew better than to interfere, ignoring them both.

"Nothing," said Nimsah, that single word somehow contriving to make her sound guilty.

"You're carrying a lot of stuff for someone off doing *nothing*," Kandilla replied, nodding at the bag over Nimsah's shoulder.

"I'm bringing some things back for Surat."

"Really? What's inside?"

"Nothing that would interest you, Kandilla. What do you want?"

Kandilla advanced on Nimsah as she took a step backwards. "You're up to something. You're usually so accomplished and composed, yet why do you look like I've caught you pilfering from Farooq's coffers? I told you to open up your bag. Show me what you're bringing to Surat."

Nimsah took another deep, slow breath, trying to stop her heart racing. She opened up her bag, pulling out the pretty red dress. "Surat wants me to wear something smart. He's organised a private party for one of his cousins later this month and I told him I could wear this. He asked to see it."

Kandilla's face twisted into a sour smile as she reached into the bag. "Yes, Surat is well-known for his love of fashion. Who's this cousin?"

"Hadeem," Nimsah replied instantly.

"Never heard of him."

"Neither had I, until Surat told me about his plans."

Kandilla took hold of the dress, running her fingers over the soft fabric. "Strange he should be arranging such a big celebration for someone none of us have ever heard of." Kandilla passed the sleeve of the dress through one hand into the other before giving it a sharp tug. The sleeve tore away from the rest of the dress with a sharp rip as Kandilla smirked. "Oops. How clumsy of me. What else have you got in there, I wonder?"

Nimsah snatched her bag away, leaving Kandilla holding the flapping red sleeve in her hands. "Get off my stuff."

"Or you'll do what?" Kandilla challenged her.

Nimsah spun on her heels and dashed off, leaving Kandilla in her wake, shouting at her to stop. She darted between the tents, weaving around people as she ran, desperate to leave Farooq's domain forever. She glanced over her shoulder and slowed a little, crying out in alarm when she saw Kandilla forcing her way through the wending main street which the tents clustered around. Kandilla's mouth curled, a lioness spying her prey, as she spotted Nimsah and pushed her way forwards.

Nimsah turned and ran faster, moving into the city of Bengarath. She knew she had to get off the main road and took to one of the twisting alleyways. Not the most direct route to the docks but it would give her the chance to lose Kandilla. She didn't want to lead her back to Jandral – she was meant to be leaving her old life, not bringing it with her.

Nimsah took a series of turns down different darkened alleys and narrow, twisting streets, going from memory, trying not to make it obvious the docks were her destination. The air tore at her lungs and after a while Nimsah had to slow down, slinking into the shadows of a passage between two houses as she peered behind her, trying to see if Kandilla was still on her tail. There was no one – just an old woman carrying washing and a trio of children playing with a brown mongrel dog. Her hair was plastered to her face with sweat and Nimsah pushed the straggling strands aside, trying to work out the best route to the southern quays.

"You think I don't know Bengarath's alleyways as well as you?" Kandilla seized Nimsah from behind, dragging her away from the entrance and pinning her back against the wall. "How dare you run away from me. You belong to me and Farooq, do you understand?"

"You're hurting me," Nimsah cried out, trying to wriggle free of Kandilla's grip. The woman was strong, nails digging into Nimsah's shoulder. She snatched Nimsah's bag and roughly emptied the contents onto the alley's dirty cobbles. The purse with her coppers fell to the ground with a soft clink next to the knife.

Kandilla's eyes met Nimsah's. "What do you need with all this?"

"Get off," Nimsah shouted, shoving Kandilla hard. The woman grunted and pushed back harder, slamming Nimsah's head into the wall.

"You're leaving, aren't you? Where are you going?"

"It's nothing to do with you," Nimsah replied, woozy from where she'd struck her head.

"We. Own. You." Kandilla snarled each word. "You're not going anywhere."

Nimsah's eyes widened as Kandilla pulled out her dagger. She imagined she looked as frightened as Denek Bel-

Haroom had been before Kandilla murdered him in his own ship.

"Farooq's going to miss his little flower," Kandilla told her with a grin. "You've given me the perfect excuse. All he needs to know is you ran away one day, like half the dirty street rats do every year. I even tried to stop you – he'll like that. He thought you were something special – always talking about his plans for you. Like I cared. He was grooming you to replace me and he thought I couldn't see it. What an idiot."

"Then … let me … go," Nimsah gasped, trying to twist out of Kandilla's hold, her fingers so tight they were gripping the bones of her shoulder through her skin. "I'll be gone from the City of Tents and … you can have Farooq … all to yourself."

"I've a better idea," hissed Kandilla, drawing back her dagger.

With a shout Nimsah slammed her head forwards, feeling her skull connect as it smashed Kandilla's nose. The back of Nimsah's head lanced with pain and she dropped to the ground, Kandilla sprawling in a heap next to her. Nimsah blinked, trying to clear her head, hands feeling on the dirty ground for Kandilla's dagger. The woman was groaning and cursing and when Nimsah looked at her she saw Kandilla was still tightly gripping her blade.

"You broke my nose, you little bitch," Kandilla snarled, words thick, as blood ran down her mouth and chin.

Nimsah scrambled backwards, trying to get back onto her feet. She didn't need her bag. She just had to get away from Kandilla and make it to the docks. Angry as she was, even Kandilla wouldn't cross Jandral and the Illesh bankers. She stumbled, legs shaky and weak as she fell. Next to her hand was the knife from her bag. Kandilla saw her looking at the blade and lunged at her with a shout.

Nimsah lashed out with the knife, hearing Kandilla grunt, using her other hand to hold off the dagger being pressed towards her throat. The pair of them wrestled on the ground and Nimsah thought she could hear children shouting nearby. Kandilla managed to get on top of her, the whites of her eyes stark as she strained to bring her dagger down. Nimsah held on to her own knife, aware there was blood on her hand. She almost let go of it when she saw her blade had slid between Kandilla's ribs.

There was a clang and Kandilla dropped her dagger, its point grazing Nimsah's ear as it span away. Kandilla's strength was fading, and when she tried to speak she choked blood out down the front of Nimsah's robes. Unsure what to do, Nimsah held her there, Kandilla pressing down onto her knife. The Zirhidan woman reached out, the tips of her fingers lightly tracing Nimsah's jawline, her eyes wide and disbelieving. With a sigh Kandilla's head lolled forwards and her dead weight settled on top of Nimsah, crushing her into the ground. She lay there for a few moments, gasping for breath, Kandilla's warm blood soaking into her clothes.

"Are you alright?" asked a small boy – one of the children she'd seen playing in the alley.

Nimsah wriggled out from under Kandilla's limp body as a girl, perhaps the boy's older sister, came and pulled him away.

"Don't talk to her. She's a street rat. She's just killed that woman."

"I think the woman was trying to kill her," said another boy.

"I'm alright," Nimsah gasped, staggering to her feet. Her knife was somewhere under Kandilla's body and she had no intention of retrieving it. She had to go. Wiping her hands on her already ruined robes she picked up her bag, hurriedly stuffed her remaining possessions inside and, ignoring the barrage of questions from the children, ran towards the docks.

CHAPTER 36

Summer 213 – Kandarah, Shekh Birizal's Palace

Shekh Birizal ate with his guests on the open air floor of his spire, the sky purpling as the sun neared the western horizon. Food was served without the usual entertainment, the lavish meal now a wake for the fallen, as Birizal fulfilled his duties as host. Birizal sought out Dojan in the mingling throng afterwards, his face sombre and full of contrition. They stood together, admiring the views across the spired city and out into the surrounding countryside.

"Crown Prince Dojan, I can only apologise for what has happened to you," Birizal began, bowing low. "That an attempt on your life should be made within the walls of my own home, the shame is too much to bear."

"You lost men as well, Shekh Birizal," Dojan pointed out. The small man nodded in a way that suggested the deaths of two guards was inconsequential when compared to the discomfort of his guest.

"We will get to the bottom of this, I swear it. I have my suspicions. The Edeen and Abitek may appear to court your favour but they are not to be trusted. Your death would have put the preparations for war into turmoil and perhaps driven a wedge between our great nations."

"Yet you eat with them, as if nothing had happened," observed Khalid a few paces behind, arms folded across his chest.

"What did your man say?" Birizal asked, moustache

twitching.

"I believe the Crown Prince's warrior was noting the strange rules of hospitality and diplomacy at times such as these," interjected Tormindah, loudly enough to speak over Khalid, who was about to repeat his statement. Dojan glared at him.

Birizal frowned. "Yes, it's difficult playing the part of a ruler. I'm always surprised at how many things I find I *cannot* do, no matter how much power and wealth my advisors tell me I have amassed."

"Meaning?" asked Khalid, not wishing to let the matter drop.

"Meaning I cannot simply throw Fasil and Narinda out of my palace based on nothing other than my suspicions. They are the ambassadors of their people and we are on the brink of war. Banishing them would likely see the dragon tribe advance from their position and attack your encampment."

"In which case they would die," Khalid replied flatly.

"As would many of your fellow warriors," Birizal countered. "We're moving into the endgame, young warrior of the spear. You may yet get your chance to prove yourself in battle, although I'm sure your emir would wish to see his army return intact, if possible."

"Agreed," said Dojan, feeling weary. He felt chilled to the marrow, despite the warm evening. "Thank you for your concern, Shekh Birizal. You know you have my support."

"Thank you. Speaking of happier things, your katib improves, I understand."

Dojan smiled. "So I heard when I returned from the funeral. Quizar has spoken to those caring for him, although he's still too weak to leave his bed. I'll need to visit him later this evening."

"I wish him a speedy recovery," Birizal replied as he took his leave.

Dojan turned to Khalid. "You do not offer your opinion unless asked, do you understand? Hadir Al-Nadim would not have spoken out of turn like that. You dishonour the memory of your mubarizun with your behaviour."

For a moment Khalid stared at Dojan, who had to resist the urge to step back for fear his bodyguard would strike him. Instead, Khalid bowed his head. "A thousand apologies, Crown Prince. I am unused to the practice of dining with my enemies whilst admiring the view. I will keep my own counsel in future, I swear."

As Shekh Birizal called for the negotiations to begin Tormindah leaned in close, whispering into Dojan's ear. "A fire to avenge his fallen friends burns hot within young Khalid. Perhaps Mubarizun Yanzin would be better placed to walk at your side until all this is over."

"The Mighty Spears serve to protect the emir and his male line," Dojan replied in a low voice. "The dishonour of stripping Khalid's traditional role from him would only make life more difficult. Better he walks at our side where we can keep an eye on him."

The delegations from each faction took their seats at a round table, surrounded by Birizal's guards. Nimsah sat with Jandral, Narinda had Ramdha of the Black Robes standing watch behind her chair, Fasil alongside her. Pasha Ulan sat at Dojan's right, Tormindah to his left. Also at the table was Khanir Shinva, Yanzin at her back.

Birizal nodded and Khan Lemarr stood up to speak. "This is the final opportunity for us to reach agreement. Fujareen stands ready to fight alongside my soldiers and enforce our claim. I've listened patiently ... *very* patiently, to the arguments put forwards by Fasil and Narinda about their various rights to claim the ancient site. Whatever may have been agreed in the past, it's important to remember that Amuran has changed beyond recognition in the aftermath of the War of the Avatars. The Abitek proudly tell me they were the first to serve the dragon race, while the Edeen claim to have guarded their knowledge for centuries, making them the true heirs to their secrets.

"Good people, none of this matters. The past is gone and we are now building a brighter future for us all. The fact is Kandarans died finding the safe route to the lost city and their sacrifice will not be forgotten. Recognising the ancient ties of the Edeen and Abitek to Amonduras, we reached out in friendship and sought your help to unlock its secrets. Your refusal speaks of a pride rooted in the Naroque of another time – a Naroque that is gone forever."

Fasil held up his hand and interrupted Lemarr's speech. "I'm sorry, I can't listen to this. Did you really say you 'reached out in friendship'? You have brought a hired army to our shores and threatened us with slaughter if we didn't allow you to steal our birthright."

"We are offering to share the spoils with you, in return for your help," Lemarr replied. "Your refusal means no one can profit."

Dojan stood up, drawing everyone's eye. He noticed Narinda was sitting quietly, deep in thought as Fasil glared at those around him. A hush fell over the assembly as they waited for him to speak. Dojan reached down and took a sip of wine, savouring the vintage and calming his nerves. Hadir's absence washed over him once more, like a cold burst of rain increasing the persistent chill gripping his body. Khalid's fierce fervour wasn't an adequate replacement for having Quizar and Hadir at his side. Dojan had never felt more alone.

"What's this?" hissed Ulan, looking up at him.

"I'm doing what I can to prevent bloodshed," Dojan replied. "Fasil. Narinda. Can I appeal to you one more time to reconsider? Please, give me a few moments." Dojan held out his hand and invited them to walk with him.

Shekh Birizal gave a nervous laugh. "Forgive me, Crown Prince. I'm unsure whether this is the time to be conducting private negotiations."

Dojan shook his head. "Please, Shekh Birizal, indulge me as your honoured guest. A few moments with the representatives of the dragon and star tribes may be the difference between war and peace."

Shekh Birizal nodded as he gave his assent, provoking a murmur from the crowd of onlookers, kept at bay by a ring of Kandaran guards. Dojan rose, Tormindah and Ulan at his side and the Mighty Spears flanking them.

"Do you know what you're doing?" muttered Ulan.

"Indulge me as well, brother to be. This won't take long."

Dojan led Fasil and Narinda to the edge of the spire, peering through the mysterious flowing glass, a nervous Ulan following a few steps behind. The sun had set and the sky was darkening, the first few faint stars appearing above them. Quizar would have known which ones, although Dojan did remember from his studies with Vizier Haman that the bright cluster to the east belonged to Altandu, avatar of light. He had deliberately chosen the side of the building that looked out over the Kandaran city wall towards the Fujareen army encampment. In the fading light he could see several units of Tireless Shields sparring and performing other manoeuvres down in the practice yards within their defensive palisade. There must have been at least a thousand of them working in the cooling air, while the rows of barracks told the story of their true numbers.

"What are we looking at?" asked Fasil. "You think this is news? I've watched your army disembark all week long."

"I've seen them fight," Dojan replied. He glanced up at the darkening hills, where the fires of the Abitek camp could be seen.

Fasil followed his gaze. "You underestimate our warriors. This is our homeland and we will not have our birthright plundered by unworthy opportunists."

Dojan held out his hand. "Fasil, I'm going to confess something I've admitted to no one else. When I was attacked I believed I was going to die. I was afraid at first, yet as the fight went on I began to feel something different. I only understood afterwards, reflecting on that day in the privacy of my chambers as night fell. I felt unworthy. The Mighty Spears dedicate their whole lives to the service of Fujareen and they fought with breathtaking skill. Did you know my brother, Saraj, now serves in the regiment? He has qualities I'll never possess. My father seized the crown in battle but, unlike Saraj, I never inherited his courage or mastery of the fighting spear. Hadir knew this – I've trained with him many times. Some would say he was the better man, the man who deserved to live that day."

"Why are you telling me this?" asked Fasil, as Narinda listened quietly. Dojan had half a hope she already understood what he was trying to explain.

"Six Mighty Spears killed four times that number, protecting a prince who has been regarded by many, including my own pasha here, as being something of a joke. I'm not as serious-minded as my youngest brother, Beneth the scholar, or sparkling company like Adina, my sister. I'm not sure why my father sent me here, but I have my suspicions it was to try and show me my own worth. I'd demonstrated little interest in ruling one day in his place, so what would it take to jolt me out of squandering my generous allowance chasing women and entertainment?"

"And your point?" said Fasil, frowning.

"If men like Hadir would die for a man like me, how do you think they will fight for the honour and glory of their emir? They serve Haraq Al-Souk, body and soul, an emir all warriors look up to with respect. They know his reputation stands or falls depending on the outcome of things in Kandarah. They will die rather than giving up an inch of foreign soil and it matters not who opposes them. Tempting as it was to think there was another way, with all our ambitious talk of alternative alliances and uncovering Birizal's secrets, time has run out. This is what I'm here to do – to state what must be obvious to you and Narinda. Your army is outmatched and outnumbered, Fasil. You will lose this war and the only choice is how to respond to Birizal's offer. Amonduras will open its gates to him, whether you're brought there in chains or walk at his side as a free man when they swing wide."

"He's right," Narinda said quietly into the growing darkness. She was still wearing her funeral henna tattoos and the circlet of stars on her brow glowed softly.

Fasil turned to her, outrage written across his face. "You're *listening* to this self-confessed wastrel's speech?"

"No, Fasil, you're *not* listening. The prince is right, we've run out of time and now the only decision we have to make is how many of our people die before we have to make an alliance with Shekh Birizal. Katib Quizar said something to me the other day, words that I've been unable to shake from my mind. He and Dojan have been trying to find a path that will preserve our traditions for the generations to come. I'll not be the elder whose pride meant our people were slaughtered, the knowledge entrusted to us lost forever."

Narinda walked up close to the flowing glass, so clear and transparent Dojan had to resist the urge to reach out and stop her falling. "We've played the game and lost, Fasil. The bankers have forced our hand. If we're to salvage anything from this situation, we must work with Birizal if we're to have a future. That's what I'm going to tell him when I return to the table. Kandarah will have the support of the Edeen and, together, we will open the gates of Amonduras."

Fasil looked shattered. "You'd betray your own cousins?"

"You teach that the Edeen betrayed the Abitek long ago. We tell a different story, that we held true to our promises when the Abitek took the wrong path. I'm trying to prevent you from making another mistake – one that will cost your people dear. Turn aside from war and help us."

Fasil groaned and pressed his head against the glass, as if trying to force himself through into the empty space beyond. "I'll not waste the lives of our people fighting these mercenaries. However, neither will I lift a finger to help Birizal and his allies lay their sullied hands on Amonduras' secrets. If you can live with betraying our heritage, so be it."

Narinda shook her head. "I'm sorry, Fasil. History will remember that your pride today cost your people their birthright." Fasil gave Dojan a baleful glance and stalked away without a word. Narinda sighed, looking exhausted, before leading the way back towards the table where Birizal was waiting.

Ulan stared at Dojan, shaking his head. "How did you know that was going to work?"

Dojan shrugged. "I didn't, but what did we have to lose by trying one last time?"

Pasha Ulan had no answer.

CHAPTER 37

Late Autumn 200 – Aboard the *Sumara* on the Strait of Bezeen

Nimsah was violently sick for the two days they spent at sea, unable to cope with the gently rolling waters of the Strait of Bezeen. Jandral was attentive, making her take little sips of water throughout the day, though he left her on her own most of the time. He could tell Nimsah was in no mood for company. When she slept she had fitful dreams, Kandilla laughing as she chased her down Bengarath's alleyways. They always ended the same way, with Nimsah plunging her knife into Kandilla's heart. Afterwards she would awake with a start, shouting and screaming.

Nimsah had slowly limped to the docks after her fight with Kandilla, head pounding, her hip and both knees sore from where she'd fallen. She must have been confused, because several times she took the wrong route despite knowing every twist and turn in the maze of Bengarath's streets. She began to panic, worried that she would miss the departure of the *Sumara* and be trapped in the city, with Farooq hunting her down. Nimsah wiped a frightened tear from the corner of her eye, took a deep breath and tried to focus on where she was. People in the street were giving her a wide berth, and when she glanced down at her blood-soaked clothes she understood why.

"Come on. *Think*. You've been to the docks hundreds of times. You know the way."

Nimsah reoriented herself, taking her lead by following the defensive outer walls in a wide circuit of the city knowing that, one way or another, this would bring her to the docks. She must have taken the long way, since it took most of the afternoon and, as the sun began to lower, Nimsah felt a stab of panic. After everything she'd been through she was going to miss Jandral. Would he come back for her after his business in Kandarah was done? He might think she'd changed her mind and decided not to come. How much interest would he take in tracking down a street child – would he even bother to find out what had happened to her?

Those thoughts whirled through her mind as she wended her way around Bengarath, fingertips lightly brushing the city walls in case she lost sight of them. She felt dizzy and sick, having to stop every now and again, knowing every delay reduced her chances of leaving the City of Tents behind. Those children had seen Kandilla's body. It was likely the alarm had been raised and the city guard might be looking for her. Nimsah knew she wouldn't be hard to find, covered in blood. Tracing the walls patrolled by the emir's own men no longer seemed like such a good idea, although Nimsah didn't trust her wayward sense of direction enough to leave them.

As she turned a corner Nimsah almost sobbed with relief when she caught sight of the distinctive triangular shape of lateen sails belonging to various dhows and baghlahs at the end of the road. She quickened her pace, unsure of the time and not really wanting to know. Jandral would either be waiting for her or he would not, and there was nothing she could do to change things.

The distant sounds of the market drifted through the air, the docks rich with the scents of salt and fish. Birds called to each other, circling high above, and Nimsah walked to the southern side of the docks, trying to work out if one of the larger ships was the *Sumara*. She blinked her eyes, trying to focus, as a man in long brown robes walked towards her. He removed the veil covering the lower part of his face, revealing

Jandral's handsome features and long black beard.

"You're late, child. I've made the *Sumara's* captain very unhappy, telling him he had to wait."

"I'm sorry," Nimsah replied. "I got lost."

Jandral's eyes flicked up and down, taking in Nimsah's battered appearance and blood-stained clothes. "All that matters is you're here. We need to leave while the tides still favour us, so let's get you aboard."

***

Nimsah felt better, although she was still weak, when they disembarked from the *Sumara*. She bent down, touching the stones making up the docks and stared in wonder at the tall buildings that reached up into the sky. This was the first time she had ever left Bengarath and she might as well have arrived in another world.

Jandral ordered a carriage to bring them to his home. Nimsah watched as his luggage was loaded aboard by the driver. She clutched her bag to her chest, shaking her head when the driver offered to take it. She sat opposite Jandral as the carriage set off, bag perched on her knees. Nimsah looked down at herself, aware she was wearing the same clothes she'd worn when boarding the ship. An unpleasant smell, supplemented by several vomit stains, only served to cement the impression that she was something Jandral had picked up off a refuse heap.

"I need to change," Nimsah told him, blinking back tears as she thought of the red dress screwed up in the bottom of her bag, now missing an arm. Her other outfit (her *only* outfit) would have to do.

Jandral leaned forwards. Perhaps he was used to her smell by now. "I'll have some of my female servants attend to you, don't worry. They'll be able to find you suitable clothes and draw you a bath. The worst is over, Nimsah. This is the start of your new life."

Nimsah tried to take that in, looking out through the windows of the carriage at the soaring buildings. It was like she had arrived in a magical forest, made of metal, stone and glass. She craned her neck, trying unsuccessfully to see the top of the giant buildings. Bengarath seemed small and mean compared with Kandarah.

"You live here?" Nimsah said, trying to take it all in.

Jandral nodded. "I was born here, going into service at the bank when I was eleven years old. Only a few years younger than you are now."

An unwelcome thought intruded into Nimsah's mind. "I don't know exactly how old I am," she admitted. "Will that matter?"

Jandral gave a soft laugh, eyes amused behind his veil. "No, the only important thing in Illesh is ability and loyalty. If it worries you, we can decide how old you are and we'll stick to that story. You told me you've lived in the City of Tents for eleven years, so my guess would be you're about fourteen. When would you like to mark your birthday?"

Nimsah thought about that, realising she'd never celebrated her birthday before. Life with Farooq had been one of existing, taking each day as it came. With Fenara, things might have been different. She closed her eyes, pain lancing through her at the sharp memory.

"I've always thought of myself as a spring child," she said with forced brightness. "Why not the first day of spring?"

Jandral chuckled. "You should have said the first day of the winter season – then you could have had your celebration earlier."

"Good things come to those who wait," Nimsah replied with a smile, inwardly kicking herself.

"Well said. There, that's the first decision you've made concerning your new life. How does it feel?"

"Good," Nimsah said, relaxing a little, although the sway of the carriage was making her nauseous. She was determined not to be ill when she arrived at … wherever Jandral was taking her.

"Is it far?" Nimsah asked.

"The good thing about Kandarah is the city is so small, nothing is very far away. We're almost there."

They rode in silence for a while, passing extravagantly crafted towers one after the other on their journey. After a short while the carriage stopped and, as the driver unloaded Jandral's luggage, Nimsah gawked at the building. The double doors, twice the height of a man, were fashioned from dark metal and decorated with a regular rectangular pattern. They radiated an aura of strength and security, in stark contrast to the lavish wealth splashed across the towers they'd passed on the way. Nimsah looked up, feeling dizzy as she saw the top of the Illesh tower, tapering off in the distance.

"Kandarah is called the City of a Thousand Spires," Jandral said, standing next to her. "This spire belongs to the Bank of Illesh. This is where we conduct much of our business and it's also where those who work for the bank are quartered."

"This is your *home*?" Nimsah asked, only remembering to close her mouth a few moments later.

Jandral nodded. "This is *your* home now, Nimsah. Dozens of floors in this building have been given over to provide chambers for those who belong to our clan. We have a school for those like you whose education we're investing in. You'll share your rooms with some of the other children, so you'll be able to make friends as you continue your studies."

"That's ... good." Nimsah's voice trailed off as she walked up to the building, placing her hand on the ... stonework? Metalwork? She didn't have the words to express what she was seeing.

Up close, the tower had a faint, lustrous hue. It was constructed of dark metal, she was fairly sure of that, although she'd only ever seen steel used so freely in the Bridge of Sorrows. The surface was warm under her fingers, absorbing the sunlight, except where it was reflected back in a tiny scattering of bright flecks that had somehow been cast into the metal.

Nimsah became aware once more of how grubby she

looked, a street urchin pressing her face up close to peer with envy at the wealth and wonders of her betters. She had to suppress a wild urge to run all the way back to where the *Sumara* was moored. Kandarah was so different to Bengarath. She'd expected Jandral to live in a palace, like Fujareen's emir, not some forest of metal.

"Are you alright?" asked Jandral, his voice soft, hand resting gently on her shoulder.

"Yes. No. I think so. I don't know …" Nimsah's words trailed off.

"You haven't eaten properly in two days," Jandral replied. "Let's get you inside, clean you up and fetch you a proper meal. While this all seems strange, you'll soon start to feel at home. This is a special day, Nimsah – more important than your new-found birthday. On this day you become part of something bigger and far older. The concerns of the Bank of Illesh have lasted for millennia. We helped build the old kingdoms of Amuran. We survived the cataclysm and rebuilt from the ashes, finding our new home here in Kandarah."

"Why me?" asked Nimsah in a small voice. "Out of all the people you've met, why pick me and bring me here?"

Jandral looked at her, his expression impossible to read behind his veil. "I saw several things in you, Nimsah. There was intelligence and potential, which would go to waste if you remained at Farooq's side. And besides your quick mind, I saw a fierce hunger and desire to become more than you were. Others saw it too – Kandilla was one. She knew you would be a threat, and she was right."

Nimsah flinched at the mention of Kandilla's name. Jandral steered her towards the door, knocking twice, the sound ringing out like a bell. The doors swung slowly open on silent hinges, revealing a well-lit chamber with high, vaulted ceilings suffused with a golden glow.

"The Bank of Illesh is your new family," Jandral told her. "You're no longer Nimsah, abandoned daughter of no one of the City of Tents. You are Nimsah of the Bank of Illesh. That is the only family name you will ever need."

With his arm wrapped around her shoulders Jandral led her inside, the doors closing silently behind them.

CHAPTER 38

Summer 213 – Kandarah, Shekh Birizal's Palace

Having planned the deployment of the Fujareen army to Kandarah, Khanir Shinva now found herself responsible for organising their swift return to Bengarath. Some of the warriors complained they'd travelled all that way for nothing, their chance to glory in battle stolen. Their officers and the more experienced warriors understood they'd already done their job – their show of strength had been enough to settle matters without needing to draw a sword. This was the best possible result; simple yet effective. Khan Gerber Al-Jalal was remaining behind with two thousand Tireless Shields, there to protect Lemarr and Narinda as they made their journey south towards Amonduras. A sufficient deterrent, should the dragon tribe change their minds.

As Dojan was explaining all this to Quizar it occurred to him that he enjoyed being the one imparting information for a change. Gods, it had happened. He was *interested* in the affairs of state. Quizar was sitting up in bed, head heavily bandaged, and today was the first time he'd been able to talk properly. He was unable to walk, although Birizal's healers assured him he would recover his strength in time. Dojan had insisted they delayed their departure for a few days until he was sure Quizar was well enough to make the sea voyage. The *Jezar* was due back in port in a couple of days' time, at which point Dojan would have to make a decision about whether to return to Bengarath or remain in Kandarah a little longer and give the ship over to Shinva to redeploy more of her troops. While Quizar's condition was a useful excuse, Dojan's main reason for delaying was to see whether the assassin Jandral had captured woke up and was in a condition to be interrogated. As Dojan had suspected, Shekh Birizal's own investigations into the attack turned up nothing.

"Hard to know what to think about that one," Quizar remarked. "If the shekh had a hand in the attempt on your life, of course he's going to tell you all his leads have led nowhere."

"It still seems unlikely Birizal was responsible," Dojan mused.

"Whilst if the Abitek or Edeen paid your assassins, that would be a rather inconvenient thing to discover, days after brokering a truce."

Dojan shrugged, already resigned to this being a dead end. "He'll tell us nothing."

"A warning from Nimsah? Remember what she said to you on the day the Fujareen army landed."

Dojan didn't want to discuss that possibility, not least because the implication was his father's newest and most powerful allies had tried to have him killed. It also meant the captured assassin was nothing more than a ruse. He smiled, remembering his conversation with Tormindah. There was a way to uncover the truth about such things – the question was what to do if Quizar's suspicions were right. Confronting Jandral and Nimsah wasn't an appealing prospect. Dojan sighed, getting up from his seat and taking a walk around Quizar's chambers. The same circular debates, the same list of suspects and same brick walls when they tried to solve the mystery. There was too much they didn't know, making it impossible to solve this puzzle.

"You don't have to stay here all day. I know it's boring," said Quizar.

Dojan turned to his katib. "After everything that's happened, I want to be here. Who else can I trust – besides Khalid, who watches me closer than my shadow, and

Tormindah, who holds the keys to my own mind? Better to spend time in your company than the snakes we've met in Kandarah."

"They outmanoeuvred us, that's for sure," noted Quizar. "Remember all our grand plans to try and seize this opportunity for ourselves? Hah – *that* came to nothing."

Dojan gave a bitter laugh. "Well, perhaps this is all a squabble over nothing. Lemarr hasn't set foot inside Amonduras yet. It could be that when Narinda opens the gates for him, all they'll find are ruins and ashes."

"In which case, all the better we didn't have to wage war on the Abitek. From what Tormindah and Ulan told me, you did an amazing job persuading Narinda to help, forcing Fasil to back down. Your father's going to be very proud of you."

"I have my uses," Dojan agreed with a wide smile, taken aback at how much his friend's good opinion mattered. "Do you know what Narinda told me? It was actually something you said, on the day we went to the Edeen embassy. Your comment about the importance of preserving their traditions for the centuries to come ..."

There was a knock at the door and Khalid stepped inside, apologising for the intrusion.

"Fasil of the Abitek wishes to speak with you," the young warrior announced.

Dojan made his excuses and with Tormindah, Khalid and his Mighty Spears he made his way to the terrace. Fasil was sitting in a comfortable chair, talking to Ulan and Arak. The tribesman rose and offered Dojan a cursory bow as he walked into the afternoon heat. Although the area was shaded it was oppressively hot outside, the air heavy and still.

"Crown Prince, please forgive me for imposing on your hospitality."

"Some tea is a small price to pay for the pleasure of your company," Dojan replied, taking a seat and waving a servant forward to pour him a cup.

"I was just telling Fasil that he made the right decision,"

Pasha Ulan said with a satisfied smile.

"Most sensible," Arak agreed. Dojan again found himself wondering how hard the Veiled Magus had really worked to try and uncover Lemarr's secrets. All academic now, of course.

"It's good to know such wise men approve of my actions," Fasil replied. "In the end, gentlemen, you won. I hope you enjoy the spoils of your victory here in Naroque."

"We were asked to support our allies and came to their aid," Ulan told him. "It's a pity you didn't take the opportunity to work with us, Fasil. You might have come away from this venture with something for all your troubles."

"And what have you got for yours, Pasha Ulan?"

Ulan frowned, confused by the question. "The Bank of Illesh is a powerful backer. Their coffers will help make Fujareen the greatest of the four emirates. In time, you'll hear that our emir has risen and united the emirates for the first time since the War of the Avatars. He'll no longer be the Emir of Fujareen. He'll be the Emir of Murtak."

Fasil gave Ulan a knowing smile, eyes clever and calculating. "I hope this venture gives you everything you deserve. Now, my friends, I wonder if I could have a moment in private with your prince? There are some things I wish to say to him before I leave Kandarah later this afternoon and re-join my tribe."

"I would prefer to stay," said Tormindah, eyeing the Sight user as Arak exchanged a glance with Ulan.

Fasil smiled at her. "You can ward your prince's mind as effectively from the other side of the door to the terrace as you can here. I promise, I'll make no use of my powers. I don't need the Sight to speak my mind."

"The Mighty Spears will remain at the side of the Crown Prince," Khalid told him, hand on his spear. "I will not leave the Fujareen prince unguarded, when an attempt was made on his life only days ago in this very building."

Dojan looked up at Tormindah. "It'll be fine – I'd like to

speak to Fasil alone. Khalid ..."

"I will not leave your side, Crown Prince. Please do not ask me again."

Dojan turned to Fasil as Tormindah, Arak and Ulan left the terrace. "You can speak freely before the Mighty Spears. I wouldn't want to place Khalid in a position where he felt he was neglecting his duty – he and his men all feel the loss of Hadir keenly." Dojan hesitated, an unexpected lump in his throat and the sound of clashing steel in his ears. He coughed to disguise the pause, wondering if Fasil had spotted the tremor in his voice.

"As you wish," replied Fasil, giving Khalid a respectful nod as the six Mighty Spears stepped away, forming a ring around the pair of them.

"So, what is it you wished to tell me?" asked Dojan, taking a sip of tea and admiring the view of Kandarah, its many spires glittering in the sunshine.

The wiry man twisted in his seat to look directly at Dojan. "When I consulted with the other elders of my tribe before coming to Kandarah they gave me two pieces of advice. The first was on no account to trust anything Shekh Birizal said. The man is an empty vassal of Illesh, Kandarah a monument to their avarice and greed as they build their towers, reaching up towards the stars. The second was they would rather surrender any claim to Amonduras, than endure being in debt to the Bank of Illesh. Thanks to you, Narinda has made a terrible mistake, thinking that Birizal and, by extension, Jandral and the rest of the Illesh banking clan, will share any of the spoils with the Edeen. Once their part has been played, Birizal will follow his orders and find a way to cast them aside."

"Why should I trust anything *you're* telling me?" Dojan asked. "You're aggrieved at the outcome of the negotiations. You had the chance of working with Birizal. This could all be some ruse to try and sow discord between the allies of my country."

"I'm talking to you because, against all my expectations, I found you were unsullied by politics. I knew from the moment I met you that your father had sent you here for the experience and to raise your status back in Fujareen. You soon worked out you had no real part to play – this wasn't diplomacy, it was the endgame. What I thought was interesting was this meant you came here with a fresh perspective and no preconceptions. Narinda and I dangled the prospect of a direct alliance and we were amazed to find you actually considering the possibility. Who knows, perhaps if you had come here a few months ago, things might have turned out differently."

"Too late now."

Fasil leaned in closer, dropping his voice. "Dojan, someone tried to kill you. Have you thought about who would be so determined to see you out of the way that they would pay two dozen assassins to carry out the task?"

"Some would argue you had the greatest motive."

Fasil gave a nonchalant shrug, as if being accused of murder was commonplace. "We'd gain nothing from your death – your army was already here. If we were responsible, it would only serve to increase the chances of war as your father took his revenge. I swear on the ancient rites of the dragon we had no part in this."

"So you say."

"Just so," replied Fasil with a nod. "Ask yourself this, Dojan. Who *does* stand to gain from your death?"

"There are a number of possibilities. I promise you, Fasil, I will get to the bottom of this."

Fasil sat back in his chair, looking thoughtful. "I hope you find the truth you're looking for. However, I'd be careful who I shared that knowledge with. Your father's advisors have led him into a bad bargain, young prince. Illesh has no interest in re-building the mighty Emirate of Murtak when their seat of power lies across the sea in Naroque. They'll bleed your emirate dry, and when your father realises what he's done it will be too late. You will never escape their grasp."

Dojan thought of the prisoner, held somewhere by Jandral. Was Fasil right and it was all misdirection? The Bank of Illesh trying to do away with the wayward prince who hadn't followed his instructions?

"They're only bankers," said Dojan, trying to inject some conviction into his voice. "We're talking about business, here, Fasil, not some grand conspiracy."

"We're talking about the men who secretly financed Morvanos' warmongering."

"Murtak fought for Morvanos in the War of the Avatars. If anything, that means our histories are closely entwined."

"Believe me, I've not forgotten," Fasil replied with a wry grin. "Murtak swallowed base lies that led the emirate into a war believing it had to defend itself against people who meant them no harm whatsoever. Morvanos was determined to destroy the dragon race and by the time the war was over, he'd succeeded, even though the price was his banishment to the Void."

"Why are you telling me this? What is it you want?"

Fasil rose from his seat and offered Dojan a low bow as he took his leave. "Crown Prince, you have a good heart. You wanted to prevent war, which I reluctantly had to accept was the right thing to do. Let me offer you some advice before you return to Fujareen. Your new friends, Jandral and Nimsah, are not to be trusted. Have a care, for their concerns rest only with their own self-interest. If they come into conflict with those of Fujareen, you will find their promises worthless."

Dojan sat for a time on the terrace after Fasil had gone, thinking about his words. The Abitek had fought and died, siding with the Avatars of Tyranny during the War. It was no surprise, even after two centuries, that someone like Fasil should hate those who'd fought against his people. Still, his words of warning wormed their way into Dojan's mind.

Dojan leaned out over the glass terrace, looking out over the splendour of Kandarah. It didn't matter what Fasil thought. His dalliance with acting the rebel was over. It was time to be the dutiful son, return to Fujareen and collect the plaudits due for his service.

CHAPTER 39

Spring 211 – Kandarah, the Bank of Illesh Spire

Nimsah enjoyed the cool morning breeze on her face, the air fresh and clean after last night's rainfall. The topmost level of the Illesh spire in Kandarah had been given over to a garden and Nimsah enjoyed spending time here amongst the carefully tended palms, ferns and flowers, which were starting to bloom. She disturbed a small flock of finches as she passed by, the startled birds flitting away in a riot of red and gold as they found somewhere safe to perch nearby.

Jandral was waiting for her on a stone bench under a tall palm, dressed in plain black robes. The last decade had been kind to him, his handsome features still firm and sharp, although his black beard was now streaked through with grey. Those dark, intelligent eyes were still the same. Nimsah always felt there was nowhere to hide when he fixed his gaze on her. Both were unveiled, since there was no need to cover their faces whilst they met together alone. The head gardener was the only other person in sight, watering a raised bed of bright yellow flowers some distance away.

"What a wonderful morning," said Jandral, smiling as she approached.

"It's been too long," Nimsah told him, taking Jandral's hand for a moment and giving it a gentle squeeze as she sat next to him.

"This is always my favourite time of the day. Up here at this time of the morning it's as if the world belongs to me alone. I do my best thinking straight after breaking my fast."

"After that it's all downhill?" Nimsah teased.

Jandral arched an eyebrow. "Remind me again why I saved you from poverty. I asked you here this morning because I've a new task for you, one that involves travel."

Nimsah felt a thrill of excitement at those words. In the past five years, since finishing her schooling, she had journeyed far and wide on business for the Bank of Illesh. At first she accompanied Jandral as his assistant, understanding for the first time the true scale of Illesh's dealings across Amuran. She'd been to all four emirates and the three Kingdoms of Kalat, as well as every port and city state in Naroque. Jandral had also taken her on several voyages north across the open ocean. There she'd been to Port Eledar in Oomrhat, the Lagashan city of Brear on the dark borders of Sommel Forest and the great port of Medan in Beria, sailing by the giant white cliffs of the Medan Spur. Nimsah also knew Jandral had business in the closed Kingdom of Sunis, although so far, despite her gentle pestering, she'd not managed to convince him to bring her along.

More recently, Jandral had trusted her to manage various affairs on her own. Nimsah had spent a year in the court of Emira Ledana in the Emirate of Amjahran, laying the foundations for a closer working partnership now the state had stabilised following the turmoil of the coup that deposed Emir Cassim. She'd also lived in the city state of Shalanar, one of the most beautiful and wealthy ports in southern Naroque, where the Halak tribe held power. Nimsah had enjoyed her independence, often walking the soft sandy beaches at dawn, admiring the crystal clear waters of the Karnac Strait. Her posting had led her to spend another year in the Kingdom of Hamda, where she'd personally negotiated on behalf of Illesh with Amisidana, their sultanah. Nimsah noticed Jandral often used her to work with the female leaders of Samarakand.

"Several things have to be put in place before I send you to your next posting," Jandral explained. "However, I wanted you to have time to prepare yourself for this next journey. It will involve a return to Fujareen, to the court of Emir Haraq Al-Souk."

Despite all of her travels across Samarakand, Jandral carefully avoided bringing her back to Bengarath. The last time she'd set foot on Fujareen soil had been two years ago, during an overnight stopover in the coastal town of Jalar on her way to the Emirate of Zirhidan. His words stirred memories of her visits to the palace all those years ago. Dojan's lonely face swam before her mind's eye, his craving for company the reason Fenara died. She closed her eyes, remembering that day in the City of Tents. Fenara's head hitting the stones … Kandilla drawing her dagger …

Jandral guessed at what she was thinking. "In time, we all have to face the ghosts of our past. I know you're ready for this."

Nimsah took a deep breath. "What do you need me to do?"

"I want you to begin drafting the terms of a contract, one which will be negotiated in secret, working personally with the emir and his vizier. We need access to the Fujareen army."

"Whatever for?" Nimsah asked.

"Kandarah's position in Naroque may become … unstable later this year. We're financing Shekh Birizal to undertake another expedition to reach Amonduras."

"Surely that will only end in failure. Only a fool tries to cross the Shimmering Way."

Jandral gave her a knowing look. "This time, I think we have a chance of succeeding. You recall we have Arak Bel-Yangash of the Veiled Magi of Fujareen secretly in our employ? We've financed his studies for many years and he has fashioned a magical device that can be used to safely navigate those poisonous forests. If he's right, our investment will have paid off handsomely."

"*If* he's right," Nimsah accentuated the word. "That will

place Kandarah in the middle of a dispute with the Abitek and Edeen tribes. They won't stand by and allow us to claim their ancient city."

"If they were so bothered, they would have crossed the Shimmering Way themselves," said Jandral with a shrug. "However, you're right. They may even try and stop the expedition, which is why it must leave in secret, tomorrow at dawn. Birizal has chosen Khan Lemarr to lead them."

"And if they're successful you want Fujareen to commit their army to defend Kandarah, should the Abitek and Edeen declare war on us. Are you sure this is wise?"

"The Council believes so," Jandral answered, as if that explained everything. "Naroque was built on the knowledge of the dragon race, and so much has been lost following the War. If anything has survived in Amonduras, we'll be in a position to lay claim to it."

"Previous expeditions have ended in disaster and financial ruin for their investors. You really think Arak's device will enable this attempt to succeed?"

Jandral nodded. "That fool Birizal thinks we'll use that knowledge to light his spires and fire his forges," he said with open contempt. "*Another* metal spire in a city that already boasts a thousand, probably named after him because his palace isn't enough. What's the point? I swear, that man is compensating for his diminutive stature and if we don't rein him in he'll bankrupt the city."

"And what are the Council's plans?"

Jandral hesitated and, to her surprise, Nimsah saw he was actually considering telling her. "Your time will come, Nimsah," he said finally. She set aside her disappointment, knowing it was dangerous to push Jandral too far – the man had a temper when roused.

Instead she bowed her head in deference. "I understand. What do you wish this agreement to contain?"

Nimsah gasped in surprise as Jandral outlined Illesh's proposed terms. The amounts of money being talked about were of a scale many *countries* would struggle to raise. If the emir of Fujareen set his seal on this contract, the emirate would as good as belong to Illesh. Nimsah thought of the privileged old families who supported Haraq Al-Souk in power, remembering Khanir Shinva Bel-Kamil. The khanir had treated Nimsah as if she was nothing. Now, with the backing of Illesh, Nimsah would own the Fujareen army. A fleeting smile crept across her face at the thought of giving Khanir Shinva orders. Nimsah paused, realising it wasn't enough. No one had paid the price for Fenara's death. The fate of a widowed basket weaver was of no concern to the ruling families like Bel-Kamil.

"Nimsah, are you listening?"

Nimsah was startled from her thoughts by Jandral's question, mollifying him by recounting word for word what he had just been saying. The older man smiled, dark eyes twinkling.

"There's something on your mind, isn't there? This is why I've delayed sending you back to Bengarath until now. What have I told you before?"

"We serve the Bank of Illesh," Nimsah recited from memory. "Our clan is older and more enduring than the short-live dynasties of the emirs, shekhs and sultans of Samarakand. We built the empires of old, advised their kings and queens and guarded the knowledge of the avatars."

"Knowledge is prized more highly than gold by the Bank of Illesh," Jandral replied. "You're part of something older and greater than the affairs of emirs, so where is your focus? Are you going to serve me and the Council well, or should I worry that you'll become distracted from your purpose in Fujareen?"

"My purpose is clear," Nimsah told him. "I won't fail you, Jandral."

"This isn't about pleasing me. This is about service to the Illesh clan – we're your family, Nimsah. You owe us your first loyalty and this is an important test, one the Council will be watching closely. I know you were wronged by Khanir

Shinva. However, I need you to set that aside for the good of your real family – the only family you'll ever need."

"Illesh has my undivided loyalty," she told him, taking his hand in hers. "What's in the past stays in the past."

Her answer satisfied Jandral, although afterwards Nimsah found herself unable to concentrate. She left the Illesh spire that evening, wandering Kandarah's streets, her veil enough to ward off any unwelcome attention. No one in Kandarah was foolish enough to cross a member of the banking clans. Nimsah knew she had been chosen deliberately for this mission. Although she wondered if Jandral was responsible, the way he had spoken made her think this was more likely an idea from the Council itself. Her performance would reflect on him, and she didn't want to let him down.

Khanir Shinva Bel-Kamil of the Blessed Swords, sworn to protect the high princess and her female line. Shinva held one of the most coveted positions in the Fujareen army. Andrals were normally selected from the khans who commanded the Blessed Swords or Mighty Spears, so when Andral Illana Bel-Jedesh stepped aside Shinva would have to opportunity to reach the absolute pinnacle of her military career. Fenara's death had been quietly swept away, ensuring Shinva's reputation was untarnished, a messy obstacle to her final promotion removed. Nimsah doubted that after all this time Shinva would even recognise her as the girl she'd left weeping over Fenara's body.

The towers of Kandarah glowed with soft light as the sun set in the western sky. A rowdy group of young Culah men passed on the other side of the street, laughing and singing, without a care in the world. Nimsah bowed her head and walked on, unseen. Jandral had understood how difficult this would be for her – knowing her better than she did herself. She thought she'd put things behind her, building a new life and accomplishing far more than she could ever have imagined when Jandral offered her passage across the Strait of Bezeen. Now she'd learned that, deep inside, part of her was still the young girl from the City of Tents.

Nimsah set her face, eyes narrowing as she walked with renewed purpose. Jandral was right. She would have to set these things aside to succeed and perhaps, one day, take one of those coveted seats on the Illesh Council. This was an opportunity to cement her position in Fujareen as the representative of Illesh in Emir Haraq's court. And if that happened to place her in a position where she could influence the ultimate fate of Khanir Shinva? Nimsah smiled behind her veil. Well, that would be a day when she could reap the rewards of her hard work and loyalty. She could hear the Culah tribesmen singing in the distance, woefully out of tune. Nimsah headed away from them, walking on through the darkening streets of Kandarah, wrapped in her thoughts.

CHAPTER 40

Summer 213 – Kandarah Slums

Dojan rode in silence in Jandral's carriage, his insides squirming, as he sat next to Tormindah and Khalid. He'd tried to engage Jandral in small talk to pass the time as their carriage rolled through the Kandaran streets, only for his words to fall flat and dead between them. Whilst the banker was unfailingly polite as usual, he looked particularly preoccupied as they headed into the night.

Their destination was a mean, low building crouching against the city walls. The edges of its sandstone blocks had been weathered round by wind and rain, mortar washed away to leave the walls crumbling, the faded blue paint on the door peeling away to reveal the grey grain of the wood underneath.

"In here?" Khalid asked, eyeing the doorway and glancing up and down the deserted streets.

Dojan hadn't realised that Kandarah had a poor quarter, although reflecting on it now it was obvious that there would be winners and losers in every society. These slums lay in the shadow of the illuminated spires, glittering in the night, elegant steel and glass reaching up into the starlit sky. Two different worlds, rubbing shoulder to shoulder yet entirely separate from one another.

Without a word Jandral knocked on the door and Dojan heard the sound of three bolts sliding back before it swung open. A veiled man ushered them inside, bowing low to Jandral. Khalid went in next with two Mighty Spears, three more watching Dojan's back as they crowded into a small room, the only features being a rickety wooden chair and some stairs descending from the far corner.

"Wait here," Khalid told two of his men as Dojan peered down a steep staircase that took them deep under the city walls.

"That won't be necessary," said Jandral.

"Wait here," Khalid repeated, before taking the lead down the stairs.

"He doesn't like this, does he?" muttered Tormindah.

"I'm not sure I do either," Dojan replied, ducking his head to avoid the low ceiling as he followed Khalid with the rest of his bodyguards.

The stairs were sparsely lit with more of those strange flameless torches set into the walls, their footsteps echoing in the crowded space. One of them flickered, buzzing as it alternated from light to dark. Even Kandaran magic wasn't perfect out here in the poor quarter.

"Have you spoken to him yourself?" Dojan asked Jandral.

The banker shook his head. "No, although one of my inquisitors has explained to our friend how much we would value his complete cooperation. So far, he has only divulged his first name. Canzar. That's all we know."

"I'm in your debt."

"Not at all," said Jandral. "On the contrary, you're only here on account of my business arrangement with your father. I'm in your debt after placing you in danger. If someone is working against us it is beholden on me to discover the truth."

"Before we start, I have a favour to ask."

"Name it."

"Tormindah has great skill with the Sight. If this man proves to be susceptible to her gifts I would like her to attempt to unlock his secrets. Every day I linger here draws more attention and questions as to why I've not already returned to Bengarath. Tormindah could save us all a great deal of time."

Jandral thought for a moment before giving a curt nod of agreement, his only condition being that Dojan and Tormindah shared anything they discovered with the Bank of Illesh and no one else. The end of the stairs led into a cold windowless gaol. There were six cells set into the walls, their spaces divided up by black iron bars, so it was possible for the gaoler to view what was happening in all of them. Only one of these was occupied. The gaoler grovelled at Jandral's feet – visitors were clearly a novelty.

Dojan walked forward with Khalid and Tormindah and stared through the bars of the cell. The man inside, presumably Canzar, looked thin and weak, staring up at them with hollow eyes. Dojan tried to recall if he'd seen him before. The fight on the white marble staircase was a blur and all he could think of was Hadir slumped against the wall, dying in a pool of his own blood. As Dojan's face hardened Canzar shrank back, pressing himself into a corner of the stone cell. He was heavily bandaged around his chest and one of his hands. His dirty legs and feet were bare and covered in bruises.

"Do you need to go inside?" Jandral asked Tormindah.

"It's better if I can be close to him," she replied, waiting as the gaoler fumbled to find the right key to open the door.

"This may not work," she said to Dojan as they entered the cell. "He may not be susceptible to the Sight and I may not be able to bring you with me, even if I can work with him."

"I want to see what you see," Dojan replied. "You told me this was possible."

"*Possible*," Tormindah emphasised the word. "Please remember, Crown Prince, that whilst you can be reached with the Sight that doesn't mean you have enough ability for me to draw you along the Path. I will take you with me if I can."

"If any harm comes to him …" growled Khalid.

"It won't," Tormindah assured the warrior.

Inside the cell, Dojan looked down at the wretched man as Tormindah sat on a low stool and indicated that Dojan should do the same. The prisoner stared at them, confused and frightened.

"You remember who this is?" asked Khalid. "This is the Crown Prince of Fujareen. You and your accomplices failed and died for nothing, do you understand? When this is over –"

The cell spun and vanished, replaced by a brightly lit and well-appointed room. Through the windows Dojan was shocked to see they looked out over the Bridge of Sorrows in Bengarath. Tormindah stood next to him and there was a group of four men sat around a low table. Dojan felt a jolt as he recognised the leader of the men who had attacked him – the older grey-bearded man with a lined face.

"I …" Dojan felt sick and had to take hold of Tormindah's arm.

"It's alright, you're with me. Nothing can happen if you're with me."

"That man …" Dojan took a breath. "That man's dead. I saw Hadir kill him."

"Yes, he's dead. We're walking through memories," Tormindah explained.

"Can they see us?"

"No. We're observing Canzar's past. We're here and yet we're not – you can't interfere in whatever's about to happen."

"Tormindah, this is Bengarath."

"I know – watch and listen."

Dojan frowned, trying to take in more details. He recognised another of the men from the scar that stretched from his eye down to his jaw, leaving a pale river of silvery skin that ran through the stubble of his beard. The other two didn't seem familiar, although after a moment Dojan saw that one of them was the prisoner. His face was fuller, beard neatly trimmed and clean and he stood up as they waited at the table, pacing with nervous energy over to the window.

"How much longer? This man insults us."

"He pays well, Canzar," the grey-bearded man answered. "You can wait patiently or you can leave and I'll find someone else to take your place."

Canzar scowled and looked out of the window. "What are we doing here?"

"Following orders," the older man replied.

"I follow the orders of my mubarizun and khan."

"These orders come from far higher than that."

"Indeed they do," Pasha Ulan announced as he swept into the room, smiling as the men stood and bowed.

"Pasha," said the group's leader.

"Nassar Al-Halaan, doughty member of the Tireless Shields, I assume?" said Ulan, clasping the man's outstretched hand in both of his.

"The same," the warrior replied.

"It's good to meet you and your men," Ulan told him, taking a seat across the table. "I only wish the circumstances were happier. This task I'm going to give you is … unpleasant. If there was another way, I would gladly take it."

Nassar nodded as the four men sat down at the table. "This isn't the first time the Emirate of Fujareen has called upon us to do what's necessary. Someone must be willing to do the inglorious tasks for the greater good of all."

"This time is different," Ulan explained. "This is a matter concerning the old families and securing the line of succession. What I'm about to tell you would be considered treason, yet it must be done for the honour of the Bel-Doshok dynasty. Before I say more, you must swear your unswerving loyalty to the Bel-Doshok house."

Canzar exchanged a look with Nassar, looking uncomfortable. Nassar leaned forwards across the table, speaking in a low voice. "I swear it. Go on."

"There are questions concerning our current emir, which have delayed negotiations with the Bel-Doshok dynasty for years. It's no secret Haraq Al-Souk wants admission to his wife's dynasty of Bel-Doshok. However, whilst our noble emir was a perfect leader during a time of war, he is considered less able when conducting himself in the diplomacy of peacetime. Haraq relies heavily on his vizier and the family name of his wife to hold Fujareen together, and the old families have always been suspicious of … Forgive me, there is no delicate way to put this. A *commoner,* who rose up and defied the old order, killing one of their own. Then there is the delicate matter of succession. Crown Prince Dojan is a pleasant young man, but his feckless nature and lack of serious-minded attention to his position is a cause for concern for his mother and the Bel-Doshok dynasty."

"What are you asking us to do?" said Nassar.

"The Bel-Doshok family would prefer to see Adina, the princess' daughter, succeed her father. Clearly, this means Dojan has to be … removed from the equation."

Nassar stared at Ulan. "You're asking us to murder one of our own, a member of the royal family. This isn't the way of the Tireless Shields. After listening to your words I should take my spear and plunge it straight into your heart, pasha or not."

Ulan's face was sombre. "Yet here we sit, and you have not so much as reached for your weapons. I know why. Nassar, you fought in the war between Haraq Al-Souk and Emir Godan Bel-Deem, fighting to protect the crown. Whilst Haraq may have offered the hand of peace and reconciliation in the aftermath of the struggle, have you or the other men loyal to Emir Godan ever seen promotion?"

"Being a warrior of the Tireless Shields is reward enough."

"Pah," Ulan scoffed. "If it was, you wouldn't seek out work as the emirate's paid assassins."

Nassar's face hardened. "I prefer to describe us as a group who deal with the emirate's enemies. Permanently."

"I meant no offence," Ulan replied, holding up a placating hand. "Think instead on this. If we do not stabilise the line of succession, the simmering resentment following Godan's death will break out once more. Dojan isn't strong enough to lead Fujareen and we risk plunging into another civil war, pitting the old families against one another. That cannot be allowed to happen. This is an uncomfortable truth, one I have the heavy duty of dealing with, for the good of Fujareen."

"This … this is different …" Nassar's voice trailed off.

"Do you know what happened when Godan died?" asked Ulan. "Godan *surrendered* to Haraq that day when the palace was stormed. Godan willingly offered up his crown to spare his people more bloodshed and horror. As a member of the old dynasty Haraq should have allowed him to leave Bengarath and go into exile. Instead? Haraq ordered Illana to execute Godan right there in the throne room, as the emir knelt before him, pleading for mercy. He rewarded Illana for the dishonourable murder of the emir by making her andral of the Fujareen army. You see, there's a weakness running through Haraq's line. His eldest son is modelled on his father, whilst the daughter takes after the older, nobler ways of Bel-Doshok. This is what we're dealing with, my friend."

Dojan watched as Nassar's knuckles whitened as he clasped his hands together under his chin, listening to Ulan's words. How could Ulan possibly know about Godan's death? His father had only confided that secret to Dojan in his private study all those years ago and, feckless as he might be, Dojan had never uttered a word of it to anyone. Regardless, he saw Ulan's clever words had swayed Nassar and the two men were now talking about how, rather than whether, the deed should be done.

"The high princess has arranged for her eldest son to join the delegation to Kandarah, making her husband think it was his own idea. The crown prince will only be protected by a small retinue of guards, with the Blessed Swords loyal, of course, to High Princess Tanah Bel-Doshok. When the time comes, you will find the prince relatively unprotected."

"The prince is guarded by the Mighty Spears," Canzar pointed out, drawing a scowl from Nassar. "Hadir Al-Nadim watches over him constantly, a man they talk about as being a future khan and andral."

"Then take enough men to do the job," hissed Ulan. "No

matter how good a warrior Hadir might be, he's only a man. He can be killed like any other."

"As can we," Canzar replied.

"You want to go to war and die in Kandarah instead?" Nassar asked Canzar. "You think Khan Gerber Al-Jalal will care if you're killed fighting in Naroque? There are ten thousand Tireless Shields and Pasha Ulan is right. Our chance to become mubarizun or khan has long gone."

Ulan gave the older man a knowing smile. "*Exactly*. This way, you will be serving your country and gaining the recognition you deserve. If you perform this task as required the money you make will be enough to retire from the army, buy a house or plot of land and live out your days with your families, knowing you secured their future as well as that of Fujareen."

"How will we get to Kandarah?" asked the scarred warrior next to Canzar.

Ulan smiled. "In a few weeks' time we'll be sending most of the army across the sea to Naroque. I can add your names to the manifest and ensure that the quartermaster knows your orders will take you directly into the city, rather than the army camp. After that, we'll find you lodgings and you will await my instructions. Word will be sent to you when there's an opportune time to strike at the prince. You need to move quickly, gathering enough men loyal to you who can be trusted to do what's required when the time comes ..."

Dojan took a deep breath, leaning on the wall, sweat running down his face. Tormindah ignored royal decorum, face full of concern as she wrapped an arm around his shoulders. Blood pounded in Dojan's skull, his vision misting and moments later he was back in that dank cell, Canzar staring at the pair of them, looking confused. Dojan staggered out of the cell, vomiting against the wall as Khalid ran towards him, shouting out with alarm.

CHAPTER 41

Summer 213 – Kandarah, Shekh Birizal's Palace

Nimsah sat listening with a combination of fascination and horror as Dojan told her what he'd learned as they sat in her private chamber on the penultimate floor of Shekh Birizal's spire. Khalid stood outside – not even he was being trusted with the truth behind the attempt on Dojan's life. Jandral's bargain with Dojan, in return for giving him access to their prisoner, meant that he was compelled to bring what he had learned to the Bank of Illesh, and them alone. Dojan had chosen to confide in Nimsah rather than Jandral, which was not entirely unexpected. However, Nimsah had never for a moment imagined the secret Tormindah uncovered would place the blame for the plot on those closest to the prince. She had removed her veil the better to empathise with Dojan's plight, suppressing a smile as she realised the young prince had made his choice and now belonged to the Bank of Illesh.

"How is this possible?" Dojan was saying. "She's my *mother*, Nimsah. My own mother ordered me killed and even devised the means to make it possible. My own mother."

Nimsah reflected that the ways of the emirs and their court wasn't so different to life in the City of Tents. Farooq had never shied away from killing anyone who challenged him or stood in his way. However, even she had to admit that Her Royal Highness Princess Tanah Bel-Doshok had displayed a shocking level of ruthlessness in trying to manipulate the line of succession.

"This is a hard truth," Nimsah told him, placing her hand gently over his, the tea on the table that separated them ignored and growing cold. "You know dynasty comes before family. Your father has long craved his elevation to become one of the Bel-Doshok, rather than merely Godan's usurper. What he failed to understand is that he challenged the old ways when he killed Godan, and the ancient dynasties never forgot the Bel-Deem line was extinguished on his orders. Haraq thinks the money from Illesh's coffers will buy his admission into the dynasty of Bel-Doshok. Money is not enough, and your mother's voice is powerful here. She is part of the dynasty and your father is not, so her ancient family will listen to her when it comes to deciding who should be admitted and when."

Dojan was shaking his head. "Ulan and I are as good as family. We've never been particularly close but I never doubted his loyalty for a moment. Adina couldn't have known about this. She's so free spirited. I always thought the two of us had more in common than I do with Saraj or Beneth."

"Adina is betrothed to Pasha Ulan," Nimsah pointed out. "He wouldn't have done this without her knowledge. No marriage can bear the weight of such a secret. Tanah would have ensured her daughter was ready and willing to accept the responsibilities of becoming emira before putting all of this in motion. Adina would have been presented to the elders of Bel-Doshok and she would have made her case to them that she was worthy of becoming part of their dynasty. I'm sorry, Dojan. I fear your sister's outward demeanour is part of an act, and she is closer in character to Ulan than you would like to believe."

Dojan put his face in his hands and wept. To give him some privacy, Nimsah left the table and walked to the window of her chamber, which opened out on to a balcony that offered one of the best views in Kandarah. There was the bay, blue waters smooth and still on this hot summer day. The *Jezar* lay moored at the dockside, ready to take Dojan back to

Bengarath, and when he left Nimsah would accompany him. Jandral had told her last week she was ready to take his place as Illesh's representative in Fujareen. Whilst it was a great honour she now understood the challenge that faced her. If this wasn't handled in the right way there was a danger that Fujareen would be torn apart by civil war and all Jandral's years of planning and the eye-watering investment of Illesh would be wasted. There was always the Emirate of Amjahran, where Illesh also held sway. However, to improve Amjahran's fortunes to the point where it rivalled Fujareen's power would take another decade. Nimsah didn't want to be the person who squandered the opportunity of consolidating Illesh's investment in Fujareen, and for the first time she wondered at Jandral's real motives for her promotion.

"I'm sorry," Dojan was saying. "This is so ... unbecoming. Crying in front of you. How embarrassing."

Nimsah sat down again and took his hand once more. "Crown Prince. Dojan. Listen to me. You've done nothing wrong, and anyone would be shaken to the core by learning something as terrible as this."

"They were never going to admit him," Dojan said, his voice thick. "The Bel-Doshok dynasty knows my father's great secret about how Godan died. I don't know how because I never breathed a word and the only other person who knew was Illana, unless she let something slip? However they uncovered the truth, they were never going to allow that stain on his honour to be washed away. They were always going to bypass him and my mother has been working on this plan for years. I thought she *loved* him."

Nimsah carefully arranged her features to hide her disappointment at how naïve Dojan was. "It was an arranged marriage – the Bel-Doshok family saw it as a way to consolidate their position and fill the void left by Bel-Deem. You know this is true. And it was a risk – the attempt on your father's life at the docks on the day we first met proves that. Fujareen's fortunes have been built on the shakiest of alliances and more than a little luck."

Dojan's eyes were distant. "You saved me that day. It seems our lives were always destined to become closely entwined. I wish I could have been a better friend to you. I wish I'd done something … anything, after that day in the City of Tents, when that poor woman died."

"Fenara."

"Yes, Fenara. I let Khanir Shinva walk away as if nothing had happened and never spoke about it to anyone. I was more worried about how angry my mother and father would be at me for absconding and, to my shame, I never gave her a second thought. Not until that day you came to the palace."

"It was a long time ago," Nimsah told him, carefully controlling her voice.

Dojan looked at her with damp, red eyes. "Please forgive me. You're the only friend I have in all of this. You're one of the few people I can trust and if I'm being completely honest, I'm afraid."

"You'd be a fool not to be scared," said Nimsah. "Make no mistake, your life is still in danger and when you return to Fujareen we'll need to work together to ensure your safety."

Dojan stiffened. "What do you mean by that?"

"I would have thought it was obvious?"

"Is it? She's my mother, Nimsah. I'll not see her harmed."

Nimsah paused before replying. "Dojan, Tanah is the woman who tried to have you killed. Do you think when you return to Bengarath she'll shrug her shoulders, reflect and decide to dote on you instead? I told you, this runs deeper than family and her first loyalty is to her dynasty."

"She's my *mother*," said Dojan. "My father loves her completely, and if this comes out it'll destroy him as effectively as any uprising or coup. There has to be another way."

Nimsah shook her head. "Dojan, you came to me with this and I thank you for trusting me. I can't help you, though, if you don't take my advice. Your mother wants you out of the way so your sister can inherit. She's not going to change her mind, and this places you in mortal danger. We have to remove that threat."

"You're talking of killing my mother and sister. That's what you mean, so why dance around the subject. Why stop there? Who knows, perhaps Saraj and Beneth heard something and we should kill them too?"

"Now you're being ridiculous."

Dojan leaned back in his chair, pulling his hand away from Nimsah. "If you're going to insult me the least you could do is address me by my proper title. I'm Crown Prince Dojan Al-Haraq and you'll remember that. We're no longer children playing tiles in my room."

Nimsah sighed. "A thousand apologies, Crown Prince. All I'm trying to say is that Tanah presents a very real threat and we need to protect you. There's no suggestion your brothers are involved, but I'm afraid your sister is implicated. Power struggles within royal families are not uncommon – history teaches us that. As you say, you're the crown prince, so with the utmost respect if you want to be worthy of that title you must be prepared to fight for it."

"Kill for it?"

"If necessary."

They sat there in silence for a time, Dojan mulling over her words. Nimsah could see the affable young man she knew wrestling with the realities of his position. What if he refused to work with her in this? There were always the younger brothers. Saraj was all muscle and, whilst he was handsome and looked the part, Beneth possessed the sharper mind. Emirs and sultans had named their younger children as their successors in the past, although it defied convention and was often unpopular. Dojan was more malleable, though, which made him attractive to the Illesh Council. Beneth would be an unknown quantity, and plucking him from his scholarly studies would mean starting again. Dojan was right – they had a shared history, and something in the young prince drew

Nimsah to him. Ignoring the fact such things were forbidden by the banking clans, there was no spark of attraction. However, she still liked Dojan – he had a kind heart and people were drawn to him. In another life he would have made a good merchant, perhaps, or a successful market trader, with his gift for putting people at ease. Yet here they were, with Dojan as the crown prince and heir apparent, unwilling to see off the threat to his position.

"I have a proposal," Dojan said finally. "My mother is the head of the Bel-Doshok dynasty. Her voice holds sway, and whatever else she might be, the honour of her dynasty is sacrosanct. We can use that to our advantage."

Nimsah leaned in towards the prince, intrigued. "Go on."

***

Jandral listened to Nimsah as she outlined her thoughts on Dojan's plan, affording her the courtesy of letting her speak without interruption as the pair sat in his chambers in the Illesh spire.

"You think this could work?" he asked, hands steepled.

"I think it has some advantages," Nimsah replied.

"Sometimes the simplest ways are the best. Dojan's proposal introduces a number of risks and uncertainties. These are things I don't like, Nimsah. These are things the Bank of Illesh does not like."

Nimsah stared hard at Jandral, arms folded across her chest. "You've given me the position in Bengarath. Are you going to undermine and question my every decision?"

"No, of course not. However, I do want to be kept informed of significant matters such as this, where I would expect my opinion to carry some weight."

"We have to bring Dojan with us," Nimsah replied. "We need to handle this with subtlety and skill, or we risk toppling the house of Haraq Al-Souk and watching as Fujareen tears itself apart. This is a better way. Why appoint me to a job if you're not willing to trust my judgement?"

315

Jandral smiled, dark eyes twinkling. "I see I've prepared you well. So be it. Follow your heart in this matter and keep me informed. You'll do well in Bengarath, I'm sure."

"This isn't a matter of the heart," Nimsah told him. "Reason dictates this is the best course."

Jandral nodded to Nimsah, conceding the point with an even wider smile.

CHAPTER 42

Summer 213 – Kandarah's Docks

Dojan stood on the deck of the *Jezar*, his robes and handari flapping in the stiff breeze coming in off the sea, watching as Quizar was brought aboard the ship on a litter carried by four Tireless Shields. The Fujareen military camp was visible from the dockside, dust rising in the air as they began to move out. Two thousand Tireless Shields under Khan Gerber's command, a formidable force to guard Khan Lemarr and Narinda as they set out for Amonduras. Dojan knew he should feel pleased, watching the expedition leave. He'd played a significant part in making it happen, something his father would be proud of. None of that mattered now, the joy of the moment stolen by the dread of what he would face upon returning to Bengarath.

Pasha Ulan was travelling with Dojan's convoy, although he was sailing on *Farah's Wings* with Nimsah. Dojan was grateful not to have to share a ship with the pasha. Whenever he spoke to the unctuous minister a creeping horror stole across him. Ulan would expect to marry Adina after his triumph in Kandarah, becoming as close to family as it was possible to be. Yet he had ordered Dojan's death with a chilling calm the prince was unable to shake from his mind. The Sight was a powerful tool, and Dojan's respect for Tormindah's quiet effectiveness had risen on this mission. How she could swim in the memories and experiences of others whilst remaining herself was impossible to comprehend.

"I wonder what they'll find?" Tormindah mused next to

him.

"The member of your Fellowship is with them, presumably?"

Tormindah nodded. "Indeed, Crown Prince. Posing as a Tireless Shield."

"A dangerous ploy if the Kandaran Sightwielders detect them."

"You wanted to learn the secret route to Amonduras. This is the best way, and certainly more effective than Arak's feeble efforts."

Dojan gave her a wry smile. "You're not a great supporter of the Veiled Magi, are you?"

Tormindah's face assumed an innocent expression. "Forgive me, Crown Prince. I'm unsure what you mean."

Dojan laughed, grateful for anything that distracted him from his thoughts. The voyage to Fujareen, and what awaited him in Bengarath, hung over him like a dark cloud. He wanted it to all be over.

***

The throne room in Bengarath Palace was crowded and noisy as people enjoyed the sumptuous banquet Emir Haraq Al-Souk laid on to mark his son's return. Dojan's sister and brothers were there, laughing and joking as they mingled with various pashas, magi and army officers. Khanir Shinva was deep in conversation with Andral Illana, Khan Hengesh watching the pair with a furrowed brow as he stood at the emir's side.

Dressed in flowing purple silks, Her Royal Highness Princess Tanah Bel-Doshok wended through the crowd towards her son, Mubarizun Yanzin at her side. The Blessed Swords had done well after the success in Kandarah, their stock rising despite the 'mishap', where they'd left the Crown Prince virtually unprotected in the moments before the assassination attempt. Dojan wondered how much Shinva and Yanzin had known about his mother's plans. As his mother enfolded him in a rare hug it came as an unwelcome shock to realise he couldn't trust *anyone* in Fujareen.

"Dojan, it's so lovely to have you back here in the palace."

"It's good to be back," he told her. "You look well."

Tanah's long hair glistened, brushed smooth by her servants to a lustrous sheen and bound together with gold and silver thread. She drew several admiring glances from ambitious pashas and katibs as they hovered on the edge of their conversation, hoping to gain her favour.

"Your father is so proud of you," said Tanah, smoothing the ruffles in Dojan's robes as she stepped away. "Poor Hadir. It must have been terrible."

Dojan stared back at her, wondering how his mother could toy with him so blatantly, though of course, she was doing nothing of the sort. Tanah had no idea Dojan had uncovered her plot and she was merely playing her part. Canzar was still rotting in a cell back in the Kandaran slums. Instead, she was spinning a web of lies and deceit, hiding her ambition to elevate Adina behind a veneer of false concern for her son. Had she ever loved him? Dojan couldn't imagine how the person he remembered from his childhood could have changed so much.

"Hadir Al-Nadim will walk into Navan's Halls with his head held high," said Khalid, filling in the silence as Dojan stared at his mother. "He was a great mubarizun, and lived and died with much honour."

"The title of Mubarizun of the Mighty Spears may pass to you, Khalid," said Yanzin, standing straight and tall, a step behind Tanah's shoulder.

"If Arkon is willing."

Tanah smiled. "I think you will find the position hotly contested. My own son, Prince Saraj, is talking of competing for the honour himself."

"As a member of the Mighty Spears that is his right, High Princess. I imagine several warriors will ask Khan Hengesh if he would consider them worthy."

"Then Khan Hengesh will have a difficult decision to make," Tanah replied with a smile before turning back to

Dojan. "We haven't spoken properly in such a long time, Dojan. You must tell me what you make of young Nimsah."

Dojan's eyes strayed to the centre of the room, where Nimsah was talking to Adina and Ulan. Besides his mother, Nimsah was wearing the most expensive clothes of those gathered there, rich silks woven into a delicate cloth of gold, even her veil glittered, hinting at the riches of Illesh. Nimsah's eyes met with Dojan's across the crowd, nodding and offering him a brief smile before turning back to listen to what Pasha Ulan was saying.

"I thought Jandral would return to our court once the Kandaran business was concluded," Tanah was saying. "Nimsah seems very young to be given the responsibility of conducting their affairs here in Fujareen."

"I can assure you, Mother, she's more than capable."

"I'm sure she is. However, she's something of a mystery. Who is she? Where does she come from? Did you learn anything more about her during your voyage?"

Dojan shook his head. "The Bank of Illesh are secretive. They set aside their family names and their past when they join the bank. I'm afraid Nimsah was all business when I spent any time with her."

Tanah's eyes glittered. "How disappointing. I'm sure I can prise more from her than that. Tell her I'd like to speak to her privately later this week. We should learn as much as possible about our new allies."

After his mother left, Dojan needed some air and asked Khalid to walk with him to the hanging gardens of the palace. The plants were in full bloom, the air rich with the scent of flowers as he sat by the side of the fountain, watching the waters cascade into the pool. The droplets created a pattern of ripples that distorted Dojan's reflection as he looked down, trying to discern if they followed any kind of predictable rhythm. All he could see was a beautiful chaos.

"I thought I'd find you here."

Dojan glanced up at the sound of Beneth's voice, and

he rose to greet his youngest brother. Now seventeen, Beneth had a slender build like Adina and their mother. However, he looked taller than when Dojan had left, of a height with Saraj. The two men embraced, Beneth holding Dojan tight, as Khalid and his men stood at a distance to allow them some privacy.

"Welcome back."

"It's good to see you, Beneth. How are your studies at the university progressing?"

Beneth smiled. "Very well, although I think all the teachers are terrified of Vizier Haman. I always get the top marks in my class, and I can't decide if that's because I'm a genius or Haman's threatened them with a whipping if I don't outshine my peers."

"You've always been bright," Dojan told him. "In the next few years I could have one brother who's a mubarizun and the other as a respected university professor."

"And Adina telling all three of us what to do," joked Beneth, not noticing how his words made Dojan wince as he continued. "I'm sorry about what happened over there. How's Quizar?"

"He'll live. You should go and see him later – he always enjoys your company. You'll have to convince him he's not lost his dashing good looks."

Beneth shrugged. "What's an ear between friends? I'm just glad … Well, you know what I mean. It could have been so much worse."

"It's strange," Dojan mused. "It was only a few short weeks, yet I feel like I've been gone forever."

"It's the journey you've been on," Beneth told him. "Your experiences have changed you."

"I've killed a man," Dojan replied.

They sat in silence for a while, watching the fountain waters and listening to the birds singing higher up on one of the mezzanine levels, hidden deep within the trailing white-flowered clematis, delicate vines and pink honeysuckle.

"What was it like?" Beneth asked. "The City of a

Thousand Spires?"

"It was another world entirely, and Bengarath seemed primitive by comparison. It made me realise how much we've lost as a result of the War."

"There's a reason they call this the Fallen Age," Beneth observed.

Dojan enjoyed talking to Beneth, describing the first time he'd seen Kandarah from the deck of the *Jezar*, Quizar at his side. Beneth looked thoughtful as Dojan recounted the negotiations between Birizal, Fasil and Narinda, and how Jandral and Nimsah had controlled events.

"I'll admit, I was a little worried when you left," said Beneth. "However, it sounds like you acquitted yourself well. Maybe you even enjoyed yourself, Crown Prince?"

Dojan shrugged. "I suppose I did. As I said, Kandarah was like another world, a melting pot of Naroque tribes and merchants from every corner of Amuran. When you stand on top of a Kandaran spire you see things from a different perspective. Amuran seemed smaller and wider all at the same time."

"You did well," Beneth told him, patting his shoulder. "Many people expected us to become embroiled in a foreign war. Avoiding that was so important – if that had dragged on and our warriors were dying for a cause few could understand, it could have started to undermine Father's position. This is good for you, Dojan, yet a stranger looking at you would think you were sitting here nursing your failures."

"Hadir *died*, Beneth. Quizar almost lost his life as well and he'll be scarred forever. That happened because of me."

Beneth looked at Dojan with bright, intelligent eyes. "No, it happened because they were faithful. They paid that price because they were loyal to you and Fujareen. This is the world we live in, Dojan. You need to seize every advantage and build on your success, so that those sacrifices mean something."

Dojan sighed and stood up, stretching his back. "You're

right, of course."

Beneth offered Dojan a wry grin. "Of course. I wouldn't be your future vizier if I wasn't always right, would I?"

CHAPTER 43

Summer 213 – Bengarath Palace

Nimsah stood outside the carved cedar door leading to Tanah's private chambers, which was guarded by two Blessed Swords. Her heart was beating fast and she had to take a few moments to regulate her breathing, slowing down and calming her nerves. She took out a silk handkerchief and dabbed at her forehead. It wouldn't do to appear anxious in front of Her Royal Highness.

The door opened and she found herself facing Pasha Ulan and Princess Adina. Ulan was dressed in his customary black robes and red Kalat handari, while Adina wore a tight-fitting white dress and sported enormous hooped golden earrings. The princess really was strikingly beautiful, the fine structure of her face closely resembling her mother – a younger version of the woman Nimsah was about to confront.

"Nimsah," Adina purred. "Mother's looking forward to her audience with you. When you're finished, come and seek me out. Ulan and I were just discussing some proposals for expanding trade with Urumesh, where the connections of Illesh could prove useful."

"It would be my pleasure," Nimsah replied, offering both of them a short bow.

Ulan smiled. "I'll make the arrangements. My katib will be in touch with you. I'm looking forward to working closely with you and the Bank of Illesh."

Nimsah politely took her leave of the pair and was

ushered inside Tanah's chambers, which were every bit as fine as anything she would expect to see in the emir's throne room. Glazed Kalat pottery, decorated with exquisite detail in a variety of bright colours, was on display as Nimsah's feet sank into a thick Oomrhani rug. Tanah was reclining on a long couch by the window, framed in a bright square of sunlight. Nimsah smiled behind her veil as she saw that Tanah had dressed for their meeting in rich silks, imprinted at great cost in the pattern of the Hunir lotus flower. Nimsah had chosen plain blue robes and whilst the light cotton fabric was good quality it ensured Tanah didn't feel outshone.

Tanah rose and walked over to welcome Nimsah, taking both of her hands in hers, greeting her warmly. The two women sat down by the window as Tanah's servants poured them tea before leaving the pair of them alone. Nimsah allowed Tanah to lead their conversation at first as she admired the view out across the palace gardens. Down by the fountains she could see Emir Haraq sharing a joke with Saraj and Khan Hengesh, their distant laughter reaching them faintly from their high vantage point.

"I've not seen Haraq this excited in a long time," Tanah remarked. "If Saraj becomes mubarizun of the Mighty Spears he'll be the youngest man to hold that title."

"He'll have to prove his skill against the other challengers, of course," Nimsah observed.

"Naturally. His rivals will show him no deference as the emir's son, which is as it should be. The title of mubarizun must be earned, and never given as a favour. However, Saraj is gifted when it comes to wielding the Samarak fighting spear, so he has a real chance. It's something his father can understand and relate to – if Saraj is successful then Haraq will act as if the honour was his own achievement. You'd think he'd never been khan in Emir Godan's army."

"How things change."

Tanah paused. "Indeed. Anyway, I'm sure you didn't come here to listen to me talk about Saraj's prospects."

Nimsah took a breath, knowing there was no going back once she spoke the words. "I'm actually here to discuss your eldest son, Dojan. I'm sure you remember conspiring to murder him, while he was away in Kandarah?"

Tanah's eyes widened as she sat on the couch, rigid with outrage. "*What* did you say to me?"

"You heard perfectly well."

"And I deny it completely. How dare you. How *dare* you come into my chambers and accuse me of such a thing. I should call my guards and have you thrown into the dungeons for showing such disrespect."

Nimsah didn't reply immediately, instead taking a sip of hot black tea. "Are you going to?"

Tanah stared and Nimsah smiled, knowing she already had her. Tanah was a proud member of the old dynastic families. However, even the high princess knew the risks of crossing the Bank of Illesh.

"I thought not," said Nimsah with a charming smile, enjoying Tanah's rigid jaw as the woman tried and failed to speak. "The evidence against you and Pasha Ulan, who I know made the arrangements personally, is compelling. You tried to manipulate the line of succession to favour your daughter over your eldest son."

Tanah leaned forwards. "Pasha Ulan made the arrangements without my knowledge. Don't you see? He's betrothed to Adina and he could have made himself grand vizier as her husband. How could you ever accuse me of harming my own son? This is Ulan's work, not mine."

Nimsah mirrored Tanah's pose, leaning in close and allowing her perfume to waft in the air between them. Tanah caught the scent, her eyes becoming distant, only snapping back into focus when Nimsah spoke again.

"Think very carefully about your next words. Are you going to continue to lie to me, or do you want me to save your life and that of your daughter?"

"Haraq would never harm me ..." Tanah's voice trailed

off as she met Nimsah's gaze.

"You committed treason, Tanah. Treason. You plotted to kill your own child, Haraq's eldest son. When he hears of this your head will adorn a spike on the palace walls. All I have to do is put you, Adina and Ulan to the question. Do you want the three of you to spend some time with the Magi of the Farseeing? I wonder what they would discover? You may not have noticed but Crown Prince Dojan has taken Tormindah El-Shan into his close confidence lately. Why should that be?"

"Dojan *knows*?" Those two careless words escaped Tanah's lips, as damning a confession as Nimsah could have hoped for. Nimsah still couldn't quite believe how readily Tanah had turned against her firstborn son. Unless there was something else. Something she was missing ...

"Adina isn't Haraq's daughter, is she?" said Nimsah in a sudden flash of inspiration. Tanah's hesitation before she replied was enough to confirm she'd guessed right. "All those years of political manoeuvres, the refusal of the Bel-Doshok family to allow Haraq Al-Souk to become one of them. Their condition was that Adina was next in line, wasn't it? Who's her father? One of your distant Bel-Doshok cousins? Someone from Ulan's extended Bel-Naraar dynasty?"

"The Bel-Doshok and Bel-Naraar families were always loyal to Godan's house of Bel-Deem," Tanah replied. "They were never going to allow an usurper to force his way to their table with Godan's blood on his hands. They'll never forgive or forget the dishonourable way Godan died or the bodies swinging from the Bridge of Sorrows when Haraq exterminated the Bel-Deem line. This was a way to regain control without Haraq ever knowing what had happened. You must understand, as the head of the Bel-Doshok dynasty this was something I had to do. I married Haraq to ensure peace and bore Adina to the Bel-Doshok house to provide a future for our people. I did what was necessary to preserve our ways and respect our history. Dojan is Haraq's son, a commoner, and the crown could never be allowed to pass to him."

Nimsah smiled, allowing the heady scent of her perfume to wash over Tanah once more. Sightwielders had their own special gifts, but so did the Bank of Illesh. She didn't need Tormindah to confirm the truth of what Tanah was telling her. She shook her head, staggered by the amount of planning that had gone into this, all taking place under Jandral's nose without him suspecting a thing. "All those years of plotting so your dynasty and their allies could enjoy a quiet vengeance, without Haraq ever suspecting a thing. Who were you going to blame for Dojan's death?"

"That was the reason why I planted the idea in Haraq's mind of sending Dojan to Kandarah. It would have been easy enough to blame the Abitek or the Edeen – a desperate roll of the dice to prevent the Fujareen army imposing their will. That could be the story still. If this comes out it will destroy Haraq. He doesn't know, does he?"

"Dojan hasn't told him anything," Nimsah assured her.

"You said you were going to save my life and help me protect Adina. You haven't come here today to see me put on trial, have you? So, what is it that you want?"

"Illesh owns Fujareen. We will not allow years of patient work and the vast sums of money we have put into this venture to go to waste. That means negotiating with the old houses to allow Haraq what he craves above all else – admission to the Bel-Doshok dynasty."

"They will never allow it – I'm only one voice."

"You're the head of Bel-Doshok. Tell them this is a condition of the Bank of Illesh, required to remove any uncertainty over Haraq Al-Souk's rule. Do whatever it takes to convince them. If you don't, the truth will come out and you'll watch your own daughter die."

Tanah swallowed. "You're not a mother. If you were, you wouldn't make such a threat."

Nimsah scowled. "Please. You intended to murder your own son. Don't try and take the moral high ground with me. What's obvious is you only care about your daughter. What about Saraj and Beneth? Is Haraq their father?" Tanah nodded. "I thought so. It appears we have considerable leverage over you, High Princess. I'm sure you'll find this motivation enough to be sufficiently convincing with the members of your house."

Tanah rose from the couch and walked to the window, peering out over the gardens, arms wrapped around her chest. The princess was cornered – would she seize the escape route offered by Nimsah or lash out? Nimsah waited for her answer.

"If I do this, what then?"

"Exile."

Tanah turned, framed in light from the open window. "My house will never accept those terms."

Nimsah shook her head. "This is *self-imposed* exile – an important distinction. Ulan will need to be stripped of his position as pasha, of course. We could contrive a story that would protect his honour, assuming Adina truly cares for him? Perhaps his health could take a turn for the worse and the doting couple could travel to the emir's summer palace in Jalar to recuperate? You could join them in order to support your daughter, enjoying a welcome break from Fujareen politics. I understand the town is particularly beautiful at this time of year."

"Jalar?" Tanah rolled the word around her mouth with distaste.

"It's unacceptable for you to remain in Bengarath with direct influence over the emir's court. Jalar will suit your needs and mine, High Princess, especially when compared with the alternative. The other thing you need to understand is that Dojan insisted there *was* an alternative. Despite everything you've done to him, he wanted to find a way to avoid the dishonour your trial and execution would bring."

"He was always weak," muttered Tanah, shaking her head.

"No," corrected Nimsah. "This isn't weakness. It's love."

CHAPTER 44

Autumn 213 – Bengarath Amphitheatre

The din in the amphitheatre echoed around the circular walls and rose up towards the grey, cloudy sky as the crowd peered to get a good look at the two remaining contestants fighting for the title of Mubarizun of the Mighty Spears. Dojan had an excellent vantage point in the private booth he was sharing with his father, now formally known as Emir Haraq Bel-Doshok. Katib Tormindah tried to look like she was enjoying her privileged position, her seat in the emir's balcony courtesy of her position as Dojan's newly appointed personal aide. Beneth was with them too, cheering Saraj as he stepped out first in front of the crowd, his black spear of polished wood held aloft. His blunt sparring weapon was more expensive than some of the actual Samarak fighting spears used by the warriors in his regiment, his armour gleaming and polished, an ornate helmet held in the crook of his arm.

"He certainly looks the part," chuckled Khan Hengesh, leaning forwards from his seat immediately behind Haraq. "The crowds love him, your highness."

Khan Hengesh was enjoying his position in court without the need to compete every day with Khanir Shinva. She'd travelled with a detachment of Blessed Swords to protect Dojan's mother whilst she remained in Jalar, leaving Yanzin in charge of the remainder of the regiment in Bengarath.

"Being popular with the commoners isn't what makes a great mubarizun," said Andral Illana. "Let's see what Khalid can do. My money's on him. No one has scored a touch in the three rounds he's fought to reach the final contest. Saraj can't make the same boast."

"Is that a wager?" asked Hengesh with a grin.

"Nimsah," Haraq called out, lifting his arm and waving her over. "You're about to miss the start. We've saved you a seat here in the royal box."

Nimsah smiled at Dojan from amid the queue of people making their way into the amphitheatre, climbing the stairs and joining them. Down below, Dojan could see Nema hissing something to her husband, Vizier Haman placing a soothing hand on her arm. Even Jandral hadn't been courted with such open favour by the emir. Dojan caught sight of Pasha Quizar, his handari carefully arranged to hide his scars, which were still healing. Dojan offered his friend a small nod of recognition, promising to himself he would make the time to visit the new pasha of the Treasury later that week. Their new duties at court took up so much more of their time and it had been too long. Dojan had heard Quizar was now courting a handsome young man from the Mighty Spears and was eager to learn all the details. As Nimsah took her seat the crowd roared out the name of Khalid Al-Shah, over and over, the sound reverberating so loudly Dojan could feel it pulsing through his chest.

"Now who's the popular one?" said Illana, giving Hengesh a sideways look as Khalid emerged from the tunnel, fist raised in salute to the crowd.

"Al-Shah. Al-Shah. Al-Shah."

The Tireless Shields were the backbone of the Fujareen army, divided into dozens of units led by junior khans and mubarizuns, each selected by their overall commander, Khan Gerber Al-Jalal. Despite being a fraction of the size with just five hundred men, the prestige of the Mighty Spears regiment meant an altogether more protracted affair was required to appoint their mubarizun. Thirty-six men had put themselves forward for the honour of taking Hadir's place, and their numbers had been whittled down through various trials of skill devised by Khan Hengesh. All of this took place in Bengarath's amphitheatre, providing entertainment for the masses and attracting the public in increasingly large numbers. The outcome of the contest was now one of the most popular topics of conversation amongst the denizens of Bengarath. The sixteen who had made it through to the latter stages of the contest were divided into pairs, each fighting for the prize of securing a place in the next round. Now only two warriors remained – Saraj and Khalid.

While Dojan knew family honour dictated he should support his brother, he had a sneaking admiration for Khalid. Khalid had been a favourite with the crowds and bookmakers for some time. No one had come near him in the three previous rounds, all of which Dojan watched. Saraj's route to the final contest had been far tighter, his opponents scoring hits against him in both the second and third rounds.

"Come on, my boy," said Haraq quietly, his face bright and animated. In private, Dojan's father had become withdrawn and irritable since Tanah's departure. It was only their visits to the amphitheatre that improved his mood. For his father's sake, Dojan hoped Saraj would emerge the winner this afternoon.

Thinking of his mother stirred a mix of emotions. He felt anger and revulsion at her betrayal, yet he also missed her and even more so the company of Adina. Dojan told himself it was better this way. He'd shown both mercy and restraint, whilst shielding his father from a truth that would have broken him. Whilst he could never imagine reconciling with his mother, this way spared his family more pain. Putting his mother on trial and executing the most senior member of the Bel-Doshok dynasty would have destroyed Fujareen. After everything he'd done to secure peace in Kandarah, he didn't want to be the one responsible for a civil war in his home country. Dojan could tell Nimsah was unconvinced, but she'd still supported his decision on how to handle this. It was

Nimsah who had finally drawn Haraq and his children into the house of Bel-Doshok, ending more than two decades of futile negotiations between the two factions. It boded well for their future working relationship, especially now Dojan had begun taking on more of his father's responsibilities. To his surprise, he was starting to enjoy it.

"The final contest," roared out the rotund ringmaster, barely making himself heard over the baying crowd. "The prize – the honour of serving in Emir Haraq Bel-Doshok's personal guard, the Mighty Spears, as their mubarizun. Only one man will prove himself worthy before you all. I give you Saraj Bel-Doshok and Khalid Al-Shah!"

At the mention of Saraj's family name a few brave souls shouted "Fix." Their voices were largely drowned out by the two sides, evenly split, who were Saraj or Khalid supporters. It was unfair to think the outcome of the contest was pre-arranged – Haraq's nervous face was proof enough. Saraj was contesting the final on merit, although he'd only scraped through the last round three touches to two. No warrior would give him quarter on account of his birth – in the fighting circle the honour of the Mighty Spears came first. If Saraj wanted to become mubarizun he would have to earn his position, just as Hadir had done before him.

The ringmaster raised both his arms and slowly the crowd fell silent, the shouts fading until all that could be heard was a nervous hum of whispers and wagers. "The final will be determined over the course of seven rounds. The first to four touches will earn the honour of becoming the next mubarizun of the Mighty Spears. Warriors – fight fair and clean, for the glory of Arkon and Fujareen. Begin."

Saraj and Khalid circled each other, the reach of their wooden practice spears keeping their opponent at bay. While Saraj was wearing a helmet, Khalid had opted against one, not wanting to impede his vision. As the two men waited for an opening the air rang with shouts of support and abuse, depending on who the crowd favoured.

The sharp crack of spear striking helmet brought the onlookers to stunned silence. Saraj took a half step backwards and almost fell over. Dojan hadn't even seen Khalid's spear move, the attack coming so quickly. Already Khalid was back in his fighting stance, spear raised, ready to start the next round.

"One strike to Al-Shah," called out the ringmaster.

"Look sharp, boy," Haraq called out from the edge of his seat, abandoning any pretence at being impartial.

"This could be over *very* quickly," muttered Tormindah into Dojan's ear.

"Just wait. Saraj's not going to give up –"

Half the crowd groaned as Khalid's spear cut through Saraj's defences with blistering speed, delivering a solid punch to Saraj's stomach that left him sprawled on the ground, winded.

"Two strikes to Al-Shah."

"Looks like Saraj will have to do things the hard way," said Illana with a satisfied grin, looking in Hengesh's direction.

Saraj got to his feet, making a show of jogging around the arena, although the blow must have hurt. When the fight resumed Saraj went on the offensive at once, wooden spears moving in a blur as strike and counter-attack blended together. Saraj was the bigger man and over this more extended exchange his strength began to tell, forcing Khalid's defences open long enough to brush the tip of his spear against his upper arm, bringing him back into the contest.

"It doesn't seem fair that's counted as a touch," Tormindah observed, shouting over the resulting din. "Khalid's strikes were both killing blows, whereas Saraj gains a point for what would merely be a graze in the real world."

"Those are the rules," laughed Beneth, on his feet applauding his brother. Dojan also stood, remembering he should be doing the same.

The next round vanished in moments, Khalid swerving around Saraj's outstretched spear and moving in close. He ducked down as Saraj brought his weapon back round in a sweeping circle, jabbing out his spear and taking out Saraj's legs from under him. As he sprawled in the sand Khalid laid the flattened bladed point of his spear at Saraj's throat, causing an uproar.

"The best of *seven* rounds," roared the ringmaster as he tried to restore order. "May I remind you this is the best of seven rounds, not five. The contest is still live."

"I bet Khalid wishes he'd met Saraj in the semi-final," breathed Beneth.

"Lucky for us he didn't, or this would already be over," Dojan replied. "Khalid's not showing any mercy. I'm sorry, Beneth, I don't think Saraj has a chance."

Saraj was dusting himself off, ignoring the jeers from Khalid's supporters as he bought some time, checking over the straps connecting his armour. Khalid watched him, a hungry look to his face, bouncing on the balls of his feet. Moments later the two clashed again, jabbing at each other as they tried to probe a way through their opponent's defences. Saraj kept on the move, often backing away out of Khalid's reach, darting to the left and right to try and keep him off-balance. It was as Khalid checked his stride and pushed off to the left that his foot gave out under him, his yelp of pain as he clutched his knee drawing a groan from the crowd as Saraj lightly touched him on the shoulder.

"Three touches to two, favouring Al-Shah," the ringmaster called out, looking worried.

"He's hurt himself," shouted Beneth, pointing excitedly as the ringmaster bent down to speak to Khalid. The warrior was shaking his head, his face a mask of misery as he continued to hold his leg.

Saraj stood a little way off, looking awkward as it became apparent that Khalid's injury would prevent their fight continuing. A large section of the crowd began to cheer when they realised this would give the title to Saraj, although a smaller group were booing at the result. Emir Haraq stood up and began applauding, Illana and Hengesh quickly following suit. Dojan rose with Beneth and the rest of the royal balcony, helping to sway the audience in Saraj's favour. After all, it probably wasn't a good idea to jeer the son of the emir for too long.

Saraj walked over to Khalid and held out his hand, helping him stand. Dojan couldn't hear what the two men were saying to one another, although Khalid looked close to tears. In a gesture that appealed to supporters on both sides, Saraj raised Khalid's hand, clasped in his own, holding it above their heads and called out "Mubarizun," over and over. The crowd joined in the chant, drawing both sides of supporters together, allowing Saraj to savour his victory while Khalid accepted the adulation, knowing he had come so close.

Nimsah reached over and took Haraq's hands in hers. "Congratulations, Emir. You must be very proud of your son."

Haraq beamed at her, unable to contain his excitement. "Of course. What a wonderful day. Please excuse me, I must go and congratulate Saraj in person."

Beneth blew out his cheeks as the sound of the crowd subsided. "That was close."

Dojan nodded. "I feel sorry for Khalid."

"He clearly angered Myshall today. The contest was there for the taking. Still, once he recovers he'll have the honour of being your personal bodyguard. Some would say the importance of your royal person is worth more than the title of mubarizun."

"You flatter me," Dojan replied. "I'm not sure that's how Khalid will see it."

"He'll get his chance. Want to place a bet on who's appointed khan when Hengesh steps down?"

Dojan laughed, hurrying to follow his father and congratulate Saraj.

CHAPTER 45

Autumn 213 – Bengarath Palace

Nimsah was working late into the evening, sitting at her writing desk as she finished the last of her correspondence. The Bank of Illesh conducted much of its business through the medium of Sightwielders, slowly rebuilding the network of instant communication that had once united the whole of Amuran during the Age of Enlightenment. *Knowledge is prized more highly than gold by the Bank of Illesh.* This was certainly true, although Nimsah had applied her own amendment to the old maxim – accuracy was to be prized over speed. A Sight user could only relay what they understood, so if they had no head for figures it was pointless asking them to summarise a balance sheet or a set of accounts. With the Sight it was all feelings, emotions and experiences, an inherent weakness Morvanos had exploited in his rebellion against the Great Tyranny.

As Nimsah waited for Tormindah to arrive she continued to pore over the ledgers Pasha Quizar had provided, detailing the wealth of Fujareen. She felt a jolt of memory as she came across Odilla's name – there was her beautiful garden full of orange and lemon trees, remembered scents filling Nimsah's senses. Odilla had re-established her connections in the Emirate of Amjahran, Illesh paving the way by easing the flow of trade between the two countries, and she was listed as the richest and most influential gold merchant in Fujareen. More importantly, the woman paid her taxes.

There was a knock at the door and Nimsah heard Tormindah's voice. Dojan's new katib was all smiles, her face warm and friendly as she came inside. Despite Tormindah's outward appearance, Nimsah still erected her inner shields to ward off any unwelcome probing by the Sight. Illesh wanted to keep hold of its secrets, so warding off Sightwielders had been one of the first things Nimsah was trained in on her arrival in Kandarah. It was simple enough in theory, creating a barrier built around an oft-repeated phrase, such as *the ancient dynasties are bound by ties stronger than love and marriage.* The real trick was to keep the phrase repeating in one part of your mind, so that was all the Sight user could hear, whilst the rest was occupied with the task in hand.

"They've made contact?" Nimsah asked, referring to the agent planted within the expedition to Amonduras. Their name was a closely-guarded secret, to which even Nimsah wasn't privy.

Tormindah nodded as she took a seat on the other side of Nimsah's writing desk. After declining Nimsah's offer of tea, Tormindah outlined the progress made by Khan Lemarr and Narinda since her last report. The journey through the dense rainforest of inner Naroque had been difficult, the old roads to Amonduras long since swallowed up by nature, making the route arduous and slow. Lemarr and Narinda had set out with an advance party whilst the remainder of their Tireless Shields established a camp on the edge of the jungle. Coordinated from this camp, Khan Gerber's task was to follow the spearhead of the expedition, his soldiers cutting through the dense vegetation and building a new road that would make easy access to Amonduras possible for the first time in two centuries.

Arak's device had guided Lemarr and Narinda safely through the Naroque jungle, although the old magic left by the War remained dangerous. People had died on the forward expedition after straying too far, consumed from within by the Shimmering Way. Nimsah hoped the secrets they discovered in Amonduras would make their sacrifice worthwhile.

"They are now camped outside the old city walls," Tormindah explained. "Narinda plans to approach the gates at first light to try and gain access."

"If the walls are still standing, that suggests a significant amount of the city within remains intact," mused Nimsah.

"It's hard to say," Tormindah replied. "The walls are covered with vines, creepers and dense foliage. The rainforest is likely to have consumed the city as well.

"Perhaps. We'll know soon enough."

Tormindah leaned forwards, lowering her voice. "Nimsah, can I ask you a question? All this effort, financed by your bank, to reach Amonduras and uncover its secrets. What if there's nothing there?"

"In that case this will have been a speculative investment that delivers a loss, rather than making a profitable return. In business, risks must be taken. The art is to balance those risks off against one another."

"By which you mean your investment in Fujareen?" guessed Tormindah.

Nimsah nodded, making a note to watch this new katib closely. Had Dojan sent her here with instructions to probe Nimsah's intentions, or was this fuelled by her own curiosity? "If Amonduras is an empty shell then in one or two generations the sun is going to set forever on the City of a Thousand Spires. The lost magic that powers the Kandaran forges will fade, and the machines of the Magi of Engineers will seize up, the flowing steels solidifying forever. The lights in the spires will go out, one by one, until Kandarah is nothing more than a museum where people will flock to marvel at the old ways. Those towers will become a monument to the folly of men who built towards the stars with no thought for what happened when their limited resources ran out. In time, those fantastical spires will crumble and one by one they will fall. And one day no one will ever know Kandarah was once called the City of a Thousand Spires."

"In which case, the Bank of Illesh will begin again, here in Fujareen," said Tormindah.

"Exactly. History teaches us that empires and countries have always risen and fallen throughout the centuries. If the future of Kandarah can be secured and their way of life maintained, that would be good, providing we control the means by which it can be achieved. If Amonduras is an empty shell then we will rebuild, abandoning Kandarah while it still, outwardly, remains a centre of opulence and wealth. Where better to start than in the richest of the four emirates?

"Fujareen represents our slow and steady profit, which we will reap for generations to come. It's ventures like this that fund riskier opportunities elsewhere, meaning we can afford to lose our coin when things don't go to plan."

Tormindah was listening intently to Nimsah. "And thus you balance the risks and swell the coffers of the Bank of Illesh."

"Exactly. You speak as if this is a bad thing. Coin is good. Coin is what makes things happen, drives change and creates a future for us all. The banking clans re-established the lost trading routes between the Amuran continents after the seas ceased to boil. We helped rebuild towns, turning them into cities and making them the seeds from which nations sprang. Morvanos may have failed in his bid to rule Amuran after he brought down the Tyranny. However, his gift to us was a world free from the shackles of the old ways, rich with opportunity."

"Cheap at the price of millions of dead," Tormindah remarked.

"I never said the War was a good thing," Nimsah replied. "Scholars will forever debate whether or not it could have been avoided. The point I'm making is that in the aftermath we had a choice – rebuild and move on or hark back in sorrow, wailing for the lost Enlightened Age. We can choose to live in the Fallen Age or we can turn this era into something else. Isn't that something you want to be part of, Tormindah?"

The katib smiled. "I can see why Jandral sent you here. You'll achieve great things with our emir."

Nimsah was about to reply when she heard shouting. It was some way off, in another part of the palace, but something in the tone of those voices sent a chill through her. Tormindah heard it too, her eyes becoming distant as she reached out instinctively with the Sight, trying to learn what was happening. Moments later she was back in the room with Nimsah, her face paling with shock.

"Something terrible has happened. I can't get a sense of exactly what, but people are running through the palace, terrified. They're rousing the emir from his bed."

Nimsah hurriedly gathered up her papers. "You'd better go to Dojan. He'll need his katib. I'll go to the emir."

Tormindah left as Nimsah continued to tidy away her ledgers and accounts, locking them in a drawer. She placed the key in a small purse and put both hands on her desk, leaning against it as she composed herself, taking in slow, steadying breaths. She knew the reason for the commotion, and understood why the palace officials and guards were so distressed. For the first time in many years Kandilla's face swam before her eyes, her form shadowy as Nimsah's chambers darkened and transformed into the narrow alleyways of Bengarath's back streets.

"We. Own. You." Kandilla snarled each word. "You're not going anywhere."

Moments later, the woman was dead. Kandilla hadn't given her any other choice, as she'd told herself every night for the first few months of her new life in Kandarah. She remembered Jandral's words, his voice calm and rational, as Nimsah wept as she finally told him what happened to her on her journey to his ship at the docks.

"Do you think you did the wrong thing?"

"I killed someone. What do you think?"

"Is it that simple? You told me she was trying to kill you, driven to hurt you by her own jealousy. So, who was in the wrong? You for defending yourself, or Kandilla for being unable to let you go?"

Nimsah wiped her cheeks with the back of her hand, looking into Jandral's dark eyes. "I know what you're saying. That doesn't make any of this easy. You can't wash away something like this with cunning words."

"I'm not trying to. Listen, Nimsah, Amuran is full of wonders, but it's also a brutal place. Sometimes we have to do hard things. If you work for Illesh you'll find yourself having to take difficult decisions. No path is easy if you want to make a difference in the world. If that's not for you then there's other things we can do. I can make arrangements for you to start a new life, here in Kandarah, far away from Bengarath if that's what you want. Not everyone is suited to the banking clans."

"No. I fought for this. I'm not giving it up because of Kandilla."

Jandral had nodded, satisfied with her answer. Nimsah took a shuddering breath, drawing herself back to the present. She'd done what was necessary all those years ago. This was no different, although it left a sick sensation in her stomach. With a heavy sigh, she straightened her back, wiped her eyes and left her room, heading straight for the emir's chambers.

CHAPTER 46

Autumn 213 – The town of Jalar on the Fujareen coast

Ignoring his advisors, Dojan's father had insisted on travelling to Jalar in person. Dojan knew he couldn't let his father make the journey on his own, telling Vizier Haman in no uncertain terms he would be joining him. Haman had looked like he might have argued the point at first, only to bow his head in submission when Saraj and Beneth announced they would also be leaving the palace.

The four of them rode together down the winding coastal road towards Jalar, Khan Hengesh leading the way. Khalid was still recuperating from his injury and, although they were travelling with all five hundred Mighty Spears, Dojan felt unprotected without him. The armoured column rode in solemn silence, all of them wearing black cloaks and robes of mourning. In the distance, Dojan could see the white buildings of Jalar, nestled in a cove amid the cliffs that rose on either side. The sky and sea were both grey, in keeping with his mood as he caught sight of the emir's summer palace.

In addition to the warriors there were representatives from the Bel-Doshok, Bel-Naraar and Bel-Kamil dynasties. Mubarizun Yanzin rode in a vanguard of Blessed Swords, while further back was a delegation of Veiled Magi, with Nimsah in attendance for the Bank of Illesh. Andral Illana sat in the saddle, her head bowed, riding alongside Vizier Haman and his wife Nema. No one spoke. The horses' hooves and the trudge of the warriors' boots were the only sound, the whole column leaving a cloud of swirling dust in their wake.

***

The summer palace commanded a fantastic view out across the bay, considered one of the most picturesque in Fujareen. Dojan knew at once that he would never return here. When the time was right, he'd suggest to his father they sold the property to one of the old families.

"Your Royal Highness, are you sure you want to do this?" asked Yanzin.

"Your emir has given his orders," rumbled Hengesh. "It's not for you to question them."

Yanzin bowed her head and led them inside. There were guards everywhere, a mixture of Blessed Swords and Tireless Shields. Saraj had his arm around his father's shoulders, each man supporting the other. Beneth walked with a quiet calm next to Dojan, wrapped up in his thoughts, looking around without really seeing what was in front of him.

The servants had tried hard to put things back in order after the attack, but as they walked down the corridor towards his mother's chambers Dojan could see spots of blood on the white ceiling. They passed servants with mops and buckets, heads bowed as they looked at their sandals. The two Blessed Swords guarding his mother's chamber had been silently cut down as they stood in the corridor. The attack had been deadly, decapitating one and piercing the other warrior through the heart and both lungs. This had taken skill, the physician concluding that the weapon used had been narrower than a scimitar. A Samarak fighting spear was thought most likely, though how the assailants had got so close to the guards without being challenged was still to be answered. The chamber doors were intact, save for a small neat hole which had blasted out the lock and handle. Haraq gently pushed them open, staring at the room.

"No one heard anything?" asked Saraj, glancing around the chamber.

"Not until Ulan fell from the window, no," Yanzin told

him.

They walked into a neat, well-appointed room where Dojan's mother would have received guests, her sleeping quarters off through another set of doors. According to the reports Yanzin had gathered, Tanah had been talking with Adina, Ulan and Shinva when the attack came. Dojan walked to the window and opened the shutters, peering down. There was a sandstone tiled courtyard several floors below, which the servants had cleaned thoroughly. Dojan winced as he saw the brown stain marking the spot where Ulan had landed, smashing in his skull. He'd been dead by the time the Blessed Swords found him.

"Father, you don't have to do this," said Saraj, placing his hand on his shoulder as Haraq eyed the wooden crossbeams holding up the roof of the chamber.

"Where were they found?" Haraq asked, ignoring his son and directing his question at Yanzin.

"Here," she said, pointing at the beam in the middle of the room. "The three of them were hung next to each other. There were a few signs of a struggle. The warriors who came in found a table knocked over by the window, a platter of dates scattered onto the floor and a broken goblet."

Haraq stared at the room and Dojan realised his father was trying to visualise what had happened inside. Beneth made a choking sound and hurried from the room. Dojan made to follow, before hesitating as his father spoke.

"Leave him. He needs some air, that's all."

Yanzin cleared her throat, clearly wishing to hurry things along. It wasn't Yanzin's fault, as she hadn't been stationed at Jalar, however the Blessed Swords would struggle to recover from the dishonour of Tanah's murder. With almost half the regiment guarding the palace and surrounding grounds the assassins had still gained access to the palace and escaped unseen. To lose their khanir in the attack only made a dreadful situation worse.

"There must have been a number of them," Haraq said,

pacing the room. "To be able to kill the guards, break through the door and move in here before my wife even knew they were under attack. It must have been quick, and there had to be enough of them to overpower four people in this room, including Khanir Shinva herself. Perhaps they took Tanah or Adina hostage, forcing the others to cooperate."

"Lynched," Saraj spat the word. "They were executed like common criminals."

Haraq nodded. "And that was deliberate. Look how the guards died – probably so quickly they never even realised they were under attack until it was too late. Whoever did this, they made my wife and daughter …"

"They made them suffer," finished Dojan. "Perhaps when Ulan realised what was about to happen he tried to get away. He could have fallen through the window in a struggle. Maybe he was so terrified he jumped."

"He was meant to be ill," muttered his father. "I wasn't told what the matter with him was. Did you know?"

Dojan shook his head, grateful for the fresh air on his face. He felt faint and he kept a tight grip on the frame of the shutters, not wanting to follow Ulan's example. Ulan being thrown to his death could simply have been a distraction, *after* his mother and sister were murdered. It would have drawn the guards away, giving the attackers time to escape. This wasn't just an assassination. There was something theatrical about the whole thing – the message clear, even if the rest of his family were unable to grasp it.

Haraq paced about the room, looking lost. "I thought coming here … I thought there might be some clue. Something the servants and your warriors had missed."

Yanzin bowed her head. "I'm sorry, your Royal Highness. The trail is already cold. I don't think we'll find the answers here."

"Isn't it obvious?" snapped Saraj. "This has to be the work of the Abitek, taking revenge for losing out in Kandarah. They killed our family for the sake of some worthless ruins in the middle of nowhere."

"There's no proof of that, Prince Saraj," Yanzin pointed out. "It may be a possibility –"

"It's the only possibility," Saraj growled.

Haraq held up his hand, looking tired. "Enough. There are other ways to learn the truth. I swear, when we discover who did this they'll rue the day they crossed Fujareen. I'll have my vengeance on those responsible, you have my solemn promise. This deed will not go unpunished."

***

Tanah, Adina, Shinva and Ulan were all cremated in Jalar, the four pyres built near a spot Tanah had enjoyed bringing her children to when they were younger, high on the cliffs looking out over the sea. Since they were all members of the extended dynasties of Fujareen, their ashes would be returned to the royal mausoleum in Bengarath, where mother would be interred with daughter, her prospective son in law next to them. If some thought Shinva's failure to protect the High Princess might have warranted a less prominent location for her remains, no one dared mention it to the emir.

With the funeral ceremony over, Dojan stood a little way off, watching the fires dying down with the last lingering members of the mourning party. Nema was crying as Haman led her away and Dojan remembered how close she'd been to his mother. He noticed Nimsah was sitting on a wall a little way off, talking to Beneth. He walked over to join them, trying to decide how to handle himself.

Beneth stood and embraced him. "Brother."

"Beneth. It'll be alright, I promise."

"Will it?"

Dojan didn't have an answer for that as the pair broke apart again. Beneth walked away, standing near the glowing pyres.

"My sincere condolences, Crown Prince," said Nimsah.

Dojan stared at her, incredulous. "How can you sit there and say those words?"

"Careful, Dojan. Lower your voice or you'll attract unwelcome attention."

"I'll say what I want."

Nimsah shook her head. "Do you really want your father to discover the truth about your mother? A truth you deliberately hid from him? Do you think he'll ever trust you again if he learns about this?"

Dojan sat down next to Nimsah, all the fight going out of him. "This isn't what I wanted. We agreed they would be exiled. What have you done?"

Nimsah looked at him, dark eyes glittering in the fading light of the flames. "You haven't changed as much as you think after your trip to Kandarah. You're still the soft young boy I met all those years ago, too cossetted and privileged to be ready to take up the mantle of emir. You shied away from your responsibilities, mistaking sparing your father pain for protecting him. I had no choice other than to act when you refused."

Dojan couldn't believe what he was hearing. "You're trying to make out this was *my* fault?"

Nimsah's voice was low, her sharp words sliding into Dojan's heart like a knife. "You said it, not me. Are you really the son of the man who stormed Emir Godan's palace and seized the crown? You don't send traitors who are planning to usurp you into exile, where they can begin to plot all over again."

"I never wanted any of this. The titles, the crown. Any of it," confessed Dojan, wishing immediately he could take the words back when he saw Nimsah shake her head in disappointment.

"You didn't hide it very well, did you? The dissolute Crown Prince, always chasing the ladies at court, never taking any interest in matters of state. No obvious skill when it came to the sword, spear or archery that might have made your father proud. No aptitude for your studies to elevate you above the ordinary. No wonder your mother made other plans."

Stung by her comments, Dojan had to turn away and wait until his voice was under control before replying. "If you think Adina would have made a better ruler, perhaps you backed the wrong side."

"This isn't about who's fit to rule," Nimsah told him. "Fujareen belongs to the Bank of Illesh, Crown Prince. You've read the agreements signed by your father. We don't need a strong ruler. We need someone who'll do what they're told, which is why you represent our long term investment."

"When you returned to Bengarath ..." Dojan gave a bitter laugh. "I really believed there might have been a chance to rekindle our old friendship. I hadn't realised my old playmate had become ... this."

Nimsah looked at Dojan with pity. "Who do you think that girl was? I was playing a role in the palace – I was even encouraged to get close to you."

"And that day at the docks?"

Nimsah hesitated. "That was different. That was a long time ago."

"I never thought that it would be possible to hate the person who once saved my life."

Nimsah stood up, the wind rippling through her black robes, wrapping them tight around her body. "You don't have to like me, Crown Prince. All you have to do is respect my position and play your part. Although you might feel betrayed now, in time you'll look back on this day and know I did what had to be done. For the good of the Emirate of Fujareen and the rest of your family."

After Nimsah left, Dojan sat on his own on the stone wall as it grew dark, aware that apart from his bodyguards waiting nearby, he was alone. He thought of talking to Quizar or Tormindah, dismissing the idea instantly. What did he expect them to do? Should he tell his father? Saraj? Beneth? How would they react, knowing he'd kept the truth from them? And if he'd told the truth from the outset? Nimsah was right, Tanah, Ulan and Adina had committed treason, for which the penalty was death by hanging. This way, his father never needed to know his wife had betrayed him or that his own daughter had plotted to seize the crown from his son. What good could come from any of this? When his mother put these events in motion through Ulan she would have known the risks. Whilst Nimsah had dispensed summary justice, both courses of action would have led to the same outcome.

What Dojan was finding hard to accept was the grief he felt at his mother's and Adina's deaths. They had been his family and their loss hurt as much, if not more, than the ultimate betrayal he had suffered at their hands. He'd avoided confronting them directly, leaving that unpleasant task up to Nimsah. He'd taken what he thought was the easy path, never realising his last conversations with them had already happened. What a fool he'd been. What a complete and utter fool.

"Crown Prince?" It was one of the Mighty Spears, his voice hesitant. It was pitch black and cold on the cliff tops and when Dojan looked up he realised he was shivering.

"Crown Prince, forgive me. It's late. We should really be back at the palace by now. After everything that's happened. Well ... Sire, it's not safe to be outside any longer."

Dojan rose and gave an apology through chattering teeth. "I'm sorry. You're quite right. Please, lead the way."

As Dojan walked with his guards he had to fight back tears. In the end, he gave up the struggle, letting them course down his cheeks as he trudged down the twisting path towards the summer palace of Jalar.

EPILOGUE

Autumn 213 – Bengarath Palace

The day after her return from Jalar, Nimsah set aside the fine clothes she'd brought with her from Kandarah, choosing an outfit at the very back of her wardrobe. She ran her hands over the coarser home-spun cotton, its nondescript tan colours a marked contrast to the striking clothes she'd favoured during her time in court. Nimsah dressed and wrapped a brown headscarf around her hair, tucking away a few dark stray strands before leaving through the servant's entrance at the rear of the palace.

Nimsah hadn't felt ready to make this journey until now. She passed through the markets, pausing at the place where Fenara's stall had once stood, noting there was now a new tradesman there, this one selling bolts of cloth – rich cottons, delicate embroidery and fine silks. Nimsah also ensured her route took her past Surat's coffeehouse. She felt a sense of relief to find it hadn't changed at all. There was Surat himself, fatter and more bent with age, although he still had the same winsome smile he used whenever he was trying to entice customers inside. He had a few more lines around his eyes, his beard whiter than she remembered. There was no recognition on his face as Nimsah declined his offer of hospitality and passed him on the street, making for the Bridge of Sorrows.

Looking like she belonged was an important part of walking safely through the City of Tents. No one challenged her as she joined the throng of hopefuls, each person queuing to gain a short audience with Farooq. Some were there to barter or trade for goods, others to repay debts or ask for his services. Nimsah kept her head down as she drew nearer the front of the crowd, watching as Farooq came into view. He was older, wearing the last thirteen years more obviously than she'd expected. The once fit, strong Naroque man was fatter, the familiar bangles tight around his arms, the golden torc sitting on a fold of flabby flesh between his neck and shoulders. At his side was a lithe Naroque woman and Nimsah started as she recognised Chandra's features, the soft-faced girl she'd shared a tent with now grown tall and beautiful. Behind Farooq stood Rogesh, muscular arms folded and sporting scars that spoke of a violent life. He looked more self-assured than Nimsah remembered, a look of calm confidence on his face as he watched over his master.

Nimsah slipped out of the queue, walking the other way before it was her turn to be called forwards. She paused at the corner of the courtyard, staring down at the cobbles where Fenara had fallen. If she'd had any doubts about giving the order to end the lives of Tanah, Adina and Ulan, the chance to make Shinva a target too was enough motivation to see the plan through. Benazar's organisation of paid assassins knew how to operate in secret, their part in the attempt on Haraq's life, which Nimsah had been caught up in all those years ago, never uncovered. When Jandral had orchestrated Emir Cassim's downfall in Amjahran they lost their paymaster. The Bank of Illesh had stepped in, Jandral making Benazar an offer that was too good to refuse.

Jandral would never have approved of Nimsah using the more sinister connections of the Bank of Illesh to serve her own private purposes. However, when Shinva was personally assigned to protect Tanah the opportunity presented to Nimsah was too good to refuse. Her only regret was Shinva never knew who was behind her death and the reasons for it. She would have died defending the High Princess and her daughter, believing her honour was intact until the very end.

Was that important? Nimsah pondered the question as she crossed to the mid-point of the Bridge of Sorrows, looking out over the wide estuary of the Namja River as its waters mixed with the sea of the Strait of Bezeen. She wrapped her hands around the slender wires that suspended the poured stone part of the bridge, leaning out across the river, trusting them to take her weight. The rust on the surface was rough against her palms, where the salt in the air had slowly corroded the steel over the years.

"Does it matter?" Nimsah whispered to herself, watching the swirling waters flowing under her, moving out fast towards the sea. She was still here and Shinva was gone, her ashes interred in the Warriors Crypt in the city. Everyone had forgotten Fenara, widow of Biwan, everyone except for the street rat who once ran with Farooq's gang.

"Tell me what you want to be." Nimsah remembered Fenara's words from long ago. She recalled that familiar gesture as Fenara tucked a stray strand of greying hair back under her green shawl. Blinking back tears as she returned to Bengarath Palace, Nimsah wondered what Fenara would think of her now.

CHARACTER LIST

Square brackets around a [name] denotes that this character has already passed into Navan's Halls at the start of A Quiet Vengeance.

The Emirate of Fujareen

Royal Family

Emir Haraq Al-Souk (b158) – ruler of Fujareen
Her Royal Highness Princess Tanah Bel-Doshok (b166) – wife of Emir Haraq Al-Souk, Tanah is from the wealthy Doshok Fujareen family
Crown Prince Dojan Al-Haraq (b188) – eldest son of Emir Haraq Al-Souk and his wife Tanah, he is the heir to his father's emirate
Princess Adina El-Haraq (b190) – only daughter of Emir Haraq Al-Souk and his wife Tanah. Betrothed to Pasha Ulan Bel-Naraar
Prince Saraj Al-Haraq (b193) – middle son of Emir Haraq Al-Souk and his wife Tanah, serving as a warrior in the *Regiment of the Mighty Spears*
Prince Beneth Al-Haraq (b196) – youngest son of Emir Haraq Al-Souk and his wife Tanah. A student at the University of Bengarath
[Emir Godan Bel-Deem] (b140 d186) – the emir of Fujareen from 179-186 until Haraq Al-Souk took power

Court Officials & Advisors

Vizier Haman Bel-Yangash (b150) – the most senior advisor of Emir Haraq Al-Souk
Nema Bel-Yangash (b160) – the wife of Vizier Haman and close friend of Tanah Bel-Doshok
Pasha Ulan Bel-Naraar (b188) – an ambitious official at the

emir's court and the personal assistant of Vizier Haman Bel-Yangash, with responsibility for foreign affairs. Betrothed to Princess Adina El-Haraq
Katib Quizar Bel-Khandir (b185) – an official at the emir's court and the personal assistant and good friend of Crown Prince Dojan
Arak Bel-Yangash (b151) – a member of the *Veiled Magi*
Veiled Magi – practitioners of magic who keep their identity hidden when in public. They wear identical white robes, so they are also referred to as 'The White'
Tormindah El-Shan (b183) – a member of the *Magi of the Farseeing*
Magi of the Farseeing – an order skilled in the Sight, used by the royal family to spy on both their enemies and allies

The Fujareen Army

Andral Illana Bel-Jedesh (b160) – andral and commander-in-chief of the emir's army, appointed following Haraq Al-Souk's conquest of Fujareen in 186, when she saved his life in battle
Khan Hengesh Bel-Daraj (b169) – captain of the *Regiment of the Mighty Spears*
Mubarizun Hadir Al-Nadim (b186) – champion of the *Regiment of the Mighty Spears*
Khalid Al-Shah (b192) – a warrior in the *Regiment of the Mighty Spears*
Khanir Shinva Bel-Kamil (b172) – captain of the *Regiment of the Blessed Swords*
Mubarizun Yanzin El-Tebir (b187) – champion of the *Regiment of the Blessed Swords*
Khan Geber Al-Jalal (b161) – captain of the *Regiment of the Tireless Shields*
Nassar Al-Halaan (b165) – a warrior in the *Regiment of the Tireless Shields*
Canzar (b180) – a warrior in the *Regiment of the Tireless Shields*
Regiment of the Mighty Spears – an elite fighting unit, sworn to protect the emir and his family, who fight with the traditional Samarak fighting spear
Regiment of the Blessed Swords – an elite fighting unit, sworn to protect Her Royal Highness Tanah Bel-Doshok and her family, who fight with the scimitar

Regiment of the Pure – the personal guard of Fujareen's andral
Regiment of the Tireless Shields – the infantry backbone of the Fujareen army organised into separate smaller units, who fight with spear, shield and short sword
Regiment of Royal Arquebusiers – a small infantry unit armed with arquebuses (an early form of heavy musket)
Regiment of the Stooping Falcon – a Fujareen regiment of expert archers

Denizens of the City of Tents – the dispossessed of Fujareen

Nimsah (b c186) – a street child who subsequently finds fortune working for the Bank of Illesh
Farooq (b c177) – a former street child, who has run a criminal gang in Bengarath since 195, of which Nimsah is a member
Kandilla (b c177) – an older member of Farooq's gang and his lover
Bizek (b c172) – Farooq's bodyguard
Raqqath (b168) – a member of Farooq's gang
Rogesh (b c185) – a street child and a member of Farooq's gang. A friend of Nimsah
Chandra (b c187) – a street child and a member of Farooq's gang. She is friends with Nimsah and Rogesh

Denizens of Bengarath, Capital City of Fujareen

Fenara (b159) – an older widowed lady who weaves and sells baskets in the market of Bengarath
[Biwan] (b154 d189) – the late husband of Fenara
Denek Bel-Haroom (b165) – a wealthy merchant
Kamjah (b170) – the leader of a rival gang, known as the Kraken, ousted from power in the City of Tents by Farooq
Surat (b147) – the owner of a coffeehouse in Bengarath
Ozmun (b176) – an ironmonger in Bengarath
Odilla (b160) – a wealthy gold merchant
Benazar – the person rumoured to be responsible for an assassination attempt on Emir Haraq's life

The Emirate of Amjahran

Emir Cassim (b130) – former emir of Amjahran

Emira Ledana (b160) – ruler of Amjahran since 200 after deposing Emir Cassim

The People of Naroque

The City State of Kandarah

Shekh Birizal (b170) – the ruler of Kandarah
Khan Lemarr (b166) – a high-ranking officer in the Kandaran army
Jandral (b160) – an employee of the Bank of Illesh and a member of its ruling council
Magi of the Order of Engineers – an order dedicated to the construction of Kandarah's spires and the power source that keeps them operational

The Abitek Tribe

Fasil (b150) – an elder and leader of the Abitek tribe, the tribe of the dragon

The Edeen Tribe

Narinda (b175) – an elder of the Edeen, the tribe of stars
Ramdha (b155) – the leader of Narinda's personal guards, the Black Robes

The Gods

The Creator – the god who, through his servants the avatars, created the world of Amuran

The Avatars, servants of the Creator

Altandu – avatar of light, sometimes referred to as the **Mother of Light**
Arkon – avatar of war
Ceren – avatar of darkness, sometimes referred to as the **Mother of Darkness**
Culdaff – avatar of the air and winds

Dinuvillan – avatar of good fortune
Garradon – general of Vellandir's forces, opposed to Morvanos
Lamornna – avatar of nature and creation
Meras – avatar of love
Morvanos – avatar of change and the natural cycle of chaos, leader of the rebellion opposed to Vellandir's tyranny, which began the War of the Avatars
Myshall – avatar of misfortune
Nanquido – avatar of the waters and the seas
Navan – avatar who guards the Halls of the Dead in the afterlife
Vellandir – avatar of unjust laws and oppression, leader of the avatars supporting the Tyranny opposed by Morvanos

GLOSSARY

Andral – commander in chief of an army, reporting directly to the Emir or Sultan

Baghlah – a large deep-sea dhow, with a crew of 30-40, with two or three triangular lateen sails

Dhow – a traditional narrow-hulled merchant ship of Samarakand, with a triangular lateen sail, normally crewed by 10-15 sailors

Emir – masculine form for the ruler of an Emirate in Murtak

Emira – feminine form for the ruler of an Emirate in Murtak

Handari – headgear worn principally by men in Murtak and less frequently in Kalat, designed to keep off the sun

Katib – writer, scribe, secretary or other official

Khan – masculine form for a captain of a regiment in the army

Khanir – feminine form for the captain of a regiment, often deployed as the guards of royal princesses

Magus – practitioner of magic and the lost sciences (plural Magi)

Mubarizun – a title of respect, referring to an experienced warrior or the champion of his or her regiment

Pasha – a high-ranking official. More senior than a Katib, though less important than a Vizier

Padishah – another word for king, derived from Shah. Used as a respectful form of address when speaking to a ruler in Kalat or Murtak

Shah – another word for king, often used interchangeably with the title of Sultan

Shekh – a local ruler or elder

Sultan – masculine title used in the Kingdoms of Kalat, referring to a sovereign ruler and religious leader

Sultanah – feminine form of Sultan

Vizier – high-ranking political advisor or minister

ACKNOWLEDGEMENTS

A Quiet Vengeance is a far better novel thanks to the input of my early test readers, Laurence Keighley and my wife Liz. Together with my agent and editor extraordinaire John Jarrold, they helped sharpen the story and bring the characters to life. There are points where, as the author, it can be difficult to see the weaknesses in your own story. Their insight, observations and suggestions have been invaluable, enabling me to give the manuscript that final, crucial polish.

The cover was created by US designer Anne Hudson. I wanted A Quiet Vengeance to look very different to my other books, making clear it was part of a new series. We explored various concepts before settling on the final one. When I read this novel now, the image that forms in my mind of Nimsah as an adult is the same picture you see on the front cover. I think Anne's captured the essence of her character perfectly.

One of the things I'm always grateful for is the support of my fellow writers and avid readers, particularly those of you who took the time to read advance copies in the run up to publication. When you get into the final stages it's good to know all those hours of writing and editing have paid off – an important confidence booster for any author ahead of a looming release date. Your quotes can be found on my website and Amazon editorial reviews section and I'm grateful for each and every one of those.

If you've enjoyed this novel, don't forget to leave a review on Amazon or Goodreads or simply tell your friends.

Recommendations, ratings and reviews help readers find new books – the process that makes my career as an author possible. Those few minutes telling others what you think makes a huge difference (and it will also make the author's day).

If you want to know more and keep up to date with all the latest news, you can sign up for my bi-monthly newsletter via my website. This will also give you exclusive access to my series of free short stories, which expand upon both the history and some of the characters in my wider fantasy world.

Twitter – @TimHardieAuthor
Facebook – @Tim.Hardie.Author.Public
Website – www.timhardieauthor.co.uk

Printed in Great Britain
by Amazon